HIS FAMILY OBJECTS
A PRIDE & PREJUDICE VARIATION

LUCY MARIN

Quills & Quartos
PUBLISHING

Copyright © 2024 by Lucy Marin

All rights reserved.

This is a work of fiction. Names, characters, businesses, places, events, locales, and incidents are either the products of the author's imagination or used in a fictitious manner. Any resemblance to actual persons, living or dead, or actual events is purely coincidental.

No part of this book may be reproduced in any form or by any electronic or mechanical means, including information storage and retrieval systems, without written permission from the author, except for the use of brief quotations in a book review.

No AI training. Without in any way limiting the author's [and publisher's] exclusive rights under copyright, any use of this publication to "train" generative artificial intelligence (AI) technologies to generate text is expressly prohibited. The author reserves all rights to license uses of this work for generative AI training and development of machine learning language models.

Ebooks are for the personal use of the purchaser. You may not share or distribute this ebook in any way, to any other person. To do so is infringing on the copyright of the author, which is against the law.

Edited Jo Abbott

Cover by Beetiful Book Designs

ISBN 978-1-963213-11-9 (ebook) and 978-1-963213-12-6 (paperback)

The plot of this story came to me while travelling through the Canadian Rocky Mountains, and so I dedicate this story to the beauty of mountains and all who work to protect them.

Whatever can give his sister any pleasure, is sure to be done in a moment. There is nothing he would not do for her.

— MRS REYNOLDS, PRIDE & PREJUDICE,
CHAPTER 43

PROLOGUE

December 1812

It seemed wholly appropriate that the clouds were thickening and the wind growing stronger as Elizabeth made her way along the path. She had slipped away from her family and prayed no one had seen her leave Longbourn. She dreaded the prospect of their questions if they had.

He was waiting for her. Elizabeth did not know how long he had been standing by the pine trees she had named as their meeting spot, and she did not care. Stopping some fifteen feet from him, she pressed her lips together, pushed her shoulders back, and silently invited him to say what he would. No matter how much it injured her, she would *not* let him see it.

"How are you?" he asked.

She shrugged. Since he was the one who wanted to meet, *he* should bear the burden of speech. As resolute as she was determined to be, she was afraid that if she opened her mouth, too much would pour out—too many emotions and accusations.

After running both hands over his face and letting out an audible gust of air, Mr Darcy paced back and forth along a short section of the path. "I...I intended to return, I truly did, but—" He made an inarticulate noise, and it was a moment before he continued. "I am sorrier than I can say that I...could not. You will want to know what happened. You have every right to know. I am aware that Lady Catherine visited you."

Elizabeth gritted her teeth, both at the remembrance of that woman's deplorable behaviour and because she began to see why Mr Darcy had abandoned her. Lady Catherine had made her displeasure clear to him, just as she had to her. A fire began to rage in her belly.

"After seeing you, she came to London," Mr Darcy said. "My aunt announced to my family that I was on the point of making an unsuitable match."

"Were you?" Elizabeth interjected, unable to keep the bitterness from her voice. At the moment, she could not believe she would accept him if he were to propose.

His feet abruptly stopped moving, and he almost stumbled. He regarded her for a long moment, and something in his eyes melted a layer of the ice that was wrapped around her heart.

The truth was that she would not have hesitated to agree to be his wife; she would have thrown herself into his arms and cried tears of joy. She loved him. It was why she was presently so wretched and nearly sick with distress. Straightening her spine, she resolved anew to be stoic.

"Lady Catherine said she had it on good authority that I was about to propose to you," Mr Darcy continued. "I do not know who told her. My family demanded to know whether what she said was true. What could I say? It was. They were not pleased by your position in life, but when they heard about your family's connexion to Wickham, they...had a great deal to say—none of it good."

"They objected?" Elizabeth had to suppress an angry bark of laughter. Her hands curled into fists.

"Strenuously and repeatedly."

"Were they as disgusted by the idea of having a woman such as me as a relation as you said they would be last spring? Was it too much for you to overcome, or did you simply remember that it would be disgraceful to connect yourself to me, given I have relations in trade? You have met my aunt and uncle, invited them into your home, showed every sign of liking them, and yet you can—"

"You do not understand," he insisted, stepping towards her.

"Shall I congratulate you on your marriage to Miss de Bourgh? It cannot be long in coming. You were quick to give in to your family's demands to forget about me. Surely you will also accede to their wishes regarding which lady you *should* make your wife."

"No!" he cried, his expression suggesting confusion. "I care nothing about my uncle and aunts' opinions, but—"

"I refuse to continue this conversation. There is nothing you could say that would make me understand the choice you have made." Elizabeth turned to walk away. She felt his hand touch her arm.

"Elizabeth—"

Spinning to face him, she hissed, "I do not give you leave to use my name! You forget that my sister is married, and I am Miss Bennet henceforth—*especially* to you. If we have the misfortune to meet again, you will address me as Miss Bennet until I find a man who will not reject me because of my

3

connexions and lack of fortune. Until I find a man who is truly worthy of me."

He blanched. "The situation is complicated. Please allow me to explain. This is not easy for me, but I have responsibilities."

"Oh yes, of course you do, and an association with a lady of my sort would preclude you from fulfilling them. I understand. Do not spend a second of your precious time worrying about it." Her tone was mocking, and as she spoke, pink spots appeared on his cheeks, either ones of anger or guilt.

"You do not understand." He spoke quietly this time, and the look he gave her was one of longing, but she was too trapped by her hurt to admit it.

"I think I do, well enough. After everything that has happened, after how horrible I felt for misjudging you last spring, everything that passed between us in Derbyshire, everything I believed, you have decided that because your family does not think I am good enough for you, you will not have me. When it comes to the point, your family objects, and I am rejected. Goodbye, Mr Darcy."

When she began to walk away, he called her name, and she heard the unmistakable sound of his boots stepping on twigs and dried leaves. There was no escaping him if he wished to pursue her. Her only hope lay in convincing him that she would not listen to more of his excuses. Without halting her steps, she spoke. She strove to keep her voice strong, though she knew it faltered.

"There is *nothing* to gain by continuing this conversation. Do not be so ungentlemanly as to force me to hear you when I do not want to!"

With that, she picked up speed and, after several minutes, accepted that he was not following her.

CHAPTER ONE

August 1812

The past four days in Derbyshire had been nothing short of magnificent, and this one would be exactly the same. Elizabeth looked into the smiling visage of Mr Fitzwilliam Darcy, and her heart fluttered. That had begun to happen the morning after their unexpected meeting at his estate. She and her aunt and uncle Gardiner were in Lambton on holiday and had decided to tour Pemberley, having been assured the family was not home. Mr Darcy had arrived that day, they had a pleasant if awkward conversation while strolling through his gardens—which Elizabeth decided were the most beautiful she had ever seen—and he asked whether he might introduce his sister to her. After their bitter exchange in Kent the previous spring, it was generous and kind, as was his treatment of the Gardiners.

But then, Elizabeth expected nothing less of him, having come to know him better.

Mr Darcy had brought his sister—and Mr Bingley, who was visiting with his family—to the inn the next morning. Elizabeth and Mrs Gardiner had returned the call the next day, and what followed seemed inevitable and natural. Without saying it was for her sake, her aunt and uncle had announced a few days earlier that they had decided to extend their stay in Lambton, and the two parties had been together a great deal since. Elizabeth and the Gardiners had dined at Pemberley twice, and the Darcys had taken Elizabeth on a more complete tour of the house and a drive through the neighbourhood.

Presently, Elizabeth, Mr Darcy, and several others were exploring a ridge path a little distance from his estate, in Castleton. The day was remarkably fine, and its glory was enhanced by the handsome gentleman by her side. Feathery clouds danced merrily across the sky, and a breeze gave relief from the summer sun. She greedily drank in the wild, untamed splendour of the countryside—all the while enjoying the company of the most interesting, enchanting man she could ever have dreamt up in her imagination, which she had always been told was particularly sharp.

"We shall soon reach a vista. The view is superior, and it will be an opportunity to rest before we return," Mr Darcy said.

"I find it difficult to believe there is yet more beauty to discover!" She laughed and revelled in his answering chuckle.

"I am glad you find Derbyshire so pleasing."

"Pleasing? That is far too meek a word, sir, for what I feel. While knowing my uncle must return to town, and the little Gardiners will be missing their parents, I shall be sorry to leave."

"Will you?" His eyes darkened as he grew serious.

"Yes." She spoke quietly and nodded, knowing what he meant and the importance of her reply.

They had so misunderstood each other. She had been more at fault, failing to recognise that he was a good man and that he was growing attached to her. To be sure, he was flawed as they all were, but in essentials, he was everything he should be. Her impression of his character had begun to change soon after their recent meeting, and the alteration in her feelings for him was swift. Upon reflection, she believed she had begun to reconsider her understanding of him after reading his letter several times after Easter, but it was meeting him again that had produced the more significant effect. He might have loved longer, but she defied anyone to say her present love was not as genuine as his.

"Would you take it amiss if I said I am relieved to hear it?" Mr Darcy asked.

"Shall I now enquire whether you would take it amiss that I am relieved that you are relieved?" She smiled, and a happy chuckle accompanied her words. This exchange was the closest they had come to acknowledging how their friendship had altered.

He too laughed. His look of pleasure, and the depth of feeling in his eyes, left her warm and embarrassed. She turned her attention to the path and remained silent for a brief moment.

"Have you taken this walk often?" she asked.

"Many times. It is a particular favourite. I believe I was eight years old the first time my father brought me here. My cousins were visiting—the colonel and his older brother. We were always very active, and my father and the earl were attempting to occupy—and exhaust—us, if only to gain some measure of peace."

"Were they successful?" Whenever he shared some part of his life with her, she felt a little fuller, a little richer. It was as though whatever bound them together was growing stronger. Beyond that, his voice was deep and entrancing, and she savoured hearing it.

He smiled in a way that spoke of fond remembrances. "They were. All three of us fell asleep in the carriage, and I recall being very quiet that evening. We were told we had to be, and everyone was serious. My mother had been ill, and the earl—her brother, with whom she was always close—had come to see her. While they could have consigned us to the care of servants, she liked to have us nearby. Some of my happiest memories are when my cousins came to Pemberley or my parents and I went to Romsley Hall."

Elizabeth wondered whether Mr George Wickham had been present during any of the pleasant times Mr Darcy was recollecting, but she would not ask. She did not want to ruin his good mood and the agreeable interlude they were sharing. And what did it matter? The men's friendship had ended long ago, and Elizabeth would be content never to see or hear of Mr Wickham again.

"You must have favourite walks near Longbourn. Will you tell me of them?" he asked.

"I would be most pleased to. As you know, I do take great enjoyment in exploring my environs, wherever I happen to find myself."

They spoke of the places she liked to go, and as she had been on other occasions recently, Elizabeth was impressed by his attentiveness and apparent desire to understand her likes and dislikes.

Elizabeth and Mr Darcy were accompanied on the walk by Miss Darcy, Mr Bingley, and Mr Gardiner; Mrs Gardiner was visiting old acquaintances in Lambton, and the Hursts and Miss Bingley had elected to remain at Pemberley. After their rest, the party began the journey down to the waiting carriage. This time, Elizabeth walked with Miss Darcy and Mr Bingley, leaving the other two gentlemen to an animated conversation. She could not hear what they spoke of, in part because Mr Bingley kept up an almost never-ending stream of words, praising Hertfordshire and the excellent people he had met there. When he asked for news of them, she told him what she could, and when he spoke about returning to Netherfield in the coming weeks, she assured him it was an excellent notion.

Beside them, Miss Darcy maintained her silence. From their first meeting, she had struck Elizabeth as not only painfully shy but also fragile. There was something in her air that hinted at a brittleness, as though one misstep—real or perceived—or one piece of bad news would shatter her. Knowing what she did of the young woman's past, Elizabeth assumed it was because of her brush with ruination after the failed elopement with Mr Wickham.

Thank goodness her brother arrived in time to prevent it! As terrible as almost marrying that scoundrel was, her situation would be so much worse had she become his wife and learnt his only interest was her fortune.

After politely laughing at the conclusion of Mr Bingley's anecdote of shooting with Sir William Lucas, Elizabeth turned to Miss Darcy. "It is growing quite hot, is it not? I shall be glad for a cool beverage. Are you fatigued?"

Miss Darcy peeked at her from around the brim of her bonnet before lowering her eyes again. "N-no." Just when it seemed she would say nothing more, she said in a rush, "There is a basket with the carriage. I hope it is suitable."

"I am sure it will be just the thing, and your brother

suggested we stop to take refreshments on the way to Pemberley. All I need is a little bit of whatever you and your housekeeper selected to pack to tide me over."

"I had only to agree to what Mrs Reynolds suggested." Miss Darcy shook her head and moved her chin even closer to her chest.

Elizabeth supposed the poor child—for such was what she seemed—would hide away, never talking to anyone, if her brother allowed it. "Even if that was the case, you still had a role in the decision by determining it was appropriate. If Mrs Reynolds had proposed something outrageous, you would have stopped her. Nothing you say to the contrary will convince me otherwise."

"Just so," Mr Bingley said, his tone jovial. "You may be unpractised at being a hostess, Miss Darcy, but you know my sisters, Hurst, and I are all very pleased with our stay. Everything that could be done for our comfort has been, and that would not be true without your efforts."

Seeing Miss Darcy's growing unease, Elizabeth decided to engage Mr Bingley in a discussion of Scarborough, where he and his family were soon going.

CHAPTER TWO

Darcy looked with satisfaction at the people gathered in his drawing room. The visit that afternoon to Castleton had been wonderful, and he was certain Elizabeth was growing to love Derbyshire—and if he were exceedingly fortunate, him. This evening, she and the Gardiners had joined them for dinner. His sister and Elizabeth were at the pianoforte, Georgiana playing while the woman he adored lent her support and turned the pages. While still very shy, his sister seldom looked like she wanted to flee the room, and she even spoke upon occasion, which was remarkable, given the presence of people she had not known a week earlier.

It was possible the Bingleys and Hursts recognised how well Georgiana responded to Elizabeth; the Gardiners and their niece could not, being unfamiliar with her. He wanted to thank them for their kindness to his sister. He knew it could be trying to be with her, requiring patience and a willingness to exert oneself to take on the burden of conversation and cheerfulness, but all three of them were wonderful to her. It pleased

Darcy immensely since he had every intention of making Elizabeth his wife. He would be glad to call the Gardiners his aunt and uncle, as much as that had surprised him at first. But they were an agreeable, polite couple and excellent company. Georgiana's life would be enriched by having them in it.

Of his other guests, his opinions were mixed. A bubble of dread settled in his stomach when he looked at Bingley. Darcy hoped he would always be a close friend, but he must tell him the truth about Miss Jane Bennet, including that she had been in town and he had concealed the news. He was determined to make the confession before his friend left for Scarborough.

Mrs Hurst and Miss Bingley sat whispering together, and Hurst appeared afflicted with ennui. It was an improvement on their behaviour while Elizabeth was performing. Then, they had spoken loudly and asked her about the militia stationed in Meryton, making an allusion to Wickham. Darcy had been ready to evict them from the estate if they dared mention the man's name. Although they did not know why he despised his childhood friend, they understood his sentiments well enough. Few knew the entire story.

How I wish there was no more to tell than what I shared with Elizabeth at Easter!

When it was time for the Gardiners and Elizabeth to depart, he walked to the carriage with them. The couple thanked him politely and stepped aside to allow him and Elizabeth a few moments alone.

Everything about her made him feel easier and more complete. Whenever he was near her, and as he grew more confident that she genuinely liked him, he felt less alone than he ever recalled feeling in his life, certainly since he became an adult. Her eyes were bright, her skin glowed, and she seemed to embody health and happiness.

"It has been a wonderful day," she said.

"What made it so enjoyable, if I may ask?"

"Do you need to?" Her eyebrows arched elegantly, and he could hear a teasing note in her voice.

"I would not like to assume, and I do have a purpose to my question. Shall I tell you what it is?"

"Please do, my good sir, for I assure you, I cannot possibly guess."

Darcy was not accustomed to flirting, and if he were being honest, it both thrilled him and made him shake with nerves. "My dearest wish is to ensure each of your days is as happy as possible. While I know I shall not always succeed, I hope to do so more often than not. Understanding what you found remarkable about today will provide me with necessary information."

Colour blossomed on her cheeks. "I find it does not take much to please me of late. I suppose the ingredients for wonderful days are a pleasant location, agreeable conversation, but most especially excellent company. *That* is what makes all the difference." Her eyes seemed to open a little wider, and she did not blink as she regarded him. What was she trying to communicate? Dare he hope it was that for which he most wished?

"We have two days before you must depart. I intend to continue doing whatever I can to convince you that Derbyshire is the best of counties. I shall be at the inn by nine o'clock tomorrow morning, if that suits."

She said nothing further but nodded and smiled at him for a long moment before curtseying and moving towards the carriage.

After watching the conveyance drive off, Darcy returned indoors ready to burst with energy. If it were possible, he would have taken a long ride or walk through the park, but he could not leave his sister for long, and he had guests to attend to. Each conversation with Elizabeth did more to convince him that she would agree to deepen their connexion. Before she left the county, he would speak. While he most desired her acceptance of an offer of marriage, he would assure her that he was prepared to wait should she require time to reflect before committing herself. He would go to Hertfordshire as soon as he could and remain as long as it took for her to be comfortable with the prospect of being his wife.

When he again joined the party, Miss Bingley called, "Oh, Mr Darcy! Louisa and I were about to send Charles to search for you. We feared Eliza Bennet and her relations had kidnapped you."

The ladies chuckled, but he found no humour in their supposed joke.

"Caroline, what a ridiculous thing to say!" Bingley snapped.

Darcy left the brother and sisters to their squabble. His immediate concern was Georgiana. With Mrs Annesley having retired, his sister was on her own and clearly uneasy.

"Would you like to take a turn on the terrace?" he asked.

She nodded and accepted his assistance to stand. He kept her hand in his until they had crossed the threshold and stepped into the open air; then he wrapped it about his elbow, keeping her close to him and offering whatever portion of his strength and love she would accept.

After strolling for a short time, he said, "I am afraid Mrs Hurst and Miss Bingley have never particularly liked Miss Elizabeth or her family. I did once think they were friends with the elder Miss Bennet, but—"

"Is her family disagreeable?" Georgiana sounded alarmed.

"No. I admit I once thought so, but I have come to realise I was being unfairly harsh in my judgment. I admit, some of the Bennets can be…a little difficult to tolerate, but it is similar to the way some of our relations are not the most pleasant companions."

"Lady Catherine," Georgiana murmured.

"The dragon of Kent. Yes, but I believe there is more kindness in the Bennets than there is in our aunt." Darcy gave a resigned chuckle.

It was a very real possibility that his anger at the world and despair over Georgiana had led to his being especially discourteous when he was in Hertfordshire, but the underlying reason for his judgment of the local people had been the arrogance he had carried with him since childhood. Elizabeth had shone a light on it, giving him the opportunity to correct the way he perceived and treated people in society. While it was not always easy, the approval—the genuine *liking*—he saw in her eyes was his reward.

"Georgiana, what is your opinion of Miss Elizabeth?" he asked gently.

His sister bit her lips together, and one hand reached for a curl hanging by her cheek. She pulled at it as she answered. "I-I like her. She is such a happy person, and I am sure it does me good to see it."

"I am glad."

"Will you marry her?"

"That, along with your continued recovery, are my most fervent wishes." He placed a kiss on her hand and led her towards the path through the rose bushes.

CHAPTER THREE

Darcy was exhilarated as he made his way to Lambton the next morning. He could hardly believe how his life had changed in the previous week, and he remarked on it to the empty carriage several times. The last year had been the most difficult of his life. He used to believe the time following his father's death would always hold that position, but between Georgiana's affliction and losing the only woman he would likely ever love, he was not sure how he managed to crawl out of bed each morning. Knowing he was to blame for both had been a bitter pill to swallow.

Then, seemingly appearing out of nowhere, Elizabeth had been there, in his gardens. They had talked pleasantly, if somewhat stiltedly, and he had discovered that her aunt and uncle—the very ones he had thought meanly of—were estimable people. Hope had blossomed in his heart, and over the course of the next few days, he had grown increasingly certain his dearest wish was becoming a reality and Elizabeth was falling in love with him. It was like a dream, and just that morning, he had stood in front of the mirror in his dressing room and taken several minutes to convince himself he was not sleeping or mad.

Today, Elizabeth, her relations, and he would spend a short time in Lambton before returning to Pemberley, where they would have a picnic by the lake. They could have simply met at his estate, but he anticipated being with Elizabeth with only the Gardiners as companions for several hours. For whatever reason, Bingley did not appear to see that Darcy wished for more than a friendly connexion to Elizabeth, and he would monopolise her conversation. Miss Bingley and the Hursts would be barely civil. Georgiana was the only person Darcy truly concerned himself with, and she was spending the morning with her companion.

At the inn, he was shown to a parlour whose lone occupant was Elizabeth; the maid said his name and left. Darcy's initial joy—this would be his opportunity to speak!—turned to fear when he saw tears streaming down Elizabeth's cheeks. He flew to her side and took the seat next to her.

"Good God, what is the matter?" he cried.

She looked at him, opened her mouth as though to speak, then closed it and her eyes, sending fresh tears down her fair skin. Darcy waited as patiently as he could manage. One of her hands held several sheets of paper, and Darcy took hold of the other. Her fingers clutched his, squeezing tightly. Part of him thought he should fetch her a glass of wine or ask where Mr and Mrs Gardiner were, knowing she might need her family's assistance, but he did not want to separate from her for even a second while she was so distressed. At length, haltingly, she spoke.

"I have received the most dreadful news."

She told him that her youngest sister, Miss Lydia, had

eloped with Wickham. Until Elizabeth had finished reciting all the news she had received from Miss Bennet, Darcy held his silence, but his mind screamed, *Must it always be Wickham?*

He swallowed the large lump that had formed in his throat before speaking. "Where are your aunt and uncle?"

"They went for a walk. To the church, if I recollect."

He supposed they had done so to give him and their niece time alone so that he could propose. Elizabeth dabbed at her cheeks with the handkerchief he gave her.

"I shall send a servant to find them." He tried to sound reassuring and calm, but his heart and mind were busy devising schemes, asking endless questions, and considering multiple possibilities. Going to the door, he spied a maid and made his request. Before returning to Elizabeth, he poured a glass of wine for her from a decanter on a table by the room's lone window. For himself, he longed to consume several bottles of strong brandy so that he might forget this horror for a short time. Was it truly less than an hour ago he was thinking that he was living in the most magnificent dream? Resuming his seat beside her, he again took one of her hands in his.

He gathered himself enough to fix his mind on what must be done to prevent the situation from becoming a disaster for the Bennets, if it was not too late already.

"I am very sorry this has happened. Unfortunately, you are correct that Miss Lydia has nothing to tempt him to marry her. He will not have taken her to Scotland. I doubt they have gone farther than London. He has, well, I hesitate to call them friends because I do not believe he knows what friendship means, but I have several ideas for where they might be found. If your sister is not at any of those places, I have people in whose discretion I trust who can help me discover her whereabouts."

"You would—? Of course you would assist my family in this." His lovely Elizabeth sniffed and pressed her fingers under her eyes as though to prevent further tears from escaping.

"There is nothing I would not do for you. Have you not yet realised that?"

She managed an understandably weak smile. Her colour was high, and although her anxiety was still evident, he saw a spark of pleasure, perhaps even affection.

"I expect you and the Gardiners will return to Longbourn at once. I shall make arrangements to travel to town as soon as possible. Tomorrow, I hope."

The Bingleys and Hursts planned to begin the journey to Scarborough in a few days, and they could easily depart sooner or stay at Pemberley, if they liked. He must make arrangements for Georgiana. Even with Mrs Annesley present, he could not leave her alone; some other family member must be with her. He would write to his relations in Warwickshire to ask that his cousin Viscount Bramwell or aunt Lady Romsley come to stay with her. Waiting to hear from them would mean a delay in his departure, but it could not be helped. Fortunately, they were in the north of the county, making the trip between the estates easy.

"As soon as I have arrived in London and begun to make enquiries, I shall call on your uncle. For now, I shall have a quick word with him to assure him of my assistance, then I ought to return to Pemberley to begin my preparations. I promise I shall see you as soon as possible."

"I understand if…circumstances prevent that." Both of Elizabeth's hands enveloped his. Her tone was serious, and she kept a steady gaze on him.

"No!" he interjected. "This changes *nothing* for me. This is not the time to discuss it, but you know what I mean."

Elizabeth nodded, but she remained sombre, stoic even. "If the situation with my sister does not improve as I pray it will, if—" Her voice broke, and she took a brief moment to compose herself. "If Lydia is lost for good, I *will* understand if you cannot—"

"I will see you soon," he reiterated and pulled her hand to his mouth to kiss it.

They sat in silence, Darcy attempting to offer comfort and strength without demanding she give him her attention when clearly she was anxious for her family, Miss Lydia especially. Knowing what Wickham was capable of, she was right to worry.

Soon, the Gardiners returned, and while Mrs Gardiner went to Elizabeth, Darcy took Mr Gardiner aside and gave him a quick explanation. He vowed his assistance until the matter was successfully resolved.

Darcy returned to Elizabeth for a final goodbye. What he could do and say were limited with her relations present, but he kissed her hand and whispered once again, "I will see you soon."

CHAPTER FOUR

Elizabeth experienced a range of emotions over the following days. The journey back to Hertfordshire was filled with signs of her sadness and anxiety and many reassurances from her aunt and uncle that they would find Lydia and put things to rights, whatever that would be in this circumstance. It did little to assuage Elizabeth. She was at once desperately worried about what would happen if Lydia was not found, doubtful that there was any good resolution to her rash actions, heartbroken at the separation from Mr Darcy, and furious with her sister for being so stupid.

Elizabeth's anger towards Mr Bennet was only slightly less acute; she had warned him that it was foolish to allow Lydia to go to Brighton, but he had not wanted to listen to his youngest daughter's complaints if she was denied the treat. They might all be ruined because of his laziness, and she and Jane robbed of excellent husbands.

Elizabeth's only solace was that Mr Darcy had vowed to do what he could. It was generous—more than generous. Most men would wash their hands of the Bennets and soon forget even an ardent love for the sister of a girl who had acted as Lydia had.

At home, Elizabeth said nothing to Jane of her time in Derbyshire or really about the holiday at all; Lydia was the only thing on their minds. Since even thinking of Mr Darcy made Elizabeth feel ill with worry, she was content to stay silent, returning to her memories of him only at night when she could not sleep. Her love and trust for him supported her during the trying days before news arrived. He was the best man she knew, and if he could help—whatever he could do—he would.

At last, an express arrived from Mr Gardiner, informing them that the couple had been found and would marry at the end of the month. Mrs Bennet's recovery was instantaneous, and she was as happy and exuberant as she ever had been. Although it was contrary to her personal wishes, Elizabeth convinced her father to invite the couple to Longbourn.

"I shall hate it as much as you, Papa," she told him one afternoon in his book-room. "I would gladly never see him, and I am afraid I shall be tempted to shake Lydia, hoping to make her see how stupid and reckless she has been. But we *must* give the appearance of acceptance—let people believe there was nothing scandalous about the affair."

Her father sighed heavily. He looked as though he had aged a decade since she embarked on her holiday with the Gardiners. "You are right, Lizzy, but let it be a short visit. Do not be surprised if I do everything possible to avoid their company, especially that…cur's."

Elizabeth moved to stand beside his chair and wrapped an arm across his shoulders. "I shall help you escape them, as long as you let me take refuge in here with you."

HIS FAMILY OBJECTS

Sitting in his bedchamber in his London house, Darcy rested his head against the back of his armchair, eyes towards the ceiling, and let out a low groan. It had been an exhausting week and a half. Only that evening had all the necessary papers been completed and signed. The business aspect of the situation—for which he had no polite name—had been concluded, and Darcy hoped it meant he would soon stop feeling perpetually sick in his stomach. That might not happen until after the couple were married and the final sums of money had exchanged hands.

Darcy fervently hoped that tonight he would sleep. Since leaving Elizabeth in Lambton, he had managed no more than two or three hours a night, with the occasional brief nap. It seemed like several months had passed since that morning, but at last, this dreadful period was almost at an end. The wedding would be soon, and Darcy would attempt to forget all about it, confident he would never see Wickham again; he hoped the same was true of Lydia Bennet. Elizabeth would understand, especially if he told her more about how Wickham had treated Georgiana.

Elizabeth. Darcy closed his eyes and let images of her flood his mind. The way she had looked at him during their last walk together, so full of life and joy, the feel of her hand in his, even her presence by his side, it was all so...*right*. They were meant to be together; he had known it at Easter when he proposed—and she had justly rejected him—and it was even more evident all these months later. She had put her trust in him, and—for her—he had found her sister and coaxed Wickham into marrying her, once it became evident the silly, ignorant girl would not leave him. Darcy had hated every minute of the endeavour, but he would do it again and again if that is what it took to win Elizabeth's hand in marriage.

"Soon," he whispered as though she would hear him. "The day after the ceremony, I leave at first light for Pemberley. I must see Georgiana and escort her to town. Once that is done, I *will* come to you, my love."

Then, the unspoken promise between them would be fulfilled, and they could look forward to a bright future.

The entirety of Lydia and Mr Wickham's visit to Longbourn was nothing short of torture for Elizabeth. Her sister was full of smiles and pride, and her mother was little better. She spent the whole time biting her tongue not to let loose her low opinion of the newly married couple.

After saying as polite a farewell as she could muster and waving at the carriage as it pulled Lydia and Mr Wickham away, Elizabeth turned towards her favourite path and began walking, not bothering to speak a word to anyone. Jane followed, calling her name, and Elizabeth waited until she was beside her before continuing, her sister's arm wrapped about hers.

"I wish you were not so angry," Jane said.

Elizabeth glanced at her. She had kept her feelings to herself, but she was not surprised her sister had noticed. "How can you not be? Lydia seems to think marriage is a great joke and that she has won some sort of prize by being the first of us to wed. She has no notion of the gravity of what she has done or how her actions might have destroyed our family—or she cares not an iota if she does—and Mama encourages her.

"As for *him*"—Elizabeth refused to speak Mr Wickham's name; the very sound of it revolted her—"he is smug, odious, and duplicitous. I am disgusted that I ever thought well of him and that I had to share a roof with him. After this visit, which I know was necessary, I will not. If Papa permits either of them at Longbourn again, I shall go elsewhere for the duration of their stay."

She hoped she would soon have a home of her own. Out of consideration for Mr and Miss Darcy, Elizabeth would not admit Mr Wickham or Lydia entry to Pemberley or the London house. Even should Mr Darcy say he would tolerate it, believing it would please her to see her youngest sister, she would refuse.

"I know it has been difficult. I pray Mr Wickham will succeed in his new position, for Lydia's sake as well as his own," Jane said in a conciliatory tone.

"I shall do likewise. He is now a husband and could possibly be a father before long. I hope he takes his new responsibilities seriously." Elizabeth spoke to please her sister, silently adding, *Though I doubt he will.*

They were quiet for a while, and Elizabeth's spirits calmed. She always found being surrounded by nature on a pleasant day improved her mood, and it worked its magic once again. She thought about Mr Darcy and how soon he would be in Meryton. It might depend on when Mr Bingley returned from Yorkshire. She expected the two men to come together, given Mr Bingley's desire to return to the neighbourhood. Mr Bingley would send word to open Netherfield, and the village gossips would ensure the news reached Longbourn.

As though knowing she was thinking of the gentleman,

Jane said, "Why would Mr Darcy have been at Lydia's wedding? I did not want to ask her, since she said it was meant to be a secret."

Lydia had accidentally mentioned it while speaking—boasting, really—of the ceremony. Elizabeth had hidden her smile. It had proved to her that Mr Darcy had done as he said he would in Lambton and assisted her uncle in resolving the distressing situation. Mrs Bennet liked to act as though Mr Wickham had always intended to marry Lydia, but Elizabeth knew that was nonsense.

"I suppose someone who knows them both informed Mr Darcy of that man running off with a young lady. Mr Darcy is too good not to intervene and attempt to rectify the situation."

"That would explain it." Jane sounded a little disappointed. The reason why was apparent when she continued. "I thought perhaps it meant they were attempting to repair their friendship. They have known each other since boyhood, and it would be a comfort to know Lydia's husband had such a gentleman as one of his connexions."

It was all Elizabeth could do not to laugh at Jane's notion. It was unthinkable that Mr Darcy would look upon Mr Wickham in any sort of amiable light. Fortunately, she was not called upon to comment; Jane posed another question.

"What did you and Mr Wickham talk of before they left? I saw him approach you on the lawn while I was speaking to Lydia."

Elizabeth rolled her eyes—not at Jane, but at Mr Wickham's impudence. "He said that we were always good friends, which we were not—not after Mr Darcy told me the truth about him when I was staying with Charlotte—and that now we were more. I told him in no uncertain terms that I had only been polite because I was forced to be in his company, but when it was just the two of us I felt no such compunction and would just as soon forget his existence. I did not stay to hear whether he had any response. It was no more than he deserved. They are gone, I am walking with my favourite sister, and I wish to put them from my thoughts and remember only that which makes me happy."

Jane patted her arm and said nothing further.

CHAPTER FIVE

True to Elizabeth's prediction, three days later, Mrs Goulding told Mrs Philips, who told Mrs Bennet, that the housekeeper at Netherfield was preparing to receive Mr Bingley. Only one guest was spoken of, and Elizabeth was certain who it would be. She was so visibly happy that even Mary noticed and asked what had her in such a good mood. Elizabeth said it was the delightful weather, although it was nothing uncommon for the season.

On the nineteenth of September, almost six weeks after last seeing him, Mr Darcy was at Longbourn. Elizabeth could hardly take her eyes off him; at the same time, she wanted desperately to hide from him, given the embarrassing display her mother was making. Mrs Bennet was all solicitousness to Mr Bingley and praised Jane excessively. In contrast, she was all rudeness to Mr Darcy, sniffing and speaking coldly when required to address him. Elizabeth wanted to blurt out that *he* was the one who had rescued her precious Lydia from a life of infamy and demand her mother treat him with the respect he deserved. Instead, knowing how much he would hate it, she took comfort in the steadiness of his gaze upon her, which seemed to say that nothing her mother did or said would alter his feelings for her.

The only thing that briefly distracted Elizabeth's attention was Jane. Her sister had sworn she would be unaffected when meeting Mr Bingley again, but her red cheeks and evident unease showed that she was not. No doubt Mrs Bennet's antics made her situation worse. A man who loved less would flee the scene, and Elizabeth gave Mr Bingley credit for remaining polite and not chuckling or rolling his eyes a single time in the face of so much provocation.

Mr Darcy and she managed only one short exchange before the gentlemen took their leave. They stood to the side while Mrs Bennet continued to speak to Mr Bingley.

"Thank you," Elizabeth said. She hoped her simple expression of gratitude would be the last time either of them had to refer to the Wickhams.

He shook his head. "I believe I once told you I would do anything to make you happy. I expect no gratitude for it. Are you well? I know your return must have been…difficult, but I pray you have been able to put the entire affair out of your mind. It need not distress you any longer."

Her heart swelled with love. "I am very well *now*." She hoped he understood that it was *his* presence that made all the difference to her well-being. "And you, sir? I am certain the weeks we were apart were not entirely pleasurable for you."

"That is all forgotten."

His fingers lightly brushed her hand just as Mary approached them. Elizabeth savoured his brief touch and thought of him incessantly for the remainder of that day and all of the next, when they did not see each other—not that he had been far from her mind since their parting in Lambton. By fortune, the following morning they happened to meet in Meryton. Kitty had begged her sisters to visit the shops with her, and soon after they reached the town, Elizabeth saw Mr Darcy and Mr Bingley riding towards them.

She believed Mr Darcy noticed her at the same moment she did him; he smiled, and the sound of her sisters' voices faded as she contemplated his fine form. A moment later, the two parties met. After the usual greetings, Mr Bingley, Jane, and Mary began to exchange pleasantries, leaving Elizabeth with Mr Darcy and Kitty, who was in an especially talkative mood.

"The weather is rather fine today, is it not? We have been particularly fortunate of late. It has hardly rained." She chattered on, evidently not noticing that her companions had no opportunity to speak, let alone that they might want to be alone. "I am glad Meryton is such an easy walk from Longbourn. *I* think we have a good selection of shops here, and Lydia was always happy enough to come, but now that she has been to Brighton, she says Meryton is dull and hardly worth visiting!"

"She is permitted her opinion, and since she is not here, it need not bother us," Elizabeth said. She doubted Mr Darcy wanted to listen to talk of Lydia, but catching her eye, he gave a slight shake of his head, which she understood meant she should not worry he was vexed. Yet, she sought some way to make her sister go and speak to the others.

"I suppose. Mr Darcy, what is the town near your estate like? My aunt Gardiner told us at Christmas that she lived there when she was a girl. Is it larger than Meryton?"

He glanced at Elizabeth, and she suspected he was puzzled. She still had not mentioned her time in Lambton. It was possible Mr Bingley had spoken of seeing her there, but if he had, it was not in Kitty's presence.

"It is similar in size and variety of shops. I admit, I have not spent very much time there."

Kitty sighed. "You are so fortunate you have been able to travel, Lizzy! I long to leave Longbourn. Anywhere would do. May I go to the haberdasher's while Jane speaks to Mr Bingley?"

"You may, if Mary accompanies you."

Kitty agreed and left them without a word. It did not look as though she asked Mary to go with her so much as took her arm to lead her away, but Elizabeth did not care. She was intent on taking advantage of her few minutes with Mr Darcy.

Lowering his voice, he said, "You have not told her you were lately in Lambton?"

Elizabeth shook her head. "I hardly wished to speak of having enjoyed myself when I first returned, and keeping those memories to myself, as closely guarded, cherished possessions, has become a habit."

His expression softened. "I am relieved it is not that recalling the visit displeases you."

"I remember telling you how much I liked Derbyshire and how happy I was there. My opinion has not changed. Do you often have difficulty recollecting events that happened not two months ago?" She arched her brow in challenge. When he chuckled, she grinned.

"Do you know how much I delight in you teasing me? I would hate it from anyone else," he said softly.

How was she expected to respond to such a statement? She

averted her eyes and took a surreptitious calming breath, hoping her cheeks would not turn bright red.

"Perhaps I only wished to hear you say it again," he said a moment later.

She lifted her eyes to his, and speaking as gently as he had, said, "Then I shall gladly repeat myself. I am very, very glad—overjoyed—that I went to Lambton and that I visited Pemberley just when its proprietor happened to be arriving."

"We ought to let the ladies continue their day, Darcy." The sound of Mr Bingley's voice was so unexpected that Elizabeth started.

The gentlemen were soon on their way, and Jane and Elizabeth went to find their sisters.

On Sunday, the gentlemen attended church and returned home with the Bennets, allowing Elizabeth and Mr Darcy to speak for a longer period without threat of being overheard or interrupted. They went for a walk with Jane and Mr Bingley. Once they were out of sight of the house, a natural separation arose between the couples.

"Your sister is happy to see Bingley again. I am glad my wrongheaded interference, and that of other parties, will not have any lasting damage. I doubt I could forgive myself if it were otherwise," Mr Darcy said.

"It is in the past, Jane is happy, and I insist we forget it ever happened. Does Mr Bingley know?" She laughed. "Perhaps I ought to have asked my question and obtained your response before saying we should forget it."

"The pleasure of hearing you laugh is enough to excuse any confusion you caused." He paused and grew more serious. "I told Bingley everything before we parted ways in August. I knew he was considering returning to Netherfield after seeing his family in Scarborough. It was important to me that he understood what your sister's sentiments had been and that I recognised I had been horribly mistaken and presumptuous—to say nothing of lying to him when I did not tell him Miss Bennet was in London last winter.

"He was…very angry. Rightly so. I apologised, but to be honest, I was not sure our friendship would survive. When he called on me in town, shortly before we came to Meryton, I was relieved. He has said he forgives me because he believes I am contrite. Naturally, he has made me promise not to behave in such an ungentlemanly manner again. Unfortunately, his sisters are not at all remorseful. They see nothing wrong in how they acted."

"I am very glad that your friendship has not ended. I believe it is important to both of you."

He nodded. "It is, and that is why he has chosen to overlook my misdeeds."

Elizabeth briefly tightened her hold on his arm; it was the only mark of affection she could offer him in their present circumstances. "I am sorry to hear his sisters maintain their opposition to Jane. I hope it does not distress him too much. He seems cheerful, but I do not know him well enough to tell whether he is simply hiding his less pleasant feelings."

"Presently, his only care is winning Miss Bennet's forgiveness for the manner in which he left and then earning her regard."

Again, Elizabeth laughed. "If he thinks either are necessary, he does not know Jane as well as I thought he did! She will see nothing to forgive, certain he had very good reasons for how he acted even if he never offers any, and she loves him as much as she ever did." Adding a serious note to her voice, she continued, "Enough about them. If you agree, I would like to have done with disagreeable topics and take this opportunity to thank you properly for what you did for Lydia. It must have been horrible for you, and I know she does not deserve it, but on her behalf and that of my entire family, thank you."

He shook his head, his gaze on the vista. "It had to be done. I wish I could have devised another end for your sister, but she refused to leave him. If only I had exposed Wickham's true nature—"

"It is not your role to protect the world and its many silly young ladies from scoundrels like him." Seeing a dark cloud pass over his countenance, Elizabeth realised he might be thinking of Miss Darcy. She had not meant to remind him that his sister had also fallen under Mr Wickham's spell; indeed, she had forgotten it for the moment, so consumed was she with her own sister's situation—and the thrilling sensation of being with Mr Darcy again. "I see no reason to speak of him further. He is married and settled far from us. There is little he can do to disrupt our peace now."

He took a deep breath and nodded. "How long do you think it will be before Miss Bennet and Bingley are engaged?"

"Hmm. I would be willing to wager he will wait one more week, then propose at the first opportunity. What say you?"

"Oh no, Miss Elizabeth, I shall not take that bet. I believe he will propose by Wednesday. Would you agree that they deserve to have their happiness to themselves for a short while —not have it overshadowed by any other similar event? If his sisters and I had left him to make his own decisions, they probably would have been betrothed nine or ten months ago."

There was no mistaking the meaning behind his question, and warmth flooded Elizabeth's body, both in anticipation of soon receiving a very welcomed second offer of marriage from him and of his thoughtfulness for her most deserving sister and his dearest friend.

"I do agree, sir. Provided, that is, Mr Bingley does not delay!"

They laughed and continued their walk until it was time to return to the house.

CHAPTER SIX

Two days later, Elizabeth again found herself walking with Mr Darcy. She had contrived to have him to herself, but she did not think anyone noticed. They were at an afternoon party at Haye-Park, the estate owned by Mr Bennet's childhood friend Mr Goulding. Since the day was warm and dry, many of the guests were spending time out of doors, Elizabeth and Mr Darcy amongst them. She took Mr Darcy into the gardens, which he had never seen. As soon as they were away from others, she laughed.

"Goodness, you are *very* popular! I have noticed how much everyone has wished to speak to you since your return, thus inconsiderately disrupting my intentions to monopolise your attention, but it was almost comical!"

He covered his face as though hiding in embarrassment. From the moment he and Mr Bingley had entered the house, two or three people had attempted to speak to him at once, usually on different subjects. "I have done nothing to deserve it, and I would thank you to stop laughing at me!"

She did her best to suppress her amusement. "You are free to tease me as much as you like should I ever find myself in a similar position. As for not deserving it, I disagree. I have never thought so highly of my neighbours as I have since seeing how much they value your company. They have excellent taste."

"Do you see why I prefer to stand at the side of the room being taciturn and disagreeable? I could hardly make sense of what everyone was saying."

"It was a bit much," she agreed. "We do not often see new people in the neighbourhood, and I admit we can be a little too eager at the prospect of hearing different voices. You bore it very well."

He shrugged. "I cannot fault your neighbours for their friendliness. I am grateful that they have welcomed me so warmly, despite how dreadful my manner was last year. Though, if I can be forgiven for saying it, I would prefer it if Mr Long did not speak so loudly, especially when he is standing beside me. I am not sure my hearing has yet recovered!"

Elizabeth brought her hand to her mouth to hide yet another laugh. Elderly Mr Long was almost entirely deaf but refused to admit it. She pointed to the left. "Shall we walk in that direction?"

He nodded, and they strolled in a companionable silence for several minutes before he spoke.

"The Gouldings have a fine property. I did not realise it was so large."

"I have always considered it one of the prettiest in the neighbourhood. Mr Goulding's mother was an avid gardener, and she is largely responsible for how the grounds look even today."

"Like my own. I often feel closer to my mother when I walk through the gardens she arranged."

She linked her arm with his and smiled gently. From the way he had spoken of Lady Anne, he had evidently loved her dearly and still grieved her death. "I wish I could have known her. Do you and Miss Darcy most resemble her or your father?"

There was a brief pause before he responded. "Georgiana reminds me of her more and more each year, though in looks I believe we both are like my father. Speaking of family, I have not heard you mention any other Bennet relations, apart from Mr Collins."

"Because there are none. My father had an older sister. She never married and died when I was still very young. We are a small family, and not a particularly illustrious one, but I am fond of them. Well, perhaps not Mr Collins, but I trust you not to tell anyone I said that!"

He earnestly vowed to keep her secret. His teasing pleased her because it showed how comfortable he was with her. They wandered a while longer until they reached a pond, where they stopped to watch a flock of ducks.

"I must go to London for a few days," Mr Darcy said. "I hope I shall be away for no more than a week, though it might be a few days beyond that. No more than a fortnight. There are meetings I must attend related to various ventures I am involved in, and more of my family will be in town. No doubt, they will wish to spend time with me and Georgiana. It has been some months since we were all together."

"Is this your mother's family or your father's? I do not recall you mentioning the latter as much as the former."

"I suppose that is true. I do not have an especially large family, though there are distant cousins I rarely see. On my mother's side, other than Lady Catherine and her daughter, it is Colonel Fitzwilliam's family—my aunt and uncle, Lord and Lady Romsley, and my older cousin, Viscount Bramwell. I am closest to them. My cousins are presently in London, and Fitzwilliam is staying with my sister, but the earl and countess are away. My father had a cousin, Mr Reed, with whom he was good friends, and I often see him, his wife, and their daughter, Rebecca. Now that I think of it, it must be six or seven months since I have, however, which is too long."

Elizabeth gave him a smile of thanks for his explanation. It would be too bold to say she looked forward to meeting them, so she did not.

"I am glad you and Miss Darcy will soon see your relations. When I was a child, I wished I had more. I still do. The idea of being surrounded by aunts and uncles and cousins appeals to me. One benefit of Jane marrying Mr Bingley, assuming he proposes"—they chuckled—"is that it means I shall have a new person to call family, one for whom I need not blush."

Their eyes met, and they shared an unspoken understanding that soon Elizabeth's family would be substantially enlarged, as would Mr Darcy's.

"I cannot promise none of my relations would make you blush," Mr Darcy said. "Two in particular, whom you have met, would almost certainly cause you vexation, if they have not already."

"And yet, I would gladly embrace them as my own."

"I hope you will have reason to before long." His fingers gently caressed hers, and she clasped his hand.

"As do I. I might even say I am counting on it," she whispered.

"As am I."

A noisy group of young people drew close, causing Mr

Darcy to withdraw his hand. They moved on, Elizabeth leading him along a path to a small copse.

"Now, sir, to return to the matter of your absence, I noticed your definition of 'a few days' does not entirely accord with my own. First, you give me reason to hope I shall have the pleasure of seeing you by Saturday, now you admit it could be a week beyond that? For shame."

He took her hand and placed it on his arm. No one would look askance at them walking thus, although anyone who knew her well—and everyone present did—would know she did not require his assistance for such an easy walk. She did not care if they commented on it. What did it matter when soon they would be sharing the happiest of news with the entire world?

"I shall make it as short an absence as possible," he vowed.

"Thank you. You will find me here, patiently awaiting you." She spoke softly.

They exchanged a long look, their gentle smiles conveying a great deal. Although part of Elizabeth wished he would speak, there was something terribly romantic about this period of their lives and the anticipation of what was to come. Her happiness was like a balloon in her stomach, slowly leaking all the emotions it contained, and once he proposed, it would burst and cover her with so much joy she would not know what to do.

Except throw myself into his arms and entice him to kiss me. She chuckled to herself. *I suspect it will not be a difficult task!*

CHAPTER SEVEN

However strong Darcy's inclination to remain by Elizabeth's side, he had responsibilities he could not neglect. As it was, the need to find Wickham had meant an unexpected separation from Georgiana. He hated to leave her for long and had only spent a significant time apart from her twice since Ramsgate. The first was when he had gone to Netherfield Park the year before; the earl and countess had insisted Georgiana would recover quicker without him nearby. The second was at Easter when he had gone to Rosings. Then, it was a matter of not giving Lady Catherine a reason to speculate on why he was changing his usual routine.

Once he and Elizabeth were engaged, Darcy would inform his family and speak to Bingley about bringing Georgiana and her companion to stay at Netherfield, as long as he could find a way to ensure she would not have to hear Wickham's name. Then he would not need to worry about neglecting his sister while also being with the woman his heart and soul most longed for. It would give the ladies an opportunity to know each other better too. At present, he was glad to spend time with Georgiana.

"Did you enjoy seeing Miss Elizabeth?" she asked.

"I did. She asked after you," Darcy answered.

It said much about Georgiana that this evidently surprised her. "Oh. Th-that was kind of her."

"She is a kind and sympathetic lady and will make you an excellent sister."

"Have you proposed to her?" Was that a spark of interest in her eyes?

"Not yet, but I shall as soon as I go back. I am anxious to settle things with her, but it was important for me to be here this week, to see you most of all, and our other relations. It always seems to be the case that I have too many meetings to attend, and there are several that will take me from home in the coming days. As soon as I have asked her, I promise I shall write to you." He explained about Bingley and Miss Bennet's impending engagement and his wish to let them celebrate it first. "As I have said before, I would prefer it if you did not mention Miss Elizabeth to Fitzwilliam or the rest of our family. I shall make an announcement after everything is settled."

"Of course, if that is what you wish, but…why?"

Darcy did not want to make too much of the matter; it would only cause her more anxiety. Thus, he kept his tone light as he responded. "I simply prefer to keep news of my interest quiet. It is possible that some of our family might oppose my choice. You should prepare yourself for it. I do not believe it will be harsh or long-lasting, especially once they have met her." Lady Catherine would object to him marrying any lady who was not her daughter, but that meant nothing to him.

"Fitzwilliam and Bramwell will be happy for me, and I am

convinced the earl and countess will be, although it might take them a little time to accustom themselves to the notion. With all four of them in town this winter, they will have the opportunity to know Miss Elizabeth, supposing she and her parents agree to her coming to London for a fortnight or so. I expect it will be similar with our Reed cousins. Rebecca will be happy for us, but her parents might need to know Miss Elizabeth before being satisfied I have made a good choice."

Georgiana nodded and kept her chin lowered. He saw her nibbling on her lip, which was a sure sign she was debating whether to say something. Experience told him it was best to wait for her to speak. At length, she did.

"Brother, what will happen to me when you and she are married? Where shall I go?"

Her tentative, fearful tone broke his heart. "It is my intention that you will live with me and my wife. Miss Elizabeth is always such a cheerful person. You remarked on it yourself this summer. Do you recall? Will it not be agreeable to be around her all the time? I am certain she already expects that you will make your home with us, at least until—*if*—you marry. If you do not, you will always have a home with me." He had assured her of the last many times. Georgiana currently stated that she had no wish to enter society or find a husband. While he hoped that would change in the future, he worried she would never fully recover.

"What if she finds out? She would hate—"

"No, Georgiana!" Darcy knelt beside his sister's chair, took her hand in his, and attempted to make her look at him. "Miss Elizabeth would no more hate you than I do, or Fitzwilliam does, or anyone who knows the truth. She would wish to be of assistance to you. She *will* wish it, even though she remains ignorant of what affects you so deeply. I could not love a lady who would not be an affectionate, caring sister to you, let alone marry one."

After a long moment, Georgiana took a deep breath and slowly released it as she had been instructed by one physician or another. She pulled her hand from his, which was Darcy's cue to return to his previous seat. Once he did, his sister told him how she was proceeding with her attempts to learn several new pieces of music.

A quarter of an hour later, Georgiana returned to her apartment, leaving Darcy to think through their conversation. It would be an exaggeration to say he was uneasy at the prospect of his relations learning of Elizabeth, but he anticipated some difficult conversations. He wanted to be done with it.

"They will all know soon enough," he said to the empty room. He would try to arrange it so that he could tell Lord and Lady Romsley in person rather than in writing. They had always been good to him and Georgiana, and they deserved the consideration. He would not take the time to go to Lady Catherine; he would not give her the opportunity to harangue him for his choice of wife.

There was another difficult conversation ahead of him; Fitzwilliam did not know of Wickham's latest antics, and while Darcy had no intention of discussing the particulars with his other relations—it would be enough to assure them Wickham would have no part in their lives—Fitzwilliam would demand to know it all. Darcy had considered writing to tell him as soon as he learnt of the elopement, but, at the time, the colonel had been in Dover, busy with his military duties, and he would not have been able to provide assistance. Later in the autumn, once he could speak of Wickham in a calmer manner, Darcy would tell him everything.

At the moment, I prefer to think of Elizabeth. Pouring himself a glass of wine, Darcy sat and stared at the empty grate. *A week from today I shall be in Meryton again, provided I can complete everything I must do by then. If not, the delay will be just another day or two. I shall then secure my happiness and that of my dearest, loveliest Elizabeth. Our misunderstandings will truly be a thing of the past and never to be repeated!*

A week after Mr Darcy left for town, Mr Bingley proposed to Jane. She accepted, and the Bennets duly celebrated the couple's good fortune. Elizabeth was exceedingly pleased for her sister and knew that when it was her turn to share similar news, Jane would be equally as delighted, if perhaps somewhat more surprised. Mrs Bennet immediately began to talk of the wedding, and Elizabeth spent a good portion of her time dreaming of Mr Darcy and the possibility of a double wedding with Jane and Mr Bingley.

On the very day Elizabeth had marked as the earliest she would permit herself to hope for Mr Darcy's return, she received an unexpected visitor: Lady Catherine de Bourgh.

Her ladyship entered the house like a tempest, her walking stick repeatedly striking the floor, sounding as though she was putting all her force into the action. Her only words were directed at Elizabeth, who was too stunned by the lady's appearance to know what to say. When Lady Catherine demanded they take a turn in the gardens, Elizabeth led the way and waited for the older woman to speak, determined to keep her temper despite her visitor's rudeness. Knowing of Lady Catherine's wish for a union between her daughter and Mr Darcy, Elizabeth wondered whether she had learnt of his intention to propose to *her* and that was the reason for this unforeseen encounter.

"Mr Collins informed me that his wife received a letter from her sister, Miss Maria Lucas." Lady Catherine paused as though she expected Elizabeth to comment, and Elizabeth obliged, unable to entirely avoid the touch of sarcasm in her tone.

"I imagine that is a common occurrence. Did Maria write something alarming? If Mrs Collins is worried about her sister or family, I can direct you to Lucas Lodge, where you can make enquiries on her behalf."

"You know exactly why I am here, Elizabeth Bennet! Mr Collins recognised the gravity of the girl's report and immediately brought it to my attention. Are you engaged to my nephew Darcy?"

"I beg your pardon?" *Why would Maria write such a thing to Charlotte?*

"Your elder sister has caught herself a good husband, one who, although lowborn, is rich. As Darcy has graciously befriended him, despite my disapproval, you have evidently turned your sights on him. Miss Maria Lucas wrote that you and he were often seen together when he was lately here. I will not permit him to marry you!"

Elizabeth's cheeks burnt at the insult to Jane, Mr Bingley, and herself. "As far as I am aware, it is not for you to permit or forbid anything Mr Darcy chooses to do. I would ask nothing of him that he would not freely give, whether it is a friendly conversation when we happen to be at the same party, or marriage."

Lady Catherine peered at her through narrowed eyes, and Elizabeth wondered whether she had spoken too warmly—had it added to the woman's suspicions of an attachment between

Mr Darcy and herself? What did it matter? Soon enough, Mr Darcy would return, they *would* be engaged, and he would inform his relations.

"If my nephew is foolhardy enough to propose to you, to actually marry you, he will not be recognised by his family. We will not share his disgrace. I see who you truly are, Elizabeth Bennet. I hoped to find you reasonable, but since you are not, I know what to do. Find another dupe to marry you. It will never be my nephew!"

With these final words, Lady Catherine turned and quickly strode about the side of the house, presumably to her carriage.

"Good riddance," Elizabeth said with a little laugh.

Shaking off her impulse to yell at the retreating figure, Elizabeth walked in the opposite direction Lady Catherine had taken, following the path to the stream. There, she found a safe spot to dip her handkerchief into the cool water, which she then pressed to her heated cheeks. It would help calm her before she returned to the house. She wished she had a way to inform Mr Darcy of his aunt's agitation. It might prepare him for whatever Lady Catherine would say to him. Elizabeth knew it would not be pleasant, but he was likely used to her manner and would manage her better than Elizabeth had.

He will be back soon, perhaps even tomorrow. We can discuss our shared experiences with the redoubtable Lady Catherine de Bourgh! Silently, she chuckled at her joke.

CHAPTER EIGHT

Every day, Elizabeth looked for Mr Darcy, hoping, even expecting, that he would accompany Mr Bingley when he came to Longbourn in time for breakfast. She listened carefully for any mention Mr Bingley made of his friend. There was nothing. At first, she thought little of it. It was disappointing, very much so, and she missed him dearly, but he had been uncertain about the length of his absence.

But a week became a fortnight and then longer still, and there was no sight of Mr Darcy, not even an offhand remark from Mr Bingley about him being held up in town for some reason. Any excuse would do; Elizabeth did not care what it was, she just wanted to know that their prolonged separation was unavoidable and would soon end.

She thought of him constantly, seemingly more so each day, and she felt herself becoming increasingly unsocial. Fortunately, the weather did not preclude walking, and she spent as much time as she could on her own, imagining her reunion with Mr Darcy and holding ever more frantic debates with herself about why he was staying away so long.

Mr Bingley and Jane had selected a date for their wedding in early December, which was six weeks away, and Mrs Bennet was managing to find a way to occupy every waking hour with planning the event and preparing Jane for her life as Mrs Bingley. Jane was understandably eager, but Elizabeth sensed her own heart had gained another crack by the time she crawled into bed each night. How could it be otherwise, when she had expected to be an engaged lady too?

No longer able to bear the growing uncertainty, at the end of October, she asked Mr Bingley about his friend. They were at a soirée at Haye-Park, and she seized a chance moment alone with him. Her heart thudded so loudly that the sound filled her ears.

"I understood Mr Darcy planned to return. Have his intentions changed, or-or do you expect to see him soon?"

Despite the dim light in the drawing room, Elizabeth thought Mr Bingley's cheeks darkened, and she sensed that he was not happy with his friend. Only then did it occur to Elizabeth that his absence could be taken as a lack of support for Jane and Mr Bingley's betrothment. Mr Darcy had been uncertain whether Mr Bingley would forgive him for his previous interference; surely he would not want to give him reason to question whether he had been wise to do so.

"Yes...that is, I *do* expect he will be here sooner or later. I hope he will be here for the wedding. I want him to stand up with me, but he would give me no promise. In truth, his explanation for why he might not was not at all clear, which is unlike him. I think he thought he might come sooner, but then he had to go to Pemberley, if I recall correctly. The harvest and what have you. Oh, there is Mr Stuart! I have been wanting to ask him something. If you will excuse me."

He hurried away. Elizabeth hardly noticed. She was too empty, too numb to feel anything. There was no mistaking that Mr Darcy had made an excuse to avoid returning to Hertfordshire—to avoid returning to her.

Elizabeth did not speak to anyone for the remainder of their time at Haye-Park. When her mother remarked on how stupid she was being, she claimed a headache and, upon reaching Longbourn, immediately excused herself. No doubt her emotions would soon overtake her, and she would not let them show until she was alone.

Mr Darcy had decided against proposing again; there was no other explanation. Really, she ought to have realised it a fortnight or three weeks ago, but she had not wanted to admit it to herself. Mr Bingley's words meant she had no choice but to accept it. Her heart shattered into a million pieces, and once she was in her room, she threw herself onto the bed and buried her face in the pillow, hoping it would muffle the noise of her sorrow.

Although she eventually fell asleep, the next morning, Elizabeth felt as though she had been awake for a week. She was still in her night clothes when Jane came into her bedchamber. A malaise had settled over her, and despite wanting to seek the comfort of the open air, she could not find it within herself to put on a day dress and go out.

"Oh, Lizzy, you look very poorly. Is it your head?" Jane caressed her cheek and sat beside her on the bed.

The only answer she could offer was a slight shrug. Attempting to do more might end with her sobbing.

Jane wrapped an arm about her shoulders. "I wish you

would tell me what troubles you. I have seen that you are not your usual self this last fortnight, but I do not know why."

"I am sorry if my mood has caused you anxiety. This is such a happy time for you, and I would not have you worry for me."

"Of course I worry for you!" Jane gave her shoulder a brief squeeze. "If you truly do not wish to, I shall not force you to confide in me, but…does it have to do with Mr Darcy?"

Elizabeth started.

"Bingley told me you asked about Mr Darcy returning. He was supposed to be here weeks ago, but now he writes that his plans are uncertain. Bingley is confused, and I admit to you alone, I think he is injured by his friend's manner." Jane paused before saying, "Bingley told me you saw each other a great deal when you were in Lambton—that you and Mr and Miss Darcy were often in company. Why did you never tell me?"

Knowing she would be unable to control her response if she spoke, Elizabeth only shook her head.

"He believes you and Mr Darcy have become friends, which gladdens him, given how little you liked each other last year. Knowing what passed between you in the spring, I wonder whether there is something more we do not know."

An involuntary whimper escaped Elizabeth.

"Lizzy, please, I beg of you, tell me."

Elizabeth's impulse to keep the truth to herself, to not disturb Jane's felicity by admitting she was desperately unhappy, crumbled when confronted with her sister's sympathy. "Before I say anything, you must promise to tell no one, not even Mr Bingley. I know it is asking a great deal, Jane, but it will make sense once I have told you."

Jane hesitated. "Very well. I shall keep your secret, so long as it does not cause you injury or keep you from being happy again."

Elizabeth stood and went to the dressing table. There, she found a handkerchief and wiped her eyes; she had not realised she had begun to cry. She kept her back to her sister as she began to tell her of the days she had spent with Mr Darcy in Derbyshire.

"I cannot describe what it was like. At first, seeing him again was awkward. We had been so angry with each other at Easter, but then, he was polite and…oh, I do not know! It was as though I was encountering someone new, yet also someone I already considered a dear friend and whose company I valued. In the days afterwards, I discovered he was everything I had ever imagined I might find in a gentleman. More than that, because he was *real*, not someone I conjured with my imagination. Aunt and Uncle Gardiner extended our stay in Lambton, and I know it was to give Mr Darcy and me more time together. They could see that we were forming an attachment."

She turned and faced Jane but did not move closer to her. Her sister's lips were parted, and her brow was arched. Elizabeth swallowed heavily before taking a deep breath and continuing her story.

"I was alone at the inn the morning your letters telling me of Lydia's elopement arrived. As I was reading the news, Mr Darcy arrived. We had arranged to…I do not recall what. I think he might have proposed that day, or at least asked whether I would consider— Well, that does not matter."

"Does not matter?" Jane cried, springing to her feet. "Lizzy, are you in love with Mr Darcy? I suspected your feelings had changed, but I-I did not think—"

"Please, Jane." Elizabeth held up a hand to prevent her sister from approaching. She also shook her head and bit the inside of her cheek, which oddly helped to control her stronger sentiments and keep her from openly weeping. "My feelings do not matter. Obviously. Reading of Lydia, I was distressed, and I confessed the whole of it to Mr Darcy. You must never tell anyone, but Mr Darcy was involved in finding Lydia and Mr Wickham and arranging their marriage. He does not wish it to be generally known." Elizabeth supposed he did not want to draw attention to his connexion to Mr Wickham. She also understood him well enough to know he would consider it a private matter.

Jane gasped.

"I was not surprised when he and Mr Bingley returned to Netherfield. The last thing Mr Darcy said to me in Lambton was that we would see each other soon. I assured him I would understand if Lydia's actions prevented him from continuing his association with me, but he said it would not. He did not use those words exactly, but everything he said and everything about how he acted that morning and when he was here in September led me to believe he would soon renew his offer."

"But…" Jane sputtered, evidently sharing Elizabeth's confusion about what had changed.

Elizabeth shrugged. "Evidently, something has altered. When he went to town, he told me he would return in a week or thereabouts, but now it is clear he has no intention of furthering our connexion."

Jane paled, and Elizabeth continued, trying to infuse her words with humour to alleviate her sister's growing unease. "I was mistaken about the strength of his regard. I have been mistaken about a great deal this past year, most especially his and Mr Wickham's characters when we first met. Perhaps Lady Catherine talked to him and convinced him he was being outrageously foolish to consider making me his wife, given my many inexcusable failings, chiefly being poor and not having a duke for a father."

"How can you jest about this?"

"Because I am tired of being unhappy!" Elizabeth exclaimed. "What more should I say? I cannot charge him with breaking a promise to me. If I am embarrassed or sad that the man I admire does not return my feelings, I shall simply have to talk myself out of it, I suppose."

They had not spoken any vows to each other, not even admitted to being in love, but in so many ways, they *had* exchanged promises. In her worst moments, Elizabeth believed his abandonment was her due for so foolishly misjudging him in the past. She did not intend to confess how deeply injured she felt even to Jane.

They were silent for a long moment. Several times, it looked as though Jane would speak, but she did not.

"I will be well, Jane," Elizabeth insisted. "I have been bewildered precisely because I allowed myself to have certain expectations. Now that I know they will not come to pass, I can put him out of my mind."

It would not be as simple as that, not when she harboured such a deep love for Mr Darcy. *I am, once again, mistaken when it comes to him, and I cannot hide it from myself. If he was the man I thought he was, the man I wanted him to be, he and I would be engaged and planning our wedding alongside Jane and Mr Bingley. If only I understood what has changed!* If she did, she was certain it would help her overcome her tender feelings all the quicker.

"Bingley was going to beg Mr Darcy to be here for the wedding and to stand up with him, but knowing all of this, I shall find a way to convince him not to," Jane said.

Elizabeth stepped towards her. "No, you must not!"

"I shall not ask you to see him and act as though he has treated you as he should!"

Elizabeth grasped her sister's hand. "You promised you would not tell him! You know his friendship with Mr Darcy is important to him, do you not?" After Jane nodded, Elizabeth continued. "If you tell him even a small part of what I have disclosed—if you even hint that Mr Darcy has injured me—Mr Bingley would sever the connexion. I am absolutely convinced of it. I would hate that to happen. As I said, it is not as though Mr Darcy has actually jilted me."

She was not certain how much Mr Bingley had told her sister of his friend's interference in their affairs—or that of his sisters'—but she suspected it had been little to avoid upsetting Jane.

"I do not like this." Jane's eyes were red, an indication she was close to crying.

"It is for the best," Elizabeth insisted. "I am absolutely certain of it. The brief period of conviviality he and I shared will one day be nothing but a pleasant memory. Little will be served by distressing Mr Bingley or anyone else, which is what would happen if they knew."

Elizabeth held her sister's gaze steady until she saw that Jane acquiesced. Some of the burden she had been carrying eased; unfortunately, she suspected she had imposed it upon Jane, but with the wedding approaching, she hoped it would soon be forgotten.

And I hope I can find a way to hide my feelings when I see him— should he actually come to the wedding. I have five weeks or thereabouts. Surely by then, I shall have talked myself out of loving him and wanting to be his wife above all else.

CHAPTER NINE

Having unburdened herself to Jane, Elizabeth found it slightly easier to act in a cheerful manner. It helped to know someone else understood she had suffered a heartache. For the first few weeks after their conversation, it was as though she entered a period of relative calm; she was still affected by the loss of Mr Darcy, but she was able to go about her daily life with relative ease. But the closer the wedding drew, the more Elizabeth felt her anxiety growing.

Mr Darcy had informed Mr Bingley he would be at the ceremony, and soon she would see him!

While admitting it was exceedingly silly, in the corner of her heart, she harboured a dream of reconciling with him. On his return to Netherfield, he would bring with him an excellent excuse for his prolonged absence and silence, and he would apologise in the most genuine, heartfelt manner possible. Elizabeth knew her weaknesses; whether she should or not, she would forgive him at once. Possibly, she would throw herself into his arms and weep. To be sure, she would eventually tell him how much his behaviour had injured her, but that would be *after* rejoicing in being with him and secure of his love again.

Jane worried for her, despite anything Elizabeth might say to convince her not to. They spoke about it one night just a few days before the wedding, while sitting on Elizabeth's bed. They were wrapped in wool shawls, and they rested side-by-side, their backs against the headboard.

"I could see that my mother's speech at dinner vexed you," Jane said.

Elizabeth gave a short laugh. "That it did."

Mrs Bennet had spent what seemed like an hour bemoaning Lydia's absence, especially that she would not be present at the wedding.

"Mama's wish to see Lydia is understandable," Jane said.

Elizabeth just managed not to roll her eyes. "Yes, I am familiar with her preference for our youngest sister. I do not have to like it, however, and I certainly do not have to anticipate seeing her or her husband ever again."

Jane remained silent, no doubt thinking what Elizabeth was—her anger was largely if not wholly because she blamed Lydia for her loss of Mr Darcy. When Jane spoke again, she raised an issue they had debated many times in recent weeks. She wanted Elizabeth to accompany her and Mr Bingley on their wedding trip to Bath, and Elizabeth had refused.

"I do wish you would change your mind, Lizzy. I truly believe it would do you good to be away from here for a time."

Elizabeth offered her a smile, though it was not long-lasting. "And I truly believe a couple should be alone after their wedding, not distracted by discontented sisters. They also deserve to have the opportunity to think of no one but themselves. I shall be well. It will be Christmas soon, and Charlotte wrote that she and Mr Collins are planning to visit. I shall enjoy seeing her again. In six short weeks, you will return, and I dare say, you will see that I am much improved." Every word she said was genuine. In addition, she wanted time to herself, perhaps partly out of a hope that she and Mr Darcy would reconcile and partly out of fear of experiencing bitter jealousy at seeing the newly married couple's happiness.

Jane's brow furrowed, and after a short pause, she sighed. "I know you are too stubborn to change your mind once you have convinced yourself you made the right decision. I hope I do find you happier when we see each other in January. I shall insist you spend a great deal of time with me then. Be forewarned!"

The ladies shared a light laugh at Jane's mock-stern tone, and soon after, they said good night.

The day before the wedding, Mr Darcy, the Hursts, and Miss Bingley arrived at Netherfield Park, and there was a celebratory dinner at Longbourn for the residents of the two houses. All day, Elizabeth was sick with apprehension—alternately chilled and overheated, unable to eat more than a morsel, and desperately praying she would not make a fool of herself, no matter what happened.

As soon as the Netherfield party entered the drawing room, Elizabeth's eyes sought Mr Darcy. Her heart ached when she saw his tall, handsome form. Their gazes met, but he had to avert his to greet her parents, which he did politely, congratulating them on Jane's engagement and thanking them for their hospitality.

A moment later, he was standing in front of her, and their eyes met. Her heart stopped beating as she waited for him to speak. When he did, she struggled to take in every nuance of how he spoke and acted.

"Miss Elizabeth, I…I hope you are well." He looked away, chagrin or perhaps embarrassment in his expression.

Her mouth was too dry to permit speech, and she made a shallow curtsey and did her best not to show how affected she was. An icy sensation overcame her, dulling her pain and fury. She would not let her true emotions show; nothing she did would mar even a moment of Jane's happiness. To mitigate her sister's anxiety, Elizabeth smiled broadly and joined her in chatting to Mr and Mrs Hurst for a few minutes until they went through to the dining room.

All through the meal, Elizabeth continued to put on a performance that would have ensured her a successful career as a stage actress, if she could repeat it. She smiled and talked animatedly and showed no sign that behind her delight for Jane lay misery. Fortunately, Mr Darcy and she were separated by two people, and it was enough that she could avoid seeing him.

Unfortunately, she could hear him perfectly well, his deep voice drawing her in as he spoke to her mother of neighbourhood news or Jane and Mr Bingley about their plans. In everything he did, apart from how he treated *her*, he was the same gentleman she had known that summer and autumn. She was glad for Mr Bingley's sake, and it confirmed her desire to keep her new brother from learning what had happened between her and his friend.

During the separation of the sexes, she remained with Mary and Kitty, having little desire to speak to Mr Bingley's sisters. When she heard the gentlemen approaching, she surreptitiously took a deep breath. *Another hour or two, and they will return to Netherfield. He will probably depart for town or Derbyshire or wherever he chooses to go after the wedding breakfast. Then and only then shall I permit myself to feel the weight of what seeing him again has meant.*

More often than not, when she peeked in his direction, she caught him regarding her, but he did not approach her, and she certainly was not going to demand he pay her any attention if he did not wish to. She noticed him speaking to several others—her father and Mr Bingley most of all but also her sisters; he had even managed to look interested during a long conversation with Kitty, although Elizabeth doubted he had contributed more than half a dozen words.

As they took tea, Miss Bingley spoke more loudly than necessary about her arrangements after the wedding. It appeared to be an attempt to capture the attention of all her companions and make them jealous.

"Louisa, Mr Hurst, and I depart the day after tomorrow. We are going to Brighton. Will that not be the most splendid way to spend the winter? We shall have ever so much fun, and it will be a wonderful change from being in town, although I adore London, of course. If I cannot be there, Brighton is the only place I would not be absolutely miserable. I can hardly sleep, such is my anticipation." She grinned, and her eyes were round with elation when she turned to Elizabeth. "What will you do, Miss Eliza, now that your sister will be so fortunately married?"

Elizabeth longed to say something sarcastic in response. To her, Miss Bingley's odious behaviour merited it, but she also knew that her disappointment regarding Mr Darcy wanted an outlet of some sort, and the other lady did not deserve to bear the brunt of Elizabeth's darker emotions.

"I have decided to remain at Longbourn at present."

Mrs Bennet scoffed. "You had much better go with them. Perhaps you would find *someone* who wanted to marry you in Bath. You certainly have had no luck here or when you went to visit Charlotte or on your travels with my brother and sister last summer."

Elizabeth could not stop herself from glancing at Mr Darcy. His expression was unreadable. How she wished she knew what he was thinking and feeling! Her mind screamed that he looked regretful, even that she saw some of the tenderness she had come to expect and treasure, but she refused to accept it.

Jane began to stammer, evidently hoping to change the subject and protect Elizabeth from any more of Mrs Bennet's talk of marriage.

To spare her the necessity, Elizabeth said in a joking manner, "I am glad to know you are so anxious to be rid of me, Mama. Mary, Kitty, you will be glad to have me here, will you not? I dare not hope my father will have an opinion on the matter."

Her sisters both answered, and from his seat near the fireplace, Mr Bennet chuckled and evidently also spoke; Elizabeth saw their lips move, but she heard none of it. She was occupied by the belief that the thoughts of at least one other person in the room mirrored hers—someone *had* wanted to marry her, and she had wanted to marry him too. The perfect gentleman for her, in fact, though she had not told anyone that was how she viewed Mr Darcy. Had events transpired as she had supposed they would, she might be seated by his side this evening, anticipating exchanging marriage vows with him on the morrow. Instead, she wanted to scream at him, beat him with her fists, and demand he tell her why he had abandoned her.

CHAPTER TEN

Elizabeth's first prayer during the wedding ceremony was for the happiness and continued well-being of her sister Jane. The second was more personal. She begged God for help forgetting her love for Mr Darcy. She struggled to keep her composure and hide how perplexed she was at what had become of their connexion; at times, she felt as though she lacked the strength to remain standing. Briefly, she wondered whether her current desolation was what he had experienced after she refused him in Kent. If so, she regretted how foolish she had been. If only they had both behaved better last autumn and spring, all of this unhappiness might have been avoided!

Watching Jane and Mr Bingley depart, Elizabeth began to calculate how soon she could steal away and seek solitude. It was not particularly cold, and she might go for a walk. Lost in her musings as she stood by a window, she did not notice Mr Darcy approach. When she felt a presence behind her, she knew it was him without even looking. Her heart began to beat quickly.

"We must talk, but not here. Somewhere alone," he whispered urgently.

She said nothing for a moment. Despite having wanted to speak to him, a part of her dreaded the notion after witnessing his behaviour over the last two days. However, it was necessary. Without a confirmation that everything between them was at an end—and ideally an explanation as to why—she would not be able to set aside her feelings for him.

"Please," he said, evidently taking her silence as an indication she would refuse.

"Meet me on the path between here and Netherfield, by the three pine trees, in an hour." She brushed past him, not liking how desperate she felt being so close to him.

Feeling the cold December wind whistling through the trees, Darcy watched Elizabeth walk away, her final words still ringing in his ears: "Do not be so ungentlemanly as to force me to hear you when I do not want to!" At once, he felt completely empty and full of something ugly and sickening. He had known their conversation would be difficult, but his imaginings had not prepared him for how terrible it was to witness her pain and fury and know it was because of his behaviour. He wanted to run after her, take back what he had said, make it as though they were beginning again—even better, travel back in time to September and propose before he left for London. Why had he entertained the ridiculous notion that Bingley and his new wife deserved a period in which everyone's attention was on them alone?

He was not usually a man who showed his emotions, but Darcy was close to tears and utterly exhausted. He stepped towards the closest tree and sat on the ground, not caring that it was cold and damp or what it would do to his clothing.

As hard as it was to live with his decision when he was away from Elizabeth, seeing her, he was not certain he could bear it. The impulse to throw himself at her feet and beg her to be his wife and confront whatever difficulties arose from their marriage together was nearly overwhelming. But surely his sister must be his priority. Even Elizabeth would agree to that if she fully understood the situation. Georgiana's welfare was a charge put upon him by his father, and it was one he endeavoured to fulfil out of love; it was not simply a duty he might seek to diminish. He had failed her in Ramsgate—oh, how he had failed her!—and he would not do it again, even though that meant giving up the woman he loved and desperately wanted as his wife.

Burying his face in his hands, Darcy dug his fingers into his skin. How had his life come to this? He had been so happy! Indeed, when he had travelled to town, a more fanciful person would say he floated above the ground. He was in love, and unlike the previous spring, he had good reason to believe—to *know*—the object of his affection loved him in return.

Then Lady Catherine had to interfere.

Darcy sighed and murmured, "I ought not to blame her." While his aunt had agitated the others, nothing she had said was truly false. The Bennets *did* have connexions in trade, and one of Elizabeth's sisters *had* married Wickham. Darcy wondered whether Lady Catherine would have hesitated to say his name if she had known how angry it would make the earl, countess, and their sons, but she did not know of the near disaster at Ramsgate.

His memories took him back to the day that had changed everything two months earlier.

Having heard that his uncle and aunt had arrived in town, Darcy called on them. The day being pleasant, he walked from his house in Berkeley Square to theirs in Grosvenor Square. The butler directed him to the sitting room reserved for the family. There, Darcy found not only Lord and Lady Romsley but also his cousins Viscount Bramwell and Fitzwilliam—and Lady Catherine.

He greeted his relations, adding, "I did not expect to see you, Lady Catherine."

The look she gave him was nearly venomous, which puzzled him.

"You did not bring Georgiana?" Fitzwilliam asked.

"She will join us later. Her music master is coming this morning."

"I am here because we have something very important to discuss," Lady Catherine announced.

"Yes, do finally tell us why you have made this unexpected visit." The earl's tone suggested he was not pleased by it.

"Darcy is on the point of making a grave mistake—one that would be a disaster for him and this entire family. He intends to make an offer of marriage to Miss Elizabeth Bennet."

Darcy was so shocked by her words that he could not immediately respond.

"Marriage?" the earl said, while the countess, eyes wide, said, "We had no idea you were interested in any lady. Who is Miss Elizabeth Bennet? Why do I not know the name?"

Fitzwilliam stared, evidently surprised; his eyebrows were

arched in silent question, and Darcy nodded to confirm Lady Catherine's information.

The earl and countess immediately began to interrogate him—who were Elizabeth's people, in which county did she live, how had he met her? Lady Catherine sat, her spine rigid, with a smug expression that further alarmed Darcy. Bramwell watched with an amused smirk; he was used to his parents quizzing him about any lady he so much as glanced at.

Darcy had hoped to put off telling them until after he had proposed and secured Mr Bennet's permission. He sought the best way to present Elizabeth to them. "Her father's estate is in Hertfordshire, neighbouring the one leased by my friend Bingley," he said.

"Her father may be a gentleman," Lady Catherine interjected, "however, her mother's people are in trade!"

"Trade?" Lord Romsley's hard gaze swung to Darcy.

"Yes, trade. One uncle is a country solicitor, the other retains a warehouse in Cheapside, and he lives nearby. Darcy would have an earl for one uncle and a lowborn salesman for another!" Lady Catherine said.

"Who are her father's family? Has he any decent connexions, someone from our circle?" Lady Romsley asked.

Lady Catherine scoffed. "That would be a miracle. The estate is exceedingly small and ill-kept. I was there just yesterday. The mother is vulgar, and as for Miss Elizabeth Bennet, she was rude and—"

"You went to Longbourn?" Darcy exclaimed. How could Lady Catherine have thought that was appropriate? *And how can I ever apologise enough to Elizabeth? No doubt Lady Catherine was unconscionably rude.* "How dare you interfere in *my* affairs!"

"That is not the material point," the earl stated, speaking loudly enough to be heard over the other voices in the room.

"Does Mr Bennet have any connexions that help make up for Miss Bennet's other deficiencies?"

While resenting the way the question was posed, Darcy knew it was best not to mention it. "No, I have not heard of Mr Bennet having any relations you might know."

Lady Romsley sighed, and Lord Romsley said, "What are you thinking, Darcy? Why would you choose—"

He got no further; Lady Catherine interrupted him to share her next objection. "This girl who has beguiled him—I need not say how—is also poor."

"Your implication is disgusting, madam, and I hardly need a bride with a large fortune!" Darcy asserted.

"Mind your manners, Nephew. Your aunt is not to blame for you becoming entangled with an unsuitable girl," the earl reprimanded.

"She is *not* unsuitable," Darcy insisted, doing his best to sound reasonable.

But then Lady Catherine told them the one thing Darcy had planned to disclose very, very carefully.

"Besides the disgraceful situation of her mother's people, her youngest sister recently eloped. Her new brother-in-law—"

"Lady Ca—" Darcy stepped forwards, his arm outstretched, hoping to stop her.

His efforts were in vain; before her name had passed his lips, she announced, "is George Wickham, the son of my brother Darcy's steward! My nephew, the brother of a servant's son? Never!"

A bomb might as well have gone off in the room. Suddenly, everyone was standing, demanding to know whether it was true and how he could possibly consider forming a connexion to Wickham. Lady Catherine calmly sat and watched; no doubt she was satisfied with the result of her interference, even if she did not understand its significance.

"Enough!" the earl barked. "Catherine, leave us. Your presence will *not* help us resolve this, not when we all know what most vexes you is that Darcy refuses to marry Anne."

Lady Catherine did not wish to leave, but after a short exchange with her brother, she returned to her chamber, saying, "If I do not have my way in this, you will hear more about it. I shall not rest until I know Darcy has given up the notion for good."

Once she was gone and the earl had ensured no one was listening at the door, he turned to Darcy. "You cannot do this. It is unthinkable!"

"Uncle—"

"Absolutely not, Darcy!" Fitzwilliam was on his feet, and his hands were clenched into fists, his face bright red. "I admit, I liked Miss Bennet when we met last spring, but how could you contemplate an alliance with her—even as a friend—when her sister is married to that beast?"

Holding his hands up in an appeasing gesture, Darcy said, "I am not proposing to marry Wickham."

"True, just his sister. I do not say that is much better," Bramwell said.

"Even if one overlooks that there was an elopement, the involvement of that-that *man*— How could you do that to Georgiana?" Lady Romsley asked.

"They would never meet, and neither would he and I. Elizabeth would not expect it of me or my sister," Darcy insisted, desperately trying to make them see the situation from his perspective. "I have considered the difficulties of the situation—of course I have! Do you not trust me to always act in Georgiana's best interests? Having a sister as kind as Elizabeth will be to her benefit. It is sure to do more to help her recover than all the doctors and other supposed experts we have consulted over the months."

Fitzwilliam gave a derisive laugh and closed the distance between them. "He is married to her sister. Of course she will want to continue to support her. I am Georgiana's guardian just as much as you are, and I will not agree to her being anywhere near the Bennets so long as Wickham is connected to them—not even if you are stupid enough to marry one of them."

"Georgiana has met Elizabeth. She likes her, and she knows I hope to marry her. I have always intended to explain the situation to her, and I am confident that—if she is told carefully and reassured that I shall never allow that man anywhere near her—she will accept Elizabeth as her sister. I truly believe she is as pleased at the prospect as she can be in her present state."

"And I am confident she will *not* accept being connected to Wickham in any manner. You cannot ask it of her!" Fitzwilliam cried.

The conversation did not improve. After perhaps half or three-quarters of an hour, the earl decided they should set aside the issue for the remainder of the day. They would take it up again after they had composed themselves enough to discuss it rationally. Darcy agreed. He departed but did not immediately return to Berkeley Square. He required a long walk to ease his agitation.

The scene he found when he arrived home was heartbreaking. Someone had told Georgiana of his intentions. They must have immediately called on her to share the news; he had not been absent that long. He suspected it was Lady Catherine, but it might have been Fitzwilliam. All of Darcy's plans to disclose Elizabeth's connexion to Wickham calmly, offer his assurances that the man was far away in the North and they would have nothing to do with him, were for naught. It was too late. Whatever Georgiana had been told, it must have been full of dire predictions of her having to share a house with Wickham when he and his wife visited Elizabeth, if not worse. She was nearly frenzied, sobbing until she was breathless, pacing, pulling at her hair, and hitting herself.

With effort, Darcy and Mrs Annesley managed to make her accept some laudanum, which eased the worst of her behaviours. She took to her bed still crying, which was distressing but an improvement.

Darcy prayed he never saw Georgiana in such a state again.

CHAPTER ELEVEN

October 1812, London

Unfortunately, Darcy's expectation that his family would regard his attachment to Elizabeth more favourably the next day was not fulfilled. Lady Romsley visited and sat with Georgiana, afterwards telling Darcy to leave his sister alone for a day or two.

"I am afraid your presence, even if you do not mention that girl's name, will be too much for her."

Darcy sighed and rubbed his forehead.

"You must be patient with her," his aunt reminded him.

"I understand that, and I shall be."

She regarded him for a long moment before saying, "There is an easy way to resolve the present...difficulty."

"You, my uncle, my cousins, and Georgiana—even Lady Catherine—can trust that I know what I am about in settling on Elizabeth." He suppressed a surge of annoyance.

Lady Romsley gave him a pitying look. "I understand you feel some affection for her, but there are other young ladies, ones who would make much better matches for you and who would meet with your family's approval."

She refused to continue the conversation, encouraging him to reflect on the matter carefully and not be guided by sentiment, then departed.

That afternoon, Darcy's cousins called, and the three men sat together in a small sitting room. Fitzwilliam was evidently still provoked.

"I thought I had better accompany him. I do not trust his present mood," Bramwell said, which earned him a stormy glance from his brother.

"Whereas I believe he has no business here. You and I are Georgiana's guardians," Fitzwilliam said. "My brother is not. Darcy, we need to discuss this asinine idea of yours."

Darcy muttered a curse before, through gritted teeth, saying, "It is not asinine. Must I remind you that you *liked* Elizabeth when you met her?"

"She was pleasant company, and I grant you, she is pretty enough, but you know as well as I do that a marriage to her would always have been frowned upon by my parents, amongst others."

"Including you?" Darcy interjected. He could feel his ire beginning to build.

"Yes, including me!"

Bramwell made a noise of disgust, but before he could speak, Fitzwilliam continued.

"Relations in trade and her lack of fortune should have been more than enough to destroy any appeal she held for you. What were you thinking to allow yourself to grow so enamoured of her?"

"It does not exactly work like that, you idiot."

Fitzwilliam rudely invited his brother to cease speaking or leave.

"It is *my* house. If anyone is going to throw someone out of it, it will be me." Darcy gave Fitzwilliam a look meant to say *he* was at risk of being evicted.

Fitzwilliam appeared not to notice, or if he had, he was unconcerned. "The most important reason why you cannot marry Elizabeth Bennet is Georgiana. *She* should be your priority, the *only* person you are thinking of at present, not some girl of no account. How could you ever dream of such a thing? It goes against every expectation—"

Bramwell barked out a curse. "Expectation! I am sick of the word. It is easy for you to say! You do not *have* to marry anyone or take their fortune into account if you choose not to." His voice altered to roughly imitate Lord Romsley's. "'Do not waste your time with this lady. Her grandfather was so and so. This lady is better than that one. Her dowry is larger, her father has these connexions, her mother was this man's daughter'." In his usual tone, he went on, "I am sick to death of expectations constantly being thrown at me, and I assume Darcy is as well. What about whether one actually likes the lady or thinks they might be happy with her? Do not throw your expectations at our cousin!"

As much as Darcy agreed with the viscount, his words only made the situation worse. Fitzwilliam stood, his posture shouting his disgust as much as his words. "You might refuse to take her fortune and connexions into consideration, but you cannot disregard Georgiana. If you did this to her, Darcy, you would be no better than Wickham!"

Before he knew what he was doing, Darcy punched Fitzwilliam in the jaw, and the two were exchanging blows.

Bramwell yelled at his brother that he had gone too far and, with some effort, managed to extricate Fitzwilliam from the tussle and drag him from the house.

No matter how hard Darcy attempted to find a way to convince his sister that she would remain safe from Wickham, and no matter how desperately he tried to convince his family to support him and join him in reassuring Georgiana, he failed again and again.

Georgiana became unsettled even at hearing Elizabeth's name. While Fitzwilliam apologised for comparing him to Wickham, he continued to insist Darcy was being unconscionably irresponsible. The earl and countess informed him that despite the match being a poor one, they *might* have agreed to meet Elizabeth before deciding against offering their support, but since Georgiana hated the idea so much, they would not. Bramwell merely shrugged as though there was nothing he could do, which, in fairness, was almost certainly true.

And so, for his sister's sake, Darcy gave up Elizabeth.

Two months later, sitting on the cold ground halfway between Netherfield and Longbourn, he still felt hopeless, remembering all that had happened.

After the conversation with Elizabeth, he could not remain at Netherfield, even though Bingley encouraged him to stay. It was a lonely journey back to town, but Darcy preferred that to company. It was full dark by the time he arrived at his town house, and only Georgiana greeted him. For that, he was thankful. He had half expected to find Fitzwilliam and perhaps the earl awaiting him to ensure he had not explained to Elizabeth why their connexion had to be broken, which they had deemed would be foolish. He would have, but Elizabeth had refused to listen. It might not have made a difference, but perhaps she would hate him a little less if she fully understood the situation. Selfishly, he wanted the comfort of speaking to her of everything that had happened; but that would mean burdening her with his sorrow, and that would be wrong. He did not blame her for hating him after how he had acted, and asking for her sympathy—as though that would excuse his behaviour—was too much.

He joined Georgiana in her private sitting room. She watched him cautiously, her lips pulled into her mouth and her body rigid as though waiting to hear bad news. He sat beside her on a settee.

"I hope my late return did not worry you."

She shook her head and tentatively asked, "H-h-how was the wedding?"

Briefly, he pressed his eyes closed in an attempt to banish the image of Elizabeth standing by her sister's side. She had given every appearance of feeling nothing other than pleasure at the happy occasion, but he had spent too many hours studying her to miss the signs of her underlying discomfort. Nevertheless, she was beautiful to his eyes, and he had not been able to keep himself from silently repeating the wedding vows to her as Bingley said them to his bride. Darcy genuinely doubted he would ever be able to marry another lady; his heart was committed to Elizabeth, and this had been a simple acknowledgement of that, a promise he could give to her, even if she never learnt of it.

Answering his sister's question, he said, "It was everything it should be. Bingley did not stop grinning the whole morning, and Mrs Bingley was lovely."

There was a long pause before Georgiana next spoke. "Did you see…*her*?"

Darcy slowly inclined his head once. "We did not speak, not more than was absolutely necessary."

"I could not bear it if you and she… To think that I might see *him*—"

"Do not, Georgiana," he interjected, grasping her hand, which had reached for her neck, the fingers curled. He suspected she would try to scratch herself as she had done in the past, once leaving long welts on her forearms. "There is no need for your anxieties. You will never have to see him again, and Miss Bennet knows whatever there once was between us is at an end. It is all…over."

Done. I have succeeded in making her hate me, and this time, there is nothing I can do to earn her forgiveness, unlike I was able to do last summer. If I were a better man, I would pray she forgets all about her affection for me and finds happiness with another. Perhaps in time, I shall be that generous, but for now, I cannot.

Georgiana rested her head against his shoulder, which lightened the heaviness of his heart, if only for the moment.

The next morning, his cousins came to call. After greeting them, Georgiana returned to her apartment. The gentlemen settled in the blue sitting room, and Darcy offered them coffee.

Bramwell slumped in a chair, his long legs stretched out and crossed at the ankle. He gave a large yawn, which Darcy interpreted as either a late night or an indication of his thoughts on the task his brother and he had likely been sent to undertake by their parents. Possibly, he had insisted on coming to prevent another battle between Fitzwilliam and Darcy.

The colonel asked about the wedding, almost exactly as Georgiana had the night before. Darcy gave a similar response.

"You saw Miss Bennet," Fitzwilliam stated rather than asked.

Darcy nodded, and Bramwell said, "Of course he did. Knowing he would is why we are here so blasted early in the day, is it not?"

Fitzwilliam glared at him before directing his next remark to Darcy. "I hope it was not too difficult."

Darcy shrugged. Fitzwilliam and he had always been close friends, and he did not want to lose that, especially when he had already lost so much. He had accepted his cousin's apology for his horrible remark; nevertheless, their previous ease was still far from restored.

"I would wager it was awful," Bramwell muttered.

Again, Darcy shrugged, this time to say his cousin was not wrong.

Fitzwilliam sighed and ran a hand through his hair, scratching his scalp a couple of times. "I am sorry about that, Darcy, but at least it is done. Now, you can…move on, find another lady. I have said it before—I liked Miss Bennet when we met at Easter. She is pretty and amusing, but you know she would never have been a great match for you. Neither would she be the best lady to help Georgiana enter society, as she must in the next few years. Miss Bennet might have been a good *friend* for Georgiana but never a sister."

"My God, you are insufferable on this point!" Bramwell cried. "If I were closer, I would kick you for that alone."

"I would prefer not to discuss it further," Darcy insisted. "I went to Hertfordshire a single man, and I returned single still. It was what you and everyone else wanted, and it is done. Let us leave it at that."

Bramwell yawned again, this time stretching his arms above his head; he then drained his cup of coffee and put it on the polished maple side table. Looking refreshed, he said, "I think the situation could have been managed. As my mother said, perhaps more time was needed to separate the younger sister's marriage and your intention to propose to the older sister, but…" He gestured as though to say it did not matter. "You know what I think about Georgiana's role in this. Allowing her to dictate whom you do or do not marry is giving her too much power. I do not believe it is to her benefit. If anything, having a sympathetic lady or two in her family would do her good."

"She has my mother," Fitzwilliam interjected.

"Yes, yes, Mother is very good to her," Bramwell conceded. "But I meant one closer to Georgiana's own age. Not a mother but a friend."

"My cousin Rebecca has done her best to befriend Georgiana in the past," Darcy said. "It has been difficult, given Georgiana's diffidence."

"A closer connexion with Rebecca would be excellent for Georgiana. It would help if she—or whichever lady we suggest Georgiana befriend, such as Darcy's eventual wife—is aware of her…special circumstances," Bramwell said.

"You ought to call her Miss Reed. She is not *your* relation." Darcy frowned at the viscount.

At the same time, Fitzwilliam said, "We are not going to share such personal information about Georgiana with anyone."

Except I did tell Elizabeth—part of it, at least. I would have disclosed the rest, once we were engaged.

In his musings, he evidently missed some of the conversation, because Fitzwilliam was facing his brother, the hardness of his features denoting a growing frustration.

"Then why do *you* not marry a sympathetic lady who can be trusted with the truth, giving Georgiana a cousin whom she could safely befriend and saving her from Darcy and me and our vicious oversight?" Bramwell's tone was biting.

Darcy did not involve himself in the brothers' bickering; instead, he contemplated Bramwell, who had mentioned Rebecca's name several times lately. *Does he have intentions towards her?*

"I still think Georgiana would have—on balance—benefited from Darcy marrying a lady even you admit was admirable," said Bramwell.

Shaking his head, Fitzwilliam argued, "The risk was too great. You did not see Georgiana much immediately after Ramsgate. You do not understand how severe her disorder can be." Bramwell had been in Scotland at the time, seeing to the management of one of Lord Romsley's estates.

Bramwell's countenance sobered. "Seeing her now, I can only imagine. But perhaps I can view the situation with more clarity than you two do *precisely* because I was not there when it happened. I do not say we should overlook her distress or tell her we do not care that she is unhappy, but—"

Abruptly, Darcy stood. He could not bear to continue the conversation, not at present. He had a sudden vision of Elizabeth, angry and hurt, when he explained that he could not propose to her because his family was against the match. The pain was too new, too raw to make the current discussion anything but agony.

"When I next see Rebecca, I shall suggest she calls on Georgiana. Until then, I hope the forthcoming Christmas festivities will be what my sister needs to cheer her. I really should…attend to some notes sent to me by my steward."

Bramwell and Fitzwilliam took the hint and departed.

CHAPTER TWELVE

The six weeks Jane and Mr Bingley were in Bath felt very long to Elizabeth. She remained content in her decision not to go with them, but she missed Jane terribly. Her sister was her dearest friend, and there was a great comfort in her steady, loving presence. Elizabeth even missed the busyness of planning for the wedding. The way it had occupied her time and thoughts would have been welcome during the endless days in December and early January. Instead, she found herself wallowing in pain and anger—towards Mr Darcy for giving in to his family's arrogance and pride and towards herself for being so foolish as to open her heart to him.

Recovering from the loss was not easy, but she did what she could, taking long walks when the weather permitted, immersing herself in new books, assisting the vicar's wife with several charitable endeavours, and the like. Mr Bennet accused her of being dispirited.

"I pray it is not because you are jealous of Jane or, heaven forbid, Lydia," he had once said. "If I suspected as much, I would think less of you."

Part of her had wanted to kick him, but instead, she had said, "It is simply the season, Papa, and how quiet we are. I want activity. Hate me for it if you like. I shall not attempt to stop you."

Mrs Bennet's behaviour was worse. She complained about Elizabeth still being at home, "…when your sister, who is five years younger, is already married. You ought to have married when you had the chance. I shall never understand why you refused Mr Collins. It would have been *you* about to have a child instead of Charlotte, and Lady Lucas tells me the Collinses' parsonage is very comfortable. I should have liked to visit you there, I am sure. Instead, look at you! You are growing thin, and you have lost your youth! No one will want you, and you will regret the choices you have made."

Elizabeth imagined she would regain some of her vigour if she did not have to listen to such condemning speeches.

As the weeks passed, she convinced herself that she *was* improving. To be sure, thinking about Mr Darcy and what might have been still caused her to suffer a pang, but she was convinced she would soon entirely forget the romantic sentiments she harboured for him.

The Bingleys' return to the neighbourhood was greeted with great fanfare. Mrs Bennet was especially vocal in her joy to see the couple again, but the pair were so well loved by everyone that there was a general increase in merriment and parties in the first weeks after they took up residence at Netherfield Park. It seemed that a fortnight passed before Elizabeth was able to have an uninterrupted conversation with her sister.

"I am so glad we can finally sit and talk together!" Jane

said. "I have told Bingley he is not to disturb us for anything less than the house falling down around us for at least an hour."

The ladies were in Jane's apartment, sharing a sofa covered in a floral-patterned silk.

"What a pretty room this is!" Elizabeth said. "You did very well with the changes you ordered. Dare I ask what my mother said when she first saw it?"

"Please do not!"

The sisters laughed together and, after Jane served them cups of tea, got down to the important business of sharing everything of importance that had happened since the wedding, even when it meant repeating what they had written to each other during Jane's time in Bath. Elizabeth insisted on hearing about the wedding trip. Unlike her previous worries about being envious, there was not even a crumb of that ugly emotion. Next to being happy herself, she most wished to see Jane live a life full of contentment and love.

"Bath sounds delightful," she said when Jane paused to drink her tea.

"Oh, it is. Caroline would say it is not as fashionable as Brighton, but I do not care for such things, as you know, and neither does Bingley. But enough about me. I want to hear about *you*. I hesitate to mention his name, but I feel I must. In your letters, you said nothing about Mr Darcy. Did you and he not speak at all when he was here?"

Elizabeth's gaze fell from her sister to the saucer in her hands. If she had not already finished her tea, she would have slowly sipped it to delay her confession. Since that was not a possibility, she told Jane what had passed between her and the gentleman on the morning of the wedding.

Jane was shocked. "How could he—? I cannot believe he truly loved you, if—"

"No, neither can I," Elizabeth interjected. She hoped to be done with the subject as quickly as possible. "I admit, it took me more than a se'nnight to come to that conclusion. It is either that or he was reminded of his pride, which I believed was his most cherished characteristic when we first met. Perhaps it was both in equal measure. Whatever the reason, he has decided I am not a worthy enough object on which to bestow his affection."

"Lizzy, do not joke about it! It must have been incredibly distressing." Jane's eyes were bright with unshed tears.

Elizabeth set aside her cup and rested a hand on her sister's arm. "None of that, please. The situation does not warrant it, and I have cried enough for both of us. But it is at an end now. I am quite determined. It *was* difficult, but given his family's past connexion to Wickham, I should not be surprised. If anything, I am astonished Mr Darcy ever considered marrying someone who must call that man brother."

"You ought to have written to me."

"I did not because, knowing you and your tender heart, you might have insisted Mr Bingley bring you home at once. I could not have that." Elizabeth smiled. "Now, enough about disagreeable gentlemen and their even more disagreeable families. Tell me truly, sister dearest, how greatly is Mama pestering you and your darling husband? Do not deny it. You marrying Mr Bingley is the great triumph of her life. She hardly talked of anything else when you were away, and I see how she likes to show you both off whenever possible."

Jane rubbed her bottom lip and opened and closed her mouth several times before finally responding. "Mama will… not always be so enthusiastic."

"Do you truly believe that?" Elizabeth asked, her tone amused. "Her daughter is mistress of the largest estate in the neighbourhood. I do not believe she will let anyone forget it."

With reluctance, Jane admitted she feared Elizabeth was correct. "I know you will not tell anyone, but Bingley and I would both prefer to not have so much attention." She hastened to add, "Everyone is so kind, and he does like to be sociable, but…"

"It is too much. I wish there was something I could do, but you know my mother would not listen to me if I told her she should leave you to yourselves. Indeed, I have already tried."

"I know you have, and I appreciate it. We shall go to town in the spring, and knowing that helps. I mean for you to come with us."

Elizabeth gave an indifferent nod; she had expected as much but was not sure what she felt about being in London. She might encounter Mr Darcy there, which would be difficult, despite her resolution to forget she had ever liked him—let alone loved him. Yet, there was no better place to seek diversion, which she knew would do a great deal to improve her spirits and return her to her former cheerful self.

Nothing more was said of London that morning; after all, there were weeks to go before any specific arrangements would have to be made. Yet, in February, they received news that encouraged Elizabeth to give her enthusiastic support to leaving Meryton. Lydia had written to her mother to say she planned to make a long visit and would be at Longbourn by the end of March. Mrs Bennet was almost faint with anticipation.

Elizabeth would do just about anything to avoid seeing her youngest sister. From everything she heard of Lydia's life, Mrs Wickham remained the silly, ignorant, selfish girl she had been before her marriage. Nothing was said of Mr Wickham accompanying Lydia to Hertfordshire, yet, after a day spent listening to her mother's recitation of the many parties she intended to arrange to ensure her daughter was well-amused, Elizabeth knew she would be miserable if she remained at Longbourn.

Jane and Mr Bingley soon decided to go to London earlier than they originally intended, which had not been until after Easter.

"I shall wait to tell my mother until closer to our departure. The news about Lydia convinced me to alter our previous arrangements," Jane explained.

"And Mama's behaviour remains overbearing. You need not admit it, sister dearest. I know it is against your nature to criticise anyone, but I can see that you and Mr Bingley both find her fatiguing. It will only be worse when Lydia is here and my mother can show off her two married daughters at once."

With evident reluctance, Jane concurred. "You must come with us."

Elizabeth opened her mouth to agree, but to her own surprise, instead hesitated.

"Are you worried you might see Mr Darcy?"

After a brief pause, Elizabeth said, "Not particularly. I see now that my infatuation for him was a grave error, and he can no longer touch my heart. How could it be otherwise, once I discovered his views are exactly what I believed them to be last spring, not what I allowed myself to believe they had become in the summer?"

Her sister looked uncertain. "I shall do whatever I must to keep you apart."

"It is generous of you to make such a promise, but you know it is impossible." Elizabeth kissed her cheek.

"I could tell Bingley," Jane said softly.

Elizabeth shook her finger at her sister. "You promised you

would not tell him of my history with his friend, and I shall hold you to it. I am disappointed in Mr Darcy, but he was always free to change his mind, and if he is so persuadable—if he is willing to listen to his family, as he evidently has—then I do not want him any more than he wants me. I must either allow you to destroy your dear husband's friendship with him or accustom myself to meeting him upon occasion. I choose the latter, though I admit I hope we do not see each other often, at least at first. It will become easier with practice, as most things do. Knowing I might be uneasy in his company is why I did not immediately assure you I would go with you to town, but of course, I shall."

"Oh, I am relieved to hear it! You know it is my wish that we shall not be separated until you find a husband who truly deserves you. Until then, Bingley and I both want you to make your home with us."

Elizabeth embraced her, whispering her thanks. "I believe my father might have a thing or two to say about it. I shall speak to him, but only about spending the spring in London with you. We should leave any discussions of the summer and beyond until later."

Jane nodded, and the sisters spent the next while imagining how they would amuse themselves in town.

CHAPTER THIRTEEN

In early March, Darcy received a letter from Bingley stating that he and his wife would soon be in town. Rather than write to arrange a meeting at their club or suggest an excursion, Darcy decided to take Georgiana to call on Mrs Bingley, assuming his friend would be there.

He had another motive, though he kept it to himself: he *wanted* to introduce Georgiana to Mrs Bingley. What he would gain from it was uncertain, but he held a faint hope that if the two formed a friendship, even if it was not particularly close, Georgiana would see that there was no harm in associating with the Bennets, despite their connexion to Wickham. If that happened, surely she would no longer object to him pursuing Elizabeth.

Although it is doubtful Elizabeth will ever forgive me for how I acted.

Darcy never should have agreed to his family's importuning; his regret left a bitter taste in his mouth. His nights were occupied reflecting on what he should have done instead, but despite debating the issue constantly, he had yet to decide what would have been a better course of action. In the end, it did not matter what he had or had not done; there was no changing the past. What was most important was how he acted at present.

Dear God, I cannot live with this emptiness inside me, the place where she belongs like a cavernous void! I must find a way to reconcile Georgiana and the rest of my family to our union—and I must find a way to convince Elizabeth to give me another chance.

He spoke to Georgiana about making the call at dinner one night. Referring to Mrs Bingley, he said, "You will like her. She is a very gentle, kind lady."

His sister held her fork and knife several inches above her plate, her hands having fallen motionless as soon as he mentioned his idea. "B-but her sister is married to...*him*! What if he is there? What if Miss Bennet is? Do you want to see *her*?"

Darcy shook his head and continued to speak in an easy, calm manner. "Bingley knows I have a low opinion of Wickham—not why exactly, of course—and would never allow him into his home. As for Miss Bennet, I read Bingley's letter very carefully, and more than once. He makes no mention of her. Would you truly object to even seeing her?"

The question was out before he could stop himself, and he knew at once it was a mistake. He sensed Georgiana withdrawing and fortifying the barriers she kept between herself and the world. He spoke on quickly.

"Georgiana—"

"Mr Bingley is a good friend to you, and I suppose he might order his wife not to be in that man's company, not in their own home, at least. But I doubt she will always hold to that." She shrugged. "It is different with Miss Bennet."

"I do not understand why. I have tried, but I cannot."

She glanced at him and took a long moment before replying. "I do not want you to see her because of your affection for her. You will find it difficult, and what if you decide I should not really mind it and propose? I could not bear it. If her younger sister arrived here or at Pemberley—with or without her husband—Miss Bennet would *not* reject her. I would be forced to see them."

Georgiana was increasingly agitated, and he sought to redirect the conversation and calm her. "As I said, I have no reason to believe Miss Bennet is in town. I am thinking of Bingley and his new wife. Unless I give up the friendship entirely, which I very much do not want to do, I should call, and it would be right for you to meet her."

Georgiana slowly lowered the fork and knife to the table and took a moment to arrange them. "I am not out."

"That is true, but in the past, you have gone with me to call on good friends or joined me in receiving them here." Believing she would find a way to refuse, he added, "We need only stay a quarter of an hour, just long enough for you to meet and offer your congratulations. Even if Mrs Bingley chooses to see the Wickhams, there is no danger that you will encounter them this winter. They are in Newcastle."

With evident reluctance, she agreed.

His sister trembled slightly as they followed the servant to the Bingleys' drawing room two days later. Darcy held her elbow and repeated his promise that they would stay only a short while. With his thoughts occupied by her as they traversed the hall, he did not initially believe he was actually *seeing* Elizabeth when they entered the drawing room. Georgiana's steps faltered as she stopped abruptly; it was this that confirmed to him that Elizabeth truly *was* there. His mind screamed her name, his lips moving as though he was speaking it aloud. Why had Bingley not told him she would accompany him and his wife to town? He glanced at Georgiana, who had grown pale, turned to Mrs Bingley and Elizabeth, and opened his mouth to greet them or say some other innocuous nothing.

Before he could form words, Elizabeth was on her feet and halfway across the room.

"Mr Darcy, Miss Darcy." Her voice and the nod she gave them were both brusque. She left through a second door, which saved her from having to approach them.

Darcy watched her go. He had the answer to one question that had plagued him since the autumn: Elizabeth *did* despise him. He had disappointed her, she could not possibly understand why, and he deserved her contempt.

He almost followed her, but Georgiana's hand on his arm prevented it. Faintly, he heard Mrs Bingley's voice; it was only when Georgiana said his name that he was able to pull his attention back to the ladies he was with and away from the one he longed to be near.

Had he suspected Elizabeth might be there, that Mrs Bingley would want her dearest sister with her? He had, but he had not allowed himself to hope he would see her. Just being near her was a balm, although her evident hatred would soon change that, the pain overtaking the pleasure.

"Mr Darcy, I am very glad to see you," Mrs Bingley said, her voice higher than usual. She looked between where he stood with Georgiana and the door through which Elizabeth had bolted. "I-I asked my sister to join me. She, um…"

Darcy cleared his throat, praying his heart would slow down and he would feel less lightheaded; it was making it difficult for him to think clearly. He bowed and felt Georgiana curtsey. "Mrs Bingley, how do you do? May I present my sister?"

After he completed the introduction, Mrs Bingley invited them to sit. He did not know what happened next, or even how much time passed. The ladies spoke, but Darcy did not add to the exchange. He sat with his eyes on the door through which Elizabeth had left, wondering where she was and what she was thinking and feeling, and imagining what he would say to her if they had a few minutes alone.

His trance ended when Bingley entered the room.

"Darcy! Miss Darcy, how wonderful to see you again. You are looking very well."

"Thank you, Mr Bingley."

While Georgiana's voice was still cautious, she appeared less timid having someone else with whom she was familiar in the room. Darcy reprimanded himself; in his distraction over Elizabeth, he had failed to pay proper attention to Georgiana and Mrs Bingley, which was rude.

"Bingley, it is good to see you too. I was glad to receive your letter saying you would be in town this month. It gave me an opportunity to introduce the ladies," Darcy said.

Bingley grinned at his wife and went to sit next to her. His smile faded slightly, and he looked around the room. "Where is Lizzy?"

"Oh, she…has a headache," Mrs Bingley said.

When her eyes flicked to Darcy, the door, and the ground, it told Darcy that she knew what had passed between him and her sister—but that her husband did not. Bingley was never the most observant man. If he was, he would have realised months ago that Darcy was deeply in love with Elizabeth.

The only reason he had not proposed before leaving Meryton in September was to allow the Bingleys the chance to have their impending engagement celebrated without any distractions. *How I wish I had not been so generous! If I had proposed and spoken to Mr Bennet before coming to town, the earl and countess—even Fitzwilliam—would have agreed there was nothing to be done about it. I would now be married to Elizabeth, and we would have managed Georgiana's anxieties together.*

Darcy and Georgiana remained only a few minutes longer. He told himself it was because he sensed his sister's growing restlessness, but really, it was his own that drove him to his feet. Elizabeth was somewhere in the house, and not being able to see her made him want to weep.

CHAPTER FOURTEEN

Elizabeth strode around her chamber, occasionally stopping to take a steadying deep breath or look out of the window at the busy street below, her hands pressed to her burning cheeks. Seeing Mr Darcy had made her feel as though a carriage had fallen on top of her. Or perhaps a house, one the size of Pemberley. She had been surprised by how compelled she had been to flee the room. They had not been together since the morning of Jane's wedding; her last sight of him had been one of bitterness, and she had walked away feeling deceived and foolish for having entrusted him with her heart. As soon as she saw him, it all came rushing back to her, a flood of emotions that was overwhelming. She wrapped her arms around her waist and hugged herself tightly, as though this might contain her sorrow.

By the time Jane came to her, she had composed herself. A cool cloth pressed to her face had helped, as had half a cup of tea, to which she had added a liberal amount of honey. She still held the cup between her hands and continued to sip from it.

"Are you well?" Jane asked.

"I am. Knowing Mr Darcy's opinion of me, I decided he and his sister would be more comfortable in my absence. It was kind of them to call on you."

"Lizzy." Jane's tone was full of reprimand.

Their eyes met, and after a brief pause, Elizabeth shrugged. "It was the shock of seeing them. I had expected we might simply encounter Mr Darcy on the street or at a party. I did not expect him to enter your drawing room. By the bye, you should talk to your housekeeper about guests being announced. Mama would be astonished you allowed such a lapse in proper behaviour."

Jane shook her head as though saying she would not allow Elizabeth to change the subject. "I wish you had not been so affected."

Elizabeth used the excuse of finishing her tea to avert her eyes. "It will not happen again. In the future, I shall be better prepared." *For the onslaught of emotions, for how dearly I wish to yell at him and then enquire if he is well and satisfied with the choice he made.*

"Do you not think you and Mr Darcy might reconcile? He was very distracted the whole time they were here, and it was not until Bingley joined us that he could do more than stare at the door you fled through."

Elizabeth began to shake her head. "I told you what he said after your wedding. His family convinced him I am not the sort of lady he should marry. Even if he changed his mind—and I doubt he would—they will not. I do not *want* him to have second thoughts. Too much has happened, and my feelings for him are not what they were last summer."

Jane's shoulders slumped. "I only want you to be happy."

"And so I shall be. If I am exceedingly fortunate, I shall

meet a gentleman worthy of my affection and one who will tolerate not only what my mother routinely assures me is an obstinate nature but also my family, with all its imperfections. It is up to you and Bingley to ensure I meet many such gentlemen while I am with you so that I can select the one most amenable to indulging my love of books and long walks in the countryside."

"I shall do my best." Jane managed a light laugh. "When you met her last summer, did you notice anything remarkable about Miss Darcy's comportment?"

Elizabeth wished that the subject of the Darcys would end. "She is very shy, and it was always difficult to make her say more than three or four words at a time."

"I think it is more than that. She is not just shy but…timid and nervous."

"Is that not part of being excessively shy? I know Mr Darcy is very careful with her. At Pemberley I often saw him encouraging her or looking at her as though he wanted to ensure she was well. Do not forget she is still young, only sixteen I believe. Not all young ladies are as lively and comfortable in society as Kitty and Lydia."

"I suppose." Jane stood and suggested they seek out Bingley and insist he find a reason to take them out. "I told him you had a headache to excuse your absence earlier. I hated lying to him."

Elizabeth clasped her sister's hand. "I am sorry to put you in such a position, but I genuinely believe it would hurt him more to lose his friendship with Mr Darcy. I shall do better from now on, and you will not have to make excuses for me to Bingley or anyone else. As for your notion of leaving the house, it is an excellent one. The distraction will help us forget they were here."

HIS FAMILY OBJECTS

The next time Elizabeth saw Mr Darcy was at a dinner party later the same week. They greeted each other but said no more than was commonplace, as though they hardly knew each other. She remained stoic, imagining she had a core of thick ice inside her, rather than her usual warm blood. It encased her sentiments, locking them away so they did not show, especially to *him*. It would give him too much power if he knew how affected she was, despite the months that had passed since there was any friendliness—let alone more—between them.

Nothing of significance happened until after dinner. In the drawing room, Jane remained close, and both she and Elizabeth enjoyed the company of the ladies while the men were absent. When the gentlemen began to join them, Elizabeth stole glimpses at the newcomers. *It is only so I know whether he is in the room. I do not want to be surprised and inadvertently draw attention by showing discomfort. He is nothing more than an acquaintance. The friend of my sister's husband.*

Their eyes met very briefly when he and Bingley made their appearance, but she quickly averted her gaze. Bingley walked towards Jane, with whom Elizabeth sat; when she saw that his friend followed him, she stood. Knowing Bingley would wonder if she always avoided Mr Darcy, she decided to remain long enough to exchange greetings. She politely curtseyed.

"How do you do this evening?" he said.

"Very well, thank you." She was on the point of excusing herself when he again spoke. The hint of eagerness in his voice astonished her; did he not share her sense that it was better for them to avoid each other as much as possible? *He must not find it as awkward as I do!*

"Bingley tells me your family are well. I am glad to hear it. I am sure your parents and sisters are missing you, yet Mrs Bingley would greatly regret not having you with her."

"That is very true," Jane said.

"We both would! I am fortunate in having her as my sister," Bingley added.

The look Mr Darcy gave her seemed to say that he also valued her company. It was too much; Elizabeth did not know how to act, and so she mentioned a desire to speak to another guest, gave her sister's arm a gentle squeeze to indicate she was well, and went to join a group of several ladies. They were discussing spring clothing fashions, which was not a subject to truly engage Elizabeth's attention, but she did her best to participate. She wanted these women to like her, and especially to like Jane. They were part of her sister's new society; Elizabeth was merely a visitor. Had Mr Darcy and she married, she would currently be taking her place as an equal amongst these ladies, but she remained simply Miss Bennet.

There was music after tea, and when their hostess asked who would like to perform, Bingley suggested Elizabeth.

"My sister-in-law is a delightful pianoforte player, and she has a lovely voice. Lizzy, you would not object to giving us a song, would you?"

"You are the kindest of brothers, but I am afraid you give a false impression of my skills," she said. "I doubt anyone here would find my humble offering especially remarkable, but I shall gladly make the attempt."

Elizabeth took her place at the pianoforte and, after a moment of consideration, decided on a Scotch air she was confident she could play without making any noticeable errors. She was some way through the song when, whether inadvertently or not, her eyes were caught by Mr Darcy's appearance.

He leant against the wall near the fireplace, perhaps a dozen feet away, and watched her. His countenance—the softness around his eyes and his smile, oh, *that* smile—threw her back in time to Derbyshire. She had seen him look at her with just such an expression before, dating at least to when they were in Kent. The first evening she and the Gardiners had dined at Pemberley, she had finally understood what it meant: it told her he loved her. Whenever she saw it, her heart answered in kind, filling her with warmth and a sense of contentment and completeness as deep as an ocean. But at present, what could it mean?

Not that *surely, and dear Lord, please do not let me feel—*

But it was too late. A torrent of sentiment flowed through her, like water filling an empty riverbed when an obstruction is removed. All the affection and admiration she had for him when they were together the previous summer and early autumn came rushing back. There was no preventing the flood.

CHAPTER FIFTEEN

Elizabeth did not confide her feelings to Jane. Why disrupt her sister's happiness when there was nothing she could do to alter what she was experiencing? Somehow, she would convince herself to stop loving Mr Darcy, to forget her good impression of him and remember all the reasons she had *not* to admire him. Time would be her cure, and to assist it, she would avoid the gentleman as much as possible.

Not long after the dinner party, the Bingleys and Elizabeth attended a ball hosted by a young couple Bingley had known for some years, the Frys. They lived in a beautiful house in Berkeley Square, which, Mrs Fry told Elizabeth, had been completely renovated following their marriage two years ago. That accounted for the interior, which was done in the latest fashion. There were many guests crowding the rooms, and Elizabeth revelled in the busyness, immersing herself in activity and meeting new people.

Mrs Fry was a generous hostess, and she and Jane were

clearly forming a friendship. Between the lady, her husband, and Bingley, they ensured Jane and Elizabeth were introduced to many of their friends. Elizabeth was asked to dance by several gentlemen, and before long, she was enjoying herself more than she had anticipated.

At the end of one set, her dance partner introduced her to a lady of about her own age named Miss Rebecca Reed. He explained that Elizabeth was new to town, soon leaving the ladies to themselves when he spotted one of his acquaintances.

"Have you been to town before? Why have you chosen to come this year?" Miss Reed asked. Her cheeks flushed. "Oh, I beg your pardon. That sounded terribly rude, did it not? I have a bad habit of blurting out whatever comes to mind."

Elizabeth smiled. "My sister is lately married to Mr Charles Bingley, and they invited me to stay with them."

Miss Reed's eyes widened. "Mr Bingley?"

"Do you know him?"

"I met him several years ago. My cousin and he are friends. You might have heard Mr Bingley mention him. Mr Darcy, from Derbyshire."

Elizabeth's mouth went dry. "Mr Darcy? Yes, he, um, that is to say we have met. He stayed at the estate Mr Bingley let in Hertfordshire, which is only a few miles from my home. It is where he and my sister met."

The news struck the two ladies very differently. Elizabeth regretted that Miss Reed, who had seemed like a possible friend, was connected to Mr Darcy, but Miss Reed grinned and launched into a speech about coincidences.

Why should I not be friends with her, just because she and Mr Darcy are cousins? There was something enchanting about Miss Reed. She seemed guileless, and Elizabeth was drawn to her—

perhaps because she still felt the sting of being deceived by Mr Darcy.

They were sharing information about Meryton and the region of Norfolk where Miss Reed's father's estate was located, when a handsome, well-dressed gentleman walked up to them.

"Miss Reed, how absolutely wonderful to see you this evening. You look especially captivating in that gown, as I believe I told you last month at the theatre."

Miss Reed sighed, though Elizabeth thought it was exaggerated.

"You know I never believe a single one of your compliments. I do not know why you waste your breath saying them," Miss Reed said.

He grinned. "I intend to convince you of my sincerity. It is all part of my plot. Do not ask what my goal is unless you are prepared for the truth. You *ought* to know, but I am sure you tell yourself you do not. Will you introduce me to your friend?"

Turning to Elizabeth, Miss Reed said, "I am so sorry! I have been neglecting you. It is this man. His nonsense is always so distracting. Miss Bennet, may I present Viscount Bramwell. Lord Bramwell, this is Miss Elizabeth Bennet. She has only lately come to town. Her sister is Mr Bingley's new wife. You know whom I mean. Darcy's friend."

Elizabeth curtseyed and was surprised by the speculative expression on the viscount's face. His head was tilted to one side, and the air around them seemed to grow more serious. Even Miss Reed apparently noticed; she furrowed her brow and shifted her gaze from one to the other.

"*You* are Miss Elizabeth Bennet?" the viscount asked.

"I am. Do you know of me?" Elizabeth was certain she had

heard his name but could not recall when. For some reason, she felt wary.

Viscount Bramwell cleared his throat and gave a low chuckle. "I do. My dearest Miss Reed failed to mention that, like her, I am cousin to Darcy."

Elizabeth's stomach fell to her shoes, suddenly remembering Mr Darcy mentioning him. "I see. You are Colonel Fitzwilliam's brother."

"Unfortunately." The viscount laughed merrily for several seconds. "I jest, but it is amusing to tease him, even when he is not present to hear it. You met him when he and Darcy had the grave misfortune of staying at Rosings last Easter, I believe."

"You recall correctly." She turned to Miss Reed. "It was lovely to meet you, but I must find my sister."

"Oh, well, yes. She may be wondering where you are. Would she object if I called on you? I suppose I should ask whether *you* would object?" Miss Reed's expression showed both disappointment and anticipation.

Elizabeth debated silently for a brief moment. "I would like that very much, and no, my sister would not mind at all. I shall try to introduce you this evening, but if I do not, I shall when you call." To the viscount, she nodded and added, "My lord."

With that, she left them.

Not long after arriving at the Frys' ball, Darcy encountered the Bingleys. They spoke for several minutes, but even without his friend mentioning Elizabeth, Darcy *knew* she was present. The air was different in some undefinable way. He had experienced a similar sensation the day Georgiana and he had called at the Bingleys' town house and when he had seen Elizabeth at a dinner party recently. Their eyes had met while she was at the pianoforte that evening, and every feeling of adoration and love he had experienced for her came rushing to the surface from the depths of his being where he had tried to bury it. He was certain Elizabeth knew what he felt and that she still cared for him.

He caught sight of her a short while after speaking to the Bingleys and found himself following her with his eyes. He attempted to approach her several times, but whenever he was within fifteen or twenty feet, she moved away, and he was afraid she was avoiding him.

And if she is? Whom do I have to blame but myself?

From what he could see, she was making new friends, and he did not doubt that she would have many admirers. If anyone deserved to be loved, it was Elizabeth, and he desired her happiness. Yet, selfishly, he also longed to spend even a few minutes in her company. Circumstance meant they could not be lovers, but might they be friends, or at least friendly acquaintances?

Immediately after supper, Darcy noticed her standing with a small group of young people and approached her. When he addressed her, she started, evidently unaware he was nearby.

"Miss Bennet, will you dance the next set with me?" He nodded and mumbled a few greetings to the other people present, all of whom he knew.

"Mr Darcy, how good to see you again," one of the women said, adding to Elizabeth, "I ought not to be surprised you have met, given Mr Darcy and your brother are friends. I am glad you know enough gentlemen to keep you dancing all night. Enjoy yourselves!"

Perhaps because the lady had taken it as given that Elizabeth would accept his offer, she nodded and allowed him to escort her to the lines of dancers that were forming.

They said nothing for several minutes. Darcy was content just being near her. He took in every inch of her, attempting to commit her appearance to memory—the shade of ivory she wore, the pattern of stitching on the sleeves, the hint of pink in her cheeks, the slope of her nose, the brightness of her eyes, and bounce of her curls.

The pain and—if he was not mistaken—longing in her eyes as they remained fixed on his. The spark that passed between them when their fingers touched that left him breathless.

Do something! Say something to make this easier for her! he silently screamed. His mind took him back to their dance at Netherfield, when she had insisted a couple ought to have some conversation.

"Shall we not look stupid if we remain silent? I recall you expressing such an opinion." He paused, hoping she might chuckle or smile. She did not, and he said, "Are you enjoying the party?"

"I am, thank you." Her tone was stiff, and she looked around rather than at him. "Are you, sir? I had the impression you did not care for such gatherings."

"Not usually, no, but one cannot always avoid them." He swallowed nervously. "And it is an excellent way to ensure I see my friends."

Her eyes flew back to his. He had emphasised the final part of his statement, in part wanting to see how she would respond and in part hoping she would like the notion of them being friends.

"You cannot be thinking of us," she whispered.

"Is it so ludicrous? I miss—"

"After you gave in to your family's demand to forget me? Yes, it is."

"Elizabeth, please, we must speak somewhere more private." He would tell her of Georgiana's illness. Although he did not know what difference it would make, he wanted her to know; at the very least, she would better understand the choice he had made.

The music stopped, signalling the end of their set. "There is no purpose when your family disapproves and you accept they have the right to interfere in your affairs." Elizabeth shook her head, the gesture angry, then gave a bark of laughter. "Oddly, I met two of your cousins earlier, Miss Reed and Viscount Bramwell. They seem to have survived the encounter. Then again, neither of them knew who I was before we were introduced. Perhaps they will change their minds and have nothing to do with me in the future. A pity. I found them, like others in your family, rather agreeable."

She dropped a shallow curtsey and walked away. Darcy recognised the implication in her final words; she meant to include him and impart the message that she no longer found him 'agreeable'. He wondered whether she would ever know how much her words cut him.

CHAPTER SIXTEEN

When Darcy first discovered that Elizabeth was in town, Fitzwilliam was off in the North. Darcy had hoped to talk to his cousin about it before Georgiana told him, but it was not to be. As they were about to depart to Grosvenor Square for dinner with their family, Georgiana revealed that Fitzwilliam had unexpectedly called earlier, during Darcy's absence. No doubt she had mentioned Elizabeth to their cousin.

Fitzwilliam will have a thing or two to say about it, Darcy reflected. Frustration and anger coursed through him at the thought.

Nothing of note happened during the meal, which suggested to Darcy that the earl and countess had not yet heard that Elizabeth was staying with the Bingleys. As far as he knew, only he and Bramwell were aware that she and he had been at the same dinner party and ball and that he had danced with her. The way gossip spread, especially when it involved encounters between an eligible gentleman such as himself and unmarried ladies, soon others in his family would hear about him seeing Elizabeth.

Fitzwilliam kept a steady, steely gaze on him, but they said no more than a few inconsequential words to each other, and Darcy hoped to escape the house unscathed; there would be another occasion to listen to his cousin recount all the reasons he must avoid Elizabeth.

As soon after dinner as he deemed polite, Darcy announced that he and Georgiana would leave. "The days are still rather short, and—"

"Good idea, Darcy," Fitzwilliam said. "You will not object to me keeping you company. There is a small matter I would like to discuss with you."

"What an excellent notion. I am at liberty, and I believe I have a thing or two to contribute to the conversation." Bramwell grinned at his brother, who looked irritated.

"I wish you boys would not be mysterious." Lady Romsley regarded them each in turn, her brow arched.

"Leave them be, my dear, unless you want to hear about whatever mischief they are planning. I trust it is nothing to worry your mother, is it?" The earl fixed his gaze on first Bramwell then Fitzwilliam.

"No, sir, not on my part. I dare not answer for him." Bramwell poked a finger in Fitzwilliam's direction.

Lady Romsley fussed over Georgiana for several minutes, going so far as to wave away the servant and help her with her coat. She then patted Darcy's cheek and said, "You are looking thin. I do not like it. Perhaps my sons can help you enjoy yourself a little more—cheer you up."

"Do not worry yourself, Mother. I shall keep an eye on him, now that I am back," Fitzwilliam said, again giving Darcy a pointed look.

His cousin and he had come to blows while arguing about Elizabeth in the autumn. Darcy wondered whether they would repeat the performance.

Georgiana went to her apartment immediately upon their arrival at Berkeley Square. She had been quiet all evening, and Darcy assumed it was because she expected Fitzwilliam to speak to him, perhaps even berate him, for making her visit Mrs Bingley and inadvertently see Elizabeth. Darcy had no intention of apologising for it. The ladies already knew each other, they had been well on their way to becoming close friends in Derbyshire, and Darcy had been entirely unaware Elizabeth was in town.

Once the three men were alone in the drawing room, Fitzwilliam said, "Were you intending to tell me Elizabeth Bennet is in London?"

They sat across from each other on matching sofas. Bramwell poured them all glasses of wine, then sat in a chair that allowed him to view both his brother and cousin easily.

"When exactly would I have had the opportunity to inform you?"

"You might have written to me," Fitzwilliam insisted.

Darcy took a slow sip, which helped to keep his temper even. "It did not occur to me. It has been only a week since I learnt she was staying with the Bingleys." He hated the note of defence in his voice and took a larger mouthful of wine, if only to stop himself from saying something he would later regret. His anger at the situation simmered beneath the surface of his being, ready to erupt at any moment.

"Have you seen her elsewhere, not just at Bingley's?" Fitzwilliam's tone was demanding.

"Tell me, why do you believe you have the right to question what I do, especially in such an accusatory manner?" Darcy asked.

"He is acting as though he were your father, is he not? I find it quite amusing." Bramwell guffawed.

"Your interference is making the situation worse!" Fitzwilliam hissed at his brother.

"Interesting. I rather believe that *yours* is," the viscount said.

Not wanting to listen to them bicker further, Darcy said, "Let us be clear. It is *my* business whom I speak to or even dance with. And yes, I have seen Elizabeth twice beyond the day Georgiana and I called on Mrs Bingley."

Fitzwilliam ran his hands over his face. "Darcy…"

"I agreed not to propose to her, did I not?" Darcy interjected. "I never said I would cut her every time we happened to be in the same place."

"I for one see no harm in you exchanging a few pleasant words with her," Bramwell said. "Spending even a short time with a pretty, charming young woman certainly improves the usual ball or dinner party. I would never attend one again if I could not do so."

Fitzwilliam gave him a contemptuous look, and he let out an exasperated breath. Darcy used his glass to hide a chuckle. Usually it was Bramwell who irritated him and Fitzwilliam who acted as the reasonable one. It was amusing the see the situation reversed, and he appreciated Bramwell attempting to calm the situation. Perhaps he would even speak in favour of Elizabeth. She had mentioned them meeting, and Darcy was certain his cousin would like her. How he wanted to speak to him of her, ask his impressions and what they had said to each other! Yet, Darcy was also unwilling to talk of her with anyone who might remind him that he could not pursue her—as Fitzwilliam obviously intended to do.

"I know this is difficult for you, Darcy," the colonel said. "I do not mean to cause you pain by reminding you that—"

"I suspect if we tried very, very hard, we could discover a way for you to have the lady you want. Truly, I doubt it would be that difficult," Bramwell said, sounding both sarcastic and indifferent.

Darcy scoffed and felt his face flush with heat. "Do you not think I have tried? Perhaps you have forgotten the endless discussions we had in the autumn, during which I offered suggestions and compromises only to be argued out of every single one of them. The simple fact is that my marrying Elizabeth is too much for Georgiana. Perhaps in five or ten years she will be sufficiently recovered, but by then, Elizabeth will be married, and I shall have lost my chance."

He stood and went to the window, keeping his back to his cousins until he regained his composure. The only sound in the room was the rhythmic tick-tock of the mantel clock until Bramwell spoke.

"I met her the other evening. I like her."

His voice less angry than previously, Fitzwilliam said, "So do I. Liking her or not has nothing to do with this."

Darcy turned to face them.

Bramwell shrugged. Looking at Darcy, he asked, "Is it about trust? Do you trust her?" He held up a hand, palm outwards, to his brother to stop him from interrupting, presumably having seen him open his mouth. "I am sure to make a remarkable observation, and I shall not have you distract me. If you trust her, Darcy, why not tell her the truth? Once that is done, she and you, aided by your loyal and caring family, will find a way to reassure Georgiana that she is safe from the man whose name none of us care to say."

"Georgiana is whom we are thinking of, in case you have forgotten!" Fitzwilliam barked. He stood and began to pace.

Directing his remark to Bramwell, Darcy said, "I am afraid of what my sister will do to herself."

"As am I, truly. But this situation cannot go on. For one, someone with more of an outside perspective might make a difference. Not much else has this past year and a half. My mother will gladly have Georgiana to stay with her, but she is too inclined to treat her niece as a small child. I do not believe that is all Georgiana requires or even that it is good for her. For two, what about *your* life, Darcy? *You* are the one who lives with her, and *you* are the only one who is being called on to sacrifice something you want so much."

It was a bizarre world in which his eldest cousin was the sympathetic, reasonable person. Darcy's head had begun throbbing, and he rubbed his temples. Bramwell was saying just what he wanted to hear, and he was afraid to believe it.

Bramwell drained the last of his wine, stood, and took a step towards his brother. "Do us a favour and hold your tongue. Let our cousin decide what he wants to do. This is *Darcy*. He is not going to seek Miss Bennet out tonight and convince her to elope." He stopped, his mouth hanging open. "That was not a well-chosen statement. My apologies. I meant there will be another occasion for you to share your opinions with him. Let us not confuse him by throwing too many ideas at him at once."

Fitzwilliam sighed audibly and threw up his hands as though asking what else he could do. Both gentlemen wished Darcy a good night and left him alone.

Darcy returned to his seat and contemplated what Bramwell had said. In December, he had meant to tell Elizabeth the entire truth about Georgiana and why he had not returned to her, but she had not let him; instead, she had run away. Since coming to town, he had not been alone with her, and he could not speak of the matter in public. Should he convince her to meet him where they might talk freely so that he could share the sad tale—as he had begun to do when they danced—or would he do better to leave her alone, as was her apparent wish? It was not about trust, despite Bramwell's suggestion. It was about…

"What exactly?" he murmured. "Hiding from what happened, finding it too difficult and embarrassing to disclose? Georgiana's privacy? She would rather no one knew."

The more appropriate answer would be fear—fear that it would damage Elizabeth's impression of Georgiana and fear that it would not make a difference to her feelings for him, given all that had happened between them.

CHAPTER SEVENTEEN

Elizabeth's chief source of happiness was seeing how joyful Jane was, and the more she knew Bingley, the more she loved him. She also revelled in being in town and knew she would have been miserable had she remained at Longbourn. There was so much more to do in London and so many more people to spend her time with, all of which suited her wonderfully.

One afternoon in the third week of March, Elizabeth was in the park with several young people she had befriended. The weather was fair and more spring-like than winter-like, and she was glad to take advantage of it by strolling amongst the elm trees while getting to know her companions better. The sun was bright and just strong enough to warm one's skin; she caught sight of several birds, and all was well with the world.

Then she saw Colonel Fitzwilliam and Miss Darcy walking towards her.

Evidently, they did not notice her at first, being caught up in their own conversation, but when they were about twenty feet away, Elizabeth could not mistake how the colonel's features hardened or how Miss Darcy tightened her hold on him and seemed to cower, as though Elizabeth would harm her.

Her own steps faltered, and she felt her sense of peace sink to her feet. She had liked Colonel Fitzwilliam when they met the previous year. Knowing he disapproved of her marrying Mr Darcy made her rethink her good impression of him. She was also injured by Miss Darcy's rejection, for she had seemed pleased by her brother's interest in her when they were together in Derbyshire.

But because Lydia married Wickham, I must suffer. If Lydia had been lost forever, I would understand, but I cannot see why I am rejected because of my connexion to him! It is not as though I intend to have anything to do with anyone by that name!

It was impossible to pass each other without speaking unless they wished to give a deliberate cut. Thus, Elizabeth approached the pair and curtseyed. "How do you do?"

Miss Darcy said nothing. She stood still, her eyes facing the ground, and clutched her cousin's arm with both hands. Colonel Fitzwilliam glanced at his young charge before nodding at Elizabeth and returning her greeting.

"I see you are also taking advantage of the fair weather. I remember how much you enjoy walking." His voice matched his stiff demeanour.

"So I do. It provides me with an excellent opportunity to spend time with some of the friendly people I have been so fortunate as to meet since coming to town. I ought to join them. I wish you both a good day."

She offered the cousins a polite smile and quick nod before walking away, satisfied she had done her duty but nothing more. Once she had anticipated calling them family. At present, she could only think of them as the sort of arrogant, disparaging people she despised.

Perhaps I ought not to be surprised. I have met Lady Catherine, and she is one of their closest relations. No doubt the remainder of their family is the same, even Viscount Bramwell, despite his seeming amiable. The sooner I forget all of them, the better.

"Are you well, Georgiana?"

Her cousin's gentle voice broke through the dark cloud that had descended over Georgiana the instant she saw Miss Bennet. It enveloped her as though it were a shroud. She bit her lip and nodded.

"Is it very difficult even to see her? You know your brother will do nothing to cause you injury, and he tells me he is avoiding her and has given up any notion of them marrying. I have no reason to suppose he is being untruthful."

He patted her hand which still rested on his arm. Part of her wanted to separate herself from him, run back to Berkeley Square, and hide in her chamber, but she knew that would be cruel when he was doing his best to be considerate of her feelings. Besides, the thought of being alone in the park, or anywhere in public, frightened her.

"Knowing she knows *him*, is his sister, when I see her—it is too much. I know how important Mr Bingley's friendship is to my brother, and I am trying to be comfortable with Mrs Bingley for his sake, but it is worse with Miss Bennet."

"It is because you know Darcy wanted to marry her, to make you accept her as his wife. He ought to have known it was a terrible idea."

Georgiana said nothing for a while. When she had first met Miss Bennet, she had liked her a great deal. She had even thought that it would be a rather wonderful thing if her brother married her. He would be happy, and she might have the sort of sister she had always dreamt of. Her cousin's objection to the match, along with that of her aunts and uncle, made her realise she was wrong to ever look upon it with favour. As kind as she was, the social gap between Miss Bennet's family and that of the Fitzwilliams and Darcys meant such a union was inappropriate, just as her own with *him* would have been. Georgiana would die if she was forced to be sister to *his* sister.

However, seeing her brother's misery made her hate herself. It was because of her, and she was to blame for all the family upset since the autumn—no, dating back to last summer, when she had so stupidly believed *his* false proclamations of love. Worst of all, Fitzwilliam and her brother were fighting, as much as they tried to hide it from her. They had been the best of friends, but their connexion was destroyed.

"I wish you and my brother were not angry with each other," she said, her voice quiet and tentative as always.

Colonel Fitzwilliam squeezed her hand. "Do not concern yourself with us. We shall be frustrated and disagreeable and believe the other is being unreasonable for a little longer, then this period will pass, and we shall be friends again. It will happen before you know it. Our only concern is you, and seeing you improve will encourage us to forget every difference of opinion we have ever had. You are doing so well, sweetheart, and that makes him, me, all of your family so very happy. Think only of what you need to continue to recover, and let Darcy and me worry about everything else, including our connexion."

Once again, Georgiana nodded. She kept her eyes on her boots as they completed their walk.

"Is something amiss, Brother? Y-you are not happy."

Darcy looked up from his almost full breakfast plate to his sister. In truth, he had been thinking about Elizabeth. He tried to keep his distress from Georgiana, knowing she would blame herself and it would interfere with her recovery, which he believed was proceeding well. He had accepted that Lady Catherine had been the one to tell her of his intentions, and he would never forgive his aunt for giving her the idea that, should he and Elizabeth marry, Georgiana would be thrown into Wickham's company regularly. It was false, but once the notion was put into her head, his sister was incapable of banishing it.

I did the right thing by giving up Elizabeth, as much as I suffer for it. Georgiana needs more time to heal, and she must *be my chief concern.*

Aloud, he said, "I am perfectly well. Do not worry yourself over me."

"Fitzwilliam and I saw her, Miss B-Bennet, during our walk the other day. Did he tell you?"

This caught Darcy's attention, and he stared at her. It was the first time she had willingly mentioned Elizabeth since learning of her youngest sister's elopement. Was she remembering how much she had liked her? Had the shock of learning of the Wickhams' marriage lessened? Would she tell him that she would gladly accept Elizabeth as her sister-in-law? Darcy prayed such a day would come to pass, but it was soon evident it would not be this day.

"He did not," he said in answer to her question. "Did you speak to her?"

Georgiana shrugged. "Our cousin did. I…" She reached for her neck and pinched herself, digging her nails into her flesh.

Quickly, Darcy stood and went to her, covering her hand with his own. "Let us not talk of her further," he said, hoping he adequately masked his disappointment and being forced to acknowledge that her objections had in no way lessened.

CHAPTER EIGHTEEN

Over the next days, Elizabeth visited Mrs Gardiner, occupied her time with new friends, and amused herself as much as possible. Bingley made a habit of introducing Elizabeth to his acquaintances, promoting her as someone with whom they could have a 'splendidly good conversation'. He once remarked that it was a shame she and Mr Darcy were not on better terms.

"Last summer, I believed you had become friends, but now you do not seem to have much to say to each other," he had said one afternoon.

He sounded disappointed, and Elizabeth was struck with regret; he did not understand because she was deliberately keeping the truth from him. Yet, she continued to believe it was for the best.

Mr Darcy and I shall continue exchanging stilted greetings where I attempt to keep my feelings hidden and not see the warmth in his eyes. Surely, in time, it will become easier. If I keep myself busy with new people and activities, perhaps I shall cease thinking of him so much.

In her heart, she knew it would not be so easy. The looks he gave her when they met were like those she had come to expect during the glorious weeks when she had anticipated marrying him. How could that be? He had decided against her, and it should be reflected in his behaviour! Once, she had spent several minutes watching him speak to Miss Reed and her mother. There was something in the way he stood and the expression on his face that was so kind and caring. It reminded her what it was like to have his attention all to herself and to know that he was truly listening and interested in what she had to say. Not questioning if it was right or not, she did not attempt to avoid him but neither did she seek him out. If nothing else, she would not want anyone to comment on her disliking her brother's dearest friend. Their conversations, when they took place, were brief and polite.

Shortly before the end of March, Bingley introduced Elizabeth to Mr Robert Grey, a friend of some ten years, who owned an estate slightly smaller than Netherfield in Northamptonshire. They were at a party at which conversation was to be the main entertainment. It was a risky choice on the part of the hostess, and Elizabeth was not sure the evening would be a success. After meeting Mr Grey, she no longer regretted attending, even if others did. He was dark-haired and handsome—though not as good-looking as Mr Darcy—and after just a few minutes' conversation, Elizabeth decided his company would be no hardship.

Bingley left them, saying, "Grey, I am trusting you with my dearest sister." He turned to Elizabeth. "Please do not tell Louisa or Caroline I said that, but they have only themselves to blame."

Elizabeth chuckled and smiled at Mr Grey. "I am afraid his sisters are not entirely happy with his choice of wife, although there is nothing objectionable about Jane. Have you met her?"

Mr Grey returned her smile, creating thin wrinkles around his startlingly blue eyes. There was something about him that spoke of an easy humour—without being devoid of seriousness when it was called for. But Elizabeth had learnt her lesson about first impressions. Thus, while she thought she could like him, she remained guarded.

"I have not, but I am looking forward to making her acquaintance. We were actually searching for her when he spotted you and insisted we must be introduced at once."

Again, Elizabeth laughed. "For some reason I do not entirely understand, he appears deeply concerned that I shall not find my sojourn in town agreeable. I suspect it is because he thinks of me as a very sociable person."

"Are you not?"

"I most certainly am, and he is very right to introduce me to as many people as possible. I am an absolute beast when I have nothing to divert me."

This time, they both laughed.

"I most sincerely doubt that, Miss Bennet. I understand you are from Hertfordshire, but I know little else of you or your family. Do you have brothers or sisters beyond Mrs Bingley?"

They spoke of their families and homes, their favourite pastimes, books, and more, spending most of the evening together. She introduced him to Jane, and the three of them and Bingley talked of places they would like to visit as the weather improved, Kew Gardens being a favourite suggestion.

Elizabeth was quiet in the carriage as they drove back to the Bingleys' house, speaking only to assure her brother-in-law that she had indeed liked Mr Grey. It took effort, but she managed not to compare him to Mr Darcy.

HIS FAMILY OBJECTS

Darcy declined several invitations to evening events in favour of staying with Georgiana; therefore, he had not seen Elizabeth for almost an entire week before they met at the theatre. He arrived with Fitzwilliam, who spotted Bramwell in the crowd and led the way to him. As they drew nearer, they discovered he was conversing with Elizabeth and Rebecca Reed. Fitzwilliam's steps slowed, but it was too late to prevent Darcy from approaching. He bowed to the ladies and gave Bramwell a brief nod while keeping his eyes on Elizabeth.

"Miss Bennet, Cousin, I hope you are both well this evening."

Elizabeth curtseyed but said nothing. She glanced at Fitzwilliam but quickly looked away. Knowing his sentiments, Darcy thought the colonel had likely been cold if not outright rude when they met in the park.

"Darcy, I did not know you would be here tonight," Rebecca said.

"We only just arrived." They had dined with Georgiana, and Fitzwilliam had been reluctant to leave. It had struck Darcy at the time, and he wondered whether his cousin had known they might encounter Elizabeth.

"I greatly appreciate your tardiness. It provided me with a delightful period during which I had these two lovely ladies to myself," Bramwell said, winking in their direction.

"Have you seen my mother and father?" Rebecca said. "You must find them this evening, perhaps at the interval."

Darcy nodded and, desperately wanting a morsel of Elizabeth's attention, asked her, "Did you come with my cousins?"

She shook her head. "Bingley, my sister, and some friends."

"Let us go and find Mr and Mrs Reed now. I would like to greet them too." Fitzwilliam tugged at his arm, but Darcy disregarded him.

"Have any of you seen *Cymbeline* performed before?" he asked. Although the question was a general one, he looked at Elizabeth as he spoke. She was acting oddly, almost contemplative, and he wondered whether she had learnt something new about his situation. Would Bramwell have spoken to her? After all, he had advised Darcy to tell her the truth. He dismissed the idea; his cousin would leave it to him to decide whether she should know.

While Elizabeth did not answer, Rebecca and Bramwell did, and they chatted about the play for several minutes until their conversation was interrupted by a young, lately married couple —the Bells. After exchanging a few commonplaces, they moved on. The viscount watched them walk away before directing his next comment to Elizabeth, who had not met them previously.

"That was Mrs Bell, who began life as Miss Ball. No doubt she will have a daughter, who will become Mrs Bill, whose own daughter must certainly grow up to become Mrs Boll."

"Let us hope the line stops there," Darcy said.

She regarded him and laughed merrily, and Darcy drank in the sight of her. She seemed to give off a light that beckoned to him, and more than anything, he wanted to answer its call. Before he knew what had happened, Fitzwilliam had succeeded in grabbing his arm and pulling him away.

"Darcy, take more care," he hissed. "Do you want everyone present tonight to know you have a *tendre* for your friend's sister-in-law? What do you imagine my parents would say if they saw you looking at her like that?"

"I do not care—"

"You might if Georgiana learnt that you were arguing with them again. You know she blames herself for the disharmony in our family. It distresses her."

Darcy freed his arm from his cousin's grasp and strode to the Romsleys' box, refusing to say another word to Fitzwilliam.

It did not take long for Elizabeth to discover that the box Bingley had secured for them was almost directly across from the one in which Mr Darcy sat with his relations. Looking around the theatre, her gaze unintentionally fell on him. He was turned towards her, and she was certain he was watching her. As she took in his appearance—handsome as always but serious and almost sombre—she felt her heart reach out to him. There always seemed to be an air of regret about him, and she wished she understood why. Earlier, for just a moment, she had imagined what it would be like if they had come to the performance together, how they would speak about the play beforehand, as they had often spoken of books. Telling herself it was ridiculous, she had the sense that his thoughts were similar, that he too was imagining what their lives might have been.

"I was very glad when Bingley invited me to join you this evening."

The sound of Mr Grey's whispered words made Elizabeth start, and she looked away from Mr Darcy, feeling her cheeks heat. "I am glad you were able to accept."

He returned her smile, and feeling self-conscious, she gave her attention to the stage. She had implied to Mr Darcy that more than one person had accompanied the Bingleys and her that evening, but in truth, it was only Mr Grey. Tonight was the third time they had been in company together.

Shortly before the interval, Elizabeth had the sensation of something crawling down her spine. When she could no longer bear it, she dared to look towards the box in which Mr Darcy sat. Instantly, her gaze was caught by that of the Countess of Romsley. She and Lord Romsley, both sitting tall and proud, were staring at her while their younger son whispered to them. It was difficult to entirely make out expressions given how far apart they were, but Elizabeth knew the Romsleys did not regard her with friendly curiosity. Acid burnt her throat, and she wrenched her eyes away and spent the remainder of the act pretending to follow the action on the stage.

At the interval, Bingley announced, "I am going to see if I can find Darcy, if you do not object, my dear."

Jane said that she did not.

"Shall I see whether I can secure us refreshments, ladies?" Mr Grey asked.

"That is very kind of you. I would appreciate it, and I am sure Lizzy would also." Jane nudged Elizabeth, who, not certain exactly what had passed, decided to simply nod.

When they were alone, Jane moved to sit next to Elizabeth and said, "I did not know Mr Darcy was here. Did you see him?"

"I did. He and Colonel Fitzwilliam arrived when I was speaking to Miss Reed and Lord Bramwell."

"And?" Jane pressed when she failed to continue.

"And nothing." Elizabeth regarded her to add emphasis to her words. "We were together for just a minute or two." While this was true in a strict sense, there was always more to her encounters with Mr Darcy—and Colonel Fitzwilliam, for that matter. It was a sort of undercurrent she was attempting to overlook.

Jane sighed and furrowed her brow.

"Stop worrying!" Elizabeth rested a hand on her sister's. "I *know* Mr Darcy and I can be nothing to each other, and while there is still a little bit of awkwardness when we meet, that will dissipate soon enough. I choose to think of what makes me happy, and that is being with you and my darling brother, and the amusing ways I have been occupying myself."

"What of Mr Grey?"

Before responding, Elizabeth glanced at the entrance to the box, listening for any sign that he was nearby. "I like him, and I anticipate knowing him better in the coming weeks. That is the most I am prepared to say."

"I like him too, and Bingley speaks highly of him," Jane said.

At the end of the evening, Mr Grey returned home with Elizabeth and the Bingleys to partake of supper. Seeing how Bingley watched them, Elizabeth was certain he hoped that more than friendship developed between them.

Clearly to further his matchmaking scheme, Bingley occupied Jane in conversation as they ate, leaving Mr Grey and Elizabeth to amuse each other.

"How did you like the play?" Mr Grey asked.

"To be honest, I am not sure what my opinion is. The actors were very good, but I tend to appreciate the history in Shakespeare's works, and perhaps *Cymbeline* has too much of the fantastical in it. Yet, I also enjoy those elements in other plays."

"Such as *A Midsummer Night's Dream?*"

"Exactly! Have you read much Shakespeare?"

"I have. I admit to being quite the voracious reader when I have time. I have been accused of neglecting my company in favour of the activity. Since inheriting the estate, I have been too busy to devote as much attention to books or friends as I would like. There is much more work involved than I expected. My father was used to arranging everything in his way, but it is now 1813, and I want to manage it in a manner that reflects today, rather than 1780 or whenever it was my father inherited. Do you understand what I mean? I fear I have not explained myself well."

He laughed, which brought out an attractive dimple in one cheek. *Mr Darcy has a similar one—two, rather, one on each side of his handsome—* Elizabeth bit the inside of her lip to still her thoughts. She *must* find a way to stop thinking of him! She regarded Mr Grey and wondered what role he would play in her life in the coming years. The more she knew him, the more she was forced to admit there was much to admire—his love of books for one, something she shared with him.

And Mr Darcy.

Again, she reprimanded her mind, her heart, whatever it was that made such thoughts intrude on her peace.

"What is the name of your estate?" she asked. "I recall that it is in Northamptonshire, but that is all."

"Graystone Manor, spelt with an a. The reason for the difference between surname and estate name is lost to history, and no one has seen fit to correct it. Can you guess what colour the house is?"

Elizabeth tapped her chin speculatively. "Hmm…violet?"

They shared a laugh, and she asked him to describe his home. While he did, she successfully kept *another gentleman* out of her thoughts.

CHAPTER NINETEEN

Elizabeth continued to be very busy as Easter approached. Jane and she often spent the morning with various ladies they had lately met, sometimes together and sometimes not. To some extent, their new circles diverged; Jane found more in common with married ladies, and Elizabeth preferred the company of those who spoke of something other than their husbands, domestic arrangements, and children. Miss Reed introduced her to other young ladies, and when the weather permitted, they enjoyed promenading in the park. Viscount Bramwell often appeared wherever Miss Reed and Elizabeth were.

"Have you known Lord Bramwell long?" Elizabeth asked one day. They had returned to Miss Reed's home to take refreshments after some shopping.

"All my life. Our fathers have been friends since boyhood, along with my cousin Darcy's."

"From the view of a relative stranger, I have the impression the viscount's interest in you—"

"Oh, please do not say it!" Miss Reed interjected, adding a nervous laugh. "I do not know whether I can bear being teased about him."

"Very well, I shall not say another word related to that gentleman."

Miss Reed squeezed her hand. "Thank you. In truth, I do not know what to make of his behaviour. I am used to thinking of him as a cousin of my cousin and…well, not exactly a rake but certainly not serious and far too much of a flirt. Not that he would misuse anyone! Oh, what a muddle I am making of it!" She took a deep breath before going on. "He is a decent sort, but one would be reckless to take any interest he shows in them seriously. Do you know, he asks me about *you* often. Not in the way of a romantic interest, you understand, but he always wants to hear about our activities and what I know of you."

Elizabeth arched her brow and managed a faint, "Oh?"

Miss Reed nodded. "Something he said led me to believe you and Darcy knew each other better than I had supposed."

"We have been in company together frequently in the past. I would not call us friends, however. At best, we are indifferent acquaintances."

Elizabeth did her best to hide her discomfort, but she doubted she was successful. The long pause before Miss Reed spoke showed as much.

"Did you and he—? I cannot believe I almost asked you that when I just begged you not to speak of Lord Bramwell."

Elizabeth offered her a little smile and shook her head. "Think nothing of it. And think nothing of my friendship—or lack thereof—with your cousin. There is truly nothing to tell." *And I suspect the viscount is only hoping to discover whether I still harbour ambitions where Mr Darcy is concerned.*

Miss Reed's expression eased, and Elizabeth saw a mischievous gleam in her eyes. "While we are speaking of gentlemen, what think you of Mr Robert Grey? He appears to be quite captivated by you."

"Captivated? We hardly know each other. He is amiable."

"You have not instantly fallen madly in love with him?"

Elizabeth laughed again. "I do not believe I am capable of being so reckless." *I was reckless when I gave Mr Darcy my heart last summer, and I suffer for it still. Never again!* "Viscount Bramwell has not made you swoon and dream of becoming his viscountess? Perhaps you endlessly scribble what could be your name? Lady Rebecca Fitzwilliam, Viscountess Bramwell."

"Could you imagine? I might have been so silly when I was twelve, but at one-and-twenty, I hope I have gained a little maturity. Perhaps we should stop discussing gentlemen."

"I agree. With all my heart!"

At breakfast one morning shortly before Easter, Bingley proposed that they attend the opera to see *Le Nozze di Figaro*. "We must invite Grey too. I know that will please one of us especially, will it not?"

He winked at Elizabeth, and Jane chastised him for teasing her. Elizabeth continued to see Mr Grey regularly, and she had yet to find anything to disapprove of in him. He was attentive, interesting, treated everyone with respect regardless of their social position, and she had never heard him say so much as one unkind word of anyone.

"I was thinking of asking Darcy," Bingley said, and Elizabeth felt her spine stiffen. "We have spent little time with him

—but perhaps I ought not, since you and he do not enjoy each other's company." He indicated Elizabeth.

"I believe we simply ran out of things to speak of and are content to let each other live our lives without feigning a closeness we shall never feel. Do not let it affect your friendship." Elizabeth chuckled and inwardly reprimanded herself. Did she want Bingley to invite Mr Darcy? She was afraid the answer was yes, although it would be much better for her if he did not. *And for Mr Darcy. I have seen that it is difficult for him to be near me, and he will refuse.*

"I suppose it feels more natural to have you dislike each other," Bingley said.

Dislike Mr Darcy? Elizabeth could never do that, not again, and their present situation did not seem at all natural to her. What *did* was being his wife, living and laughing with him and striving together to build their family and future.

"Oh, I think it is too much to say Lizzy *dislikes* Mr Darcy. They simply…are not friends," Jane said.

He appeared to think about it for a moment, his lower lip jutted out, before nodding. "Well, I shall not invite him, but I shall invite Grey. How does that sound?"

Jane—echoed by Elizabeth—agreed that it was a very good plan.

In the end, Mr Darcy *did* attend the opera, though he was with his own party. Elizabeth saw him before the performance began, but they were already in their separate boxes. She was not certain whom he had accompanied, so quickly had she looked away when she glimpsed his tall, unmistakable form.

HIS FAMILY OBJECTS

She did not leave the box during the interval lest she encounter him, and when Mr Grey mentioned seeing him to Bingley, she expressed disinterested surprise.

All this changed during the third act. As the Countessa Almaviva sang of her betrayal and heartache during the *Dove Sono i Bei Momenti* aria, tears formed in Elizabeth's eyes, and her throat tightened. Her gaze drifted to Mr Darcy, who she found was watching her in return. Some of the song's lyrics struck her like a knife through the heart.

> *Where are the beautiful moments of sweetness and pleasure, where have they gone, those vows of a deceiving tongue?*
> *Why has everything changed into tears and pain for me?*

Elizabeth's situation with Mr Darcy was not the same as the Contessa's with her husband, but Elizabeth *did* feel that he had betrayed her. Like the fictional woman, she remembered the moments during which she and Mr Darcy had been in concord, when she had felt they perfectly understood each other and shared a beautiful love. But unlike Almaviva, Elizabeth had no thoughts of changing Mr Darcy's mind, of attempting to make him love her again.

What would be the use, when he has proved his feelings for me are so easily set aside? Regardless of the looks he gives me, I cannot believe he truly loves me. If he did, his family's opinion would not matter. That is how he has betrayed me.

Darcy knew Elizabeth was in attendance that evening. There was something in the air that assured him she was nearby, a certain lightness or rightness that told him the world was not as dour as it had seemed. He glanced at her during the performance, attempting to overlook Mr Grey's presence. Darcy had met him but would not call him a friend; their paths had not crossed frequently.

Seeing how easy he was with Elizabeth, Darcy loathed him. It was jealousy, as he was perfectly willing to admit, but that did not change how much Darcy wished Mr Grey would be called away to the country, or say something Elizabeth would find objectionable, or really that *anything* would happen that might disrupt their growing friendship.

I ought to wish her happy, hope she finds another man who is free to love her as I am not, but that is asking entirely too much of me.

Weeks ago, Bramwell had offered the opinion that there was no reason Darcy should not marry Elizabeth. He advised Darcy to tell her the truth of what had transpired at Ramsgate and its effect on Georgiana. What would it do to his sister if he did? The earl and countess would certainly berate him, as would Fitzwilliam, but he cared nothing for their angry words. Would it be more than Elizabeth could bear—both the ugliness of his tale and what they would have to confront to be together?

Seeing the utter dejection on her beautiful face as they looked at each other during the aria, he knew something had to change. The only way it would was if Elizabeth fully understood the situation.

As the opera ended, he used the crush of the crowd to hide his actions. Without drawing the attention of Elizabeth's companions, Darcy approached her from behind, lightly touched her arm, and whispered into her ear. "We must talk. Meet me tomorrow, in the park by the gate."

She started and met his eye, shaking her head.

"I beg of you. Early—before the breakfast hour. There is much you do not understand."

"Darcy!" Bingley called, as jovial as ever.

Darcy's hand dropped to his side, and he hoped no one had noticed him grasping Elizabeth's elbow.

"Bingley." Darcy bowed to the others. "Mrs Bingley, Mr Grey."

"You must join us for supper." To his wife, Bingley continued, "I told him that at the interval, but I think he worries he is imposing. Tell him he is not, my dear."

Before Mrs Bingley could be convinced to do so, Darcy spoke. "I cannot, but thank you. I am meeting some friends. It was a pleasure to see you all, but if you will excuse me, I must find them."

Darcy gave Elizabeth an imploring look before she averted her gaze, and as he walked away, he prayed she would not leave him waiting alone the next morning.

CHAPTER TWENTY

Darcy reached the gate long before he expected Elizabeth would come. He feared that if she arrived first and did not see him, she would leave. He had been awake the night through, planning the words he would say to her with a mix of anticipation and trepidation. If he were exceedingly fortunate, he would leave the meeting an engaged man, or, at the very least, reconciled with Elizabeth and with an idea of how—*together*—they would convince Georgiana and his family that their union would harm no one, especially not his sister.

He watched her approach, her long, deep-red coat making her look even lovelier than usual. Her steps were assured, and when she saw Darcy, she said a few words to the footman trailing her, who remained where he was while she continued forwards. He led her to a quiet, out-of-the-way spot where they were unlikely to be interrupted, the servant moving slightly to keep his mistress in sight. Once they stopped, Elizabeth fixed Darcy with a look that said she was listening. However, his words failed him, and he remained silent.

Either she was impatient or the pause was longer than he had realised, because she spoke. "I cannot remain long. Jane and Bingley will miss me, and I would rather not explain this to them." She gestured between them, her action and tone dismissive.

Licking his lips to give them much-needed moisture, he said, "It is about why I said what I did in December. I did not tell you everything."

Elizabeth stilled instantly, her expression wary.

"The reason why I could not, why I did not, return to Hertfordshire as expected was Georgiana. Not-not simply because she does not think you would be an appropriate wife for me but because...because it was *you*. I am explaining this very poorly. It is about that summer and Wickham." He tasted bile just thinking of it.

Her expression eased, and she seemed attentive and curious.

"My sister suffered greatly after Ramsgate. I did not know whether she would recover, whether she would wish to...go on living or find a way to do it. My mother was the same. She felt things, difficult things, too much for her health. She was often despondent, unable to leave her bed, and she...she hurt herself." At little more than a whisper, he added, "As does Georgiana."

Elizabeth gasped, and a hand flew to her mouth.

"When she found out about your sister and Wickham, it was more than she could bear. I had planned to tell her gently, assure her he would never be part of our lives. I am certain I would have succeeded in convincing her there was no need for alarm. She liked you and knew I wanted to marry you. When I returned to town in September, she even asked me whether I had proposed.

"Instead, she learnt of it in the worst possible manner. Lady Catherine told her. Georgiana was inconsolable. She begged me not to marry you, acted as terrified as if Wickham were at the door, ready to drag her away or murder us all. Nothing eased her fear other than my family promising I would never ask her to accept you as her sister. Fitzwilliam and his parents refused to listen to any argument I offered, any suggestion for how the situation could be remedied. By the middle of November, I had given up all hope."

"Why did you never tell me?" Elizabeth demanded. She looked almost wild, her eyes round with shock. "I have four sisters. Do you not think I understand the impulse to do *anything* for them, if their well-being is at risk? If someone had told me I could protect Lydia and secure the reputations of Mary and Kitty and Jane by rejecting you, I might have done it, despite how difficult it would have been. I like to think I would have, to shield my innocent sisters, if not poor, stupid Lydia."

"I wanted to," he interjected. "I tried to, but it was impossible to find the words to explain. It was easier to let you believe it was my family, not Georgiana. I did not want you of all people to think poorly of her."

"Think poorly of her?" Elizabeth cried. "How could I? She was a child, and that man abused her!"

Darcy covered his eyes with a hand and bowed his head, hiding from the reality that he had not yet told Elizabeth just how terribly Wickham had treated his beloved sister. Speaking through his fingers, his voice sounding as weak and tired as a newborn kitten, he admitted, "I am afraid for her. Every day since then—a year and a half now—I have been frightened she might not find the strength to go on, that I could lose her as I did my parents. I certainly would have lost her had she married him. With her delicate nature, she would not long have survived exchanging vows with him. I would have done everything in my power to prevent their marriage. I *did* do everything possible for your sister, but she would not leave him. I told her I would arrange everything, even if there was a child."

Elizabeth made a noise of disgust. "I am thankful she has not had to contend with *that* yet. She is so young! In truth, I hope they never have children. Neither of them should be responsible for an innocent baby."

Darcy spent a moment looking at her, torn between telling her the next, most awful, part. He wanted her to know it all and yearned for her sympathy and understanding, but he hated to burden her with the knowledge of what Georgiana had suffered. In the end, he *had* decided to be open with her, and keeping back anything would be wrong.

"I thank God Georgiana was spared that particular horror too."

She recoiled, almost stumbling backwards, and he reached out a hand to steady her. She brushed it away and gaped at him. "Oh no! She—?"

With a nod, he admitted, "I wrote to her in Ramsgate, telling her to expect me. From what I have discerned, when she received my letter, she told him that she wanted me to know of their engagement. They argued and..." He shrugged, although there was nothing light-hearted about the matter. "I do not believe he gave her a choice, but I am not sure. He might have cajoled more than forced, if you believe that makes a material difference. She refuses to give a direct answer no matter who asks."

Elizabeth pressed a hand to her mouth again, and for a

moment, he thought she might sink to the ground. "Oh, dear Lord!"

"When I arrived in Ramsgate, I saw at once that she was nervous. When she told me she had seen Wickham and they wanted to marry, I naturally believed that explained her agitation. I met him and conveyed that Georgiana is not entitled to her dowry until she is one-and-twenty, that I would do nothing to have it released earlier, and that he would be solely responsible for her care. I would give him nothing. The part about her dowry is not true, but I knew the effect it would have on him. He advised me to speak to Georgiana, said I did not know everything and that if I did, I would insist on them marrying.

"I imparted the substance of this conversation to her. That was when I became aware that *more* had happened between them." He paused to take several calming breaths. "It made no difference to me. I would *never* have permitted their marriage, even less so, knowing he might have— Since that day, whenever his name is mentioned, she becomes…distraught." He ran his hands across his forehead, almost dislodging his hat.

"I confronted him again, as you might imagine. I made an agreement that Fitzwilliam and I would not attempt to destroy him as long as he did not attempt to ruin my sister. Had I suspected his treatment of her was not a unique occurrence, I would have done more to protect unsuspecting ladies."

"There is no sign that he forced Lydia into anything," Elizabeth said. "I have no idea how he persuaded her to elope, but knowing my sister, it would not have taken more than a promise of amusement and something she might boast of to her friends and family. She showed no signs of regretting her actions when she was at Longbourn."

"In singling out your sister, I think he knew it would hurt me."

"Or he saw a pretty, silly girl who would readily accede to whatever he wanted. It is not your fault, and you were generous to go after them and ensure he married her."

Darcy waved this off. "I took Georgiana to Romsley Hall as soon as we left Ramsgate. She was only at ease with Lady Romsley, and she and the earl insisted I should leave her with them. Seeing me upset her. They said it was because she believed I must hate her, but of course, I never could. Fitzwilliam all but forced me into the carriage, and despite my reluctance, I left and went to Netherfield, as you know. I had promised Bingley, and I did not want to draw attention to Georgiana by changing my previous arrangements. We met you, and I was drawn to you almost from the first. I told myself it was because you were so lively and happy, and my mind was craving such company in light of the disorder in my family. It was nothing more, or so I believed until we met again in Kent. Then fate threw us together again in Derbyshire."

"Do not forget the next part, Mr Darcy," she said, her voice a touch cold. "Fate, your sister, your circumstances—whatever you choose to call it—then tore us apart. You should have told me! Instead, you lied to me by implying it was because of your family. Do you have any idea how it made me feel to think that you gave me up for no more reason than that your relations believe I am unworthy of being your wife? I decided you had reverted to your previous arrogant views and succumbed to their prejudice against me. I felt like such a fool because I had trusted you, had allowed myself to care for you, to dream of a future with you as my husband."

"I wanted to tell you, but—"

"What excuse can you possibly have for not doing so, for leaving me to wonder why you abandoned me? I would have understood. It would have hurt, but it would have been better than to think you decided I was not good enough for you. Thank you for your explanation, but this changes nothing between us."

Alarmed by the final statement, Darcy said, "I cannot bear being apart from you. I will find a way to rectify everything. I cannot deny what I want, and I know if I find the right words, I can—I *will*—make Georgiana understand that our marrying does not mean she will ever see him. It is not right that I should have to give you up, that we cannot have our share of happiness."

But Elizabeth only shook her head. "Nothing is resolved with your sister or family. I should marry you and watch it tear you apart? I should enter into marriage knowing my new sister, who is still so young and will live with us, hates me?"

"She does not hate you."

"She disapproves of me and would hate her brother's marriage. How could that be good for any of us? I would never want to be responsible for causing her more pain. You cannot simply erase the past eight months and reconcile Miss Darcy and your other relations to an alliance with Wickham, even an indirect one. It is better for both of us to-to put aside any feelings we have. Clinging to them will just make us miserable."

She inhaled sharply, and he had the impression she was finding it very difficult not to cry. He felt the same way.

"It is not that easy."

"Is it not what you decided to do months ago?" she demanded.

Unconsciously, he tried to grasp her hand. "Seeing you again has made it impossible."

"Then we must avoid each other, at least until such a time as—"

"As it no longer rips my heart from my body? I have loved

you for eighteen months, even when I had no reason to hope I would ever see you again, when I thought you despised me. Do you really think I shall simply forget now, especially knowing you return my feelings?"

Her beautiful eyes were red with unshed tears, and she shrugged sadly, as if to say they had no choice. "It is enough that Lydia faces a terrible future. I shall not risk another young woman's well-being by making her accept a sister-in-law with a connexion to the man who terrifies her." She held up a hand to forestall his next words and walked away, the footman throwing him a daring expression when he made to follow.

Darcy let her go yet again.

CHAPTER TWENTY-ONE

Elizabeth strode back to the house, intent on reaching it as quickly as possible. She barely managed to contain her strong emotions until she was alone in her chamber, having impatiently waved away the maid who had greeted her at the door. Her heart beat thunderously against her ribs, which almost felt as though they would bruise, and her hands shook such that it was difficult to undo the buttons of her coat.

What should she make of everything Mr Darcy had told her? Naturally, she believed him, but she immediately dismissed his claim that he would find a way for them to be together. She would never accept him without Miss Darcy's full, freely given support, and that seemed unlikely to ever occur, given her understandable reluctance to have any tie to Mr Wickham.

How greatly Miss Darcy had suffered! Even when Elizabeth believed Mr Wickham had only deceived the young lady, she had pitied her, but with this new information, she longed to hold Miss Darcy within her protective embrace and act as a shield against the world which had treated her so cruelly. Briefly, she worried about Lydia married to a man who could behave in such a reprehensible manner, but at the present time, Mr Darcy's disclosures took precedence. Later, she would decide whether there was anything she could do to assist Lydia should Mr Wickham show signs of abusing her.

Elizabeth's mind took her back to the summer and meeting Miss Darcy. She had thought her exceedingly shy and even fearful at times. She recalled seeing her pulling her hair or squeezing her hands together until her knuckles were white—clear evidence of the girl wanting to harm herself, just as Mr Darcy had said. Elizabeth could not conceive of feeling so hurt, so unhappy that you wanted to cause yourself pain. What a dreadful way to live!

Elizabeth was angry and disappointed in Mr Darcy. Why had he not told her the truth when they talked in December? He had humiliated and misled her by not being more forthright. This last was particularly difficult to accept. If he had not waited so long to talk to her, leaving her to wonder why he had not come—she would still have been heartbroken, but she liked to believe she would have understood.

Part of Elizabeth's anger was because she felt as though she was being punished for Lydia's reckless actions. It was not a new sentiment, but it returned stronger than ever. She suffered for her sister's thoughtless deeds and would in one fashion or another for the rest of her life because, distressingly, knowing how much Mr Darcy had given up for his sister, how far he would go to protect her well-being, Elizabeth loved him more than ever.

The Hursts and Miss Bingley returned to town the week after Easter, and Jane, Bingley, and Elizabeth set out to call on them at Mr Hurst's town house in Grosvenor Square.

As the carriage slowed to a stop, Bingley said, "There is no escaping this visit or their company while we all remain in London. We shall see them as little as possible, and I promise you both that I shall not allow them to be unkind."

His sullen manner showed how much his sisters' behaviour towards Jane had injured him and how easy it was for those who were supposed to be our nearest and dearest loved ones to wound us. The realisation made Elizabeth think of the Darcys, though she could not blame either of them for hurting the other—him because he wished to marry a woman his sister did not like and her for being so unwell that he was required to put her needs above his own desires.

Mrs Hurst and Miss Bingley greeted Jane with what Elizabeth saw as obvious false sincerity, though she doubted her sister would recognise it.

"Are you not looking well? Your day dress is…pretty. Now that Caroline and I are in town, we shall take you to the best dressmakers and ensure your wardrobe does credit to my brother," Mrs Hurst said.

"Going shopping together would be lovely. I am sure we can find a morning that suits us all, though I admit, I am terribly busy." Jane smiled contentedly.

"Miss Eliza, I had no notion you intended to stay with my brother *so* long," Miss Bingley said.

"Enough," Bingley hissed. "I am *very* pleased to have Lizzy with us, and she is here because both Jane and I begged her to accept a home with us."

Miss Bingley's cheeks flushed, but she refrained from addressing Elizabeth or Jane again. While they drank tea and nibbled on lemon cake, the ladies told them of their time in Brighton. Jane spoke a little, but no one else did. The Bingleys and Elizabeth departed soon after, but not before Jane offered them an invitation.

"We are having a dinner party soon. I hope you will come."

"Thank you. We shall be delighted," Mrs Hurst said, though to Elizabeth's ear, her tone did not match her words.

The dinner party was much like any other, in Elizabeth's opinion. She enjoyed *most* of the company, which included Mr Grey and Miss Reed, two people she found it especially easy to talk to. The meal itself was delicious, the choice of dishes carefully considered, and the after-dinner entertainment amusing.

Mr Darcy was also in attendance. She hardly knew how to look at him, let alone speak to him, after their conversation in the park. During dinner, she sat beside Mr Grey, and she felt guilty because of the attention he was paying her. She imagined it injured Mr Darcy to see it. There was no denying that he still cared for her—loved her—but their situation was impossible.

Although they had greeted each other earlier, they did not speak until later in the evening. Finding herself alone, she had stepped into a corner where she was unlikely to be seen, assuring herself she was not deliberately seeking solitude in the hope that he would join her but suspecting that is exactly what she meant to do.

Sure enough, he was beside her almost at once. They said nothing for a long moment. She kept her eyes averted, peeking at him occasionally. Presently, her anger towards him was out of mind; all she could think of was how much he had to bear. Her fingers itched to reach for him, to comfort him, and she clasped her hands together to prevent herself from doing so.

"I…I hope you are well," he said softly. "That you are not distressed after the other day."

Knowing he must be referring to their conversation in the park, she said, "How could I not be? I am horrified by what your sister and family have had to endure." *And that* my *sister is married to such a man!*

"I know you said it changes nothing, but do you not think we might find some way?"

She shook her head. "If there were such a way, you would have found it by now. Is Miss Darcy well? Does knowing you and I shall not marry help her?"

With evident reluctance, he nodded.

"I am glad for that. She *must* be your priority. That is why you did not return to me last autumn, and I understand," she assured him sincerely. "It is better that we both accept that *this* is how our lives will be, as difficult as that is."

They gazed into each other's eyes until Elizabeth worried that she would act imprudently and turned away. Several minutes passed before she went to speak to someone else.

Elizabeth continued to spend time with Miss Reed and, in so doing, saw Lord Bramwell several times. He was always amiable, which was a marked contrast to Colonel Fitzwilliam, who tended to regard her coldly. She never saw Miss Darcy, though she did spy Lord and Lady Romsley at one event or another but was not introduced to them—until the afternoon she was walking in the park with Miss Reed. The couple and the viscount were walking towards them.

"Miss Reed, Miss Bennet, what a wonderful surprise to meet the two most charming young ladies in London on this fair day." The viscount made an exaggerated bow and turned to his parents. "You remember Miss Reed, I am sure."

"Naturally. I *have* known her father since we were boys. If you paid attention to what I said upon occasion, you might recall I mentioned having dinner with him last week." Lord Romsley's tone was droll, and there was a certain lightness in his demeanour that Elizabeth found agreeable.

Viscount Bramwell did not seem to hear his father's remark and went on. "And this is Miss Elizabeth Bennet. Miss Reed and she have become good friends since they met earlier in the year, which does not surprise me in the least."

"You seem to want one of us to ask why, and I shall, to spare the young ladies a measure of your teasing," the countess said.

Lady Romsley was a tall, slender woman, with an air of confidence Elizabeth currently envied. She was used to thinking poorly of the couple, comparing them to Lady Catherine in her mind, but she could see that they were not the same. Consequently, she was embarrassed for having judged them before they had ever met. Would they have raised objections to her marrying Mr Darcy regardless of his sister's health? If she made a good impression, would they think differently of the matter and encourage their niece to do likewise?

The earl chuckled, and Lord Bramwell added an awkward noise that might have been meant as a laugh.

"They are both admirable, as you would know if you knew them as well as I have come to, and I believe they have a great deal in common, besides being equals in beauty. They are each caring, well-informed ladies and not silly or conceited, as so many are."

"I am very glad to hear it. Now, we ought to let them continue their walk. Miss Reed, it was lovely to see you again. Please give our regards to your mother and father," Lady Romsley said. She regarded Elizabeth for a moment before adding, "Miss Bennet, it was a pleasure to meet you."

Before they parted company, Lord Bramwell met Elizabeth's eye and gave her a quick smile, leaving her once again with the impression that he did not share his family's concerns regarding her connexion to Mr Darcy. He gave Miss Reed a longer look and one of a rather different character.

CHAPTER TWENTY-TWO

Almost two weeks after his meeting in the park with Elizabeth, Darcy was with his cousins in a sitting room at Grosvenor Square. The three of them had been riding earlier and had just finished a light repast.

"I introduced your Miss Bennet to Mother and Father. We were promenading in the park and met her and Miss Reed quite by accident," Bramwell said, obviously attempting to act as though it was an insignificant event, although clearly it was not.

"Accident, was it?" Fitzwilliam asked, his voice indicating he was dubious.

Bramwell shrugged. Darcy did not know what to think. His cousin surely could not have known that Elizabeth and Rebecca would be in the park, but then, Bramwell had a way of knowing things.

"She is not my Miss Bennet," he said.

"Are you sure about that?" Bramwell waggled his eyebrows.

Fitzwilliam, who sat beside his brother, punched his arm. "Leave it."

"If it were not for Georgiana, would you be against him marrying Miss Bennet?" Bramwell asked bluntly.

Fitzwilliam scowled and hesitated before admitting, "I suppose not, despite it being a poor match for him. But the fact is, we *do* have to consider Georgiana."

"*We* have to help Georgiana see that she is not a wicked little girl who deserves endless punishment and thus seeks it from herself since she is not going to receive it from either of you, as her guardians, or the rest of us, as her family." Bramwell took his fob watch from his pocket and began to polish it with a handkerchief. "I have decided to marry. Since Georgiana spends a fair amount of time at Romsley Hall, and I expect my wife and I shall receive many invitations to Pemberley, she will spend more time with my dearest wife, which will aid her. Georgiana, that is. My wife will like it too, needless to say."

Fitzwilliam sighed. "Whom have you decided to marry? I notice you do not name her, which can only mean you hope we shall tease you into telling us. I warn you, I shall only ask this once."

"Do you not know?" Darcy asked. He had guessed Bramwell's interest in his cousin Rebecca weeks earlier.

"Do you?" the brothers said at the same time.

Darcy shrugged, and if he were not so melancholic at the thought of Elizabeth, he might have laughed at the petulant look Bramwell sent his way.

"I refuse to identify the lady until everything is settled." Bramwell watched Darcy until he shrugged again to signal that he would keep his suspicions to himself. "Once Georgiana has regained a little of her strength, I see no reason why you and

Miss Bennet should not likewise marry. She would be an excellent sister."

"Just how well do you know her?" Fitzwilliam demanded.

"Well enough. Darcy, explain the situation to her and give her—and yourself—hope."

While Darcy affirmed that he had, Fitzwilliam again ordered his brother, "Leave it alone. The matter is settled. Darcy will find another lady, one more acceptable to the family and especially to Georgiana, and Miss Bennet will attract another gentleman. In fact, I hear Robert Grey has been spending a great deal of time with her and the Bingleys."

Darcy stood and walked to the door. Before he left the room, he heard Bramwell say to his brother, "You are an insensible imbecile—"

Several days later, Darcy escorted Georgiana and Mrs Annesley shopping. They were leaving a warehouse just as Mrs Bingley and Elizabeth were entering, and naturally they stopped to greet each other. He doffed his hat, introduced Mrs Bingley to Mrs Annesley, and thereafter observed Elizabeth and his sister.

"Miss Bennet, how good it is to see you again," Mrs Annesley said. They had met in Derbyshire.

"And you. Are you finding your time in town pleasurable? I recall you telling my aunt that you have a sister who lives here."

They talked about Mrs Annesley's family and similar matters. Other than greeting Georgiana and Darcy politely, Elizabeth did not even glance their way. It was a kindness as far as Georgiana went. As soon as they had seen Elizabeth and

Mrs Bingley, his sister had stiffened, and Darcy suspected Elizabeth meant to make the encounter as easy as possible for her. He wished she would at least look at him, but Georgiana might notice; Elizabeth would worry that she might find even that disturbing. If only his sister understood how much she was doing for her—her kindness this morning, the way she refused to consider a future with him, despite her wishes! Perhaps then Georgiana would be more willing to accept the possibility of their marriage.

The previous Sunday, Darcy had mentioned returning to Derbyshire soon, but Fitzwilliam had been against it. He did not want to be separated from Georgiana before he must be, and he could not leave town at present. The earl and countess also did not like the idea, believing it was better for them to remain together at what was a difficult time for the Darcys. Seeing Elizabeth renewed Darcy's desire to leave London. It was too hard to be in her presence. She had said that it would be better if they both accepted that their situation would not change, and as much as he hated to admit it, she was correct.

In two or three weeks, I shall inform my family that Georgiana and I are going home. There, I shall immerse myself in work and long rides across the park.

At breakfast one morning in early May, Bingley spoke of how much he had enjoyed the last weeks and sought reassurance that Elizabeth and Jane had likewise. In truth, as they moved through the end of April and into the early weeks of the new month, Elizabeth found herself growing weary of being in town. It was diverting in its own way, to be sure, but the spring weather made her long for the country.

Nevertheless, she said, "For my part, I certainly have. Next to spending so much time with you and my sister, I have liked meeting so many new people."

"Perhaps Grey especially?" Bingley laughed and waved a hand to indicate she need not reply. "I am only teasing you, Lizzy. I know he likes you very much, but even though I introduced you to him—"

"And every other single man of your acquaintance," she remarked archly.

He laughed. "It is *not* because I am anxious for you to marry him or any other man. Jane and I would only wish for you to know the happiness we have found. Is that not right, my dear?"

"Yes, of course, but Lizzy will know when…well, when she is prepared to marry." Jane's expression was remorseful, probably because she knew the thought of giving her heart to any man was presently distasteful to Elizabeth. Jane cleared her throat and said, "Bingley and I were discussing leaving town soon. Not immediately, but perhaps in three or four weeks. What do you think?"

Elizabeth gave a light laugh. "Just last night, I realised that I was beginning to yearn for the country."

"Did I not tell you she would be longing for a good country ramble, Jane?" Bingley said. "There is one other matter for you to consider, Lizzy."

"Oh?" She hoped it was that Jane suspected she was with child, and she was a little disappointed when no such disclosure was made, despite having seen no sign of it herself.

"We have talked of finding a new estate. Bingley has heard of several potential properties," Jane explained.

"We thought it would be fun to embark on a tour to see them so that we can decide which one we like best. My experience at Netherfield taught me it was important to consider the house, grounds, how well the estate has been managed, the neighbourhood, et cetera, et cetera. I could not possibly make such an important decision without hearing Jane's opinion. Most of those my agent has suggested are north of London, and we could plan our route to end in Scarborough so that we could visit my family. I am *not* asking Louisa and Caroline to join us."

"But we hope you will." Jane reached across the table to clasp Elizabeth's hand.

"Of course we do! Did I not say that?" Bingley asked.

Jane and Elizabeth both shook their heads.

"Well, you must," he went on. "Remember, we are determined that you will stay with us until you marry or grow fatigued of our company."

"It is impossible that I would ever grow tired of your company," Elizabeth interjected.

Jane squeezed her hand. "We have spoken of it a great deal and have decided we do not wish to remain at Netherfield. I know Mama will be disappointed."

Elizabeth laughed before her sister could continue. "She will simply have to accept that it is *your* decision to make." She looked between Jane and Bingley. "I love my mother dearly—I truly do—but we all know that if you lived so close to her, she would not be content to let you live your lives without interfering at every turn! You have made a wise decision. Now, please, I beg of you, tell me about these estates. I find the notion of you choosing a new home delightful!"

CHAPTER TWENTY-THREE

The Bingleys and Elizabeth were invited to a ball at the beginning of June, not long before they were to depart town. Mr Darcy was also in attendance with his cousins. To Elizabeth's relief, he did not ask her for a set or even approach her. The thought of standing opposite him for half an hour, of having to take his hand and being expected to talk amicably with him, was too much to bear, even for one such as she who always attempted to face the world and all its trials with courage. It was especially difficult knowing they would soon be separated and she would not have even the comfort of seeing him. She imagined Colonel Fitzwilliam's position by his side prevented him from attempting to speak to her. Whenever she happened to look their way, she often noticed their gazes upon her—one with what she could only interpret as regret mixed with longing, the other with his customary suspicion.

She spoke to Miss Reed, whom she had seen dancing the first set with Viscount Bramwell. It was clear the couple was growing closer, and Miss Reed confided that he had asked her for a second set. When Elizabeth regarded her with a knowing look, her friend blushed.

"He has been very attentive. I asked him what he meant by it."

"Did you? What did he say?"

The colour in Miss Reed's cheeks deepened. "He said he was attempting to make me fall in love with him. Will you blame me if I admit we argued?"

"Why?" Elizabeth asked. "I could have told you his purpose weeks ago. He is madly in love with you and hopes to gain your affection and make you his viscountess. I hope you will not think I am not good enough to be your friend when that happy day arrives." The last was said in a teasing tone and only because she had discerned the lady's growing feelings for Lord Bramwell.

Miss Reed looked shocked, but her demeanour soon eased, and she laughed. "Naturally, I shall not—should he ever propose, and I accept. I shall forever be enormously glad you and I met, and I intend for us to be friends for the rest of our lives." After chuckling, she added, "After such a speech, perhaps it is time for us to call each other by our Christian names?"

Elizabeth clasped her hand. "I agree without reservation. My only regret in leaving town is that we shall not be able to meet as often, but we shall write. As for the viscount proposing…" She kept her eyes fixed on her friend's and was satisfied when she nodded. "Will your parents be pleased?"

"As long as I am happy, I do not anticipate any objections on their part. Lord and Lady Romsley might feel differently. Lord Bramwell could make a much better match. But they are such good people, and I have always believed what they most want is their sons' happiness. And that of my Darcy cousins, whom they are very fond of." Miss Reed hesitated before continuing, "I have been concerned for Darcy these past months. He has seemed despondent. Elizabeth, I would never ask you to tell me something you are not comfortable sharing, but I have seen him observing you a great deal, and I wondered whether there was more to your connexion than not especially liking each other, as you once told me."

It was Elizabeth's turn to blush and avert her eyes. "Goodness, I hardly know what to say. I wish he would stop. I have been afraid people might notice." She took a deep breath to bolster her courage. "Yes, there is much more to our past, but this is not the time or place to explain. Will you be satisfied if I promise to write out the sad tale of our history—as much as I am able to share—in a letter?" She would have to craft it carefully to avoid revealing Miss Darcy's secrets or inadvertently altering Miss Reed's—Rebecca's—favourable opinion of the Romsleys and their sons.

"Of course! Please do not feel you must tell me if it is so painful. I am sorry for both of you—because clearly it is distressing and because I believe you would suit each other very well."

Elizabeth blinked quickly several times to hold back the tears that threatened to fill her eyes.

"Enough of gentlemen! If I remember correctly, last time we discussed them, it was you who ended the conversation, and tonight it is my turn," Rebecca said with forced cheer. "I see Miss Watson. Shall we go and talk to her?"

Elizabeth agreed, and they walked through the ballroom hand in hand to avoid being separated.

Later in the evening, Elizabeth was standing by an open

window, taking in the fresh air and contemplating the busy street, when Viscount Bramwell approached her.

"I find you alone. How strange."

"I do not see why." She furrowed her brow in confusion.

"Because it means my cousin has not managed to escape my brother and seize the opportunity to speak to you."

Elizabeth swallowed heavily. "He and I both know it is better if we do not spend time together needlessly. I do not believe we should discuss that particular subject further."

Lord Bramwell sighed. "Very well, but only after I say that I am sorry. I do not believe what has happened is necessary." He glanced around them, evidently to see whether anyone was in proximity. "I told Darcy he ought to explain exactly what occurred, and he said he had."

"He did. Thank you for encouraging him to do so, but it really makes little difference."

He sighed again. "So I gather. I heard from Bingley that you are leaving town soon, and before you do, I wanted you to know that not all of us are pleased with what has happened. Even my parents called it regrettable. After meeting you, my mother said that you seemed like an estimable young woman, and my father agreed."

Elizabeth smiled, but it did not last long. She supposed it was pleasant to know that the earl and countess might not have attempted to convince Mr Darcy she was unsuitable if the circumstances had been different. Feeling it was necessary to say something, she managed, "Thank you."

He gave an awkward shrug and looked about them again. Leaning closer, he said, "While I have your undivided attention, I wanted your opinion of Miss Reed. Not-not *of* her, exactly, but…"

She would have supposed it impossible a moment ago, but

a bubble of amusement lightened her mood. "I take your meaning, but you ought to know I would not share any of her confidences. I shall only say I look forward to writing to her at her new home in the not-too-distant future. I would like to hear her impressions of Warwickshire."

He grinned and asked whether she had a set open and would dance with him. She did, and it was one of the more pleasurable parts of the ball, thanks to the viscount being an amiable partner who also happened to be in a very happy mood.

Mr Grey had asked Elizabeth for the supper set, and after the meal—which they ate in company with Jane and Bingley—they stepped onto a balcony. They shared some general remarks on the ball and their satisfaction at the unfolding spring, which they agreed was one of their preferred times of the year.

There was a brief silence before he spoke. "I have long counted Bingley amongst my good friends, and I am glad we have been able to spend so much time together, even more to see how happy he is. He is very fortunate to have gained such a prize as your sister."

She thanked him for the compliment to Jane, and he continued. "I hope you know how much I have enjoyed meeting *you*. A man at my time of life finds the company of young ladies of particular interest, as we look to the future. To meet one such as you, with whom I have felt an affinity from the beginning, has been…especially agreeable. Dare I hope you have felt the same?"

Elizabeth's mouth grew dry, and she said a silent prayer that he was not about to propose. As much as she liked him, she was far from prepared for such a step. He was a kind gentleman, and she would hate to disappoint him. "I have."

His shoulders seemed to relax, and he smiled. "I have no wish to intrude upon your private affairs, but if you will excuse me being indelicate for a moment, I have noticed that you… have not appeared as easy of late. I believe I must date the change to the night we went to *The Marriage of Figaro*. Mr Darcy was there, and I have seen how he looks at you. If there is some reason I should alter my hopes, I would appreciate knowing of it."

Elizabeth took a long moment to consider her response. While she did not owe him her secrets, she understood why he was asking, and she was the sort of person who believed it was better to be open, whenever possible. As well, she genuinely felt—or wished to—that their friendship could become something more in the future; she would not want him to withdraw his attention because he misunderstood her connexion to Mr Darcy. Knowing the truth, Mr Grey might decide he was not interested in pursuing her, but at least he would have made the decision based on facts rather than suspicions.

"There was a very brief period during which…well, our relationship might have become quite different from what it is today. But he and I shall never be more than acquaintances. We both accept it. Nothing untoward occurred, and I do not blame him. I do not believe he blames me either. We…had a difference of opinion, which must be the source of discomfort you have seen."

He studied her for a moment, and she remained silent, leaving him to his thoughts. His serious expression soon lightened. "Bingley and I have spoken of your tour. Your route will bring you within an easy distance of Graystone. I had thought to invite your party to break your journey there. You might remain a few days or a week, though I would certainly not object if it were longer. I would like to show you my estate, but if it is too much, I shall say nothing of it to your brother or sister."

Elizabeth's cheeks warmed. She sensed that an important decision was before her. If she said she wanted to see his home, it was as a possible future mistress, not just as a friend. Was she prepared for such an admission, even though she was not being asked to commit herself to any course of action other than a sojourn under his roof? She wanted to believe that she was, although deep in her heart, she was afraid she may never feel enough to marry Mr Grey or any man other than Mr Darcy.

"I should like that, should Bingley say it does not interfere with his arrangements to view possible estates." She felt a little lightheaded and held on to the balustrade. Out of the corner of her eye, she saw him grin and was glad her response had pleased him.

But what has it done to me? she wondered as he described the delightful villages and towns she would encounter as they made their way through his county.

CHAPTER TWENTY-FOUR

Darcy was at the breakfast table, sitting opposite Georgiana. He was lost in thought, sullenly recalling observing Elizabeth the night before. He had watched her chatting with her friends and felt dispirited seeing various gentlemen claim her for a set. Jealousy ate at his insides because it was increasingly obvious that Mr Grey intended to win her regard. She and Bramwell had laughed while dancing together. Darcy had asked his cousin what they spoke of, but the infernal jackanapes had refused to say. She and the Bingleys were departing town shortly, and it depressed his already low spirits even further. While it was dreadful to see her and know a gap as wide as an ocean stood between them, it would be worse *not* to see her.

He was beginning to hate being in town and was no longer content to wait until the end of the month to travel north with Lord and Lady Romsley, as they wished. The earl, countess, and Fitzwilliam frequently spoke of it being good for Georgiana to be close to family, and Darcy did not disagree with them. He had noticed it himself when they spent a day recently with the Reeds, and Georgiana had been in a reasonably lively mood. She had even admitted to finding it agreeable.

"Brother," she said, pulling him from his reflections. She only continued once he met her eyes and nodded for her to go on. "I was thinking of our cousin Rebecca. You know that she called on me yesterday?"

"I do." He took a sip of his coffee and hoped nothing she said would interfere with the plans he was silently forming to travel north as soon as possible.

"I like spending time with her. Her company is…easy. Have you…have you ever considered that you and she might—?" She shrugged. "She would make a very good wife and sister."

Darcy laughed, only just managing to keep it light enough not to embarrass Georgiana. "I am pleased you and she are becoming closer, but it is quite impossible for there to be more between her and me. We do not have those sorts of feelings for each other. But I believe she and another cousin of ours do. I would not be surprised were we to receive news of an engagement before the summer is over."

Her face fell; he was sorry to disappoint her and even more regretful that he intended to separate her from Rebecca's company just when she was open to establishing a friendship with her. He might invite the Reeds to Pemberley that summer, but if Bramwell and Rebecca did soon become betrothed, they might be occupied preparing for a wedding. Yet surely the earl and countess would want them to visit Romsley Hall, and Pemberley was an easy distance away; they could go to Derbyshire before or after staying in Warwickshire.

"Bramwell will be a fortunate man, should she accept his proposal, as I expect she will. You know how often we are at Romsley Hall and how much our cousins like to come to

Pemberley. You will see a great deal of her—more than you currently do." He took another sip of coffee to give her a moment to reflect on his words. "What do you say to returning home as soon as it can be arranged? I long to be in the country again, and as you are aware, I always seem to have an abundance of work to do during the summer. We shall see the earl, countess, and Fitzwilliam before too long."

But please not too soon! I could use a month or two apart from them—especially from Fitzwilliam!

Georgiana agreed. Darcy pretended not to notice her reluctance, even though it made him feel like the selfish creature he knew Elizabeth had once believed him to be.

"What does Papa write?" Jane asked Elizabeth.

They were sitting together one rainy afternoon, drinking tea and attending to their needlework, when the post arrived. Elizabeth had received a reply to her letter announcing her intention to travel with the Bingleys that summer rather than return to Longbourn. She folded the sheet of paper and tucked it beside her dish on the mahogany side table.

"He wishes me to return home, there has not been a word of sense in the house since I left, and so on. In other words, exactly what he always writes when I am away. He proposed a compromise, which is that I go to Gracechurch Street for a week or so first, thus giving me additional time in town to amuse myself. The Gardiners would be pleased to have me, et cetera."

"But *I* am not content to leave you there." Jane regarded her for a long moment, her head tilted and brow furrowed. "I think a change of scenery and the delights of travel would do you good. I know how agreeable you found your journey with our aunt and uncle last summer, even before you reached Lambton."

Where I met Mr Darcy again and fell in love…

"It has not escaped my notice or Bingley's that you have not yet agreed to make your home with us. I would always want your opinion of the estates we shall tour, but since you *will* live there too, I must have it."

"Jane…" Elizabeth was not certain what she meant to say.

"I insist, Lizzy," her sister said, sounding remarkably stern. "I want you to be happy again, and you will not be if you return to Longbourn. I do not care how much Papa says he needs you. If he will not forbid Lydia and Wickham from visiting or insist Mama is kind to you, then-then I will not allow you to live there!" Her cheeks were red, and her gaze darted guiltily from side to side.

Elizabeth laughed affectionately and gave her hand a squeeze. "Have I ever told you that you are the best sister a headstrong girl could ever hope to have?"

Jane waved this off. "You know Mr Grey has invited us to stay for a week. He told Bingley we might even extend it, if our arrangements allow. You would have a chance to know him better, especially in a setting where we shall not always be surrounded by other people. Perhaps you will discover you can learn to care for him enough to—"

"Perhaps," Elizabeth interjected. Then she quickly changed the subject and engaged Jane in a discussion of what she most hoped to find in a new home.

The following day, which was a Sunday, Miss Bingley joined them to attend church and take breakfast. Mr and Mrs Hurst were with his family, and Miss Bingley claimed they were rude to her; thus, she avoided them. Instead, she would spend the morning being uncivil to Jane and Elizabeth.

Bingley announced their plans for the summer months, having avoided doing so until their departure was imminent. Otherwise, his sisters might attempt to interfere with their arrangements, perhaps insert themselves by insisting their views must be taken into consideration. Elizabeth imagined them desperately attempting to follow behind in Hurst's carriage, and Bingley, Jane, and she taking drastic measures to evade them. It sounded like a silly fear for her brother to have, but Elizabeth accepted it as a sign of his ongoing unhappiness with his sisters.

"*She* is going with you?" Miss Bingley said, pointing at Elizabeth.

"She is," Bingley confirmed.

Pouting, his sister said, "*I* should be the one accompanying you, not her! It will be *my* home, the *Bingley* family estate." She glanced at Jane out of the corner of her eye while pronouncing the name, and Elizabeth's hands curled into fists.

"It will be *my* home and that of my wife and eventually our children."

"But I do not wish to live with Hurst any longer! He is odious! You know I have never liked him, no matter who his family is. I want to go with you and help to find a suitable home for us. You are *my* brother, and it is only right that I live with you. Jane does not know what to look for! Our family's reputation must be upheld—"

"That is enough, Caroline," Bingley interjected. "If you cannot refrain from insulting my wife or her sister through even a single meal, you are welcome to return to Hurst's. Let me be clear—only Jane's and my opinions matter, and we shall greatly value Lizzy's because *she* has our best interests at heart and always treats us with respect."

"There is no need for you to be cruel to me! You would not be if Louisa were here."

He snorted. "Of course I would, if she took your part. I dare say Hurst would support me too. Jane, Lizzy, and I shall leave as planned, and I shall be sure to write to you or Louisa to let you know once we have secured a new estate. Or perhaps I shall write to Hurst instead. *He* is more agreeable company of late than either of you. If you and Louisa wish an invitation to see my new home, you will have to learn to be kinder to Jane and to Lizzy, whom I love dearly and consider just as much my sister as you." When Miss Bingley opened her mouth to respond, he held up a hand to her and made a warning noise. "I suggest you stay in town and find a husband. *That* is the only route through which you will gain your wish not to live with Hurst any longer."

Miss Bingley huffed and complained, and before the meal was completed, Bingley had the carriage readied to carry her back to Grosvenor Square. Elizabeth rejoiced that he had succeeded in saving them from her company over the coming days.

Less than a fortnight later, they left London. Through Bingley, Elizabeth learnt that Mr Darcy and his sister had likewise departed. She supposed it would be many months before she saw him again, perhaps not until they were all next in town. By then, she might be engaged or even married to Mr Grey, if only she could convince herself she could be happy with him and make him a good wife.

CHAPTER TWENTY-FIVE

The journey to Pemberley had been easy, at least as far as the roads and weather went. Georgiana was not inclined to engage in much conversation—at least with Darcy; she showed no such reluctance when it came to Mrs Annesley. His sister grew less petulant the closer they drew to Pemberley, and he supposed her pleasure at being home was finally stronger than her upset that he had given her little say in the decision to quit town when they did.

Darcy would never say it aloud, but he blamed Fitzwilliam for a portion of the distance between himself and his sister. He also found himself giving greater and greater importance to Bramwell's assertion that Georgiana would do better if they—especially Fitzwilliam—did not coddle her so much. It was what he wanted to believe because he continued to cling to the hope that Georgiana would change her opinion of his marrying Elizabeth. She only had to permit herself to trust they would keep her safe from Wickham. If his sister showed any improvement along these lines, he would immediately set out to earn

Elizabeth's forgiveness and remind her of the reasons she had once loved him and anticipated a joyful future as his wife. Only her marriage to another would stop him from dreaming of such an outcome to their tortuous history.

A fortnight after they arrived at Pemberley, they welcomed the earl, the countess, and Fitzwilliam. Lord and Lady Romsley would spend a week with them before settling at Romsley Hall for the summer. Fitzwilliam would be obliged to return to town almost at once, and this allowed him to spend an interval with Georgiana; it might be later in the summer or even autumn before they were reunited. The earl reported that Bramwell had elected to extend his time in London and travel north with the Reeds, whose estate was in Shropshire.

"If he thinks I do not know what he is about, he is a fool, and I would hate to think that of my heir," the earl said at dinner on the first night.

Fitzwilliam regarded his father, a puzzled expression on his face. It surprised Darcy that he had not yet discerned that his brother was in love with Rebecca, and he derived an odd satisfaction from it, given his still-simmering resentment. He regretted the feeling; he had once considered Fitzwilliam his dearest friend. With luck, he would be able to claim it again one day.

If I put more effort into it and saw the situation through his eyes, it might happen sooner. Then again, he could try to understand my perspective and at least show a little sympathy.

Darcy wrote to Mrs Reed and suggested she, Mr Reed, and Rebecca visit later in the summer. Georgiana and Rebecca were exchanging letters regularly, and he wished to do everything he could to encourage their friendship. He attempted to interest his sister in making friends with some of the young ladies in their vicinity. Unfortunately, Georgiana did not like to leave the estate, and whenever one of the ladies came to call, she said as little as possible. He knew some of that was due to her natural reserve, and he dreamt of how much better she would feel if she had Elizabeth by her side. Elizabeth would be such a supportive, sympathetic sister—especially since she knew Georgiana's entire history—and not even the tiniest part of Darcy doubted that Georgiana would improve remarkably under her care.

Yet who knows when, or even if, they will ever be in company again. I do not imagine it will be until Georgiana is out, and by then, I shall surely have lost all opportunity to reconcile with Elizabeth.

The thought prompted Darcy to close the treatise on sheep rearing he had been reading and turn his mind to the more demanding activity of reviewing the account books. He had to find a way to stop dwelling on Elizabeth, and especially he had to stop feeling that Fitzwilliam and—worse—Georgiana were to blame for their separation. After all, Darcy had agreed not to pursue her. Bramwell might be correct that it would have been wiser to tell Elizabeth the truth from the very beginning, but he had not, and he must bear the consequences of his actions.

I shall use the summer to find a way to accept that she is lost to me forever. This dream of earning her forgiveness and love and that, somehow, we shall be able to marry is doing me, Georgiana, Fitzwilliam, and even Elizabeth no favours. He could not lie to himself that Elizabeth had not seen him staring at her in town, and likely he had caused her some discomfort. Mr Grey had begun giving him dark looks, suggesting he had also noticed. *If she can find happiness with him or another man, I must wish her well.*

In the first few weeks of their tour, Jane, Bingley, and Elizabeth viewed three estates. There was nothing particularly wrong with any of them, but likewise, there was nothing remarkable either. Along the way, they stopped here and there to partake of local sights of interest, but the only significant break on their journey was at Graystone Manor.

Mr Grey welcomed them warmly, and if there was something more to his greeting of Elizabeth, she pretended not to notice. When she was alone later that day, she questioned why she had acted thus.

If I am certain I could never care for him enough to accept his proposal, I must find a way to tell him. If I am unwilling to do so, then I must open my mind and my heart fully to the possibility of a future with him. She still might decide she could not become his wife; for that matter, he might never choose to propose. But she knew that was where his interest lay at present, and it frustrated her that, no matter how much she tried, she could reach no firm decision about what she hoped their future would be. She worried she would injure his feelings.

During the nine days they were at Graystone, Elizabeth explored the estate and neighbourhood with Mr Grey. Often, Jane and Bingley were with them, but they also left Mr Grey and her to themselves so that they could get to know each other better without interference. The house was well-maintained and decorated in a manner that would offend no one, unless they were very particular. Elizabeth could imagine how she might change this room or that to make it more to her personal taste, but there was nothing she disliked. The gardens were a little too orderly for her, but the grounds included a wide, picturesque stream and a copse, and the nearest town was pleasant and contained a good variety of shops. Mr Grey spoke well of his neighbours and those he regularly met at dinners and other social events.

As much as Elizabeth admired his estate, she admired the man even more. He was handsome, friendly, well-read, responsible, and respectful. He would make an excellent husband and father, and it would be a very good match for her from a practical point of view. In addition, he and Bingley were close friends, and Jane liked him. Should Elizabeth marry him, she was certain there would be no impediment to seeing her dearest sister.

I would be a fool to let a daydream rob me of a life with such a man. I may not be in love with him at present, but there is no reason why I should not fall in love with him. Had I never met Mr Darcy, or if we had not encountered each other again last summer, it is probable I would have by now. Indeed, I believe I would be floating ten feet off the ground to think that this man cared for me so much that he wished to marry me despite my lack of fortune and connexions. I will conquer my feelings for Mr Darcy, then perhaps I could love Mr Grey.

Because she was alone, she whispered, "Why must it be so hard?"

The night before the Bingleys and she were to leave, Mr Grey and Elizabeth went for a walk after dinner. It was not excessively hot, and the sun was low in the sky, the last light of the day just peeking through the trees. They remained on the terrace and the gardens with the clearest paths.

"I wish you could stay longer," he admitted. "I hope you have enjoyed your time here."

"I have. Your estate is wonderful, and the company is even better."

He had such a look of joy on his face that Elizabeth regretted having spoken so warmly. It might lead him to believe she was ready to receive his proposal. His next words suggested as much.

"Perhaps if there was a good reason for it, Bingley and your sister might be willing to extend your stay."

She forced a laugh, infusing it with as much humour as she could, and sought for a way to hint to him that she required additional time before being able to commit herself. "Oh, I do not know that I could ask it of them. They are eager to find a new home. Netherfield Park is lovely, but I am confident they will find a situation more to their liking, one in which they will raise their children and spend their lives. Do you know that they met soon after Bingley let the estate? It was evident that they liked each other at once. They met at an assembly, and they danced twice!" She laughed again. "It was much talked of, and many people were convinced they would marry before they had known each other two months, my mother included. Events transpired that separated them for a time, but they were engaged soon after meeting again last September. As much as I know my sister was saddened during the time they were apart, on the whole, I think they are better off for it. I have always believed a couple should know each other at least half a year before committing themselves. It gives them an opportunity for sober reflection and for first impressions to be confirmed."

His response was long in coming, and he spoke slowly, suggesting he was disappointed. "I believe I do, and that is wise of you, Miss Bennet."

She slipped her arm around his. "Will you tell me more about the herb garden? I seem to recall you mentioning it was a special interest of your mother's."

He nodded, and as they continued to stroll, they talked of the garden, his late parents, and her interest in plants of all sorts. It was full dark before they returned to the house. Jane sent her a questioning look. Elizabeth did not expect either gentleman would recognise its import, but she knew her sister was silently asking whether Mr Grey had proposed. In reply, Elizabeth gave a quick shake of her head.

If he took her at her word, she had delayed a proposal until September, coincidentally a year after she had expected to receive one from a different gentleman.

CHAPTER TWENTY-SIX

Elizabeth experienced an odd assortment of sentiments upon entering Derbyshire. Since leaving Graystone, she had spent a great deal of time during the long carriage rides and quiet nights contemplating the two gentlemen fighting for space in her heart. She had almost determined that she could gladly marry Mr Grey.

"I might not feel the same overwhelming draw to him that I do—*did*—to Mr Darcy, but I could be happy with him, if I allowed myself," she whispered to herself shortly before dawn on what would be their first full day in Derbyshire.

Jane and she had not talked of Mr Darcy since leaving London, but during their time at Graystone, Jane had asked what she felt for Mr Grey. Elizabeth suspected her brother and sister would be pleased if she married him, which added to her confusion, and she would only admit that she liked him.

To date, Bingley had said nothing of making a trip to Mr Darcy's part of the county, and Elizabeth was relieved.

The silence ended when he announced at breakfast several days later that he had received word from his agent.

"He has discovered not one but *two* estates that sound like just what we are looking for! Do you want to know the best thing about them?" He continued without waiting for a response. "They are both within twenty miles of Pemberley! I wrote to Darcy and told him we would trespass on his kindness."

Elizabeth's eyes flew to Jane, who was staring at her, her expression mirroring the same alarm. Fortunately, in his happy mood, Bingley did not notice.

"He will not object. Indeed, he would be insulted if he learnt we were nearby and did not stay with him. You will love Pemberley, Jane. I know Lizzy does, and I certainly have always thought it one of the most marvellous estates I have ever visited. If we like one or both properties—and they both sound perfect for us—Darcy can give us his opinion. He knows a great deal more about estates than I do. How good it would be to settle near him!"

Elizabeth was horrified by the prospect of returning to Pemberley. Not only did Bingley expect her to go there, he expected her to *stay* there, to sleep under *his* roof! Desperately, she sought a way to avoid it, but there was none. She had no friend thereabouts she might claim a desire to visit, and how could she explain a sudden, urgent need to return to Hertfordshire? Bingley would never agree to her taking a public conveyance and would insist on driving her in his carriage, which would mean disrupting his and Jane's tour and journey to Scarborough, and Elizabeth would not be responsible for such an outcome.

She left Jane to say all that was proper in answer to Bingley's enthusiasm, though if her sister heard the details of the estates they were to visit any better than Elizabeth did, she would be shocked. Jane was pale, and her voice was weak when she spoke. It was astonishing that Bingley did not notice. Then again, thought Elizabeth, he had failed to recognise his friend's love for her or how awkward they were towards each other all the months they were in town. Today, his enthusiasm must partly account for his overlooking what seemed glaringly obvious to her.

Later that same day, Bingley left the ladies at the inn while he went for a walk. No sooner was he gone than Jane took a seat next to Elizabeth. Their hands found each other's, and they remained thus connected as they discussed his announcement.

"It is time to tell him the truth about you and Mr Darcy. Then he will understand why we cannot go to Pemberley," Jane insisted.

Elizabeth was shaking her head before the last syllable of his name left her sister's lips. "There is no need for it. Miss Darcy will have him refuse if she finds the notion too daunting, and unless Mr Darcy puts us off, I can manage a few days at his estate. He and I—all three of us, really—must accustom ourselves to sometimes being in company. Should we divulge the truth, I truly do believe that Bingley would sever his friendship with Mr Darcy. Perhaps I am mistaken, but I do not think that I am, and I would hate to be the cause of it."

"You think too much of it! Bingley loves you, and he would choose your happiness and comfort over his friendship with Mr Darcy without a second's hesitation. Yes, it has been significant to him, but he has different priorities now—me and our family, which you are a very important part of, as you surely know."

Elizabeth embraced her. "I do, and it is because he is such a good man that I want to do this for him. It is just a few days—supposing Mr Darcy agrees to us staying, which I doubt he will. What harm could there be in it?"

Jane took a long moment to think, during which she kept her gaze fixed on Elizabeth. At length, she said, "If you are absolutely certain."

Elizabeth nodded.

"Very well, I shall say nothing to Bingley. However, if at any time you change your mind, if you find it too difficult once we are there, you must promise to tell me. Bingley would be very angry if he discovered we remained there despite you being miserable. Worse, he would be hurt I did not tell him sooner."

"I would hate to cause any strife between you, and I promise I shall tell you if I find it would be better for us to leave."

Privately, Elizabeth desperately sought to understand why she despised the notion of Bingley knowing the extent of her history with his friend. Was it embarrassment? Or was it because, if he knew, she would surely see less of Mr Darcy? She refused to believe that a part of her longed to go to Pemberley and be near him again, but a persistent little voice in her head suggested that might be the case.

And if it is true, I am a horrible person. How could she think otherwise, knowing the visit would only cause Mr Darcy and her pain, to say nothing of Miss Darcy? And then there was Mr Grey to consider. If her feelings for Mr Darcy were still so strong, she *must* ask Bingley to write to Mr Grey to inform him that he should have no hope where she was concerned. To do otherwise would be unconscionable.

The post arrived in time for Darcy to peruse it at the breakfast table. He set aside two that were related to business affairs and one from the earl in favour of reading Bingley's. His friend was making a slow journey to tour vacant estates and had sent previous letters in which he had expressed his disappointment in those he had viewed. Bingley's passing mentions of Elizabeth, which were always sprinkled throughout his notes, were what made Darcy particularly anxious to receive his news. He was not surprised that Bingley had come to appreciate Elizabeth, and he was glad for her that she had such a caring brother.

The opening paragraph contained the usual sort of information—where they had been, that they were all healthy, and that he hoped Darcy and Georgiana were well and enjoying the summer. It was what followed that made Darcy softly gasp and gape at the paper, his vision clouded and heart thudding.

They were coming to Pemberley. *Elizabeth* was coming to Pemberley.

> *You will not mind putting us up for a few days, will you? It is presumptuous of me to assume you will, but I know you would be upset if we did not impose upon you and you later discovered how close we had been.*

He most assuredly did not object. Once again, he would have the exquisite joy of seeing her in his home, sitting in his drawing room, strolling in his gardens. She had been delighted with his corner of Derbyshire last year. What would she think currently? Immediately, he began to plan. Which rooms would he give her—and Bingley and his wife? What would he do for her amusement? She had particularly liked the path beside the stream; had it been tended to properly of late? Then there were meals to consider. He would ensure her favourites were included, and—

And he had to tell Georgiana of Bingley's request.

He looked across the table at her, a sheet of paper still clutched in his hand. She was reading a letter from Fitzwilliam, her features brightened by a slight smile.

Please let her be strong enough to bear their visit. I want—oh, how I desperately want—Elizabeth here. Perhaps it will help alter Georgiana's views of her becoming my wife.

His vow to give up that dream had vanished the moment he knew he might see her. It was reckless of him, and he would not burden Elizabeth with his desires until he could abolish the barrier between them. But if Georgiana did well during Elizabeth's stay…

He delayed speaking to Georgiana of Bingley's letter until that afternoon. It gave him several hours to anticipate seeing Elizabeth without having to confront his sister's possible—even probable—dislike of the scheme. It also meant he had time to contemplate how best to tell her and make her see that it would be pleasant to have guests. He truly believed it would be better for her to see more people, and since she remained disinclined to involve herself in the neighbourhood, people must come to her.

She was in her sitting room, working on a drawing of a colourful blossom when he went to her. Mrs Annesley had gone into Lambton on errands; thus Georgiana was alone.

"Do I disturb you, my dear?" he said.

She shook her head and set aside her pencil and paper.

"May I see it?" Darcy took a seat beside her and indicated the drawing.

Silently, she gave it to him; he spent a long moment examining it, intending to show her that he was genuinely interested in her pursuits. So often, she seemed to feel she was an inconvenience and that none of them particularly cared for her, save perhaps Fitzwilliam and Lady Romsley.

"It is lovely. You have made remarkable progress. I especially like how you have captured the subtle variations in colour in the petals." He smiled and placed the sketch on the table.

"Mrs Annesley has taught me a great deal," she said, her voice hardly above a whisper.

"I am glad you have such a useful and sympathetic companion."

She nodded but said nothing.

"I had a letter from Bingley this morning. It contained interesting news." Georgiana kept her eyes lowered and gave no sign of curiosity. "You know they are on their way to Scarborough and are viewing estates along the way, searching for one they like enough to purchase. It so happens that he has learnt of two that are near Pemberley."

At this, his sister met his gaze. Her eyes were opened a little wider than usual, as though she suspected what he would say next. Gently, he placed his hand over hers.

"He has asked if they can stay here while they are in the neighbourhood. It will be agreeable to have company, will it not?"

"I-I do not need company, and, Brother, *them*? *She* is with them, and—"

"And it has been a year, or close enough, since…everything that happened last autumn. There is no harm in either Mrs Bingley or Miss Bennet. You said yourself that Mrs Bingley is pleasant company, and when you first met Miss Bennet, you found her agreeable."

She bit her lips together and turned away from him.

"I can give him no good excuse, Georgiana. At present, he does not know what I once hoped, but avoiding them might just make him realise something significant occurred between Miss Bennet and me. If he knew, I am afraid it would be the end of our friendship. I disappointed him once before, and this would be too much for him to overlook. I would prefer to avoid taking that risk."

He might be overstating the situation, but he had to make his sister accept the inevitability of seeing the Bingleys and Elizabeth. It was true that he expected Bingley would view him differently if he knew how he had treated Elizabeth, but it would be easy enough to devise a reason to keep Bingley and his family from coming to Pemberley.

When Georgiana remained silent, he added, "It is just for a few days. You will hardly see them. Your youth and studies with Mrs Annesley can be an excuse to absent yourself during the mornings, if you feel it is necessary. Besides, they will be occupied with their search for an estate."

He overlooked her evident reluctance when she nodded her consent.

CHAPTER TWENTY-SEVEN

Four days after Bingley's announcement, they went to Pemberley. Bingley spent what felt like every minute from when they stepped out of the inn until they pulled to a stop outside Pemberley chattering about their forthcoming interlude with Mr and Miss Darcy. He was particularly animated, seeming almost to bounce in his seat and showing uncommon signs of impatience.

"It will be very good to see Darcy again. Being at Pemberley is always agreeable. It really is the most wonderful estate, as you will soon see, my dear Jane." He laughed. "Perhaps we ought not to go. Nothing we see will satisfy you afterwards. Caroline has compared every place we ever were to Darcy's estate." He rolled his eyes. "But then, she always hoped to interest him, if you know what I mean. Darcy never showed any particular affection for her, which is just as well. I do not think they would have been a good match. I suppose he will want to marry soon though. He is eight- or nine-and-twenty now."

Nine-and-twenty, Elizabeth thought. It had been his birthday at the beginning of the month. She knew because they had once spoken of how they celebrated birthdays and other special occasions. She remembered telling him an anecdote of one particularly disastrous birthday dinner that had resulted in a ruined cake, many broken plates and glasses, and Kitty and Lydia screaming—Kitty in confusion and Lydia, then an adorable two-year-old, because she had been desperate to eat the dessert. Elizabeth felt a pang thinking of her youngest sister, but it was Mr Darcy who truly occupied her thoughts. He had laughed. It had been the first time she had witnessed him unabashedly express his amusement, and the moment had made her fall more deeply in love with him. That was when she had truly begun to dream of being his wife and the joy they would share in the years ahead. She would teach him to be livelier and share his happiness with those he most cared for and trusted.

Perhaps that is why it hurt so greatly when I realised he would not return for me. Surely, if he had felt the same connexion, he could not have simply discarded me.

The hole left by the severing of the bond was almost unbearable, and all these months later, she was still attempting to fill it.

But I shall. I was not formed for unhappiness, and I refuse to let anyone rob me of what I want for myself, including to find pleasure in every day and to surround myself with people whom I love and who love me in return.

She met Jane's eye and smiled, hoping it communicated how greatly she loved and appreciated her. If they were alone, she would tell her sister; but Bingley was present, and he continued to express how glad he was that they would soon see his friend.

HIS FAMILY OBJECTS

Darcy was more agitated than he recalled being in months. In truth, he could only remember feeling thus on three other occasions in his life—as he awaited the doctor's opinion on what had been his father's final illness, after Georgiana's misadventure in Ramsgate, and as he walked from Rosings to the parsonage to make his ill-fated, poorly thought-out proposal to Elizabeth. Again and again, he consulted his pocket watch or the nearest clock and cursed how slowly time was passing. He should not anticipate seeing Elizabeth as much as he did, but it was proving impossible not to. He had loved her for so long, and he *knew* to the core of his being that they were meant to be man and wife.

I suppose I should say I know she is the only woman with whom I could be happy. As matters currently stand, she is free to seek the comfort and security I would have given her with another. I, who have often remarked what a wonderful mother she would be, should want her to find a good man who would care for her and give her the children God surely intends her to have.

As best he could, he attended to various pieces of estate business his steward presented to him, including a contract to sell wool produced on the estate to a local mill, but it gave him a headache. He sat with Georgiana and Mrs Annesley at breakfast and told them of the news he had lately read. Later in the morning, he listened to his sister perform a new piece on the pianoforte.

"Your playing was delightful, my dear. Your skill is growing by the day, and I commend you for practising as much as you do."

She lowered her chin and shook her head. "I am glad you

are pleased, but if the music sounded especially good, it is because of the instrument. It was such a generous gift." He had surprised her with the pianoforte the previous summer.

She turned around in her seat to face him before speaking again. Although her chin was lifted, her gaze was directed to the side, not at Darcy. "They will arrive soon."

Darcy rubbed the back of his neck. "They will. I hope you are not nervous. Nothing ill will come of their presence, I promise you. You know Bingley well, and the ladies are good people."

She glanced at him, her eyes seeming to ask if he was a fool; they both knew why she was anxious.

"Some days they will only be here for dinner, and I am sure they want to begin the drive to Yorkshire as soon as possible. They will not linger in the neighbourhood. Should you wish it, Mrs Bingley would be pleasant company."

He expected that Elizabeth would avoid them both as much as possible, Georgiana especially, in an effort to spare her discomfort. As for him, Elizabeth believed it best if the two of them did not spend time together. Nothing about their situation had changed—unless it was even more hopeless because she was forming an attachment to Mr Grey—and while either one of them still loved the other, attempting to act as though they were friends was painful. For his part, he would never stop loving her. He was certain he would know in an instant if her sentiments for him had altered.

Georgiana remained silent, and thus he added, "If you find it difficult to be with them, do not hesitate to excuse yourself and return to your apartment. They will not expect you to act as their hostess, given your age. Consider them my guests, not ours. Now, what do you say we ask Mrs Reynolds to send us tea?"

Elizabeth's heart raced and her legs felt weak as she stepped down from the carriage. She let her eyes take in the smooth white stone of the manor, noted the sweetness in the air as the breeze carried the scent from the nearby flower beds, and savoured the warmth of the sun on her face. What she avoided seeing was the couple standing by the door awaiting them.

"Darcy! Miss Darcy, how do you do?" Bingley cried. "I cannot thank you enough for accommodating us."

"Georgiana and I are pleased to see you."

Elizabeth felt Mr Darcy's gaze on her, and his deep voice resonated within her.

"It is very kind of you. I own I was worried it would be an imposition, though Bingley insisted it was not," Jane said.

"Not at all," Mr Darcy assured her. "Please, will you come in? We have refreshments waiting."

Bingley stepped to Miss Darcy's side and, as they began walking towards the entry, said something too quiet for Elizabeth to hear. Jane began to remark on their drive, her voice trembling subtly, but stopped when her husband looked over his shoulder and beckoned to her to join them.

"Come and tell Miss Darcy the name of that pretty village we saw the other day, the one you liked so much," he said.

With a regretful look at Elizabeth, Jane did as he had asked, leaving her alone with Mr Darcy.

Glancing up, Elizabeth's eyes met his, and a surge of energy coursed through her, beginning in her toes and travelling up until it seemed to burst from her.

"Elizabeth." He seemed to whisper the word, making it sound like a sigh of relief. "I am glad to see you."

She could not look away. She *should* do so, but she did not have the necessary strength. "I…" The backs of her eyes began to burn, and she hoped she managed to avoid crying in front of him.

"Please do not say that I should not rejoice that you are at Pemberley again. I know it, just as I know that it is right that you are." He shrugged.

She nodded, wondering if that was what she was feeling also. It was difficult to make sense of her confused emotions, but she had to admit it was most credible. "Are you well, and your sister? I was certain she would object and you would write to Bingley to put him off."

"I would not like to do that, and Georgiana is improving."

There was something in his tone that told her he was overstating the matter, and she knew it was because he had wanted to see her. Had she not also wanted to see him? She might not like to admit it, but was that not why she had refused to explain enough of the situation to Bingley to make him understand? Before she could speak, he suggested they enter the house; they would not wish their delay to be noted. She agreed, and as they began to walk, she was reminded of her dreams of returning to Pemberley as his wife, of him escorting her indoors for the first time as Mrs Darcy. Instead of that exquisite happiness, there was the crushing pain of loss.

Coming to Pemberley had been a terrible idea. *How am I to survive three or four days of this?*

CHAPTER TWENTY-EIGHT

Alone in her chamber later, Elizabeth was able to regain her equilibrium and convince herself that all would be well. To be sure, walking through the house had been difficult. Everywhere she looked, she remembered the previous year, talking and laughing with Mr Darcy and the delicious sensation of falling in love with him. It had been as though the world was brighter each day, as though the sky was slowly clearing, allowing the sun to shine through, the air was lighter, and every care she had in the world was gone because he was with her. She had felt complete even though she was not conscious of anything missing from her life before.

"But that was last year," she whispered, hoping that hearing the words aloud would convince her recalcitrant heart, which stubbornly clung to her affection for the gentleman. How she regretted their brief exchange upon her arrival. If only Bingley had not wanted Jane by his side, then she and Mr Darcy would not have been left alone, and then—

"He would not have seen that I still...that my feelings for

him are still so strong." If she could convince him that she viewed him only as a friend, he might learn to see her that way, and if he no longer looked at her with so much love and heartache in his eyes, she might finally be able to accept that there was no hope that they would ever reconcile.

She rolled her eyes, knowing her plan, if one could call it that, was nonsensical. Instead of worrying about what he felt, she needed to vanquish whatever was inside her that clung to him. Surely she could continue to think of him as the most caring, dedicated man of her acquaintance—as well as the most interesting and handsome—without denying the possibility of giving her heart to another gentleman?

She stood at the opened window, the gentle breeze refreshing, and took in the magnificent view of the park with its stream, pond, and copse in the distance. There was no denying Pemberley was a remarkable place, but she forced herself to recall Graystone and the agreeable company provided by Mr Grey. Her stay there had been enjoyable in a quiet, comfortable sort of way. There would be no ease at Pemberley. Instead, there would be awkwardness and acting as though nothing was amiss.

A soft voice in her mind said, *Yet, would you not rather be here, no matter the difficulties and discomforts?*

"No," she insisted, the word coming out weaker than she liked. "I want to be happy. I shall make my happiness where I can and have what I want in life."

Mr Grey was everything she could want in a husband. Of every gentleman she had met, he was the most suited to her—apart from Mr Darcy. Since she could not have *him*, she would be a fool to give up Mr Grey.

To help with her resolve, she spent the next few minutes compiling a list of what she most liked about him. Amongst his many good qualities, he made Elizabeth laugh, and she dearly wished she had cause to do so presently. Another of his attractions was that he did not have a sister with a tragic past to prevent him from marrying her.

Shame made Elizabeth's cheeks burn. She went to the wash basin and pressed a cloth that had been dipped in the cool water to her face, then prepared for dinner.

Before and during the evening meal, Darcy found it difficult to look at anyone other than Elizabeth, as much as he attempted to. She was unusually quiet, but he caught her glancing in his direction now and again. From the moment she had stepped out of the carriage and their eyes had met, he had known she still cared deeply for him. If she had ceased to love him, she would be awkward; instead, she seemed dispirited and perhaps a little angry, though he believed it was because of their situation rather than being directed at him.

Despite not being her usual happy, lively self, she was the most welcomed sight in the world to him, as she always was. He revelled in her being at Pemberley again, but at the same time, it was heart-breaking. They ought to have been married for months by this time and would have greeted the Bingleys as *their* guests. He did not expect that the next few days would change anything for them, but he prayed that he was mistaken, that he would see something, anything, that he might use to convince Elizabeth to trust him—and Georgiana to accept his marriage.

At the conclusion of dinner, Bingley and he immediately accompanied the ladies to the drawing room. Bingley talked to him of their travels and the estates they had viewed, and Darcy did his best to listen. He was pleased to see Mrs Bingley engage Georgiana, and his sister appeared to listen attentively, although she did not say much. Elizabeth remained apart from the rest of the company. Darcy considered ways to gain her attention, longing to have her to himself for a short while. If he did not know it would disturb Georgiana, he would ask Elizabeth to take a walk on the terrace with him. She enjoyed exercise, and she might accept. If they could speak openly, build on the understanding that had passed between them earlier, together they might be able to devise a scheme that would allow them to marry. Perhaps once his sister retired, he would try; Georgiana seldom remained in the drawing room for more than an hour in the evenings, and since he had encouraged her to consider Elizabeth and the Bingleys *his* guests, not theirs, she would feel little obligation to change her habits.

When he saw Elizabeth step out of the room for a few minutes, he made an excuse to do likewise. He waited for her in the hall, determined to speak to her alone. When he saw her, he stepped towards her, blocking her path, and whispered her name.

She started. Looking at him briefly, she shook her head. "Please, do not do this. Being here will be difficult enough without us having private conversations."

Darcy hesitated, suddenly not sure what to say. Away from the others, she allowed him to see how unhappy she was; he was not sure whether it was inadvertent or not. If he demanded too much, she might decide she hated him more than she liked him, and he feared where that would lead. Without meaning to, he asked, "Bingley does not know, does he?"

"No. I feared if he learnt of it, he would feel obligated to end your friendship, and I did not want to be the cause of that."

His fingers ached with the desire to touch her. Had she thought only of Bingley, or had she worried for *his* feelings, knowing that losing his friend as well as her would add yet more disappointment and regret to his life? "I have worried about that too. I am not convinced he will ever entirely forgive my interference in his relationship with your sister. Thank you."

She gave an offhanded shrug, keeping her eyes lowered.

"I wish things could be different."

Her head jerked up, and she silenced him with a hard expression. "They cannot be, and wishes are meaningless in such a case. I have accepted it, and you must as well. What purpose is served by us having these conversations? They will do more harm than good, especially if your sister learns of them," she hissed.

With that, she swept past him, her arm briefly brushing against his. A spark of electricity passed through him, and he wondered whether she felt it too.

The next day, Bingley, Jane, and Elizabeth were to tour an estate. Bingley suggested Elizabeth need not go with them if she did not want to.

"We would like to have you with us, of course, but I thought you might find staying at Pemberley more agreeable than another day in the carriage. Darcy and his sister would be good company for you."

To Elizabeth, he seemed to observe her carefully as he spoke, his eyes slightly narrowed.

"I am sure they would. However, I would value your opinion, Lizzy," Jane said in a calm tone.

If they had been alone, Elizabeth would have kissed her for providing such an easy excuse for why she certainly would accompany them. They had not been at Pemberley a full day, and already she had endured two unpleasant, bewildering conversations with Mr Darcy, and when Miss Darcy was not pretending Elizabeth was not there, she was staring at her suspiciously. As much fortitude as she believed she possessed, Elizabeth knew it was not enough to tolerate more of the same without the comfort of Jane and Bingley's presence.

The estate was the farthest of the two properties they wished to see, and they left Pemberley early. It was a pleasant day, although the estate did not strike any of them as suitable. They did not linger and returned to Pemberley in time for dinner. All the ease Elizabeth had felt when she was with only her sister and brother vanished at the first glimpse of Miss Darcy, who was all but glaring at her. Mr Darcy had indeed exaggerated when he implied his sister's health had improved —at least in regard to her willingness to view Elizabeth favourably; she prayed it did not end in disaster for all of them. Jane attempted to draw Miss Darcy out while they were at the table and again later in the drawing room, and Elizabeth suspected her motive was to keep her from dwelling on Elizabeth's presence. Bingley and Mr Darcy spoke to each other, which was preferable to the latter approaching her, but it left Elizabeth not knowing what to do with herself. She wished Mrs Annesley had chosen to remain with them, but Mr Darcy had explained that she had decided to leave the party to themselves. Elizabeth was a little surprised Miss Darcy had not insisted her companion remain by her side.

Perhaps she was worried Mrs Annesley would reprimand her for the way she is observing me so closely. If Miss Darcy needs to see that I have no intention of tempting her brother into being my friend—let alone something more—I invite her to stare as much as she likes. Whatever eases her anxiety.

Not long after Elizabeth retired for the night, Jane joined her in her apartment.

"Are you too tired for company?" Jane asked.

"Not at all. I was going to read for a while, but I would be happy to spend time with you."

Jane's answering smile was weak, and she nibbled her lip as they moved to the settee.

"Is something amiss?" Elizabeth said.

Her sister shook her head and took one of Elizabeth's hands in hers. "No, not exactly. I wanted to tell you of a conversation between Bingley and I earlier."

"Oh?" Trepidation made her long to stand and pace about the room.

"He has noticed that you are not in spirits, that you seemed…ill at ease yesterday and for several days before then. Although he knows you and Mr Darcy are not on good terms any longer, compared to last summer, he was surprised by how awkward you were with each other, to say nothing of you and Miss Darcy. He asked me whether you had argued."

Elizabeth gave her sister's hand a gentle squeeze. "I am sorry. What did you tell him?"

Jane gave an impatient shake of the head. "I hardly know exactly, but I made some excuse or another. I told him nothing of what truly happened, but I felt terrible about it."

"Do you wish to tell Bingley everything? Would that be better for you?"

Jane appeared to ponder the question seriously for a long moment. "I do not know. What is your opinion?"

"I know that Mr Darcy believes that Bingley will not forgive him. He told me as much recently."

"Recently?" Jane's brow arched.

Elizabeth regretted not being more careful with her words; she did not want her sister to question her about Mr Darcy. "We spoke of it yesterday evening. It was a very brief exchange."

Jane regarded her for a moment before evidently deciding not to pursue the subject. "Bingley has such a high opinion of him, and very likely he would be disappointed in how he acted. It would sadden my husband, and I would hate to see it. I would hate to see Mr Darcy lose his friend. I suppose we shall continue to keep it our secret."

"I promise to do better at hiding my discomfort," Elizabeth said. "We shall not remain long, and after a good night's sleep, you will see that I can act as though I am delighted with everything and everyone I see about me. Bingley will have no cause to question you again."

"I am less worried about that than I am your unhappiness."

"I am not unhappy. Have you not seen how lovely Pemberley is? And I am with you and Bingley, two of my very favourite people. I have great hopes that the next property we see will be just what you are hoping to find. Then, once you have decided on it and Bingley undertakes whatever business is necessary to purchase an estate, we shall make our way to Scarborough. You know how much I relish seeing new places and meeting new people, and from what your husband has said, his family is delightful, so I am sure to enjoy every moment we spend with them."

Elizabeth successfully kept the subject on their journey. In about a quarter of an hour, Jane said good night, leaving Elizabeth to her thoughts.

CHAPTER TWENTY-NINE

Elizabeth woke to the sound of a steady rain and the faint headache that always accompanied unsettled weather. She lay in bed for a long while, staring at the ceiling and wondering whether she should remain in her chamber all morning. Bingley had arranged for them to see the second estate on the morrow, wishing instead to show Jane the neighbourhood today; Elizabeth was to go with them. They had talked of it on the way back to Pemberley the day before, and Bingley had said he would invite the Darcys. Even if one or both were to accompany them, Elizabeth had been looking forward to the distraction. As much as anywhere in the area would revive memories that were best left buried, going to Lambton and seeing some of the picturesque and otherwise interesting spots near Pemberley would be preferable to staying at the estate with little to do. But given the strength of the rain, the excursion would have to be postponed.

There is nothing else for it! She pushed herself out of bed and asked the maid to fetch some tea; that was usually enough to ease her headaches. As she sipped, she considered what she might do during the coming hours that would allow her to avoid the Darcys.

It was a quiet day and one Elizabeth spent largely alone. Her hopes that the rain would cease long enough for her to take a walk in the open air were never fulfilled, though she managed a short excursion that involved pacing back and forth on a sheltered terrace. Jane and Bingley walked about the house, and Elizabeth did likewise but on her own, wanting not to intrude on the couple's time together. Jane also sat with Miss Darcy and Mrs Annesley, and Bingley and Mr Darcy amused themselves somehow, while Elizabeth sneaked into the library for long enough to find several volumes to occupy herself. She would not remain there to read, however, fearing Mr Darcy would find her and attempt to have another private conversation.

While she succeeded in avoiding him, she was not so fortunate as to avoid his sister. Elizabeth almost ran into Miss Darcy as she rounded a corner in a corridor.

"Oh! Pardon me." Elizabeth gave a quick nod and continued, but Miss Darcy spoke, arresting her movement.

"You must hate me." Her tone was odd to Elizabeth, almost as if she spoke a challenge.

Elizabeth turned to face her, puzzled by the young lady's intentions. "I do not. It is not my right to judge you." She struggled for a polite way to express herself. "I know how disagreeable it is to have that man in one's family. I wish I could forget it, and I have not suffered at his hands as you did."

"You *ought* to hate me. I know you expected to marry my brother, and because I said I could not bear it, he did not propose. It must have made you very unhappy."

Again, it was more *how* Miss Darcy spoke rather than what she said that drew Elizabeth's notice. She sounded as though she *wanted* Elizabeth to be angry with her and blame her, but Elizabeth could not understand why.

"What purpose would that serve? Should I convince myself to despise you despite understanding why you do not want me as a sister-in-law? I am not so foolish as to think it will remain thus always, not unless I let it, and I shall not." It was only after she fell silent that she realised what she had said. She had not wanted to admit she was unhappy, though if pressed, she would say it was only because she was at Pemberley and knew she ought not to have come.

Miss Darcy scratched at her arm, and Elizabeth almost took a step forwards, wanting to stop her, but she was afraid she would scare the girl.

"What he did to you was horrible! I cannot even imagine—I wish there was some way I could be of use to you. Perhaps the only way I can is to tell you I do not judge you or hate you. You should not judge or hate yourself," she said.

Red splotches appeared on Miss Darcy's face, and her entire body looked taut enough to snap in half if disturbed by the barest whisper of wind. "How can I not?"

Elizabeth longed to embrace her but only allowed herself a brief touch to direct Miss Darcy's hand away from its task of digging into her skin. Speaking as softly and gently as she ever had in her life, Elizabeth said, "Because he was a grown man, and you were little more than a child. What did you know of the world compared to him?" Miss Darcy bristled at this, but Elizabeth continued, insisting on being heard. "Unfortunately, I have met the man. He excels at deceiving people, and he set out to use you. A lady older than you could easily be taken in by him and soon find herself behaving in a manner she knew was wrong."

Her cheeks bright pink, Miss Darcy spun round and strode away. Elizabeth remained where she was a moment longer, her head bowed, rubbing her forehead and hoping she had not made Miss Darcy's suffering worse.

All day, Darcy said silent prayers that he would find an occasion to speak to Elizabeth again, if only for a moment. Her unexpected visit had been a gift to him, a gift of time, but he knew his opportunities to have her to himself were rapidly diminishing. She and the Bingleys would depart soon, and he had no notion when they would next see each other.

His hopes were fulfilled shortly before dinner. Once prepared for the evening, he had gone to the drawing room, intending to be present whenever his guests or sister appeared. It was then that he noticed the clouds had cleared, and he stepped out to take the fresh air for a few minutes. Although intending to remain on the terrace, when he stood at its edge, he saw a figure on the stone path through the nearest garden, and his heart cried out that it was Elizabeth. Before he knew what he was about, he was walking towards her.

"I see you also decided to take advantage of the improving weather," he said when they met.

"I did." Her eyes were directed to the side rather than at him.

"If I recall correctly, it was close to here where we saw each other last year. I was never so surprised in my life. I knew at once that I must seize the moment to show you that I had attended to the reproofs you so rightly gave me in Kent. Within a minute, I knew I wanted more than to demonstrate I could behave as a gentleman ought," he said.

His wonderful Elizabeth offered him a smile that he interpreted as combining fond remembrance and sorrow. "I was surprised that you were so welcoming, despite how I had abused you the last time we met, that you were kind to my aunt and uncle, and…"

"Pray, go on."

She shook her head, her dark curls gently swaying. "I should not. It serves no purpose."

"Perhaps not, but I would still like to know."

"It was all so long ago. So much has happened since then. Does it not feel like an age has passed?"

Something in her voice struck him, and he immediately thought of Mr Grey and how attentive he had been to her in town. Darcy leapt to the conclusion that he might have already offered for her, that she had promised herself to another, despite her lingering feelings for him, and his heart began to race.

But if she was engaged, Bingley would have told me!

No, he decided, she could not be betrothed, but possibly she was anticipating receiving a proposal soon. At present, he would not concern himself with the future; he would relish every second they had together.

"To me, it feels like it was only yesterday," he said, meaning to imply that his love for her had not changed. That day, he had known that what he wanted most was to win her regard, and it was still true. "Will you walk with me? We have only a minute or two before the others come down."

She hesitated, looking about them and evidently struggling with her response. "I-I should not. What if someone sees us?"

He knew she meant Georgiana. "My sister was still in her apartment when I came down, and she will not make an appearance until after everyone else has."

Elizabeth regarded him for a long moment before nodding. They strolled side-by-side, Darcy adjusting his long stride to match hers. She kept her hands clasped behind her back, while his hung by his side, ever ready to reach for her should an excuse appear—perhaps an uneven stone or puddle she might need his support to traverse without getting wet. He glanced at her as often as he could while watching the path ahead of him.

For a minute or two, nothing was said. The simple act of being beside her calmed him in a way nothing else could, and as much as he wanted to clasp her hand and declare his love, he knew a serious conversation would drive her away. Besides, what he most wanted currently was to prolong the sense of peace he felt.

"Are you feeling better?" he asked. She gave him a puzzled look, and he explained. "This morning, at breakfast, I believe you had a headache. I recall you telling me last year that unsettled weather often left you feeling ill."

Her eyes still on him, she graced him with a smile. "You remember that?"

"Of course I do."

She blushed and averted her gaze. "You are correct about this morning, but it is gone now." There was a slight pause before she continued. "Thank you for-for asking and remembering."

Again, they strolled without speaking. He wanted to tell her that everything she had ever told him was securely locked into his memory. How often had he sought comfort in their past, the all too brief period they had enjoyed when they were happy! Elizabeth next broke the silence.

"It is very beautiful here, and I have always found that the world seems brighter, the air fresher after a heavy rain. I might not like the rain because it stops me from going out as I would like, but apart from recognising the necessity of such weather, I truly do appreciate how it…I am not sure of the best word to use. Perhaps restores or rejuvenates the world."

He made a noise that signified agreement, at first feeling too much to respond properly. Her comment was like one she would have made before he disappointed her, and it gave him hope at the same time that it emphasised how much he had lost. She was sharing a piece of herself, and listening to her observations and thoughts had always enticed him.

"I cannot claim I appreciate winter storms, but I understand what you mean about summer ones," Darcy said at length. He chuckled. "Once, when Bramwell and Fitzwilliam were staying here, there was a mighty storm, and we sneaked out of the nursery to run about in it. I must have been seven or eight years old. It had been so hot for days, and it only began to rain after nightfall. I have no notion what time it was when Fitzwilliam woke me, but he and Bramwell wanted to go out of doors, and I thought it was an excellent idea."

She laughed and covered her mouth with a hand. "Did you? Were you discovered?"

"Oh yes, and our parents were *very* displeased. My father and the earl went on and on about the danger we had put ourselves in, and I do not know what else. By that time, I was too tired to really listen—to say nothing of uncomfortable, given I was drenched and my feet and legs were covered with mud."

"I see how it is," she said. "When I have a little bit of mud on my skirts because I dared to walk to Netherfield to tend my ill sister, I am judged, but it is perfectly acceptable for you—"

"I was a child!" he interjected.

Elizabeth had stopped walking. Her eyes danced, and one of her fingers was pointed in his direction. By instinct, he grabbed it and kept her hand in his. It was such a small thing, this interlude in which he told a silly story of his past, but they had spent so much of her time in Derbyshire the previous summer doing just that. It had allowed them to grow closer, to know more about each other, and, oh, how he wanted that feeling again!

They stood where they were, their eyes fixed upon each other's. Her chest began to rise and fall quickly, and her lips were parted. If he dared, Darcy would kiss her. He believed she would let him, but foreseeing she would later regret it, he did not. What he did permit himself, however, was to caress her cheek, feel her warmth and the shape of her beloved visage. Her eyes closed, and she gently sighed.

Soon, they had no choice but to return to the house. As they walked, Elizabeth kept her arm wrapped around his, only removing it when they were within sight of the manor.

CHAPTER THIRTY

Elizabeth and the Bingleys left to view the second estate the following morning. Georgiana kept to her apartment or the music room and was always in company with Mrs Annesley. While they and Darcy took refreshments together after noon, he asked his sister if she would take a walk with him. She shook her head, maintaining a silence that had lasted all day—at least in his presence. He supposed it was her way of telling him how displeased she was that he had allowed Elizabeth to come to Pemberley. She might even have spied the two of them walking together the day before; after all, her apartment overlooked the gardens in which they had been.

Bingley's enthusiasm for the estate, named Larch Lane, was evident from the moment he, his wife, and his sister returned.

"It is perfect, Darcy, absolutely perfect!" he continued to exclaim at dinner. "Is it not, my dear? Lizzy, I know you agree with me, if only because of the number of trees and rocks we saw." He began to describe Larch Lane's manor and grounds, which to Darcy sounded exactly as they should be.

"Were you as pleased with it as your husband," Darcy asked Mrs Bingley in an effort to encourage his friend to eat, lest the meal last until the next morning.

She smiled, reminding Darcy that he had once believed she smiled too much. He still thought it was true, but he no longer criticised her for it. She was simply a kindly lady who preferred to see the best in the world. He was glad for Elizabeth that she had such a sister.

"I was. We have seen many estates since leaving town, and this is the first one I felt could be our home."

"You did too, did you not, Lizzy?" Before she could respond, Bingley continued, directing his remarks to Georgiana. "Although she has not yet actually agreed to it, Jane and I expect Lizzy to make her home with us. That is, until she is claimed by a worthy gentleman, which I suppose means it will not be for all that long!"

"Bingley…" Pink covered Mrs Bingley's cheeks, and she looked between him, her sister, and Darcy, her expression suggesting she wished she could make his words unsaid.

Or perhaps it is only that I wish I had not heard them.

Bingley grimaced good-humouredly by way of apologising. "It is only sixteen miles from Pemberley, and the road is good. Would that not be something, Darcy? You and I settled so close to each other! Jane and I agree it is a distinct advantage of this estate, to know we have you nearby, and we have other friends not so far away. I do not recall whether I mentioned it, but we stopped in Northamptonshire and spent a week with my friend Grey." He looked first at Mrs Bingley, then Elizabeth, saying, "The drive was very easy, was it not? It took hardly any time."

"The roads were very good," Mrs Bingley said, and Darcy saw her eyes dart to her sister.

"It took two days, Bingley," Elizabeth said, but Bingley spoke on, evidently not hearing her.

"Graystone—Grey's estate, you know—is a fine one. Very comfortable. Do you not agree, Lizzy?"

He winked at her, and she responded with a brief, hesitant smile. Fortunately, before Darcy was tempted to strangle him, Mrs Bingley spoke.

"Ought you not to attend to your dinner, my dear? After so long in the carriage, I hoped you would take me to view the gardens afterwards. I would hate for it to be too dark when the meal ends."

Her husband agreed at once, and nothing more was said about estates, apart from Bingley requesting Darcy accompany him to Larch Lane in two days' time to give his opinion of it.

"If it is not an inconvenience, Jane, Lizzy, and I shall extend our visit a little longer, Miss Darcy. If it is, we shall find an inn nearby."

"Not at all," Darcy said before Georgiana had the opportunity to respond—if she intended to, which was doubtful. "My sister and I are happy to have you remain for as long as your business keeps you in the neighbourhood."

Darcy knew his assurances would not please Georgiana and possibly would be contrary to Elizabeth's wishes as well, but he did not believe he had a choice. How would he explain it to Bingley? Neither, he admitted to himself, did he wish to end Elizabeth's time at Pemberley before it was necessary. As far as he could tell, the situation was not particularly burdensome to his sister. She hardly spent time with them apart from at meals and for an hour or so in the evening. While she was not treating Elizabeth with the friendliness she had when they first met, she was not displaying any of her worrying behaviours either; thus he felt justified in his confidence that her health was improving.

Elizabeth was pleased for Jane and Bingley. Currently, all there was for her to do was hope that Larch Lane proved to be just as attractive upon second viewing and study of the estate details—tasks Bingley would undertake with Mr Darcy's assistance. Larch Lane was by far the most suitable property they had encountered, offered everything Jane particularly wanted regarding size and number of rooms, and, having been well-maintained, would require little renovation. As for Elizabeth, she would be happy to live there, should that be her future. Its proximity to Pemberley meant nothing to her. She knew Bingley would maintain his friendship with Mr Darcy, but that did not mean she would have to join him and Jane when they visited or do more than exchange polite nothings with him should he visit Larch Lane. If she had learnt anything from the walk she had taken the day before with Mr Darcy, it was that she *had* to be more resolute, to put a firmer barrier between them.

In the drawing room that evening, weary and annoyed by feeling awkward, she decided to play the pianoforte. She asked if anyone objected, and no one did. Much of the music by the instrument was unfamiliar to her, some of it far beyond her skill level, but she found a few pieces she was familiar with and began with a sonata by Corelli. She was some way through it when Mr Darcy appeared by her side.

"Shall I turn the pages for you?"

His voice was low and warm. It was improbable anyone would overhear their conversation, given the pianoforte was at the opposite side of the long room from where their families sat, but still, despite how much she was enticed by his presence, she did not want him there. It frustrated her that he had come, but she refrained from ordering him to leave her be.

"That is very kind of you but not necessary."

"Yet, I would like to."

Elizabeth did not respond and continued playing. The instrument was far superior to any in Meryton, and she recalled how delighted she had been to use it the previous year and the occasions she had turned the pages for Miss Darcy while she performed. The evenings the Gardiners and she had spent at Pemberley had meant so much to her. She had begun to imagine how happy they would be living there together, she and Mr Darcy in love and creating a prosperous future for their family, and Miss Darcy as her younger sister, whom she would guide and support as she emerged from the blanket of reserve and anxiety under which she had sought refuge. Little had Elizabeth understood at the time what was behind Miss Darcy's demeanour!

Glancing in her direction, Elizabeth saw that the young woman's eyes were fixed on her, her brow furrowed and lips pinched tightly. "You should go to your sister. She is uneasy."

He looked over his shoulder at Miss Darcy before turning again to the music he was supposedly following to assist her, though she had needed to remind him when to turn the last page. He sighed.

"If you worry it distresses me, you need not," Elizabeth said.

"This entire situation distresses *me*."

"It is not your sister's fault," she insisted, despite doubting he blamed her.

"I never thought otherwise. She is entitled to her feelings, and I know she cannot simply alter them. My difficulty is in wanting to have a reasoned discussion of the situation and finding it impossible. Not only with Georgiana but also with Fitzwilliam."

"He is attempting to protect her and make her well. That is surely his purpose, as I know it is yours." Elizabeth found herself wanting to assure him she understood his actions and that he was doing the best he could, given the circumstances.

He gave a dark laugh. "I have done little else the past two years but strive to do just that. She requires it, I do not deny that, nor do I resent it. I would do *anything* to ensure her well-being. I have consulted every doctor, every person who believes they can help her, and I shall continue to do so. You know better than anyone what I have given up to protect her delicate health. We are all protecting Bingley from discovering what happened, and I am beginning to fear where that will end. Do you never think we are so busy protecting others that we have forgotten what is best for *us* and that there must be a compromise between the two? I will *never* abandon Georgiana, neither do I expect her to miraculously be strong after a good night's sleep, but I do not believe the current situation and how my cousin and aunt and uncle insist on acting is in her best interest."

Elizabeth unintentionally played the wrong notes, and she busied herself looking through the music as though searching for a different piece to play, despite not having finished the last one. "You are angry."

"Of course I am!" he said. "I am angry that I failed my sister and left her exposed to Wickham, and I am angry that I can do so little to help her, and I am angry that because of how he acted, I have lost my chance of happiness. I long to beg you to promise yourself to me, even though I do not know when we would be able to marry. I do not do so because it would be wrong of me to expect you to give up your life for a dream that I can only hope will one day become possible—not that you would agree to such an arrangement. And because I shall not ask, and you would not agree, I have lost you. Or do you deny it?"

The conversation was clearly increasingly agitating him, and it was little different for Elizabeth. She gathered the sheets of music into a neat pile and stood. Before leaving him, she said, "Do you not realise your sister knows you are unhappy and that is making her even more wretched? She loves you dearly. I could see that last summer, and it must be tearing her apart to feel she is the cause of your present ill temper. I assume she believes it is *her* you are angry with, and *she* who has most disappointed you."

This realisation was born of the conversation Miss Darcy and Elizabeth had shared two days earlier. Elizabeth had thought Miss Darcy wanted Elizabeth to blame her, and it struck her that the poor girl truly expected that everyone did, or at least that they should, because she did herself. This was not the time or place for her to discuss the matter further with Mr Darcy, and possibly there never would be one. What she did know was that it was wrong for them to continue their present discussion where Miss Darcy and Bingley would see that they had grown serious and wonder why.

CHAPTER THIRTY-ONE

Darcy took a long, solitary ride early the next morning. He needed the time alone to clear his thoughts and prepare for another day of seeing Elizabeth. Her being at Pemberley was more difficult than he had imagined it would be. It seemed that each hour he was growing more vexed by the situation, but he had nowhere to safely direct his destructive sentiments, which meant he kept them inside himself, an ugly malevolent mass growing steadily larger.

Bingley and he would go to Larch Lane the next day, and Darcy had decided to hint that his friend should not extend his stay at Pemberley much longer. It would pain him to say goodbye to Elizabeth again, but it would be for the best—for her, for him, and certainly for Georgiana, who was growing increasingly uncomfortable. He had tried to avoid admitting it, but it was irresponsible not to; his first duty must be to her.

The ride helped, and he was much better prepared to be with his guests and sister when they met at breakfast. He asked Mrs Bingley whether she had settled on any plans for the day.

"Bingley has promised to take me on a tour of the neighbourhood and to Lambton. Did he not tell you? He was supposed to ask whether you and Miss Darcy would like to join us." She gave her husband a look of fond reproof, and Darcy envied their easy relationship.

Bingley chuckled and finished chewing and swallowing the large piece of toast he had just eaten. "It appears I forgot. My apologies. What better way to occupy ourselves on such a fine day, eh? Lizzy will come with us. What say you? Does it not sound amusing?"

Darcy did not need to ask Georgiana's opinion. "I thank you for inviting us, but I believe we should remain behind. My steward has left me some letters and such to review." Making an excuse for Georgiana was on the tip of his tongue, but it would be false and doubtless evidently so. He did not wish to insult their companions.

"Oh, that is a shame. We understand, of course. We would not wish to disrupt your work or Miss Darcy's studies more than necessary," Mrs Bingley said. To Georgiana, she continued, "I promise we shall not trespass on your hospitality much longer, shall we, Bingley?"

The look she gave her husband suggested it was a conversation they had already had. Darcy could have kissed her; he might not be required to have an awkward conversation with his friend after all. He wondered how often he had underrated Mrs Bingley. He could never view her as favourably as he did Elizabeth, but beneath her beauty and smiles, the lady was intelligent and sensible. While she coaxed Georgiana into telling her a little of her favourite places around Pemberley, Darcy surreptitiously observed Elizabeth, who met his eye several times. She looked tired and sad, and he hated to see it. It confirmed to him that she must leave as soon as possible, as distressing as their separation would be.

The Bingleys and Elizabeth were still out when an unexpected guest arrived: Fitzwilliam. The butler, Hudson, brought Darcy the news. Darcy stared at the servant for a moment, wondering whether he had heard him correctly. Sufficiently regaining his composure, he set aside his pen.

"Where have you put him? Have you informed Miss Darcy?"

"The colonel is in the blue drawing room, sir. Mrs Reynolds is having his usual apartment prepared. And, no, I have not yet told Miss Darcy."

Darcy thanked and dismissed him, saying he would inform his sister himself. Why was his cousin here? He guessed that Georgiana had asked him to come, and it distressed him that she would write to Fitzwilliam and claim a need for his company without telling Darcy what she had done.

He found Georgiana in the sitting room she had taken as her own. She and Mrs Annesley were practising Italian. He apologised for interrupting them, then directed his attention to his sister, watching her carefully as he spoke.

"Hudson just informed me that our cousin Fitzwilliam has arrived. I had no notion he intended to visit."

The flash in Georgiana's eyes and short-lived smile on her face spoke of more than delight that he was there. Darcy turned to the older lady.

"I trust you will excuse my sister from her studies for the remainder of the day."

The look Mrs Annesley gave Georgiana was disapproving, and he had the impression she suspected Georgiana had known Fitzwilliam was expected. He took his sister away. Her steps were lighter than usual, and as they approached the stairs, he indicated they should stop for a moment.

"Did you ask him to come?"

She bit her lips together and did not seem inclined to speak.

Keeping his tone even to show he was not angry, he said, "I would like an answer, please."

Darcy was left with the view of the top of Georgiana's head for what felt like a full minute before she lifted her chin and glanced at him, their eyes meeting for a second.

"I wrote to him when you told me she would be at Pemberley."

Darcy sighed. It was ridiculous to him that she would not even say Elizabeth's name. "To which 'she' do you refer? Miss Bennet, I assume?" When she nodded, he continued. "What harm has she done you since she and the Bingleys have been here? She does not even ask that you speak to her. I wish I understood why even seeing her disturbs you so greatly, and I wish you had told me that you had written to Fitzwilliam."

Again, she was silent, and Darcy wondered when he would no longer worry that every word he spoke, every action he took, would cause his sister an injury.

"Well, let us go and greet him, shall we?" He held out an arm to her, offering his support as they descended the stairs and went to their cousin together.

As soon as she saw him, Georgiana flung herself into Fitzwilliam's arms, greeting him as though he had come to rescue her from a horde of highwaymen. Darcy gritted his teeth.

I suppose I have only myself to blame if that is how she feels. I convinced her that having Elizabeth and the Bingleys here for a few days would not be difficult. Who am I to say what she can and cannot bear?

The spiteful looks his cousin gave him only worsened Darcy's mood. Fortunately, while the three of them were together, no mention was made of Elizabeth. That changed when Fitzwilliam asked Georgiana to return to her apartment.

"I want to have a chat with your brother." As soon as they were alone, Fitzwilliam said, "Are you mad?" He sat across from Darcy, his arms spread and one foot resting on the opposite knee, taking up as much space as possible.

"No, I am not mad, and you had no reason to come here in such haste." A deep fatigue settled over Darcy. How many times had he and his cousin spoken of Elizabeth over the last year? He had no desire to listen to Fitzwilliam again tell him why a union between them would be wrong.

"Elizabeth Bennet is staying under your roof, and you think there is nothing amiss with the situation? Forget how difficult it is for you to see her—you are free to cause yourself as much distress as you like, though I fail to see the charm in it—asking Georgiana to play hostess to Wickham's sisters—"

"We both know it is Elizabeth's presence you—and Georgiana—object to, not Mrs Bingley's. Georgiana is letting an irrational fear rob her—and, yes, me—of the opportunity to have Elizabeth as part of our family. Why do you refuse to understand how much Georgiana would benefit by it? There is no more sympathetic, understanding woman."

Fitzwilliam gave a dismissive wave. "I know you believe it, but it is too great a risk to take. What if you were wrong? Consider what that would do to her."

"I am *not* wrong. Georgiana says she is afraid she would have to see Wickham. Since that is the sum of her argument—"

"You cannot say it would not happen. If Elizabeth were your wife, and her sister turned up at the door, seeking shelter, do you think she would turn her away, even if Wickham was with her?"

"Yes." Speaking over Fitzwilliam, who surely intended to call him a fool, Darcy continued. "For Georgiana's sake and for mine, she would, even without me asking it of her."

Fitzwilliam shook his head. "We are never going to agree. Well, like it or not, if she and the Bingleys are at Pemberley, so shall I be. The only other choice is that I take Georgiana to Romsley Hall with me today."

"What my father was thinking to make you one of her guardians—" Darcy ran his hands through his hair. "Have it your own way, but remember they are my guests—people I consider friends. If you cannot treat them with respect and politeness, you will leave—*without* my sister. Elizabeth and the Bingleys will not be here much longer." Darcy stood and strode from the room, wanting to be far away from his cousin.

Jane, Bingley, and Elizabeth were informed of Colonel Fitzwilliam's arrival upon their return that afternoon, but Elizabeth did not see him until dinner. She delayed joining the others until directly before they would go into the dining room. She and the colonel greeted each other politely but exchanged no other words.

Miss Darcy was more animated than she had been previously, though she confined her attention to her cousin. Bingley began to talk of his and Mr Darcy's estate visit the next day, and the colonel evidently overheard something of it.

"Oh yes, I had heard you were looking for a new estate. I did not know it was in this county."

Bingley nodded, but it was Jane who responded. "We did not choose Derbyshire particularly. We have seen half a dozen or more since leaving town. We are making our way to Scarborough, to see my husband's family."

"We were nearby when I received notice from my agent about two prospects close to Pemberley. I knew at once we had to see them, and I wrote to Darcy about staying with him. What a happy coincidence that the estate we like best is the one closest to his!" Bingley said.

Turning to Elizabeth, Colonel Fitzwilliam asked, "And you decided to accompany them rather than return to Hertfordshire?" His voice hinted at disapproval.

"I did." Elizabeth sipped her wine, refusing to say more.

"We insisted, did we not, my dear?" Bingley said. Jane nodded, and he went on to explain that Elizabeth would live with them. "Until some fortunate gentleman takes her from us. I told you we had a very pleasant visit with Grey, did I not, Darcy? Do you know him, Colonel? We stayed a week with him. There is nothing to fault in his estate. The situation is just what it should be, the house and grounds lovely and well-maintained." He laughed. "I have had my mind turned to purchasing a property for so long, I view them all by such measures now. If Graystone Manor had been on the list of possibilities, I would have put in an offer immediately. One could not help but be happy there. I am in no rush for Lizzy to marry, but I do not believe we shall have her with us for very long." He winked at Elizabeth.

Elizabeth wished she could sink into the floor. She was too mortified to look at her companions, but she knew several sets of eyes were on her. Jane spoke, but her voice sounded remote.

"Bingley, you ought not to tease Lizzy. You know it might give people the wrong impression."

"Is she engaged to Mr Grey?" Miss Darcy whispered to her cousin.

Elizabeth imagined she was not supposed to hear the remark; nevertheless, she looked at the girl and shook her head, not knowing whether Miss Darcy would take it as a response to her question but finding it difficult to give a firmer response.

I expect it disappoints her, she thought bitterly. *She would not need to worry that her brother and I might marry if I had accepted another man's proposal.*

"The estate the Bingleys favour is not twenty miles from here. Bingley has asked me for my impression of it, thus our visit tomorrow." Mr Darcy's deep voice carried an edge of challenge.

Colonel Fitzwilliam kept his gaze fixed on him for a long moment before again attending to his dinner.

Elizabeth refused to listen to any more of the conversation. Instead, she ate as much of her meal as possible, afterwards retiring for the night, making a vague excuse. She doubted anyone believed her.

CHAPTER THIRTY-TWO

Elizabeth was not sure whether going to Larch Lane with Bingley and Mr Darcy would be better or worse than remaining at Pemberley with Miss Darcy and Colonel Fitzwilliam. If Jane had wanted to accompany the gentlemen, Elizabeth would have gone, but Jane had made the decision to remain behind, clearly unaware how uncomfortable Elizabeth would be around the colonel. Elizabeth had not told her about her encounters with the gentleman in town, and Jane knew Viscount Bramwell was pleasant to her; thus she believed the same was true of his brother. The truth came out when the two ladies spoke before breakfast.

"I am glad not to spend so much time in the carriage today," Jane confessed as the sisters took a slow stroll through the gardens. "Once we are done with our business in the neighbourhood, it will be a long journey still to Scarborough."

"I am sure the day will pass agreeably. Miss Darcy and Colonel Fitzwilliam have each other for company. Likely we shall not see them all morning, and I need not worry about talking to them."

"What do you mean?"

The confusion in Jane's voice warned Elizabeth that she had said more than she meant to. She made light of the matter but admitted that, "When the colonel and I first met, we had many engaging conversations, but when we saw each other in town, it was the exact opposite. He treats me with suspicion, though what he thinks I shall do, I have no notion."

Jane made a noise suggesting she found that disappointing. "I do not understand why your situation with Mr Darcy should influence how anyone acts. You and he are not engaged, and there is no question of it. You have done nothing to make any of that family believe you will attempt to persuade him—or his sister—that he should marry you."

Elizabeth linked her arm with her sister's. "You need not convince me that I do not deserve his present disdain. I am content to avoid him and Miss Darcy. I hope Bingley can make a decision about Larch Lane today. Once he has, I believe it would be best if we leave. Do you think we could devise an excuse to satisfy your husband? Our presence is evidently worrying Miss Darcy."

And I do not know how much more of this oppressive atmosphere I can bear!

"Yes, of course, Lizzy. Is it very difficult to be here?"

"No, not at all." It was a prevarication; it was increasingly painful to see Mr Darcy and not remember how much she cared for him, but no good was served by telling Jane how she really felt. "Shall we return indoors? What will you do after breakfast? I am considering taking a long walk across the park, but I do not think you will want to go that far."

Jane said she would not and indicated a desire to rest. "I

might sit with Mrs Annesley. You should take your walk. You have not had enough exercise to satisfy yourself of late, and you will regret it if you do not. Who knows when there will be another occasion once we leave Pemberley?"

Elizabeth was returning to the house from her walk when she came across Miss Darcy, who was sitting on a bench, ostensibly sketching. Elizabeth could not be certain, but from the glimpse she managed, the page looked empty. She was content to nod and continue into the house, but Miss Darcy virtually leapt to her feet and blocked her way.

"Will you marry Mr Grey?" She spoke quickly, as though she had been waiting to ask and was grasping at an opportunity that might not come again.

"I do not know. He has not asked me, and I would not like to assume he ever will."

Miss Darcy lightly tapped her mouth, giving the impression she was contemplating Elizabeth's answer. "If Mr and Mrs Bingley buy Larch Lane, you and my brother will see each other. How can you bear it?"

"What cannot be cured must be endured. It will become easier in time, and we shall both move on with our lives." Elizabeth shrugged. She did not know why she was less inclined to hide her feelings from Miss Darcy than anyone else, even Jane. It was as though she understood the young woman would recognise the lie, or perhaps it was just that she thought Miss Darcy—who had been so cruelly deceived—should not be asked to tolerate similar behaviours again.

"I shall not allow them to bring your sister and *him* here or go to see them when they are in the neighbourhood." She spoke bravely, lifting her chin an inch or two.

Elizabeth laughed without humour. "You need have no worries. Jane will not admit them to her home, especially when I am there. Do you think anyone in my family rejoices in their union or would choose to associate with them if it were possible to avoid it? My father allows them into his presence only to protect our family's reputation, including Lydia's, though I am afraid she is too stupid to understand why it is necessary. I pity my sister and dread the day she understands the sort of man she has married. Do you want to know whom I truly blame for my unhappiness, because as I said the other day, it is *not* you? I blame my parents for the ways they failed Lydia. And I blame him. I need not explain why. If you will excuse me, Miss Darcy, I have said too much and feel the need to…calm myself."

She was just walking by her, when Miss Darcy spoke again, causing Elizabeth's steps to falter.

"You could make him marry you. It would take nothing."

Elizabeth did not know what to say, and after a brief pause, managed only, "I beg your pardon?"

"My brother. He loves you. I used to think he would forget you and find another lady, but now I am not certain that is true."

"A lady more worthy of him?" A heaviness behind her eyes told Elizabeth she was in danger of crying. It was a weakness she did not wish to show in front of Miss Darcy.

With an impatient shake of her head, Miss Darcy said, "I care nothing for that sort of thing. I know that is what Lady Catherine said, and probably Lord and Lady Romsley think similarly, but *I* do not. I see now that I was mistaken. My brother cares for you very deeply, and I am sure he wants to marry you."

Elizabeth happened to know that he had held that view not very long ago, and she had no reason to suppose his wishes had changed. She could not speak and said a silent plea that Miss Darcy would soon reach an end to whatever she wished to impart so that they could separate.

"You could, oh, I do not know." Miss Darcy stepped a little closer to Elizabeth. "He agreed not to ask you last autumn, but now I understand it was only because I frightened him and asked him not to. I do not believe what my aunt said had any effect on him. He *would* marry you. Do you not love him?"

Elizabeth blinked several times in a last, futile attempt to stave off the evidence of just how much she felt. "It is *because* I love him that I shall not, as you say, make him marry me. It would tear him in half to be the cause of your unhappiness. How could I knowingly do that to him? Why would I act in a way that would make *you* miserable, when you have already suffered enough?"

Miss Darcy's chin quivered, and blotches appeared on her face.

"What happened to you was horrible, and I cannot imagine what it has been like for you. Naturally, your brother—and the colonel and your entire family—are concerned for you. I will not do anything to make the situation worse for you and thus for them." Elizabeth was conscious of their conversation traversing some of the same ground as their earlier one, but it was apparent the poor girl needed reassurance and to be told that she was not at fault for the violence and betrayal she had experienced. "I am only sorry I did not find a way to prevent my brother, sister, and I coming to Pemberley. I had hoped when Mr Darcy raised no objection, it meant you would not find it distressing."

Fat tears fell down Miss Darcy's cheeks, and Elizabeth felt several of her own falling too. She would embrace her young companion, but she did not believe Miss Darcy would allow it or receive the comfort she wanted to give. They stood, not two feet apart, for several long minutes, until Miss Darcy walked away.

CHAPTER THIRTY-THREE

Rather than return to the house, Elizabeth extended her time in the open air. She did not want to encounter Jane until she had regained her composure.

When she saw Colonel Fitzwilliam walking towards her, she wished she had gone to her chamber. She brusquely nodded and walked past him, but he called her name. She stopped and turned to regard him, arching her brow in invitation for him to say what he liked.

"Will you not walk with me? We strolled together often enough in Kent."

Elizabeth was incredulous. "A great deal has changed since then. I was under the impression you had no desire to see me, let alone speak to me."

His countenance took on a light dusting of colour. "I regret that. We were always friends."

She laughed, infusing it with more humour than she felt. "Do you know, Mr Wickham said almost exactly that to me when he brought my sister to Longbourn." She could see her arrow had hit its mark, and while that was satisfying, she more kindly added, "Unlike him, I believe you are an honourable man, Colonel, and you have done what you considered best for Miss Darcy. But I cannot pretend not to feel it. Do you truly expect me to wander the paths, perhaps make the occasional remark on the fineness of the view or how I have spent the last few months, as though nothing has happened? It is far too much to ask of me."

"You say you understand, but your demeanour suggests otherwise." He spoke as if challenging her, and she responded in kind.

"Very well. I *accept* that you and others in your family believed your cousin would be wrong to marry me, given how greatly the thought of it distressed Miss Darcy. While I do not agree that she has any reason to fear me or that she would have to see that despicable man, I *understand* she cannot view the situation as I do. What I shall never comprehend is why you acted towards me as you did whenever we saw each other last winter."

"Why were you there?"

"In town?" He nodded once, and she continued. "Surely you know I went to be with my sister. If you next ask why I am here, I assure you, it is not out of some nefarious plot to ensnare Mr Darcy or entice him to propose. What manner of person do you think I am? I wish we had not come to Pemberley, but I genuinely did not know how much it would disturb Miss Darcy's peace. Was there something else you wished to say to me, or might I continue my walk?"

He regarded her for a moment. "It would be better if you and your family left as soon as possible."

"My sister and I agree with you."

"Good. I *will* do everything in my power to protect Georgiana."

"From me?"

He gave a little jerk of his head as though saying that was exactly what he meant, and Elizabeth let out an exasperated gush of air.

"I ask again, what manner of person do you think I am? How exactly do you think *I* would hurt her? Do you believe I would ask either of your cousins to sit down to tea with Mr Wickham, knowing what I do of their past? *Nothing* about me has altered since you and I first met, other than me now having the great misfortune of calling Mr Wickham a brother-in-law—one I would gladly never see again. I do not understand how *I* have become the person to blame for what my sister did, why I have had to give up *my* happiness because of it. *She* eloped with that man, not I. Yet, you act as though my presence in Miss Darcy's life would introduce evil to it. Let us resolve to avoid each other for the time I remain at Pemberley. I fervently hope it will not be long."

She strode away without giving him a chance to say anything else that would anger her.

"I am pleased for you, Bingley," Darcy said for what felt like the thousandth time. Surreptitiously, he sighed in relief at the first glimpse of Pemberley House as they returned from their visit to Larch Lane. While some improvements were necessary, it was nothing extraordinary. His advice had been to proceed with the purchase. For his part, Darcy was pleased at the prospect of his friend being settled so close to him, though now, what he most fervently wanted was five minutes of quiet. Bingley was understandably gleeful, but there were only so many times Darcy could assure him of his approval.

Once the carriage had stopped in the courtyard, Bingley leapt out, hardly waiting for the steps to be lowered.

"I shall just find Jane and tell her you agree with us. We shall be settled in our new home by Christmas—sooner, I expect. How wonderful!"

"Wonderful indeed," Darcy murmured as he rubbed one temple.

He followed his friend into the house and, upon encountering Mrs Reynolds, enquired where his sister was and asked her to send tea to his apartment in a quarter of an hour, hoping it would ease the slight headache that had formed during the carriage ride. "I shall go there after I have a quick word with Miss Darcy."

Georgiana refused to see him.

"She is resting. I am afraid she is having a difficult afternoon," Mrs Annesley said. They were in the corridor outside Georgiana's bedchamber.

"What has happened?" Darcy demanded.

"I do not rightly know, sir. I enquired, of course, but she would only say she did not feel well and wanted to sleep."

Anxiety clouded Darcy's ability to think clearly. *After all these months, how can I not know what to say or do under these circumstances?*

"I am not unduly worried," the older lady assured him. "She was not upset as she often gets—no crying or…other unfortunate behaviours. It is possible she truly is simply tired. She is not used to being around so many people who are not relations."

Darcy nodded. "Very well. Thank you. Please do have me

informed at once should anything further happen and send for me the moment she is prepared to see me."

Mrs Annesley had been invaluable, and he knew he could trust her to keep Georgiana safe. With both him and Fitzwilliam close at hand, his sister was in no danger of doing herself any true harm. It meant he was not particularly worried when he went to the drawing room an hour later to wait for his guests and cousin.

Fitzwilliam entered first. "Day with Bingley go well?"

"It did. Were you aware that Georgiana will not come down tonight?"

Fitzwilliam gave him a look that silently asked whether Darcy was an idiot. "You can hardly blame her for not wanting to sit at the table with them. When are they leaving?"

"I might ask you the same thing." Darcy crossed his arms over his chest and regarded his cousin, who stood near the fireplace.

"*My presence does not disrupt Georgiana's well-being.*"

"Perhaps if you did not constantly tell her that she is justified in shunning Elizabeth, and society as a whole, she would not find it so impossible. Enough. I hear Bingley and the ladies approaching."

Sure enough, the trio entered the room. Oddly, Bingley was subdued. Darcy expected such behaviour of Elizabeth, who only offered him a brief glance and nod in greeting; she disregarded Fitzwilliam entirely. Mrs Bingley's gaze darted from her husband to her sister to Darcy again and again. She spoke primarily to Fitzwilliam, asking him how he had spent the afternoon; her voice was tight.

Nothing changed once they moved to the dining parlour. Bingley slowly moved food from his plate to his mouth. If spoken to, he answered offhandedly, but otherwise, he appeared to observe the rest of them, his brow furrowed. Mrs Bingley remained the only person who said more than the odd few words. Her chatter was uncommon for her, and much of what she said served no purpose other than to fill the silence.

As soon as the meal could reasonably be considered at an end, Mrs Bingley stood. "I think Lizzy and I should leave you gentlemen to enjoy your…whatever you prefer. She and I have something to discuss. Um…family business. But-but nothing serious."

The way her tone became higher pitched belied her words. Elizabeth regarded her sister with concern—indeed, both Bingleys had looked ill at ease all evening—and rose and went with her. Darcy turned to Bingley, who watched him steadily, his eyes flickering to Fitzwilliam.

Why do I have the distinct impression something grave has taken place, and why am I afraid to find out what it is?

CHAPTER THIRTY-FOUR

Jane led the way to Elizabeth's bedchamber. She refused to answer any questions until they were alone, shaking her head whenever Elizabeth so much as said her name.

As soon as they were in the room, her expression became one of regret, and she grasped Elizabeth's hands. "Oh, Lizzy, I am so sorry."

"What has happened? Jane, you are worrying me. Is it news from Longbourn?"

Jane shook her head, and Elizabeth pulled her to the settee. Once they were seated, she wiped her sister's cheeks with a linen handkerchief. Then, she insisted Jane tell her what had occurred.

"Bingley was so happy when he returned. Mr Darcy sees no reason he should not purchase Larch Lane, and Bingley liked it even more today than he did when we went together."

"But that is good news, is it not? Have you decided you do not want to be settled at such a distance from Longbourn?" Elizabeth enquired when her sister failed to go on.

"No, it is not that. I am afraid you will be very angry with me."

"Why? I could never—"

"I told him, Lizzy," Jane interjected, then covered her mouth with a hand and looked aghast as she awaited Elizabeth's response.

"Told him? What are you talking…" Her voice faded as her sister's meaning occurred to her.

In a rush, Jane continued. "I was glad for Mr Darcy's good opinion, of course I was, but then Bingley said something about us staying at Pemberley longer so that he could meet with the seller's solicitor, or whomever one sees about such things, and I knew we could not. You and I talked of needing to depart as soon as possible, and I tried to tell Bingley that I thought we had asked too much of Mr and Miss Darcy as it was and they would want their house to themselves again, but he did not agree.

"When I tried to insist, he wanted to know why I did not want to stay. Did I dislike Pemberley, or perhaps it was Mr Darcy or his sister I did not care for? I could not agree to that! He kept insisting on an explanation for why I wanted to leave, and I had to tell him about you and his friend. I bungled the whole thing so terribly, and I am sorry. He was shocked and so angry, more than I have ever seen, even more than he has been with his sisters. He says he does not blame us, but…I know you did not want him to know."

"Never mind it, Jane." Elizabeth's voice sounded flat to her ears. She stood and went to look out of the window. It was dusk and difficult to make out more than shapes on the horizon.

Jane continued to apologise, but she stopped when Elizabeth shook her head and said, "He would have found out sooner or later."

But now that he has, it changes so much. It felt like an ending—and not of Bingley and Mr Darcy's friendship alone, if Bingley truly was as angry as Jane presently believed. The end was for something between *her* and Mr Darcy. While she had accepted months ago that they would never be married, Bingley knowing forced her to accept it in a different manner. It was subtle, but she felt it deep within herself.

Swallowing heavily, Elizabeth returned to her sister's side and embraced her, whispering into her ear. "It is immaterial. It is not such a bad thing that Bingley knows, even though I did not want him to. It is not as though my mother learnt of my past with Mr Darcy. *That* would be another matter altogether." She tried to laugh, as much for Jane as for herself. "Your husband is an excellent man, and I trust him completely. My only regret will be if it affects their friendship. I shall speak to him and convince him it need not."

They spoke for a few minutes about Larch Lane and where they might go from Pemberley, agreeing that an inn close to the estate would be the most convenient choice for several days. Then they could continue on their way to Scarborough. What would happen after that, Elizabeth could not speculate, but she knew it would not involve Mr Darcy.

"Colonel, do you mind if I have a word with Darcy alone?" Bingley said.

Fitzwilliam caught Darcy's eye; he shook his head, indicating he had no notion what Bingley wanted to say to him.

"Very well. I shall be in the library." The colonel swallowed the last of his wine and left the room.

As soon as they were alone, Bingley's expression changed. It became colder and accusatory, not unlike it had when Darcy told him of his interference in his relationship with Miss Jane Bennet, as she had then been.

"I had the most extraordinary conversation with my wife. She spoke of us needing to leave Pemberley as soon as possible, and naturally, I asked why."

I can answer for her. Elizabeth can no longer tolerate my company. No doubt Fitzwilliam's arrival has made it worse, but it is me *she wishes to escape.*

"It was not easy to convince her to tell me the entire tale, but I believe it was a relief for her to unburden herself of the secret. Can you imagine how stupid I feel—how stupid I *know* I am—for never realising you were in love with Lizzy?"

"Bingley—"

"No, Darcy, you have had more than a year to tell me of your attachment. You did not wish to then, even after all the times you listened to me talk of Jane, and so I ask that you let me say what I will before you attempt to justify yourself."

Darcy lowered his chin, both to acknowledge Bingley's request and to avoid seeing his anger. He had always known that their friendship was at risk if Bingley discovered how he had treated Elizabeth. She and her sister had both considered it a possibility too, which is why they had said nothing of it to him. In less than five minutes listening to Bingley, Darcy knew they had all been correct.

Bingley's fingers drummed on the mahogany tabletop as he spoke. "I cannot recall how many times I asked Jane if all was well with Lizzy. Even last winter—no, before that. Last autumn, I could see that her spirits were not what they should be. Not long after we arrived at Pemberley, I asked Jane again. Each time, she assured me there was nothing for me to worry about, Lizzy was simply fatigued, required more exercise, et cetera. I readily admit, I am not the most observant chap, but you would think I would have noticed a pattern. When she and the Gardiners were here last summer, she was lively and as joyful as any person has a right to be. Even when you and I returned to Hertfordshire, she was happy, especially considering what the family had just gone through with the Wickhams."

The sound of the hated name made Darcy recoil, and Bingley evidently noticed. He paused and regarded Darcy for a long moment before nodding.

"Yes, I can see how little you like the mention of him. You never have, but it has worsened, has it not?" He paused briefly. "This is what I have been told. You will be good enough to tell me if there is anything essential I have misunderstood or that Jane has chosen not to disclose.

"You have been in love with Lizzy for well over a year, perhaps dating back to when we first met the Bennets. The two of you had some sort of disagreement when you met in Kent the Easter before last, but when you saw each other again in Derbyshire, you forgave each other. She is or was—I do not pretend to know what she feels at present—in love with you, and you gave her reason to expect a proposal when we returned to Hertfordshire last September. But then, you went to town and did not come back until directly before my wedding. You all but promised yourself to her, then you left her, knowing how she felt and what she had every reason to anticipate."

"It is not so simple," Darcy interjected. He leant forwards, his chest touching the edge of the table, as though closing the distance between the two of them would make Bingley believe him. "It was because of the youngest Miss Bennet's marriage. You know a little of my history with Wickham, but there is more to it." He provided a rough explanation of Wickham convincing Georgiana to agree to an elopement. He said nothing about Wickham injuring more than his sister's heart. "She cannot bear to hear his name, and when she learnt that he was now Elizabeth's brother, she became convinced that she would have to see him if we were married. She and my family begged me to consider Georgiana's happiness above my personal wishes, and…" He held his arms aloft as though asking what he could have done.

Bingley took a deep breath and slowly released it. His voice might have been slightly less angry when he next spoke, or that might have been only what Darcy wished to hear.

"I see, and I am very sorry for Miss Darcy and you. But once I brought Lizzy into your house, once I *suggested* doing so, you ought to have told me. I am responsible for her well-being, and I can hardly protect her properly if I am kept in the dark about such important matters. I wish she or Jane had told me, but when it was clear they would not, *you* ought to have done it."

Darcy nodded, accepting the rebuke.

"I understand you decided you could not offer for Lizzy. You did not want to distress your sister, and if you told me your uncle and aunts raised objections, I would not be surprised. But I cannot believe *you*, of all men, could not find a better way, especially since—from everything I have heard—you were honour bound to her, even if not actually engaged."

Heat suffused Darcy's cheeks, and he was glad the gentle candlelight meant Bingley was unlikely to notice. "You are correct. Are you surprised that I agree with you? Elizabeth knew I intended to propose after what was supposed to be a brief trip to town last autumn. I placed myself in an untenable position. In a moment of panic, I promised Georgiana I would not marry Elizabeth unless she was comfortable with me doing so. She was not, and in truth, meeting Mrs Bingley and having you all to stay here has been difficult for her. I believe she only acquiesced to you coming because, like your wife and Elizabeth, she did not want to damage our friendship. She does not fear being near your wife as she does Elizabeth, for some reason I only vaguely understand, and she has always liked you, which helped, I suppose."

Bingley watched him for a long moment. Darcy could not guess what he was thinking, but he doubted it was anything pleasant. At length, Bingley pushed himself away from the table and stood.

"We cannot remain. Jane, Lizzy, and I shall leave first thing in the morning."

Darcy also got to his feet. He jerked his head in acknowledgement. "I want you to know—"

"I am grateful for everything you have done for me, Darcy, but Lizzy is my responsibility, as your sister is yours. I shall always put Lizzy's happiness—and Jane's, needless to say—above any friend. You would expect nothing less of me, and you would act exactly the same in my position. You *did* exactly that when you rejected Lizzy for your sister and other relations. I expected better of you. I used to consider you the best of gentlemen, the most honourable, and one whom I could trust to always do what was right. I forgave you for lying to me about Jane, and you vowed never to behave in such a manner again. And yet, here we are. It is not even myself I am angry for. First, you injured Jane—the woman I love more than I do my life—and then to discover you also injured Lizzy! I do not know what to say to you. I do not know whether I shall ever have anything to say to you again." Bingley strode from the room.

The Bingleys and Elizabeth left Pemberley before breakfast the next day. Darcy did not attempt to speak to any of them, choosing instead to discreetly watch from a window as the carriage drove away.

CHAPTER THIRTY-FIVE

Bingley directed his coachman to take them to Buxton. It was a sizeable town and close to Larch Lane. He said very little during the drive, other than asking Jane and Elizabeth whether they required anything. Jane kept her head lowered and only shook it. Elizabeth, likewise, remained quiet. She felt guilty for everything that had happened—for Bingley's unhappiness and simmering anger and for having begged Jane to keep secrets from her husband. Bingley had assured them both that he knew they had acted as they thought best, and he appreciated the impulse to spare his feelings.

"Do not mind Bingley's mood," Jane told her when they stopped near Bakewell to take breakfast. "He is disappointed in Mr Darcy and uncertain whether he will be able to overlook it."

In other words, Bingley was mourning what might be the severing of the connexion, just as Elizabeth had feared he might.

"I ought never to have asked you to keep the truth from him. I am to blame for this. Surely, if I had only tried, I could have found a way to tell him enough so that he understood why I would prefer not to see the Darcys but that it need not affect their friendship."

"Everything will be well, for all of us. I am certain of it. You will say I am being fanciful and only seeing the good in everything and everyone, but I feel in my heart that it is a very good thing that this has come out now. Somehow, you and Mr and Miss Darcy will all be better for it."

Elizabeth laughed, though it sounded sad rather than amused. "I cannot see how that is possible, and it absolutely is not if you mean to imply the three of us shall be friends. I am glad we are gone from Pemberley and that you no longer have to keep secrets from Bingley. Let us resolve to do what we can to cheer him. You will have your own ways of doing so, and you are his best comfort. As for me, I shall ensure he knows that I am as enthusiastic about our tour as I have ever been, and I am sure I have a joke or two or an amusing anecdote tucked away up here." She tapped her forehead with a finger. "Before the morning is up, we shall have him smiling and laughing again."

Jane regarded her for a moment. "And you, my dearest sister, will *you* be happy again?"

"I shall, and much quicker than you might imagine. I shall be my usual self before you know it." To ease Jane's disquiet—and for herself—Elizabeth silently vowed to do whatever she could to be more cheerful.

They made good time to Buxton, and after arranging for rooms at an inn, spent the day quietly exploring the town. Bingley said little until dinner.

"I know we came to Buxton because it is close to Larch Lane, but I am questioning whether it would be a good idea to proceed with the purchase."

Elizabeth saw the same questioning expression on her sister's face as she knew she herself wore. They turned as one to Bingley.

"You are?" Jane said.

Less hesitant to ask what had possessed him to say such a thing—and rather suspecting the reason—Elizabeth said, "Have you changed your mind about its suitability, or is something else worrying you?"

Bingley poured himself more wine, though he did not drink it. "It is so close to Pemberley. That was an attraction not so long ago, but now, I do not know. Does it not seem…wrong to you?"

"Not at all." Elizabeth stated firmly. All three of them had agreed that Larch Lane would make the perfect home, and she was not about to let anything other than discovering some fundamental flaw with it dissuade Bingley. "If you are thinking of my feelings, I appreciate it, but it is not necessary. My situation should not affect your choice of estate at all. It is not as though Mr Darcy and I would have to see each other. I admit that it has not always been easy when we have been together, but it will become easier in time—for both him and me." Elizabeth reached across the table and rested her hand on his. "Listen carefully to me about this. You should not make a decision that has long-term consequences for your family based on something that is short-lived, as is the discomfort Mr and Miss Darcy and I feel when we are together."

Bingley furrowed his brow and turned to Jane. "What do you think, my dear?"

Jane glanced at Elizabeth before responding. "Recollect, I approved of Larch Lane knowing of…everything, but the choice is yours."

"Would it prevent you from living with us, Lizzy?"

Elizabeth shook her head. "You are far more concerned for my feelings than the circumstances warrant. I understand why. It was a shock to you, and I apologise again and again for deciding it should be kept from you." He waved this off, and she continued. "Remember that Mr Darcy and I have known there was no future for us apart from as acquaintances for months. The secrecy of the thing made being under the same roof much worse than it needed to be. Thus, Bingley, dearest brother, I demand you purchase Larch Lane at once and present it to my dearest sister as her new home. Then I, your dearest sister-in-law, will set about exploring every inch of the grounds and rejoicing in calling such a place *my* home, for as long as I live with you."

In a more serious tone, she added, "Please, do not give up on your friendship with Mr Darcy. I know it is important to both of you. Nothing that has happened between him and me needs to alter it."

He sighed. "It is not only that he did not tell me of his feelings for you."

"I understand," Elizabeth said, surreptitiously glancing at Jane to indicate that she knew the gentlemen had previously argued. "But Mr Darcy is not the only person who kept this information from you. I begged Jane last autumn not to tell you. I admit, I did so in part because it embarrassed me, but it was also because I feared exactly this would happen—that you would believe you could not be friends with him and a good brother to me. If you can forgive me for the deception, can you not also forgive him?"

"You know Lizzy has a great deal of common sense. We have both remarked on it, and I think we ought to heed her advice," Jane said.

Bingley kissed Jane's hand. "If it will make my *dearest* wife and *dearest* sister happy, then I agree. I shall proceed with the purchase of Larch Lane, and regarding Darcy...I shall allow my anger to dissipate."

"I propose we set aside the matter of Mr Darcy and think only of you two finding your new home, one I shall be happy to share," Elizabeth said. "Let us celebrate. Shall I enquire whether the innkeeper can offer us any special treats to add sweetness to the end of our day?"

Jane and Bingley agreed, and when the three of them retired later that night, they were all in much improved moods.

Darcy knocked at the door to his sister's chamber. About an hour had passed since the Bingleys and Elizabeth had left Pemberley. Her maid gave him entry and took herself off.

"How are you this morning?" he asked.

Georgiana gave a lopsided shrug, one shoulder nearly touching her ear, and Darcy supposed that was all the answer he was to receive. He approached her, a cloud of caution hovering around him as it so often did when he wanted to talk to her of anything more than innocuous topics such as the weather or her enjoyment of a meal—though even they could be controversial if she happened to decide he would be disappointed in her response. He perched on the edge of a delicate bergère chair that had once been in their mother's apartment.

"Mr and Mrs Bingley and Miss Bennet left earlier today."

"Why? Did you ask them to go?" Georgiana's gaze met his.

Darcy swallowed heavily before admitting that he had not. "I believe they felt they had remained long enough and wanted to give us time to ourselves."

"Does that mean he decided against Larch Lane? Did you tell him you did not approve of it?"

"I did not. It is a fine estate and would suit them well. I cannot say what Bingley will do about it." *But whether he purchases it or not, I doubt we shall see much of him and his family in the future.* On another occasion, he would tell her as much, but it was anyone's guess whether this would reassure his sister or cause her distress. She might believe she was the cause of his friendship's end. Had he not suggested that might be the outcome if he told Bingley not to come to Pemberley?

Georgiana looked away, and while her eyes remained averted, she said, "I expected you would propose to her while she was here."

You have no idea how much I wish I had—or that I had done it ten months ago, as I had planned, or even last spring in town. "I do not know why you would." Left unsaid was that she and their relations had made him vow not to.

Again, she shrugged. When the silence between them felt oppressive, he asked whether she would join him and Fitzwilliam for breakfast. "Later, if you like, we might take a ride or go for a walk. Which would you prefer?"

"If you insist. It does not matter to me which one. Are you certain they have gone for good? Mr Bingley did not simply take them out to-to tour the neighbourhood or visit Larch Lane again?" She watched him out of the corner of her eye.

"No, Georgiana. They are gone, and they will not return."

She made an odd sound, almost as though she did not

really believe it. He was too weary and heartsick to puzzle out her meaning, and instead he suggested they find Fitzwilliam and make arrangements for how they would spend the day.

CHAPTER THIRTY-SIX

Like at so many other points over the last two years, Darcy found the strength to set aside his personal sentiments in favour of his sister's needs. By dinner, she seemed to be in good spirits, and as they ate, she and Fitzwilliam chatted about how they might amuse themselves for the next week, after which, he would return to his military duties.

"Perhaps once our cousin leaves, we should go to Romsley Hall for a time. Our cousin Reed wrote that they hope to visit later this month or early next month, but we could spend a week or so with the earl and countess before then. What do you think, Georgiana?" Darcy asked.

"They would be very happy to see you. You ought to go, if not immediately, then after the Reeds have been," Fitzwilliam said before Georgiana had a chance to express her opinion. To Darcy, he added, "If you cannot remain, you know Mother would happily keep Georgiana with her."

Darcy hoped his sister did not hear the disapproval with

which their cousin spoke to him. Fitzwilliam was far from reconciled to Darcy's reasons for welcoming the Bingleys and Elizabeth to Pemberley.

"I suppose I would like it, but only if my brother was there too."

Darcy smiled at Georgiana and nodded, silently saying that of course he would remain with her if that was her wish.

They went into the drawing room together after eating, and Georgiana spent above an hour playing the pianoforte. When she announced her intention of retiring for the night, Darcy said that he would do likewise.

"Unfortunately, I might be occupied with estate matters tomorrow," Darcy said. "Fitzwilliam, you will not mind entertaining Georgiana on your own, will you?"

"We shall hardly miss you."

Fitzwilliam chuckled, but Darcy doubted he was joking. He stood aside as his cousin and sister said their good nights, then wrapped Georgiana's hand around his elbow and led her to her apartment.

"Must you attend to your work all day?" Georgiana asked.

"I shall attempt to finish it as expeditiously as possible, but I can make no promises. If Fitzwilliam were not here to keep you company, I would arrange my time differently, but this way, I hope it will free me from needing to do much for the rest of his stay."

She accepted his explanation, clumsy though it sounded to his ears. In truth, Darcy desperately wanted to be alone to wallow in his misery over Elizabeth and Bingley. If he could do that for four or five hours, he was almost certain he would soon feel much more capable of being the brother his sister deserved.

Darcy spent an hour or two with his steward the next morning and spoke to Mrs Annesley about his sister and what they might try to improve her health, but what he most sought during Georgiana and Fitzwilliam's absence was solitude. He sat in his study and informed the butler he was not to be disturbed unless Pemberley was collapsing around him. He wrote a long letter to Elizabeth, apologising and vowing that he would be happy for her if she married Mr Grey or another gentleman, despite accepting that he would love only her for the rest of his life and could never marry another.

Excising her from his heart had never been a possibility once she entered it; he was certain she was the lady he was meant to be with, and nothing would alter that. He wrote a shorter note to Bingley, thanking him for the years of their friendship and wishing him well. Once that was done, he burnt both letters. The writing exercises helped to settle his mind, but only a little.

Some time later, Fitzwilliam entered the study, poured himself a glass of wine, and sat in a leather armchair on the other side of the desk from Darcy, all without saying a word.

"Where is Georgiana?" Darcy asked.

"With Mrs Annesley. What really happened with Bingley?"

Darcy sighed and ran a hand over his forehead. "He learnt of my history with Elizabeth and did not feel it was right for them to stay. He is angry and disappointed that I did not tell him myself."

"Good." The word was clipped, and Fitzwilliam paused to sip his wine before going on. "I was sorely tempted to tell him that their presence here was inappropriate and ask him to leave myself since *you* would not do it. Do you feel better for taking the day to wallow in your misery?"

"I had work to tend to," he insisted, resenting the accusatory tone of his cousin's question.

Fitzwilliam gave a snort of laughter. "I am sure there were one or two things demanding your attention, but do not lie to me, Darcy. You wanted to be alone to think about your tragic lost love. You know I think highly of Elizabeth Bennet—"

"Do I?" Darcy's head jerked backwards, and his brow arched. "You have spoken against her often enough since last October."

The colonel's features tightened. "I spoke against you marrying her. If it were just a matter of it being a poor match for you, I would have said nothing, but given how much it distresses Georgiana, it would have been unconscionable on your part."

"Why are we speaking of this again?" Darcy interjected. "If it has escaped your notice, I did *not* marry her."

"No, you did not, and indeed, we have spoken of it too often. We would not have to if you would accept that she is part of your past. Unfortunately, so might your friendship with Bingley be. It seemed unlikely it would survive, given he married another Bennet."

"You, who have never been in love, are telling me to simply, what, forget about her?" Growing agitated, Darcy stood and went to the window because it gave him a ready excuse to turn his back to Fitzwilliam. Heat was building in his body, beginning in his gut and spreading outwards.

"Yes. Do you have any idea what it is doing to Georgiana to see you like this? You are a fool if you believe she remains ignorant of your unhappiness. She spoke of little else during our excursion."

Without meaning for it to happen, Darcy spoke with more raw feeling than he usually did. Still taking in the view from the window, he said, "Am I not even allowed this? A few hours to experience my regrets in private rather than impose them on Georgiana and you? I might have lost an old, dear friend—to say nothing of Elizabeth, whom I might never see again."

Darcy turned and regarded Fitzwilliam. Pressure was building behind his eyes; it would be humiliating to cry in front of his cousin, but it might finally make him understand just how deeply he had been injured by recent events. "You speak as though it should be easy for me to forget my attachment to Elizabeth. I love her and have loved her for *two years*. She is the only woman I have ever met that I dreamt of spending my life with, having children with, and growing old with her by my side. I am very sorry I could not set aside my sentiments to take a pleasant drive about the estate with you and Georgiana—that I dared to take a few hours to myself, knowing you were here to care for her. Not for the world do I want my sister to see how…how difficult this is for me. She suffers enough. She suffers, I suffer, Elizabeth suffers—when does it end? How much more shall I be asked to sacrifice? I have already given up Elizabeth."

Georgiana stood with her hand outstretched, almost touching the door to her brother's study. She had come to find him and Fitzwilliam. She had enjoyed herself that day, more than she had in over a week—really, since her brother told her Miss Bennet and the Bingleys would be staying at Pemberley. As always, her cousin was solicitous, and he understood why she had disliked seeing Miss Bennet constantly. He listened patiently while she told him of being worried for her brother and said everything reassuring. They had talked of convincing him to go to Romsley early, perhaps in two- or three-days' time. With more people around, his spirits would recover faster, as would hers.

Georgiana did not tell her cousin that she knew *she* was to blame for her brother's dark mood, or that she was very confused by Miss Bennet. Did she or did she not love Darcy? Why had she agreed to come to Pemberley? She must have known it would hurt him! Perhaps it was to punish her for preventing their marriage, but she did not want to believe that. Miss Bennet had been unexpectedly kind on the two occasions they had spoken, and she *had* tried to avoid her, which she appreciated. While Miss Bennet might not hate her—or so she claimed—Georgiana knew that she should.

At present, hearing her brother's speech about sacrificing his future, the fleeting moments of feeling almost like herself again that she had experienced earlier were gone, blown away by the strong gust of self-recrimination, and replaced with a black cloud.

If she were not here, her adored brother could seek his happiness. He could go to Miss Bennet and propose, tell her there were no more obstacles between them. She would be overjoyed, and any thought of another man would be gone. Miss Bennet should not marry Mr Grey or anyone other than Darcy. It would break his heart, and he had given up enough, borne enough sorrow and loneliness because of Georgiana.

Unconsciously, she began to bite one of her knuckles as she turned away from the door and slowly made her way to her chamber. She needed to free Darcy from the burden of caring for her, of having to order his life for her, whatever that meant to his own happiness. There was only one way Georgiana knew to do it. She could not hurt herself, not in a final way. Even though he should not, Darcy would feel guilty, as though he might have stopped her. He would have to live with the memory of burying her, and she remembered how he had looked the day of their father's funeral. He had seemed lost and so much *smaller* than usual.

The best thing she could do for him would be to go away. She would leave, and then Darcy might do whatever he liked with his life, beginning with marrying Miss Bennet. He would have the future he had spent so long dreaming of.

Alone in her bedroom, Georgiana plotted her departure. She was not exactly sure where she would go or how to arrange her travel, but she was clever enough to sort it out.

The next morning, she slipped out of the house, leaving a note for Darcy, assuring him she would be well and he should forget about her. She thanked him for everything he had done for her and apologised for not being a better sister to him.

CHAPTER THIRTY-SEVEN

It was more of a relief to be away from Pemberley than Elizabeth had expected. As much as she did not want to admit it, she felt a powerful and uncomfortable tether connecting her to Mr Darcy, and being in such close proximity to Miss Darcy was confusing and distressing. It was apparent the young lady was deeply unwell, which made Elizabeth long to help her, but she did not know how.

Which is the dilemma Mr Darcy and his family have faced all these months. The experience allowed her to better appreciate why he was adamant about doing whatever brought his sister a measure of relief. He was an excellent brother and was understandably protective of her fragile well-being. Elizabeth would expect nothing less of him. His caring nature was one of the reasons she loved him as much as she did.

Bingley estimated that they would need to spend two or three days in Buxton. That morning, Elizabeth decided to stay at the inn while Jane and Bingley went to view Larch Lane again to decide what renovations they would like done to the house. She had told the couple that she had been neglecting her correspondence, and it was an excellent opportunity to tend to it. It had taken a bit of convincing, but at last, they had departed.

She wrote to her family and to Rebecca Reed and Charlotte Collins, extolling the beauty of the places she had lately been and never once mentioning Pemberley or Mr Darcy. A substantial part of her morning was spent in her thoughts. She wondered how he was, whether he felt as confused as she did, and whether she could encourage Bingley to write to him and say that they would remain friends. It would ease some of Mr Darcy's disappointment. If Miss Darcy was happier, given Elizabeth was no longer there, that too would gladden him.

Finishing a letter to her mother, she sealed it and went to the window, which overlooked the courtyard. It was bustling with people as always, with carriages arriving and departing in a seemingly endless procession.

With her mind so much on the Darcys, she dismissed her initial impression that a young lady in the street below resembled Miss Darcy. Her gaze remained on the unknown woman, although it was a leisurely regard. There was nothing that immediately made her especially interesting, but over the next few minutes, her behaviour increasingly worried Elizabeth. At first, it was because she appeared unsure what to do or where to go, and when Elizabeth looked for her companions, she could not spot any. Yet, a relation or servant or friend must be with her. She was evidently wealthy, from what Elizabeth could make of her clothing, and would not be unaccompanied.

Then, as Elizabeth continued to watch her, she became more and more convinced the young woman actually *was* Miss Georgiana Darcy! Her hand flew to her chest. *No. It cannot be! What is she doing in Buxton? Where is her brother or the colonel?*

Elizabeth hastily made her way out, excusing herself to a trio who were walking up the stairs as she ran down them. It took a moment to find the girl, and as Elizabeth approached her, she noted how dazed and frightened she appeared.

"Miss Darcy?" Elizabeth spoke softly. Miss Darcy's wide eyes met Elizabeth's, and she was breathing quickly. "Come, let us go into the inn. I am staying here with my sister and brother." Elizabeth touched Miss Darcy's elbow, her fingers barely making contact, to guide her in the proper direction. Fortunately, she did not hesitate; if anything, Elizabeth would have said she was relieved to have someone tell her what to do.

As they moved towards the door, they encountered Bingley's valet, who had evidently seen Elizabeth leave from wherever he had been passing his time; he asked whether she needed assistance.

"My friend and I shall be in my chamber. I shall call you if you are needed," she told him.

The man would recognise Miss Darcy, but Elizabeth saw no reason to mention her name in such a crowded locale. She smiled reassuringly at Miss Darcy, who had started when the valet spoke.

Silently, they climbed the stairs and entered Elizabeth's small room. Jane's maid heard them and, like the valet, asked whether she needed anything. Elizabeth dismissed her, then insisted Miss Darcy sit beside her on the edge of the bed. She desperately sought the appropriate words to say to the fragile young woman.

"I am surprised to see you. Does your brother know where you are?"

Tears pooled in Miss Darcy's eyes, and she shook her head. Her voice sounded strangled when she admitted, "I-I-I left."

"Left? Where are you going?" The questions had blurted from Elizabeth's mouth before she knew what she intended to say.

A few sounds emerged from between Miss Darcy's lips, but they were little more than stutters, and Elizabeth worried her exclamation had added to the girl's confusion. Silently, she ordered herself to remain calm—or at least sound thus despite the rapid beating of her heart.

"Are you perhaps going to a friend or-or your aunt? But Romsley Hall is in Warwickshire, is it not?" Wherever Miss Darcy was intending to go, she would not be travelling alone. At the very least her maid or Mrs Annesley ought to be with her, but Elizabeth had seen no sign of them. Might the younger woman have been separated from whomever accompanied her?

"I do not know. I needed to—" Her voice was as squeaky as a hinge needing a good oiling. She grabbed Elizabeth's arm with both hands, the movement so sudden, Elizabeth's breath caught in her throat. "Please, no one must know where I am. You cannot tell Mr Bingley or your sister I am here."

It was Elizabeth's turn to stammer. "T-they are out at the moment, but Bingley could return you to—"

"No, no, no." She shook her head vigorously. "I cannot go back. I shall find somewhere else. I simply left too quickly, without knowing where I should go, but I knew I *must* leave. But once I was here, I had no notion how to do *anything*. There was no one to help me, and some man— Oh, he was beastly! He said he could take me somewhere, but I knew I should not go with him. What do I do? I cannot go home."

The more Miss Darcy spoke, the more agitated she became. Tears streamed down her face and fell unchecked from her jaw. Most alarming was the way her breathing became faster and shallower. Fearing she would make herself faint, Elizabeth lowered her voice until she was almost whispering and spoke with exaggerated calmness.

"Everything will be well. Follow what I do. Breathe as I do, Miss Darcy." She inhaled deeply, only slowly releasing the air in her lungs.

It took what felt like a quarter of an hour and a great deal of coaxing, but at last her companion became less frantic. Elizabeth wiped Miss Darcy's cheeks. She would have liked to go to the wash basin for a cool cloth to bathe the young woman's face and ring for tea, but she did not want to leave her side just yet.

"Now, can you tell me why you left Pemberley?" Elizabeth took Miss Darcy's hands in hers and kept her tone as sedate as possible.

Fresh tears began to spill from Miss Darcy's red, puffy eyes. Fortunately, she did not entirely lose her composure, as she had come close to doing earlier. "I heard my brother and cousin speaking. I have ruined my brother's life. He would be better off without me, but I know if I...if I *hurt* myself, he might never forgive himself. He would think he could have stopped me." She gasped as though swallowing a sob. "I do not want to be me, to feel this way and see him and know I have taken *everything* from him, but I cannot do *that*. I do not want to die."

Elizabeth said a hasty silent prayer at that admission.

"If I go away, then my brother will finally be happy again." Miss Darcy wrenched her hands free from Elizabeth and began to strike her head, wailing, "I am so stupid! I cannot do anything correctly. All I do is injure others. Even in trying to free him, I failed."

Shocked and not knowing what else to do, Elizabeth embraced her, trapping her hands where she could no longer hit herself. While Miss Darcy sobbed, Elizabeth continued to hold her, whispering soothing sounds and words. Never had she been more aware of what Mr Darcy and his family had to deal with, of just how ill the poor girl truly was. Despite her overarching concern for Miss Darcy, Elizabeth sensed her own anger—at what had happened between Mr Darcy and herself—lessen.

Shortly, she felt Miss Darcy's arms around her waist. She began to speak of Mr Wickham.

"I told him my brother was coming to Ramsgate and I would inform him of our engagement. I believed my family would be happy for me, but he said my brother would never give his consent. I thought he was mistaken and insisted my brother ought to know. He claimed he was only concerned there would be a delay. It was because he loved me so much and *needed* to marry me right away. What if my brother and cousin said I was too young? We would have to wait years until I was seventeen or eighteen, and he could not bear that. Then he said he knew what would make them have to let us marry."

She let out a long whimpering sound. "I did not know what he meant, but he asked me whether I loved him—whether I wanted to marry him and make him happy. I said I did. He had been so charming, did everything to convince me he truly loved me, despite me being so much younger than him. I was not like other girls. He-he said it was the only way, and he…he *did* things. I did not know what he would do to me. I did not like it, it hurt, and I wanted him to stop. It felt *wrong*, and I was sure it was, but he was so strong, and he said that I *had* to let him, that it would make me his wife, and that after telling him I wanted to marry him, I could not change my mind and say no. It would be too cruel, impossible for any man, but I did not know what he intended and-and…"

Mr Darcy had told Elizabeth much of what had happened after his arrival in Ramsgate, how he had informed Mr Wickham he would not obtain Miss Darcy's dowry for years and that, regardless of what had happened between them, he would not force a marriage. Nevertheless, Elizabeth listened in silence as Miss Darcy explained it in fits and starts. She was distraught at present, and it must have been so much worse at the time. It was no wonder that Mr Darcy had been quick to do whatever necessary to bring his sister some relief.

After letting her cry for a while longer, Elizabeth made the girl look at her without entirely releasing their hold on each other.

"What he did to you was very, very wrong. He was unforgivably cruel and used you for his own gain. I can well imagine how easily he was able to convince you of what he wanted you to believe. He lied to me, and because he is handsome and charming, and I liked what he said, I did not question a word of it—and I was five years older than you were when I met him. The only person to blame in this is him. I know it, your brother, the colonel, your aunt and uncle, everyone familiar with the situation knows it—except you, and more than anything, I wish I could convince you."

Miss Darcy's brow furrowed, almost—if Elizabeth dared to believe it—as though she was carefully contemplating what Elizabeth had said.

CHAPTER THIRTY-EIGHT

A few minutes later, Elizabeth judged that Miss Darcy was sufficiently composed and stepped to the washstand to fetch a cool cloth for her. Miss Darcy willingly took the cotton square and wiped her cheeks, then withdrew a handkerchief from her pocket and rubbed it under her nose.

"What say I call for tea? I would wager you could use a cup, and perhaps something to eat?" Without meaning to, Elizabeth spoke as though addressing a child.

Miss Darcy nodded. "I suppose I ought to eat. I have not since yesterday."

"You must be very hungry."

When Miss Darcy shrugged, Elizabeth fought to keep from frowning, concerned the younger woman would see the disapproval and it would make it more difficult for her to accept Elizabeth's help. Not eating would only make her feel worse, and she was determined to see that Miss Darcy consumed a good meal.

Elizabeth summoned Jane's maid, requested she arrange for tea and food, and asked that Bingley's valet be informed she would require his services in five or ten minutes. She then sat beside Miss Darcy once again. "You heard me say I would need my brother's valet?"

Miss Darcy regarded her suspiciously and nodded.

"I feel we must send word to your brother to inform him of your whereabouts." When Miss Darcy began to shake her head and opened her mouth to speak, Elizabeth gently laid a hand over hers. "It must be done. I understand you acted in the manner you believed best for him, but I promise you, he has never wanted you gone. I am as certain of that as I am that we are here together. He and the colonel will be frantic not knowing where you are and that you are safe—and you *are* safe with me."

Elizabeth could have done the deed surreptitiously, but she believed she had earned some of Miss Darcy's trust and she did not want to lose it by keeping her intentions a secret. Miss Darcy had confided in her, perhaps in a way she had not any other person. That she had felt able to tell Elizabeth what had happened in Ramsgate was a responsibility and, in its own way, a privilege. Miss Darcy hung her head and kept her gaze downwards, but she did not withdraw her hand; Elizabeth considered it a victory, and she dared to forge ahead.

"Your brother loves you dearly, as does your entire family. They are good, caring people and want only the best for you. Do you know that your cousin Rebecca and I have become friends?" Miss Darcy nodded without looking up. "She speaks so well of you and hopes that you and she will grow closer now that you are older. You may not know this, but Viscount Bramwell is in love with her."

"My brother said he thought they would marry."

Elizabeth gave a soft chuckle. "I would be very surprised if they did not. Since you spend a great deal of time with the earl and countess, you will see her more often. Would that not be lovely?"

Miss Darcy nodded.

"It can be difficult to recognise how much the people closest to us love us. Even before I met you, I knew that your brother adored you. Nothing has changed that, not even having to give up his hope of marrying me. When we met last summer, I liked you very much, and I knew that, if I did marry your brother, I would soon grow to love you as much as I do my other sisters. I still believe that is true and that you and I could become good friends one day."

Miss Darcy glanced at her, and Elizabeth saw that her cheeks had taken on a little colour.

"Your brother wishes the *situation* were different, absolutely not that you were gone from his life."

"I know what he wishes. He wishes he could have you, and if I were not here, he could." Miss Darcy spoke quietly but with conviction.

"And I know that he wishes he had never let you go to Ramsgate, that he had never hired Mrs Younge, that he had told you why he was no longer friends with that man. In other words, he wishes he had better protected you, and he wishes he knew how to help you be well again."

There was a pause in their conversation as tea and plates of pie, fruit, and cake arrived. As Miss Darcy began to nibble at the food, Elizabeth wrote a short note to inform Mr Darcy that his sister was well and at the inn where she and the Bingleys were staying. She asked the valet to send it express, impressing on him that it must reach Pemberley as quickly as possible, and to apprise Jane and Bingley of the situation when they returned.

Elizabeth took a cup of tea and once again sat on the bed. The room had only one chair, and Miss Darcy was occupying it as she ate. For her part, Elizabeth had no appetite, and she suspected her companion needed the sustenance far more than she did. Miss Darcy watched her from the corner of her eye. Her expression was guarded. Elizabeth allowed instinct to guide her words and hoped she would not make the situation worse.

"I understand if you distrust what I said earlier, but your brother and I have spoken about everything. Last spring, he wanted me to understand why our…friendship had to end. My impression was that he needed someone to speak to candidly, someone he trusted and who was not as affected by what happened as your family is."

"I thought he told you in December."

Elizabeth shook her head. Later, she would review their conversation on the day of Jane and Bingley's wedding; she suspected she had done him—and herself—a disservice. "You might believe you have failed in some manner, but he would say the failure was all his—that he was not a good enough brother to you."

Miss Darcy held a forkful of lemon cake aloft and gaped at Elizabeth. "But he is *too* good to me. He always has been, especially after I was so reckless."

"I do not say I agree with him, but neither do I agree with you blaming yourself. I suppose you might have acted differently that summer, but I understand why you trusted Mr Wickham." When Miss Darcy flinched at the name, Elizabeth gave her a reassuring smile. "Do not be afraid of his name. It is a word and meaningless. I despise him as I never have anyone else and as I hope I never shall again, but I refuse to give him so much power over me that even his name affects me. I pray that one day you will be strong enough to say the same." She allowed Miss Darcy a moment to contemplate this before continuing. "Do you feel your brother and Colonel Fitzwilliam are to blame for failing to examine Mrs Younge's character sufficiently or not better preparing you to go out into the world?"

Miss Darcy placed the fork on the table, having consumed most of the food. She turned the chair so that she was more directly facing Elizabeth. "They did nothing wrong. They have always been very careful with me, and I know they consult Lady Romsley all the time. She approved of Mrs Younge."

"I am sure she and Wickham planned their scheme very carefully. Unfortunately, they were able to accomplish part of it, but I am grateful beyond measure that it did not entirely succeed."

"What do you mean?"

"Mr Darcy believes Mr Wickham wanted revenge because your brother had refused to give him money in the past. By injuring you, he succeeded. But you are not married to him, which he must see as a failure. What you have endured these last two years has been difficult, but your suffering would have lasted your lifetime had your brother not refused to force a marriage."

There was a long pause before Miss Darcy said, "I had not considered that. But if my brother had made me marry him, he would not have been free to pursue your sister."

Elizabeth shrugged. "I suppose that is true, but I see a difference in the situations. Do not mistake me—I *do* worry for her. But Lydia views eloping as a good joke, and she was content to live with him despite being unmarried. She sees nothing wrong with what she did. Your brother attempted to convince her to leave him and go to my aunt and uncle Gardiner, promising to arrange a better future for her. Did you know that, or of his role in her marriage?"

Miss Darcy shook her head. She listened attentively as Elizabeth explained about having received Jane's letters and Mr Darcy arriving at the inn in Lambton just as she had read the dreadful news. "That is why the Gardiners and I left so unexpectedly. Your brother vowed to assist in finding Lydia, and he was the one who did. When she refused to leave Mr Wickham, your brother convinced him to marry her and purchased a commission for him in a northern regiment.

"I wish Lydia were not bound to him. But my relief that you are not is greater than my regret that she is. She may come to despise the consequences of her actions, but for now she is content. They might get on together reasonably well in the future, especially if they do not expect much in the way of love and companionship from each other." To herself, Elizabeth added, *Or fidelity*. "In other words, it is possible Lydia will do well. You would not have. Taken all together—the people involved, the particulars of what happened—it is better this way."

Miss Darcy leant forwards and regarded her with wide eyes. "You really believe everything you have said to me?"

"I do. Every word of it."

They continued to look at each other, Elizabeth struggling not to speak and instead leave Miss Darcy to her contemplations. Eventually, Miss Darcy yawned widely.

"You are tired. That is hardly to be wondered at. Would you like to rest for a while?" Elizabeth asked.

When Miss Darcy nodded, Elizabeth helped her into the bed. She was asleep almost immediately.

CHAPTER THIRTY-NINE

Darcy rose before dawn the morning after his latest disagreeable conversation with Fitzwilliam. He took a long ride, then went to his study to attend to some work. The reading he did was complicated enough that it helped to occupy his mind, keeping thoughts of Elizabeth on the periphery rather than overtaking him entirely. He was still hard at work when Mrs Reynolds entered the room.

"I am sorry to disturb you, sir, but—" She approached the desk and held out a note to him with a shaking hand. "Miss Darcy's maid found this when she went into her chamber this morning."

Darcy's heart began to race. He virtually tore the slip of paper from his housekeeper's hands. As he read the short message, everything around him faded except the words written in Georgiana's hand; they seemed too large and bright and as though they were screaming at him.

I am leaving. It is for the best for you, my dear brother, and all my family. This is the only way I can free you from the responsibility of my care. I want you to be happy, and now you can be.

"Before bringing it to me, the silly girl searched everywhere in the house she thought Miss Darcy might be, and even spoke to several of the gardeners. No one has seen her. I have asked that a more thorough search begin," Mrs Reynolds said.

For a second, Darcy stared at her, letting her words penetrate the thick, panic-formed shell that enveloped him. He then gave one brusque nod and stepped past her and into the hall, where he bellowed for Fitzwilliam.

"Where the hell could she be? What was she thinking?" Fitzwilliam all but shouted. He began to pace around Darcy's study.

It was about a quarter of an hour since Mrs Reynolds had brought the news to him. He had shared the note with his cousin, who was understandably agitated. Unfortunately, it meant he had thus far been of no use in deciding what to do. Mrs Reynolds had every servant she could spare searching the house and grounds, but there was no sign of Georgiana. All the horses were accounted for, so she had not taken one to ride off somewhere. Darcy had sent men to enquire in the villages. She must have made her way to one—though God only knew how and at what hour since he had been awake since five o'clock and had not seen her.

"I have no answers," Darcy said. "Should one or both of us stay here to receive word of what is found and arrange other searches? Should you or I go after her ourselves, although I do not know which direction she took? That is what I long to do. I shall go mad if I do nothing!"

As it was, Darcy felt sick with worry. He had actually been sick soon after first reading the note when the implications of it became clear to him. Georgiana had run off on her own without even a trusted servant. After everything his sister had already experienced, and given how fragile and sheltered she was, she was in grave danger. He leant against the desk, his legs too weak to fully support him.

Fitzwilliam stopped walking and thrust a finger in Darcy's direction. "This is because of you. I told you yesterday that she knew you were unhappy, and you knew how much she hated having Elizabeth here."

Weariness and anxiety for his sister prevented Darcy from retorting. Instead, he said, "Are we truly going to quarrel now? I would much rather put my energy into finding Georgiana. I give you leave to recite all my failings *after* she is safely with us again."

Fitzwilliam made an inarticulate sound that expressed his deep frustration. He ran both hands through his hair. "You are correct. This is not the time, and I know my remarks were not fair. I apologise. This…I do not know what to say. We have disagreed about what is best for Georgiana, but I know you would never purposely injure her. I never thought she would do something like this. What if she is hurt? What if we cannot find her?"

"I refuse to believe that. She cannot have gone far."

"Assuming she left this morning and not last night."

At Fitzwilliam's words, Darcy felt lightheaded. He had not considered the possibility that his sister had left so many hours ago. He wanted to dismiss it, but he knew to do so would jeopardise their search. He swallowed, attempting to create enough moisture in his suddenly dry mouth to make speech easier.

"Let us think rationally. Only that way can we ensure we are doing everything possible to retrieve her as quickly as possible."

"Yes. Yes." Fitzwilliam nodded and again ran his hands over his face and through his hair. "Very well. First, I need coffee and something to eat. A drink or two might help, but it is not yet nine o'clock, and I would not risk becoming inebriated at such a time."

"Breakfast must be nearly ready. We can talk while we eat."

The men went to the breakfast room. After much discussion, they decided they had best remain at Pemberley to direct the search so that they were ready to leap into action once there was word of Georgiana's whereabouts.

The morning wore on, unfortunately with little news that told Darcy where his sister was. He and Fitzwilliam questioned the servants, as did Mrs Reynolds and Hudson in case they knew something they were reluctant to disclose to their master. Mrs Annesley was shocked by Georgiana's rash actions, and she claimed that, just the day before, Georgiana had spoken highly of Elizabeth. The lady was so distraught that Darcy had insisted she drink a glass of wine. Fitzwilliam had sent word to Romsley Hall, both of them hoping their ward had decided to go to the countess but not truly believing it. Darcy had men asking at the posting inns, but he was determined to go himself if the next set of reports yielded nothing.

Fitzwilliam and he were walking back and forth on the terrace, all argument between them forgotten for the moment. In a startling echo of the earlier scene with Mrs Reynolds,

Hudson rushed towards them, a piece of paper clutched in his hand. He held it out and spoke, his hand trembling.

"An express, sir, from Buxton."

Darcy took it from the butler's hand and tore it open. "It is from Elizabeth!" he exclaimed.

He read the missive aloud to impart the information to Fitzwilliam; Hudson remained nearby as well.

Mr Darcy,

Your sister is safe and with me. Somehow, she made her way to Buxton. Fortunately, I remained at the inn this morning, and I happened to see her from the window of my room. Naturally, I brought her inside, and she told me of running away from Pemberley. She is well. I promise you with everything that I am, she is well, and I shall ensure she remains here until you and Colonel Fitzwilliam arrive.

Elizabeth Bennet

To Hudson, Darcy said, "Have the carriage prepared as quickly as possible."

The butler was already turning away when Fitzwilliam said, "We ought to ride! It will be faster."

"We shall need the carriage to bring Georgiana home. See to it, please, Hudson."

With a nod of acceptance, Hudson hastily left them. Darcy was faint with relief. Somehow, his beloved sister had come across a person he knew with certainty would treat her with the gentle sympathy she so clearly needed. There was no one better for Georgiana to be with at this moment, and although Darcy was not the most devout man, he truly believed God had led his sister to Elizabeth in what must have been a dreadfully low moment for her.

Fitzwilliam muttered his agreement, and as soon as he and

Darcy were alone, he exclaimed, "What in blazes is Georgiana doing in Buxton? And how is Eliz—"

Darcy turned to him, fury surging through him. "Do not dare say a single word against Elizabeth. Use your head, man! You know her and know she would never do anything to harm Georgiana!"

Fitzwilliam appeared to shake himself. "No, that is not what I meant." He let out a gust of air. "Perhaps it was, but… you are correct. I am *extremely* glad she found Georgiana. I do not want to think what might have become of her had she *not* encountered a friend like Elizabeth. I cannot imagine *how* it happened."

"Neither can I, but currently, I do not care. You might take what has transpired and use it to recall Elizabeth Bennet's worth. At the very least, let it remind you to treat her with the respect and consideration she deserves."

"I do not know what to say. Everything I have done has been to protect Georgiana. You would argue I have gone too far. My brother has told me that often enough. Believe it or not, I have considered what you said yesterday, about the price you have paid. If I was wrong to oppose your marriage to Elizabeth so strongly, I apologise. I do not want you or her to be unhappy, but Georgiana…" He sighed and slowly shook his head, appearing abashed.

Darcy understood what he meant. "Her situation has required that we place her well-being foremost in our thoughts."

"But determining what is best for her has not been easy."

Darcy made a noise of agreement. As much as this was not the time for them to be having this conversation, he was glad for the reconciliation it promised. They had been at odds far too often, and he missed their friendship, the brotherly accord they had enjoyed since childhood. "No, it has not been. I have no answers even now, but in my heart, I have always believed—and expect I always will—that she would benefit from having Elizabeth as her sister."

Fitzwilliam lifted one shoulder in a half-shrug. "How long will it take for the carriage to come round?"

Darcy could not say, but he suggested they make themselves ready so that they could leave as soon as it was. Hudson informed them that Mrs Reynolds was having a basket of food prepared for them. Mrs Annesley rushed down the stairs carrying a small bag. It contained several of Georgiana's things—a shawl, handkerchiefs, a small cushion, a tincture, and some powders, one to ease her agitation and the other for headaches. It was a somewhat odd assortment, but Darcy assumed the lady had quickly gathered what she thought might comfort his sister.

Shortly, Fitzwilliam and he were on their way to Buxton, Darcy silently urging the horses to hurry.

CHAPTER FORTY

It took Elizabeth a long time, and another cup of strong tea, to begin to regain her composure. She was certain that it would take days before the task was complete. Miss Darcy slept peacefully, while Elizabeth sat in the chair, acting as a guard, a book in her hands. But her thoughts were too much of a jumble for it to hold her attention.

Please let me have helped her. Even if my words were not what they ought to have been, at least let them have not caused her greater injury.

It was shocking to realise how ill Miss Darcy was—not in her body but in her mind. Elizabeth had to believe there was a way back to health for her, though what it was, she did not know.

Whatever it is, I know Mr Darcy will discover it. He will continue to search for every possible treatment, consult every possible source until he does. That is his life's purpose, and I would never, could never, interfere in it.

Had circumstances been different, she would gladly have assisted him. But her sister had married the man who was responsible for Miss Darcy's present state. Elizabeth could not wish Lydia's marriage undone; that would have meant ruin for her family, and she had been truthful when she said she believed it was better, even though only slightly, that Lydia and not Miss Darcy was Mrs Wickham. Mr Wickham would have done everything in his power to make Miss Darcy miserable to cause her brother greater distress. He had no incentive to mistreat Lydia—not more than he otherwise would a wife he did not want—and Elizabeth prayed he was a better man than she believed him to be.

Elizabeth's sentiments towards Lydia had softened after speaking to Miss Darcy. Both girls were very young and had come up against a man who would take what he wanted—whether that was a wealthy wife or the companionship of a willing woman. Elizabeth spent the next while wondering what she might do to help her sister, if anything.

I should begin by not blaming her for destroying my chance of happiness with Mr Darcy. She was reckless, but she will bear the consequences of her actions for the remainder of her life. I need not add to her burden with my anger. I shall always despise Mr Wickham, but likewise, I shall always love Lydia.

That did not mean she would allow her sister to be part of her life in any substantial manner. She could not imagine the day would come when she would no longer refuse to see Mr Wickham. While she presently had no desire to see Lydia either, she would attempt to maintain a correspondence with her. In that way, Lydia might be comfortable approaching her for help if she ever required it.

She was in the midst of devising ways Lydia might gain her freedom from Mr Wickham when she heard sounds in the corridor that signalled Jane and Bingley's return. She quietly slipped from the room, hoping not to disturb Miss Darcy. It would be better for her to remain asleep for as long as possible. That way, she would not have an opportunity to grow restless while waiting for her brother and cousin's arrival.

Elizabeth held a finger to her lips to warn Jane and Bingley to speak softly. The surprise and unease on their faces suggested that Bingley's valet had informed them of Miss Darcy's presence. They went into Jane's chamber, leaving the maid and valet outside Elizabeth's room to ensure Miss Darcy did not wake and leave.

Elizabeth explained how she had espied Miss Darcy in the courtyard and that she had left Pemberley alone. "I am not sure what else I should say at the moment. I ought to return to her side lest she wake up."

"Should I send for a doctor?" Bingley asked.

Elizabeth said there was no need. "I expect Mr Darcy and Colonel Fitzwilliam will be here soon. They will best know what to do for her. It may be a false hope, but I almost believe her adventure and speaking to me as candidly as she did has... released a burden from her shoulders. I pray it has, for her sake and that of her family."

Jane began to quietly cry. "Oh, Lizzy, what you have been through! And Miss Darcy, the poor girl. Her brother and cousin must have been sick with worry when they discovered she was missing!"

"I do not doubt it, but I am well." When her sister looked sceptical, she continued. "I am very glad I was here, but I did little other than listen and feed her." She accepted Jane's embrace.

Bingley kissed her cheek. "It is fortunate she met you. I know you are made of stern-enough stuff to manage it all quite well. Still, I wish you had not been alone all day."

Elizabeth offered him a fond smile and shrugged to say it

did not much matter. It had been a difficult day, but she had done her best and would be no worse for it. She excused herself to go back to Miss Darcy, refusing Jane's offer to accompany her. "Once she is awake, we shall join you in the parlour as soon as she feels able to see you."

It was little more than sixteen miles from Pemberley to Buxton, but the distance might as well have been the one hundred and fifty between the estate and London. Darcy felt tired and weak until he saw the inn. As the carriage began to slow, he saw Bingley's valet standing by the entry. He pointed him out to Fitzwilliam, who had been surprisingly quiet during the drive.

"Good. He can direct us to Georgiana at once."

Darcy nodded and stepped down from the carriage, his energy fully restored.

The servant showed them to a private parlour, leaving them outside the door. Darcy's hand shook as he reached for the latch; he felt Fitzwilliam's hand on his shoulder in what he took as giving and seeking reassurance. They would confront Georgiana's illness together, as they had done in the months directly after Ramsgate and as they had failed to do since Lady Catherine had shared the news of his intention to propose to Elizabeth.

The Bingleys, Elizabeth, and Georgiana were seated at a table on which a tea service was arranged. The curtains were a startling shade of yellow, and they flapped in the wind entering through the window. Darcy noticed these inconsequential details in an instant, after which all he saw was Georgiana and his beautiful Elizabeth, who was doing an admirable job of acting as though nothing unusual was taking place, probably to avoid adding to his sister's unease.

He closed the distance between them in several long strides. Georgiana stood, and he swept her up in his embrace, holding her tightly. If he could, he would gather Elizabeth into his arms too. Fitzwilliam was there immediately after he was, his frail little sister surrounded by the two men charged by her father with protecting her.

"Thank God you are safe," Darcy whispered. "I love you, Georgiana, and nothing you could ever do will change that."

"We both do," Fitzwilliam said. As soon as Darcy released her, he also embraced her.

They spent several minutes assuring themselves that she was well.

"We have much to discuss," Fitzwilliam said. "For the moment, all that matters is that we are together again. Neither your brother nor I would ever forgive ourselves if you came to harm."

Darcy agreed. "We shall return to Pemberley anon. First, I would like to speak to our friends. Do you object?" He held her by the shoulders, peering into her face and taking in every slight alteration to her expression, trying to judge her true response as well as what she admitted aloud, knowing that her spoken sentiments did not always match what she felt. As it happened, she did not speak; she only shook her head. Her chin was lowered, and Fitzwilliam gently lifted it with a single finger, forcing her to look at him.

"All is well, dear girl. We are not angry, only very, very worried for you and gladder than either of us can say that you are here with people we know, respect, and trust as much as the Bingleys and Miss Bennet." Fitzwilliam looked in Elizabeth's direction.

When she nodded, Darcy knew she had understood his cousin's attempt to apologise.

Mrs Bingley stood and said, "Miss Darcy, would you like to come to my chamber and prepare yourself for the drive? Mr Darcy, Colonel Fitzwilliam, I imagined you would not wish to tarry. I have asked that a basket be prepared for you for your return journey."

"You are very good, madam. Thank you," Fitzwilliam said. To Georgiana, he added, "Go with Mrs Bingley. By the time you are ready, your brother and I shall be too."

Georgiana glanced at Darcy, who nodded his agreement and gently caressed her cheek. She was pale yet did not seem as fragile as he had expected her to be. Mrs Bingley held out a hand to her; to Darcy's surprise, she readily took it, and the two ladies quit the parlour.

CHAPTER FORTY-ONE

Once Jane and Miss Darcy were gone, the gentlemen sat. Elizabeth longed to comfort Mr Darcy. It was for the best that they would not have a private conversation; she might say more than was wise, even promise to always love him. She expected that she would, but what would be the good in burdening him with the notion that she would never be happy because he was unable to marry her? He kept his gaze steadily on her, and she could not look away.

"Miss Bennet, will you please tell us what happened?" Colonel Fitzwilliam said.

At the same time as she nodded and began to say that naturally she would, Bingley spoke.

"I understand why you ask, but my sister has been through a great deal today. If she does not wish—"

Elizabeth rested a hand on his arm. "It is kind of you to worry for me, but it is not necessary. Miss Darcy's needs are far more important."

Bingley frowned. While they had waited for the gentlemen's arrival, he had taken her aside to say that she did not need to see Mr Darcy if she did not wish to. He was evidently still upset with his friend, but she expected that, as soon as he had a greater understanding of the situation, his disappointment would lessen.

"Thank you," Colonel Fitzwilliam said. "I do not know how much Bingley already knows, but please speak freely. The time for secrets amongst us here today has ended."

Elizabeth nodded. She had noticed his tacit apology. It was welcomed, but it would take much more than that for her to overlook how he had treated her since the winter.

Not knowing how long they had before Jane and Miss Darcy returned, Elizabeth quickly and efficiently explained as much of what Georgiana and she had spoken of as she could recall. In particular, she wanted Mr Darcy and Colonel Fitzwilliam to know what their ward had told her about Mr Wickham. The colonel covered his eyes with his hands and bowed his head for a long moment. Mr Darcy allowed her to see the tears that formed in his eyes. Bingley, pale and looking like he wanted to vomit, also noticed and clasped his shoulder; he then did the same to the colonel.

"I do not know if anything I said to her helped," Elizabeth admitted. "She and I had two brief conversations when I was lately at Pemberley during which I urged her not to blame herself."

"We have told her the same more times than I can count," the colonel interjected, sounding as though it was important to him that she knew they had.

"I expected as much," she said. "I know she did not believe me previously, but today, I think she might have…oh, I do not know, understood, perhaps even accepted what I said—not fully but a little. It might be only a wish on my part, but I genuinely believe there was a significant difference in her demeanour after she slept."

Indeed, after Miss Darcy awoke from her long nap, she had seemed a great deal stronger and more at ease than she had when Elizabeth first found her, perhaps since Elizabeth had first *met* her. If anything, the young woman was embarrassed.

Colonel Fitzwilliam slowly took a deep breath. "Thank you. I hope you are correct, but even if you are mistaken, please know that it is not because you did not say the right words. My parents, Bramwell, Darcy, and I have all talked to her extensively, promised her we do not fault her for what happened. Mrs Annesley has also attempted to help her see the event as we do. None of it has had the desired effect. My cousin and I are both grateful for the care you provided her, and I cannot express our profound relief that *you* found her. She is far calmer and more composed than I feared she would be."

Bingley had been quiet throughout her explanation, his chin lowered. As the colonel fell silent, he looked up and said, "Darcy, I owe you an apology. I had no notion what you and Miss Darcy have been experiencing these last two years. *Two years!* It has lately come to my attention that I do not notice a great deal. I wish I had known so that I might have been of use to you. Jane has vowed to help me become more observant, if only so that I can be a better husband and brother. I shall add friend to that." Bingley looked between Mr Darcy and Elizabeth. She guessed he was thinking that one of the matters he had overlooked was that the two of them loved each other.

"You think too much of it. I ought to have told you…something. We did not want people to suspect thus did our best to act as though nothing had changed, but especially after last summer, I should have confided part of it," Mr Darcy said.

Bingley waved this away, and when the colonel asked what

he meant, Mr Darcy promised to explain it another time. Elizabeth knew he had been referring to their disagreement when he had informed Bingley of his lies regarding Jane.

Her sister and Miss Darcy returned before more could be said, and the party from Pemberley prepared to take their leave. They exchanged subdued farewells, and Miss Darcy, standing between her guardians, addressed Elizabeth, her voice sombre.

"Thank you. I-I am very glad you were here. I do not know what would have become of me otherwise."

"I am very glad that I was here too." Elizabeth stepped forwards and gripped Miss Darcy's hand. "Be well."

Miss Darcy gave her a tremulous smile and a nod. Elizabeth felt a gentle pressure on her hand as Miss Darcy briefly returned her clasp. Then, with Colonel Fitzwilliam's arm across her shoulders, Miss Darcy turned and left the room.

Mr Darcy remained, his eyes lingering on Elizabeth; she could not—did not want to—look away. At length, he could no longer delay following his sister and cousin, and he walked out of her life for what she expected was the final time.

Jane and Bingley immediately began to ask whether she was well and offer all manner of comforts. Elizabeth refused them all, assuring them there was no need. At length, she agreed to take a walk with Bingley while her sister rested. Contrary to his garrulous nature, he said little, which suited Elizabeth.

They were almost at the inn again, when he surprised her by saying, "He is a good man. Darcy, I mean."

"I never doubted it. That might not be strictly true, but when I did, I was angry and disappointed. Now, I know he is the best of men, the best of brothers—next to you, of course—and he will be the best of friends, if you allow him."

Bingley nodded.

She retired soon after they ate, only to lie awake far into the night, occasionally sitting at the window and staring into the courtyard, thinking of Mr Darcy and what he was doing at that moment.

The following morning, Bingley absented himself to allow the sisters to speak privately. Elizabeth assumed the couple had planned it in advance, expecting she would be franker if it were just her and Jane. They sat side-by-side upon an old but well-maintained sofa in the parlour, the remnants of their breakfast having just been cleared away by a maid.

"What would you like to do?" Jane asked. "Bingley and I have completed everything that requires our presence in Derbyshire for the moment. However, we could remain longer if you wish to be near Pemberley."

It was an effort not to gape at her sister. Elizabeth had not expected her or Bingley to think she wanted to intrude on the Darcys. She shook her head. "No. I am glad I was able to…do whatever I could for Miss Darcy, but nothing has changed. We ought to continue to Scarborough, do you not think? After which, you must return to Hertfordshire to see to closing Netherfield Park and arranging to remove to Larch Lane as soon as possible."

"As soon as possible? W-why?" Jane's brow gently furrowed.

Elizabeth chuckled and held her sister's hand. "My darling sister, *Bingley* is the unobservant one. You are with child, are you not? I have suspected it this last fortnight, or perhaps a little longer."

Jane's joy was evident in the pinkness of her cheeks and softening of her features. "I ought to have told you, but it is very soon. From what my maid and I estimate, I am weeks away from feeling the quickening, but yes, I do believe I am. I would like to be settled in our new home before winter begins."

"Christmas at Larch Lane. It sounds wonderful. How much we shall have to celebrate."

"I hope we shall. But be serious for a moment, Lizzy. Are you certain about leaving the neighbourhood so soon? If Miss Darcy's health was the chief impediment to you and Mr Darcy—"

"It was and still is," Elizabeth interjected gently. "You must see that nothing has changed. Miss Darcy's needs *must* come first."

Evidently, her troubled thoughts were reflected in her demeanour because Jane asked, "What is it? Please tell me."

Elizabeth sighed. "My feelings were injured that he was not honest with me at the beginning. Last night, I dreamt of seeing him at your wedding. I woke up and was unable to sleep further. It left me reflecting on that day, and I think he was going to explain it all to me, but I did not allow him to speak. I heard only that his family were against his marrying me, and he had given in to their persuasion. I was furious and refused to listen to more. If he had told me then of his sister's situation and what it meant for us, I would still have been disappointed, but I like to believe I would have understood, and my anger would not have been directed at him as it was for so many weeks. Even after he told me the truth last spring, I was still angry, then because he had not done it sooner! What is worse is that I know I interrupted him that day too. I do not know whether he had more to tell me, but I do recognise that I must learn to listen to people more carefully and let them speak, especially when the conversation is such an important one." She rolled her eyes. "So much of my anguish might have been spared. I loved him still. I knew it soon after we met in town. I think I hated myself a little for that. How could I possibly still care so deeply for someone who would give me up just because his family objects to my lack of high connexions and fortune? I might have spared some of his sorrow too. He knows what I believed of him, what my sentiments have been, and it must have affected him."

"If he came to you today and told you he had resolved it, that Miss Darcy accepted your union, would you marry him?"

How could she possibly answer such a question? In some ways, it was easy. She would say yes immediately, likely cry out in joy and throw herself into his arms. But imagining it might be possible was too painful to bear. After a long pause, she said, "I do not want or need to remain in the vicinity. Leaving aside what happened yesterday, you and Bingley had expected to continue to Scarborough tomorrow or the day after, if I recollect."

Jane nodded. "I have been anticipating meeting Bingley's family. After that, we have a long journey to Hertfordshire. My mother has been urging us to return. Since she does not yet know we have been searching for a new estate, she does not understand why it is taking us so long. I am growing anxious to tell her. I do not like to keep it from her or my father and sisters, but I do not feel it is right to give the news in a letter. I know you were unhappy in Hertfordshire last winter, and if you do not wish to go…"

"I admit that for just a second, I considered asking that you leave me in town with Aunt and Uncle Gardiner, but that is not fair to our parents or Mary and Kitty. I have not seen them in months. Papa has actually written to say he misses my company, and he assures me Lydia has returned to her lamentable husband."

"You will stay with us at Netherfield," Jane said decidedly, then her voice turned hesitant. "What of Mr Grey?"

Elizabeth took a deep breath and ran a hand over her face. There was no question of Mr Grey, and looking back on it, she acknowledged that there never had been, not unless he was content to wait a very long time. "Please ask Bingley to inform him that I do not anticipate marrying for at least the next year or two, possibly longer. I expect he will understand why without my brother needing to explain further. I genuinely admire him, but I cannot promise him anything at present. He deserves someone who can love him as devotedly as I know he will love his wife, and that will never be me."

"You ought not to give up on finding love just because you and Mr Darcy cannot marry." Jane's brow furrowed.

"I have not. I am giving up on the notion that I might learn to love Mr Grey. There was a time I thought I might, and if we were to meet again in three or four years, and neither of us were married, then perhaps we would be able to find happiness together. I very much doubt he will remain single so long, however. He wants to have a family of his own, and he deserves it. I did not say I would never marry, just that it would not be for some time. If you do not take care, Jane, I shall accuse you of not listening to me. I begin to think you wish to encourage me to accept the first man who proposes so that you and Bingley will be relieved of my company!"

"Of all the times to make a joke!" Jane shook her head. "You know you will always have a welcoming home with us. We have said it often enough."

"You have, and the only reason I have not accepted before now was my stubbornness and how disordered I have felt because of the situation with Mr Darcy. That is at an end. I shall endeavour to be useful at Larch Lane. Perhaps I shall teach your adorable children to be mischievous. I am certain they will be as beautiful and handsome as their parents and just as desirous of pleasing everyone. It will do them good to explore a way of being contrary to their natures."

Jane laughed and so did Elizabeth. It felt good, and she determined to set aside her sombreness and embrace cheerfulness instead. It might not be easy, but she was tired of being unhappy, and believing she had done Miss Darcy a good turn, Elizabeth had reason to be satisfied with her sojourn in Derbyshire.

CHAPTER FORTY-TWO

The carriage ride back to Pemberley was quiet. It was not the appropriate time for a serious conversation, and soon after arriving home, Georgiana had retired. The following morning, she, Fitzwilliam, and Darcy sat together in one of Pemberley's small sitting rooms. Darcy had chosen it because it was particularly bright and cheerful. Georgiana's hands were folded together in her lap, and she did not look directly at either Fitzwilliam or him.

"I believe what Fitzwilliam and I would most like to know is why you felt compelled to leave the way you did," Darcy said.

Georgiana visibly swallowed. "The day before, I overheard the two of you. You spoke of Miss Bennet and having to sacrifice a future with her. It was plain how much it hurt you to do so, and how much it still did, despite all the months that have passed. I thought if I were no longer here, you could marry her and be happy. I wanted that for you. I cannot explain why it affected me so much all of a sudden. I have always known that you did not propose to her because of me."

"I must bear some of the responsibility for this situation—perhaps most of it," Fitzwilliam said.

"What?" Darcy was too surprised to stop himself from blurting the word.

Fitzwilliam offered him a regretful shrug before explaining. "I have realised how unfair I have been about and to Miss Bennet. I regret that it took recent events to make me see it. Georgiana, do you recall that I met her previously, in the spring of 1812 in Kent?"

She nodded, and he went on. "I liked her a great deal, and I was quick to forget that or accept that she and your brother loved each other as much as I now believe they do."

"When I met her, I liked her too, and I looked forward to the day she would be my sister," Georgiana said. She turned to Darcy. "I knew she would make you happy, and I was very glad for you. You deserve someone who loves you and makes you laugh, as I saw she did last year."

He murmured his thanks, and she continued. "Even when I was most frightened of being near her, I never once thought meanly of her, only of her connexion to him." She paused and visibly straightened her spine. "Wickham. I ought not to be afraid to say his name. It cannot harm me unless I let it."

Fitzwilliam pulled her hand to his mouth to kiss, demonstrating his approbation. "I know I said I disapproved of her because she is not rich or part of the *ton*, but I never cared about that. As soon as you learnt from our aunt that Darcy intended to marry her, you were distraught, and that was enough for me. I did not need to know more, and I acted accordingly. I was not kind. I argued with Darcy, and I treated this whole thing as a simple matter. You did not want him to marry her, and that was the end of it."

"And it was," Darcy interjected. "I would never do anything that truly made you unhappy, Georgiana. I hope you know that. I could not live with myself if I did."

Georgiana's cheeks turned pink, and her lips turned upwards in a small smile.

Addressing Darcy, Fitzwilliam said, "I know you would not, and it may have been necessary to postpone any plans you and Miss Bennet made, which is exactly what you and Bramwell suggested. Where I absolutely failed was that I did not take into account how difficult it would be for you—that your attachment to her was deep and long-lasting. I could say it is because I have never felt such for a lady, but in reality, I simply did not think of you—I only thought of Georgiana. Bramwell told me I was being stupid about it often enough, but I disregarded him because I did not like what he was saying. I made the situation worse for you, Darcy. If we had spoken of it more, if I had not simply argued with you, if I had talked to Georgiana of the situation in a more reasonable fashion instead of just saying that yes, of course it would be a terrible thing for you and Miss Bennet to marry—"

"I appreciate what you are saying, but perhaps we ought to move on. Nothing can change the past. We all made mistakes, and we all shall again in our lives," Darcy said. He reached across to clap his cousin on the shoulder as a way to emphasise the verity of his words. It was satisfying to know Fitzwilliam regretted his behaviour, but at this late date, it made no material difference, other than making it easier for them to return to being friends. He and Elizabeth were still as far apart as ever. Elizabeth would never agree to marry him if she had even the tiniest concern that their union would cause Georgiana a moment's unease.

"What would you like to do?" Darcy asked his sister. "We could go to Romsley Hall or to town, visit some other place, if you like, or we might stay here."

"Do not answer in the manner you believe would most please us," Fitzwilliam said. "Take a moment—or longer, if necessary—and tell us what *you* need."

Georgiana looked from one of them to the other and back again several times, all the while nibbling her lower lip. At length, she said, "I am not sure what I need at present. I know that I do not want to always feel this way."

They spent the next interval speaking of what they had been advised to do by various people who claimed to be experts in nervous disorders.

"I have recently learnt of several other doctors, and I shall write to them. They might not have anything different to suggest or that we are prepared to try," Darcy said, "but…"

"I shall gladly consult with anyone you can find who might aid me. I am determined to believe that someone knows what will help me, and I vow to truly put my mind and effort into feeling better, whatever it takes. I know it will not be easy, but I shall not let that deter me."

Darcy took her hand in his. "Do not think we believe this is completely in your control. We know it is not, any more than you could simply wish away a bad cold."

"We shall do our best to support you. As will the rest of your family, all of whom will rejoice with each step you take towards health," Fitzwilliam added.

Looking less downtrodden than Darcy recalled seeing her in over two years, Georgiana smiled—genuinely smiled!—at him and Fitzwilliam. With a little more discussion, they decided to remain at Pemberley to enjoy more of the summer before travelling to town in about a month. Fitzwilliam would keep them company for as long as he was able, though he could be absent from his military duties only so long.

"I recall you saying the Reeds would visit us at the end of August," Georgiana said, "but now we wish to return to town in early September. Do you think Rebecca might be able to come sooner, either with or without her parents? That would be agreeable, do you not think? Perhaps Lord and Lady Romsley and Bramwell would also like to visit."

"I think it is a wonderful idea. I shall write to Mr Reed today and do my best to arrange it. As for Bramwell, if we tell him that Rebecca will be here, he will certainly come," Darcy said.

Fitzwilliam turned a puzzled expression on him, which Darcy held with a steady gaze. It took perhaps half a minute until Fitzwilliam hit himself on the forehead with the palm of his hand.

"My brother is in love with Rebecca Reed? You hinted as much in town. My mother did too, come to think of it. Does she return his regard? Good Lord. Can you imagine what Lady Catherine will say of *that* match?"

Georgiana giggled, and the sound was like the finest music to Darcy's ears.

CHAPTER FORTY-THREE

After spending an agreeable fortnight in Scarborough, Jane, Bingley, and Elizabeth returned to Hertfordshire in early September. Bingley might have liked to remain in Yorkshire longer, but Mr and Mrs Bennet's pleas that they return were growing increasingly urgent, and they were all conscious of having to inform the family that they were removing to Larch Lane.

Upon entering the neighbourhood, they first went to Netherfield Park, where Elizabeth would remain. That same afternoon, the three of them journeyed to Longbourn to take dinner. Mrs Bennet fussed over Jane, but when she at last addressed her second daughter, Elizabeth knew she had been right to agree to stay with the Bingleys.

"I had hoped *someone* would take an interest in you. Did I not warn you those town gentlemen would not take kindly to you always acting as though you are cleverer than the rest of us? Mark my words, if you do not change your ways, you will end up a spinster." Mrs Bennet shook her head, seeming both sad and disappointed.

"All the better. She can remain at home and keep her old father company. One of our daughters must." Mr Bennet winked at Elizabeth. "I did just happen to notice, Lizzy, that no trunks were brought into the house."

"I insisted she stay with me." It was unlike Jane to speak up, especially when she knew what she said would displease someone. Doing so was a mark of her concern for Elizabeth.

Mr Bennet scowled but said nothing more.

Worse was to come several days later when Jane gently broke the news that Bingley had purchased an estate in Derbyshire and they would soon be removing to it—and that Elizabeth would live with them. Mrs Bennet spent two days in her room, claiming the announcement had caused a severe nervous fit. She spent several more constantly dabbing a handkerchief under her eyes and saying that Jane and Bingley had broken her heart. Mr Bennet accepted the news as well as could be expected, and Mary and Kitty had little response to it.

One morning soon after, Elizabeth sat with her father in his book-room. He observed her from behind his desk, his fingers steepled together, as he so often had over the years.

"Are you certain you wish to go north with Jane? You do not seem particularly pleased about it."

Elizabeth was taken aback that he had noticed her mood. "Do I not?" she said, attempting to suggest she felt *he* had said something outrageous rather than that *she* had betrayed her struggle to be cheerful.

It might help if I knew how Miss Darcy fared. Surely if Bingley had any news, he would tell me. She worried that if she enquired, he—and especially Jane—would think too much of it.

He shook his head. "I do not doubt that Jane wants you

with her, but you need not give in if you do not like the notion."

"I am grateful to her and Bingley, and I *do* want to live with them. It will be better for me, Papa. I know you might not like to hear that, and I shall miss you, but I shall be happier at Larch Lane than I could be here," Elizabeth insisted.

"Hmm. Next you will remind me that you are of age and do not need my permission." He took a sip from a cup of tea. "Well, you are old enough to know what suits you best. I trust you appreciate that I have *not* asked if there is a gentleman behind your present mood, which no matter what you say, is not at all as lively as I would expect."

Rather than say more, Elizabeth stood, kissed his cheek, and left him to his books.

Correspondence occupied a fair amount of Elizabeth's time during the first week she was in Meryton. She received and wrote letters to her aunt Gardiner, Charlotte Collins, and various friends. The one she found most heartening was from Rebecca Reed. As she had promised before leaving town, Elizabeth had provided Rebecca with an account of her connexion to Mr Darcy, though she left out many details and softened how and why it had ended, simply saying they had a disagreement. She had also mentioned the sojourn at Pemberley, but only in passing.

September 4, 1813

My dear Elizabeth,

I hope that you and your family are well and your journey from Yorkshire to Hertfordshire was as easy as possible. I am very happy for your sister and brother-in-law that they found a new estate. Derbyshire is a wonderful county, and I hope you and they will be very happy there.

Thank you again for telling me of your past with my cousin Darcy. I find myself often thinking of it and you, especially after you said you were at Pemberley last month. I can only imagine it was very difficult and awkward for both of you. I shall not burden you with my wishes for the two of you. Only know that I am very sorry you could not reconcile your differences.

As I mentioned in my last letter, my parents and I went to Pemberley to see my cousins. Viscount Bramwell and the earl and countess visited at the same time, and Colonel Fitzwilliam was there for several days as well. I was pleased to spend more time with Georgiana. She appeared more willing to speak and partake in conversations and activities. It might simply be because she was at home and surrounded by her family again. She and I spoke of you one morning. My cousin has a high opinion of you, which shows she is wise beyond her tender years.

While at Pemberley, the viscount, whom I suppose I may now address as Bramwell, proposed. We went for a walk in the gardens after dinner, and whether he meant it to be or not, it was very romantic. The light was hazy, the air was full of floral scents, and some species of bird was singing in the distance. He immediately spoke to my father, and we were all awake into the early hours of the next morning celebrating. Apparently, the earl and countess already knew he planned to ask me to marry him, and I am pleased to announce that they show every sign of being happy with their son's choice. I suppose it helps that Lord Romsley and my father are friends.

We have returned to London. If Mr and Mrs Bingley do not intend to spend time here before removing to Derbyshire, I hope you will come and stay with me. I am sure between your brother and my father we could make arrangements for you to safely travel to them later in the autumn.

Your friend,
Rebecca Reed

Elizabeth was delighted to hear of the engagement, but what most affected her was the news of Miss Darcy. It took several minutes for her head to stop swimming, such was her relief. It sounded as though the young lady had made a genuine improvement, and Elizabeth fervently hoped it was so. It would ease the heavy weight on Mr Darcy's shoulders, and she would dearly love to see him be happy. She would greatly value knowing more about Miss Darcy's present circumstances. Was Rebecca correct that her health was improving? What had led to such a change?

Perhaps I shall obtain more news from Bingley. He and Mr Darcy must write to each other, and they will see each other in town. At least, she hoped that was the case. She hated that their friendship had been damaged, despite what she and Jane had done to protect it.

Another notable letter she received was from Lydia. While in Scarborough, Elizabeth had written to her sister. She was determined to view her with more compassion than she had since her elopement. They would never be as close as she and Jane were, but still Elizabeth might be a better friend to her than she had been in the past. In her missive, she had expressed a wish to exchange letters—something they had never done. She did not mention her concerns or explain her changing views, knowing Lydia would overlook them.

> *I would like to know how you are. You can tell me anything, whether you think I shall like or approve of it or not. I think it is valuable to have someone in whom we can confide without fear of what they will say in response. I do not know whether you have someone such as this already in your life. Kitty is the only possibility I can think of, but whether she is or not, I am offering to be that person for you.*

She had not expected to receive a reply for weeks, possibly months, if one ever arrived, yet a letter from Lydia was delivered soon after Elizabeth's return to Meryton. It was full of glee and assurances that she had never been happier than she was since marrying her 'dear Wickham'.

> *I do not know why you were so serious. Lord, it is almost as though you expected me to tell you that he beats me. I would never let any man treat me so infamously, and Wickham would never behave in such a manner. Being a wife is the most wonderful thing in the world, and if you were as quick-witted as Papa always says you are, you would find a husband as soon as you might. I know you envy me mine, but I am sure you can find another man who will suit you almost as well as he does me.*

There was a certain falseness to Lydia's claims of being pleased with her life, but Elizabeth could not compel her to be franker. At least half of the letter was filled with Lydia's complaints about being short of funds. Elizabeth chose to overlook that part of it; she had no intention of sending Lydia money, being certain Mr Wickham would pocket it all, then gamble or drink it away.

The least expected and most satisfying letter arrived a few days later. As Bingley was distributing that day's post, he handed Elizabeth a missive in an unknown hand. Her curiosity excited, she immediately broke the seal and sought the name of the sender.

Georgiana Darcy

Elizabeth stared at the two words for a long while, Bingley and Jane's voices fading as she seemed to slip to a different place where the loudest sound was the blood rushing through her body. Why would Miss Darcy write to her? Quickly, she excused herself and went to her apartment where she could read in peace. She sat in a wide armchair, her legs tucked beside her, and with some trepidation, began.

September 8, 1813

Dear Miss Bennet,

I hope you are well, and I beg you will forgive me for writing to you in such a fashion. My aunt encouraged me to do so. She said that, from what she had heard of you, you would forgive the presumption. I wished to convey certain messages, and as I do not know when we might next meet, this seemed like the best means of saying what I wished. I do not know whether I would be brave enough to express it all were we sitting together; thus a letter is more practical as well.

First, I must offer you an apology. I know the last day we were together was unpleasant for you, and indeed I made those you passed at Pemberley last month difficult. I am very sorry for my behaviour. Regarding Buxton, I am extremely grateful that you were there when I most needed a friend.

As you can see from the direction, we are now in town. My brother and I remained at Pemberley until four days ago. You may have learnt already that my cousins—the Reeds—came to visit us, as did Lord and Lady Romsley and Bramwell. Having them all there made the house so much livelier. For the first time in years, I liked being amongst them. After my stupid decision to run away from those who love and care for me, everything changed. I was very glad to see my relations, especially Rebecca. It provided us with an opportunity to grow closer—enough that I believe she would call me a friend. It was amusing and heartening to see her and Bramwell together, especially to see him in love. I am very happy for them. I am not sure I would have been able to enjoy it two or three months ago—their visit or the celebration that came with their engagement, about which she told me she would write to you. She told me how much she enjoyed meeting you last winter and that you had become good friends. I was not surprised by that. I, who can appreciate your worth in a way I imagine few others can, know that she is fortunate to have gained your friendship.

I have rambled long enough. The true reason for disturbing you with my letter is to thank you. I do not know exactly what it was you said to me that day, but your words have helped me more than I can express. Long ago, my brother told me what a sympathetic lady you are, and that is what I found in you during that horrible morning when I was in desperate need of help.

Since my silly, ill-planned escapade, there has been a great deal of talking—with my brother, cousin, Mrs Annesley, and my aunt and uncle. I find it all uncomfortable, but I am determined to continue it. I know it is necessary if I am to grow stronger. Beyond that, my brother arranged for a new doctor to come to Pemberley. He is a young man, not yet thirty, and I liked him. I cannot explain why exactly, but his manner was reassuring, more so than the older gentlemen we have consulted. He prescribed more exercise, especially in the open air, and certain changes to my diet. I do not know whether they are making a difference, but I suppose they cannot hurt and are far less displeasing than the various powders and elixirs thrust upon me by others over the last two years. I am following his instructions carefully, and I do feel more myself. I know I have a long road ahead of me, but for the first time since Ramsgate, I am hopeful. I tell you all of this so that you know I am truly trying to be well again.

Miss Bennet, I owe you a debt I can never repay. Your goodness to me cannot be praised enough, especially when I have treated you so poorly this past year. I was lost the day you found me at the inn, in more than one way, but with your assistance, I believe I have been set upon the correct path towards recovery. I will only add, God bless you.

Georgiana Darcy

"Well, the Darcys are certainly superior letter writers," Elizabeth quipped, although no one was nearby to hear her.

Her hands trembled as she folded the paper. Doing so was pointless; she would read and reread it many times in the coming days, just as she had the one Mr Darcy gave her in Kent. Was she destined to have her life altered by letters from that family? How many more times would it happen?

"I do not know why, but her letter *has* changed me," Elizabeth whispered. She wiped her cheek, only vaguely acknowledging the moisture she felt.

Elizabeth felt set free. *That* is what had changed after reading just a few paragraphs.

It was over. Truths had been revealed—Miss Darcy's regarding what happened with Mr Wickham and Elizabeth's in how she had harboured anger and disappointment rather than compassion for Mr Darcy and her own sister. *I pray Miss Darcy's dark cloud truly is dissipating. I have the strong sense that it is, and with it, so is the hold the Darcys had on me, and have had since Mr Darcy and I met two years ago.*

With that thought, she buried her face in her hands, Miss Darcy's letter still clutched in one, and began to cry. She did not know whether it was from relief or sorrow.

CHAPTER FORTY-FOUR

Darcy could not decide whether he was glad to be in town again. On the whole, he thought not. It had the benefit of allowing him to see friends and be closer to his family, who were all in London, and it allowed Georgiana greater access to masters, which was reassuring after her disinterest over the past two years. On the less beneficial side, he might see Elizabeth. He longed to—he would *always* want to be near her—but it was also painful because he could not be with her. At present, she remained in Hertfordshire, but from what he had learnt from Rebecca and the one letter he had received from Bingley since their parting in Derbyshire, she would likely spend some weeks in town that autumn. It was his fate to love her for as long as he lived. Surely, if it were possible for his sentiments to fade, they would have during the months—years—of knowing he could not have her as his wife. But he expected her to move on with her life. He wanted her to be happy, and he had no reason to suppose Robert Grey had lost interest in her; thus, if he saw

Elizabeth in town, he must also be prepared to see Mr Grey chasing after her.

Sitting alone in his study, several important letters of business neatly piled on his desk, Darcy pressed his eyes closed and attempted to force the morose thoughts aside.

I ought to remind myself of what adds pleasure to my life—Georgiana, most of all. There was no denying that her health *was* improving. The relief he, Fitzwilliam, and others in their family felt was immeasurable. She was by no means fully recovered, but if she continued to show so much progress over the next few months, he believed she might be one day. At the very least, she would gain greater control of her emotions, and all of them—herself included—would not need to be so worried for her.

He selected the letter from his steward to review and was writing a response when the butler announced a caller: Bingley. Darcy did his best to hide his surprise; he had not known Bingley was in town or that he would call. He did not know whether Bingley still considered them friends—if his understandable anger when they last spoke at Pemberley had lessened with time. When they were in Buxton, Bingley had apologised, which was completely unnecessary. It had given Darcy hope that he had not lost their connexion. He would know for certain in a few minutes, which made him nervous. He told the butler he would join Bingley in the drawing room and asked for a tray of refreshments to be sent there.

The gentlemen greeted each other, and Bingley said, "I had to come to town for a couple of days to see to some minor business. I shall not weary you with the details. I also wanted to see my sisters in person and remind them to behave properly when Jane, Lizzy, and I return later this month."

"They are not with you." Was it disappointment or relief

Darcy felt? His words were not a question, but Bingley treated them as such and shook his head.

"We shall be leaving Meryton soon enough, and once we do, who knows when we shall visit? Jane is going to have a child in the late winter or early spring."

"Bingley, that is wonderful news," Darcy exclaimed. "I congratulate you both."

Bingley gave an awkward chuckle and blushed. "We have not told that many people. My sisters do not yet know. I only arrived yesterday, and thus far, they have not wanted to listen to anything I have to say. Rather, they wished to share their many, many complaints, chiefly that I would dare to purchase an estate without consulting them, let alone decide on renovations. It will not be *their* home, so I do not know why they believe they should have a say in it." He waved a hand as though dismissing the topic. "That does not matter. I knew you were in town and thought I would come to see you." He paused. "Miss Darcy's letter. Lizzy told us about it. Not *what* she wrote, just that you were in town and your sister was doing well. Is she?"

"I am happy to say that Georgiana is doing very well." Darcy knew Georgiana had written to Elizabeth. She had asked his opinion on the wisdom of doing so, especially whether Elizabeth would be affronted, and he had assured her that she would not be. Like Bingley, he did not know what his sister had written. She had only told him that she wanted to thank Elizabeth for her kindness.

Bingley let out a gush of air. "That is the best news I have heard in a very long time. Apart from becoming a father, that is." He laughed. "And you, Darcy, are you well? I spoke harshly to you before leaving Pemberley, and I regret it, but at the time

—well, no need to go over all that again. I admit that a part of me is still vexed, but with Jane's assistance—I truly have the most excellent wife—and after that last morning, I understand that you were in a very difficult situation. What I want most of all is for my wife and Lizzy to be happy. You too. That is why I am here."

"You were right to be angry, and I am sorry I did not confide in you about Georgiana or Elizabeth."

He was stopped from saying more when the refreshments arrived, and as Bingley partook of a glass of lemonade and a piece of chicken pie, they chatted about nothing in particular.

"I ought not to stay much longer. We have not yet decided exactly what day we shall leave Netherfield, but I shall let you know. Jane is looking forward to seeing some of the ladies she met earlier this year. If you and Miss Darcy do not object, I am sure she would like to call on her," Bingley said.

Darcy noticed that Bingley did not mention Elizabeth calling on Georgiana. He had not expected it; after all, his sister had made it plain she did not appreciate Elizabeth's company, and apparently, nothing in her letter suggested she had changed her mind.

"I shall ask her, but I hope she agrees. I would be glad to see Mrs Bingley and her become friends. Please give her my thanks for her consideration, regardless of what Georgiana decides."

Bingley made a noise of agreement, and there was a brief silence before he continued. "Lizzy is looking forward to returning to town too. She will live with Jane and me. But you already know that." He scratched the back of his neck and averted his eyes.

"Say what you will."

With a single curt nod, Bingley said, "Lizzy is really why I came this morning, though I did want to see you. You must remember me speaking of us going to see my friend Grey and—I am sorry if this pains you, Darcy—hinting about him and my sister-in-law."

An anvil settled in his stomach. He could not respond.

"Soon after everything that happened in Derbyshire, Lizzy asked me to tell Grey that she did not anticipate marrying for the next year, if not longer. She might be reconsidering, especially after Miss Darcy's letter. It is something she said to Jane. Grey has not given up hope. He has become attached to her—they have always had a great deal to say to each other, lots of interests in common and what have you—and he says she is exactly the sort of woman he wants as his wife. He would be good to her. Jane believes that once they become reacquainted, and if Grey treats her with patience and holds off proposing for even a few months, Lizzy will accept him."

Darcy felt as cold as if he had just taken a long walk through the Derbyshire winter weather. "I see."

"*Do* you?" Bingley asked.

There was a certain emphasis in his voice that made Darcy pay attention. He opened his mouth to ask what his friend meant, but just at that moment, a knock interrupted their solitude. It was Georgiana, who opened the door enough to peek around it.

"May I come in, or do I disturb you?" she said.

Bingley was already on his feet and approaching her. "Miss Darcy, how good it is to see you! Please do join us."

Darcy stood and watched as they exchanged pleasantries. Georgiana coming downstairs to greet Bingley was a sign of how much progress she had made, and it gladdened his heart, although it still remained heavy. In a few minutes, the mantel clock chimed the hour.

"Is that really the time?" Bingley exclaimed and pulled out his fob watch to consult it. "I am afraid I must go. I have an appointment at the bank. I shall see you both before long."

Darcy thanked him for coming, Georgiana offered him a shy smile, and Bingley departed.

"Brother?"

Darcy shook himself out of his stupor and looked into his sister's face. She was beside him, which she had not been when Bingley left. From the tone of her voice, she had not only moved across the room, she had also previously spoken to him.

"I am sorry, dearest. What did you say?"

Her brow furrowed, and she sat on the sofa, watching him carefully as he took a place next to her.

"I said I did not know Mr Bingley was in town. Do you mind that I intruded?"

"Not at all." He lifted her hand to his lips for a kiss. "I also did not know he was here. He came alone, but all three of them will return within the next fortnight, I imagine. He mentioned that Mrs Bingley would like to call on you, if you will allow it."

"Oh." She sat a little straighter, and her eyes met his. "That is very kind of her. I-I would like it. Did…did he mention Miss Bennet?"

He certainly did, Darcy thought, but it was not in the way he suspected Georgiana meant.

"I understand she might not like to see me," Georgiana said when he failed to speak.

"I do not think it is that. She would consider *your* feelings, not her own wishes." He squeezed her hand.

Georgiana nodded, and they were silent for a long moment. Darcy's thoughts remained heavy, and it was difficult to form words. It was odd that his sister was the more willing or able of them to talk when it had been the other way round for so long.

"Did Mr Bingley have news of her that upset you?"

He ran both hands over his face and through his hair. "In a manner of speaking, though it is no more than I expected. You recall he hinted about a growing attachment between her and Mr Grey?"

Georgiana's features seemed to crumple, as though she had been told something distressing. She nodded and kept her eyes on his, silently asking him to continue.

"Nothing has been settled between them, and it might not be for several months, but Bingley clearly feels it is inevitable."

"I do not understand. As you said, he *did* speak of it at Pemberley. Why would he tell you again? Did he want to warn you away from her?" She sounded incredulous, which *he* did not understand, unless it was that she could not imagine Bingley behaving in such a way.

He thought for a moment. "Actually, I am not sure what he really wanted to say. He talked of her accepting him, and I said I understood. He asked if I did, and I was just about to enquire what he meant when you knocked at the door."

Georgiana requested that he go over it all once again; she listened intently as he attempted to recall exactly what Bingley had said, after which she exclaimed, "Oh, Brother, do you not see? He was hinting that she is not in love with Mr Grey and that if you are at all interested in pursuing her, you had best get to it."

A sudden tightness in his chest made him swallow and look away. He felt Georgiana's soft touch on his arm.

"I would not object if you did," she said.

His gaze flew to meet hers. "Georgiana—"

"I would not," she repeated. "I-I-I know you did not propose to her because of me, and I appreciate it, but I am doing much better now. I see that my fears were unfounded. Ridiculous really." She shook her head when he opened his mouth to speak. "They were. You told me so, but I did not want to hear it. I know Miss Bennet would never expect me to see Mr Wickham or even Mrs Wickham. I *like* Miss Bennet. I did when we first met, and nothing has happened to change that. If anything, I think more highly of her now than I did then. How could I not, after how kind she was to me in Buxton—even before, when she was at Pemberley? There is no reason for you not to marry her, not for my sake, not any longer."

Darcy sighed. "I am afraid it is too late. I was not entirely honest with her last autumn. She was understandably angry and hurt, and when I at last did tell her everything, it made little difference."

"You believe she cannot forgive you, that she would not accept you, even if she was assured I would be pleased with your marriage?"

He shrugged. He had given up dreaming of a reconciliation with Elizabeth the day he last saw her. The looks she had given him at the inn in Buxton had clearly communicated two things to him: she understood the struggles he had faced with Georgiana and pitied him, and, as far as she was concerned, their connexion was irrevocably at an end.

"Do you still love her?"

He made a noise that suggested the question was ridiculous and unnecessary.

"Then should you not go to her before it is too late and find out whether she still loves you and whether she can forgive you?"

Once again, Darcy regarded her. Slowly, she smiled and nodded, which he took as her silent assurance that she was being truthful and *not* acting simply to please him. His heart raced. He gathered her into his arms and began to make plans for a trip to Meryton.

CHAPTER FORTY-FIVE

Elizabeth sat on an iron bench on the terrace. She had been in Hertfordshire for two weeks, and she was already anticipating leaving. It felt odd and awkward being in her old neighbourhood.

A confined society. Mr Darcy had once used that phrase, or near enough. Her mother had taken it as an insult, but Elizabeth had understood what he meant then, and she understood it even better at present. She continued to care for the people she had known for years, such as the Lucases and Gouldings, and she valued her family dearly. Seeing them again was the best part of being here. Walking the familiar paths was refreshing and made her wistful in a way, but her life was no longer here. She had been desperately unhappy when she was last at Longbourn, and returning brought back those old feelings. So much had happened to her during the months of her absence. It meant it was difficult to feel a connexion to what was taking place around her, to take an interest in the same topics that had occupied people for years.

I shall have a new home soon enough.

At present, that would be Larch Lane, but for how long? Would Mr Grey remain patient and steadfast, as he had suggested in his letters to Bingley? In six months or a year, would her feelings for him be strong enough—and those for Mr Darcy diminished enough—that she would welcome his proposal? At present, it did not seem possible that such a day would ever come to pass, but she had ceased trying to guess what her future would be like.

Her thoughts were often with Mr Darcy. Bingley had received only one letter from him since they last saw each other in Buxton, and it was largely filled with his thanks. She supposed she continued to dwell on him because, as much as Miss Darcy's letter suggested *she* was doing well, Elizabeth did not know how *he* fared.

Perhaps Bingley will see him while he is in town. Bingley had claimed a need to go to London for reasons that could not wait until the end of the month. Unless his plans had changed, he would be home later that day. Elizabeth hoped he would voluntarily tell her about Mr Darcy; she did not want to betray herself by asking after him.

Betray myself? She supposed she was hiding her feelings from him and Jane in a way. But how could she admit how often she felt Mr Darcy beside her, his large, solid form warming her more slender frame with his presence. His shadow always there because, while reading Miss Darcy's letter had freed her, she had discovered she was wrong about all the ties between her and the Darcys being severed. There was one bond that remained—that of her affection for him. Her stubborn heart would not give it up.

What she needed was exercise—a long walk, during which she immersed herself in the sights, scents, and sounds of the countryside, would help her banish Mr Darcy from her mind, at least for the remainder of the day. She left her book on the bench and strode away from the house. She had no particular destination in mind.

Perhaps an hour later, she saw a figure walking towards her on the path, but it was too far away to recognise. Elizabeth's first inclination was to turn around; she had no interest in encountering anyone. As she had hoped, the pleasant scenery was having a soothing effect on her, and she did not want it disrupted.

Just as she was about to continue her stroll, her feet already partly pointed in the opposite direction to the one in which she had been walking, something stopped her. She stared into the distance, not truly seeing anything. Her heart began to beat more quickly, and her mouth went dry.

It was Mr Darcy. She was convinced of it, although she could not explain why. Slowly, oh so slowly, she turned to look at him and watched as he continued his steady approach.

She said nothing as he drew close and stopped about a yard away from her. There was a long moment of silence as they looked at each other, his eyes appearing to take in every inch of her. She wore a pink day dress and straw bonnet, neither of which were special in any way, yet the soft, warm expression on his face—one she had seen many times—made it seem as though he found her beautiful despite the plainness of her attire.

"I have been hoping to come across you. Your sister told me where I might find you," he said.

Elizabeth swallowed against the continued dryness of her mouth. "Why are you here?"

"I wanted, *needed* to talk to you. I…" He held out a hand but let it fall again before actually touching her. "I am hoping and praying that I can earn your forgiveness and love again. I am willing to beg if that is what it takes. Elizabeth, I have loved you for so long, longed for you more than I can ever express, and at the risk of sounding selfish—and I admit I am a selfish being—I have needed you with me. You cannot imagine how much. The entire situation with my sister would have been immeasurably easier for me to bear if I had you beside me to comfort me, talk to me, help me understand her and what I should do. Most of all, I have wanted you with me simply because I adore you, and I feel happier and more complete when we are together."

Tears pooled in Elizabeth's eyes, and she blinked to clear them. His words were like a beautiful song to her soul, but they did not erase the barriers that stood between them. "It was the exact opposite of selfish when you gave me up to care for your sister."

He shook his head. "You have no notion how difficult that was—how I debated and argued with Fitzwilliam about it. He said I was trying too hard to convince Georgiana that she would be helped, not hurt, by having you as her sister—that you would enrich our lives. When I saw what she was doing to herself, I could no longer tell myself there was a way I could both help her and marry you."

"Her behaviour frightened you. I understand that so much better after seeing her in Buxton, and I know you have witnessed far worse than I did that day. Why are you here, saying these things to me now?"

"Is it too late? My love for you and my hopes and dreams have never wavered. I shall do whatever I must to earn your forgiveness if you believe you could give me the honour of your love once again."

"Why now?" she repeated. She wanted to shake him, as

though that would make him finally answer the question. She might have attempted it if she was not afraid that touching him would cause her to lose all reason and cling to him, promising him anything he liked. "Miss Darcy wrote to me, and I am thrilled she feels that her health is improving, but nothing she said led me to believe the situation had materially altered. Does she know you have come?"

He nodded and took a small step closer. "Bingley called on me two days ago. I know Robert Grey has shown a strong preference for you, and Bingley believes you would accept him. As much as it pains me to say it, he would be a good husband to you, perhaps even love you as you deserve, but…but *I* love you, with everything I am and will ever be, and I could not step aside without making one final attempt."

"Your sister—" Elizabeth interjected, only to be interrupted by Mr Darcy.

"I told Georgiana what Bingley said. *She* was the one who helped me understand his true purpose—or what we assume it was. We believe he wanted me to know that I have very little time left to pursue you, to attempt to convince you to forgive and marry *me*, not Grey. I had been telling myself that I have made too many mistakes, caused you too much heartache, but…have I? Georgiana gave me reason to hope that it was not too late, and she immediately told me that I should come to you. She admires you, has remembered how much she liked you last summer and anticipated having you as a sister, knows you would never cause her harm, and"—he took a deep breath, almost as though he could not believe what he was about to say—"she has no objections. None of my family do. I spoke to all of them, to inform them of my intentions and insist they welcome you as you deserve if I succeeded in convincing you to have me. Of course, Lady Catherine still might not, but her opinion does not matter."

Even as tears steadily fell down her cheeks, Elizabeth felt a tiny bubble of amusement rise up her body and emerge as a chuckle. She was dizzy with the mix of emotions coursing through her and with the difficulty of maintaining her refusal to believe Mr Darcy was truly saying they could have the future they had both dreamt of, one in which they were husband and wife and lived happily ever after. "You do realise it is ridiculous that our future is dependent on the permission of your seventeen-year-old sister?"

Mr Darcy gave a slight groan. "I have badly mishandled this entire affair. I ought to have been open with you from the beginning."

"And last year, at Jane and Bingley's wedding, I ought to have given you a chance to fully explain. I know I did not—just as I interrupted you now."

He smiled at her slight tease. "I was going to tell you then about Georgiana, but I was so…I cannot describe it. Perplexed, frantic, confused, despondent. The weeks we were apart were dreadful, full of anxiety for my sister and quarrels with my family, until I felt I had no other choice but to agree with them that you and I had no future together. I believe part of me hoped that if you knew the entire ugly story, you would see a way to resolve it even though I could not. Yet, I also did not want you to know. It is such a horrible event to recall. At the very least, had I told you, you would have understood why I was acting as I was. It would not have been right or fair to you, but at one time, I contemplated asking you to agree to a secret engagement until Georgiana was stronger and I could convince her Wickham would never be part of our lives. Can you forgive me, dearest, loveliest Elizabeth? Can you love me again?"

Elizabeth contemplated him for a second, seeing the anxiety in his dark eyes and the way his chest rose and fell in quick succession. She did not doubt what her response would be; her heart had always known the truth, as much as she had fought against it. Her inability to speak at once was because, at last, she was able to drink in the sight of him. This—*this*—was true freedom, not that emotion she had felt after reading Miss Darcy's letter. In a sense, perhaps the bonds between them *had* been broken, as she had then thought, but only so that they could be re-formed into something stronger and longer lasting.

She stepped forwards and took his hand in hers. It was still summer, and the day was warm. Neither of them wore gloves, and when their skin touched, she felt a jolt of something powerful pass through her, something that promised that everything was finally as it was meant to be. She raised his hand to her mouth and kissed it. He whispered her name.

"I have spent the past ten or eleven months maintaining a barrier around my heart when it comes to you. It is going to take some time to fully dismantle it," she said softly.

"But?"

Her cheeks heated. "But that barrier would not be needed if I no longer loved you as much as I did this time last year, if not even more."

Before she had time to know what was going to happen, she was being kissed and then apologised to.

"I ought not to have done that," he said.

"Silly man." Taking hold of his lapels, Elizabeth pulled him to her for another kiss. She broke it in less than a minute and, meeting his gaze, sternly said, "This does *not* mean we have nothing left to speak of. After everything—"

"But you *will* marry me?"

"Yes, of course I will. Oh yes, I will!"

Elizabeth saw that his eyes were red, either from the effort of not crying or as a prelude to doing just that. He seemed incapable of speech, and instead, he gathered her in his arms and held her tightly. She rested her head against his chest and whispered his name, at last feeling like all was right with the world.

CHAPTER FORTY-SIX

Walking back to the house with Elizabeth, their hands clasped together, Darcy learnt that Bingley had not yet returned from London but was expected later that day. They spoke further; however, they did not touch on any difficult subjects. For his part, it was enough to be with her and to know that she still loved him. It was a miracle, but she assured him he had understood her perfectly and that they would be married. Whether that was in a day or a year, she was his forevermore.

She said, "I cannot tell you how many times I have told myself to forget about what we had, that I had to put you into my past, only to realise my heart still belonged to you. After last month, I was certain I would be able to do it, but all it took was seeing you walk towards me to know I was mistaken once again."

He kissed her hand. "I often made similar vows. I did not try to convince myself that I did not love you, but rather that I was a fool to hold on to hope that our marriage would ever be possible."

Once at Netherfield, they sat with Mrs Bingley, who observed both of them carefully but asked no questions. She sat a little too stiffly until Elizabeth whispered something to her, then she grinned. As they drank lemonade and partook of a light meal, Mrs Bingley led them in an easy, friendly conversation.

Bingley arrived in the early afternoon and burst into the drawing room. He took in the three occupants, then strode in Darcy's direction.

"I am glad you are here!" He thrust out a hand, and when Darcy took it, he shook it vigorously. "I was delighted when the butler told me. I believe my response shocked him. Oh!"

He swung around to face his wife.

"My dear Jane, can you forgive me for not greeting you first? How inconsiderate I am! It is just that—"

"I understand," Mrs Bingley said, sounding and looking serene, as she usually did.

In her place, his Elizabeth would have made a joke at his expense. Darcy knew which approach he preferred. He met Elizabeth's eye, and they exchanged a smile that said more than words would have.

"And everything is as it should be?" Bingley looked between Elizabeth and him. "Everyone is…pleased?"

Elizabeth laughed, stood, and went to embrace her brother-in-law. "Yes, everything is exactly as it was always meant to be." Meeting Darcy's eye and then her sister's, she added, "For the remainder of today, I would like to simply enjoy the four of us being together. I cannot tell you how often I have imagined this—three of the people I care most for in the world and I doing nothing more than talking and being happy."

She reserved her largest smile for him, and for perhaps the twelfth time that day, Darcy was close to crying in relief and joy. She would be his wife, the Bingleys his brother and sister, their children would grow up together, Georgiana *would* be well, and all was right with his world.

Elizabeth did not sleep much that night. Her life had taken a drastic turn, one she genuinely had not foreseen happening, and, once again, she had to redraw what her future would be. For the first time in almost a year, she was overjoyed with the prospect. She was at liberty to love her Mr Darcy and anticipate their life together.

There were no more obstacles in their path. Or just about none. She could not forget his sister's fragility, and as much as she wanted to marry him as soon as it could be arranged, she needed to ensure nothing they did would pose a threat to Miss Darcy's well-being.

Her joy was compounded by Jane and Bingley's satisfaction with the situation. Elizabeth had found a private moment to speak to Jane and had a longer conversation with Bingley after dinner.

"I suppose you know I encouraged Darcy to come and see you. Did I do right?" Bingley had said.

"Yes, my darling brother, you most certainly did. Have you forgiven him for not telling you about our attachment and Miss Darcy's struggles?"

"Goodness, yes." Bingley had laughed. "I could hardly not be friends with him when you are going to marry him. I have an inkling you and Darcy belong together the same way Jane and I do. I may not have known you and Darcy loved each other until last month, but now I do, and when you told us of Miss Darcy's letter, it made me wonder whether perhaps the two people I most admire, apart from Jane, could find happiness together. Darcy deserves it, and you deserve a man who will love you as much as he does."

"I shall endeavour to be worthy of him, but I know that—as much effort as I put into it—I shall never deserve such a wonderful brother," Elizabeth had said, accompanying her statement with a hug.

Throughout the night, Elizabeth debated with herself what the following weeks and months should be like. Her situation with Mr Darcy was not easy, but she did not want to add more complications to it than were necessary. She supposed she felt a little bruised after everything that had happened, but her chief concern was Miss Darcy.

I want to know that she will not change her mind, ending with me facing the anxious countenances of her family, all of whom want me to disappear as a consequence.

That might be unfair to Miss Darcy, but everything she knew and had witnessed of her struggles left Elizabeth feeling unusually cautious. At the same time, she wanted to be Mrs Darcy and have the right to call Mr Darcy her husband, to enter Pemberley as his wife, and to—at long last—begin their lives together.

Before much longer, she devised a scheme she would suggest to him in the morning. Then, she spent the rest of the night dreaming of him, both when she was awake and when she finally drifted off to sleep.

As he had crawled into bed, Darcy had been certain sleep would be impossible. Yet, he slept very well and had sweet dreams of his future with Elizabeth all night. He supposed he had been over-exhausted after having spent the previous two days worrying about what he would say to her and having serious conversations with his family, especially Georgiana and Fitzwilliam. His sister had been even more resolved the day after their initial discussion.

"I have hoped for weeks that you and Miss Bennet might reconcile. Even when she was at Pemberley, I hated the thought that she might marry Mr Grey, because she was meant to marry you," she had said. "If there is anything I can do to assure her I would be glad to have her as my sister, I shall."

He and Fitzwilliam had spoken for above an hour, and he was more hopeful than ever that they would be friends again and find a way to overcome the disagreements of the past year.

Darcy was out of bed and sitting in a conspicuous spot early the following morning. The housekeeper had been kind enough to bring him tea, toast, and some fruit in the drawing room. He wanted to be where Elizabeth could easily find him.

Sure enough, she came down shortly after seven o'clock. The smile she gave him was almost enough to make him forget his gentlemanly manners. Instantly, the world was brighter. He leapt out of his chair, closed the distance between them, and drew both of her hands to his mouth to kiss. If he were not worried about being seen and creating gossip, he would have kissed her properly.

Her eyes danced with merriment. "Good morning," she said, still smiling.

"Good morning, my love. Did you sleep well?"

She did her best to suppress a yawn, then laughed. "I did not. I was too happy for sleep. But if you say you did sleep well, I promise I shall not take it as a sign that your sentiments are less fervent than mine."

She quickly finished the cup of tea he prepared for her and ate half a piece of toast then said, "Shall we go for a walk? It looks like the weather will be fine today."

It had been far too long since Darcy had the pleasure of a gentle stroll with Elizabeth, her arm wrapped around his—apart from the day before, when in truth he had been too disbelieving that she had forgiven him to fully appreciate it. He had struggled to accept he was not trapped in a fantasy while also drinking in each moment of the first truly joyful day he had experienced in longer than he could recall. This morning, he would have relished their walk if they talked of nothing other than the clear cerulean sky or the birds and other small animals they saw as they wandered aimlessly. But she had more to say than that, and he was not at all displeased by it.

After they had been walking for perhaps ten minutes, she said, "Since you are here and Bingley, Jane, and I are leaving Netherfield soon, you should speak to my father. I do not need his permission, being of age, but still, you should request it, and his blessing, of him. He might be surprised, but he will not say no."

She stopped walking, caressed his cheek, and gently kissed him. They broke apart just as it was on the cusp of becoming too passionate.

"I love you, Fitzwilliam Darcy, and nothing will bring me more joy than to be your wife."

Darcy rested his forehead against hers and closed his eyes for a brief moment before kissing her and saying, "I love you, Elizabeth Bennet, and nothing would make me happier than to be your husband."

With one more kiss, they resumed their walk.

"Now, I do have a condition. Or it might be more properly considered a related series of stipulations," she said.

He encouraged her to continue, knowing he would agree to whatever she had decided was necessary or appropriate.

"The most important one is that I believe we should delay actually getting married for a short while."

"You do?" If she felt it was necessary to wait, he would, though he would like to understand why.

"I do," she repeated. "While part of me would like nothing more than to march to the church this minute and demand the vicar marry us, I believe it would be wrong. I should spend more time with your sister. The more she becomes familiar with me, the easier she will be, and, truthfully, I shall worry less that she will…perhaps not change her opinion but be uncomfortable with me, and I do not wish that. It would make all three of us unhappy. There is the matter of your other relations, but that is not as significant. Except for Colonel Fitzwilliam, given how close he and Miss Darcy are."

"He feels terrible for how he acted. We had a long conversation two days ago, and he fully supports our marriage. He asked me to tell you that he intends to apologise when next you see each other. As for Lord and Lady Romsley, they will love you."

"I hope you are correct. I even believe that you are, but I shall be far more confident entering into my new life as your wife *after* we have an opportunity to know each other better. Besides, another couple will soon be married, and it is enough to have one wedding in a family at a time. I am very happy for Rebecca and Lord Bramwell."

"As am I. You do know that Bramwell already likes you, do you not?"

"I like him too, and I am delighted he will be my cousin. Do not tell him, but I am even more pleased that Rebecca will be."

"Oh, I certainly shall ensure he knows that you prefer Rebecca to him. Bramwell needs taking down a peg or two, though he is so enamoured of my cousin, he might simply agree with you and spend the following hour explaining all the reasons he admires her. He forgets sometimes that I have known her since she was an infant."

"Ah, but he is in love. I shall be offended if you do not send at least one person to sleep by sermonising on my finer qualities." They both chuckled, and she continued. "Does what I propose sound reasonable? I really would like to be married as soon as it can be arranged, but when I think of the situation rationally, waiting makes more sense."

"With some regret, I agree. It would give me great pleasure to take you to Pemberley this winter as my wife and to celebrate Christmas there as a family. But, yes, given the circumstances, it is better to wait."

Having settled this point, they spoke of other matters and made arrangements to partake of several amusements while they remained in town before returning to the manor.

CHAPTER FORTY-SEVEN

Jane had already agreed to Mrs Bennet's request that they go to Longbourn that afternoon; they would stay until after dinner. Bingley had sent a note before breakfast asking whether Darcy would also be welcome, and the response had been that he was. Elizabeth had suggested he speak to Mr Bennet as soon as possible and warned him that her father might scowl, look at Darcy as though he were mad, and demand to speak to her at once. She did not want her betrothed to be taken aback, and most of all, she did not want anything to mar how happy they were that day.

Soon enough, they were at Longbourn. After greeting her mother and sisters, Darcy surreptitiously left to seek out Mr Bennet. In less than ten minutes, he was whispering to Elizabeth that her father wanted to talk to her.

When she entered the book-room, she watched her father with arched eyebrows until he spoke.

"So, you wish to marry Mr Darcy. That was a surprise."

"If it makes you feel better about not knowing that he and I love each other, I truly did not expect there would ever be an occasion for us to have this conversation." Elizabeth sat in a worn armchair across the desk from Mr Bennet.

"Love, is it? I recall your young man mentioning the word, but to hear it from you as well... I suppose there is no need for me to ask whether you are certain you wish to have him as your husband?"

"No, Papa, there is no need at all. Mr Darcy and I have had a rather tumultuous history—why is not important—but our affection for each other has endured. I absolutely, completely, utterly know that marrying him is what I want and what will bring me the most satisfaction in my life." He opened his mouth to speak, but before he could, she held up a restraining finger. "Before you ask, the reasons we did not come to an agreement sooner have all been resolved. At first, it was because we misunderstood each other, and after that, I cannot tell you because it involves someone else."

"And you wish to protect their privacy?"

"I shall always protect them as best I can."

Her father made an expression that seemed to accept defeat and concession. "If you expect me to say that I am glad you and Jane will both be settled in Derbyshire, you are mistaken. When you have a moment, pity me. Now, dearest daughter, Mr Darcy mentioned you waiting until next spring to marry?"

Elizabeth confirmed that was their preference. "I prefer not to tell my mother and sisters today. I shall do so before we go to town. What do you think?"

He laughed. "Knowing how thrilled your mother will be to have another daughter married to a rich gentleman, you wish to postpone exposing him to her...excesses? I hope your young man is made of stronger stuff than that implies."

Elizabeth rolled her eyes. "She will wish to discuss nothing other than the wedding all day, and Mr Darcy and I have not had much opportunity to decide what we want. I would like to speak to him about it first. Then, I shall explain it all to my mother."

"Very well. I shall be from home tomorrow morning between the hours of eleven and one. Please do the deed then." Her father grinned and pushed himself to his feet, adding, "Well, as we have settled everything that needs to be discussed today, I suppose we ought to join the rest of the party. Your mother will come to drag me there by the ear if I do not do Bingley the honour of greeting him at once. You would think a man would have to be gone a week or more before I am required to treat his absence as notable, but there we have it."

Before they descended the stairs, her father patted her cheek. "You are a good girl, Lizzy, and I shall sorely miss you."

Elizabeth offered him a loving smile and wrapped her hand around his arm for the remainder of their short walk.

The day passed as those at Longbourn usually do—it was a little too loud and chaotic for anyone not accustomed to it, though fortunately, the only disagreeable moment was when Kitty wanted to know why Elizabeth was going to town with Jane again and *she* was not invited instead. Mr Bennet told her that he would not give his permission, even if Jane had asked, so there was no need to discuss it further. Mrs Bennet remarked that Elizabeth *needed* to go because she was "not getting any younger or prettier" and had to find a husband. It was all Elizabeth could do not to laugh, and from what she saw, Bingley fared little better; Jane looked aghast and Darcy stoic.

It was probably with that in mind that, as they drove back to Netherfield that evening, Bingley asked when Jane thought they would be prepared to depart for London. Jane looked from him to Darcy and lastly to Elizabeth, then said, "Would this Saturday suit?"

The remaining days in Meryton were busy. Elizabeth told her mother and sisters of her engagement and that she and Darcy would like the wedding to be in Derbyshire.

"We could not possibly be married without Jane and Bingley there, and you know Jane will not be able to travel for months after we remove to Larch Lane," Elizabeth had said to Mrs Bennet to ease her complaints. "You would not want me to delay marrying him until next summer, would you? Besides, it is a wonderful excuse to make Papa take you and Mary and Kitty to Derbyshire. You will all see Jane's new home and meet your grandchild."

Mrs Bennet reluctantly agreed after Elizabeth promised to write to her 'constantly' about the arrangements.

Upon arriving in town, Elizabeth found a note from Colonel Fitzwilliam requesting a private interview. If she accepted, he would call the next morning.

"I shall join you," Darcy said. He had accompanied them to Bingley's house and come in so that they could settle their plans for the following days. Presently, they were sitting together, Jane and Bingley having left them alone for a few minutes.

Elizabeth regarded him, her brow arched. "You will? I believe he wishes to speak to me, not you."

"And I would like to be present."

"Whereas I believe he and I would speak more freely if you were not." She held up a hand to stop him when he opened his mouth to respond. "He has not been pleasant to me for many months, and I understand you wish to protect me. I adore you for it, but it is not necessary."

He sighed, and she wrapped her arm around his and rested her head on his shoulder.

"This first meeting with the colonel since Buxton will be awkward, and I would like to have it done as soon as possible. He and I shall resolve our differences and, I hope, find a way to be friends again. If you are here, I shall be distracted. I would want to give all my attention to you, and I shall be minding my manners lest you think poorly of me rather than speaking as openly as I would like to your cousin. Then the business will be only half complete, and he and I shall have to meet *again* so that he can apologise."

"You are teasing me," Darcy said. Elizabeth laughed, and he added, "I have missed you doing it. I do worry about you seeing him."

"I know you do. Will it help if I promise to recount everything we say to each other, even if it makes me seem like a shrew?"

Their eyes met, and he smiled. "I suppose."

"Now, I beg of you, before Jane or Bingley interrupt us, kiss me!"

She did not have to ask him again.

Bingley insisted on greeting the colonel with Elizabeth. She supposed it was his way of reminding her visitor that she had family who would not allow her to be mistreated.

"I believe you wish to review your correspondence or read a book or something—anything—else?" Elizabeth said to him.

Her brother-in-law chuckled. "That is her way of telling me to go away. I shall be in my study."

She smiled at him as he left the room, then turned her gaze

to Colonel Fitzwilliam and stood still while waiting for him to speak. He cleared his throat.

"Miss Bennet, I owe you an apology, and I offer it to you without reservation. My behaviour has been unconscionable, and I am ashamed of it."

"Thank you," she said when he paused. "Why did you feel it was necessary—or appropriate? Was there something in my behaviour that concerned you? Did I give you reason to suppose I would attempt to convince Miss Darcy that she must tell her brother to marry me, or that I would trick him into it? Perhaps you thought I would deliberately ensnare him—"

"No, of course not," he interjected. He sighed. "May we sit?"

She nodded, and they took seats opposite each other.

"I liked you very much when we met in Kent. I still do," he said. "I…I do not know if I can tell you how distressing it has been to see Georgiana as distraught and self-destructive as she has been since Wickham. You must have witnessed some of it yourself in Buxton, perhaps at Pemberley."

"I did. After that last morning, I understood better than I had before what your family have had to contend with. Yet, it does not explain how I became the villain in your mind."

"I am afraid the answer will do me no favours," he admitted.

Elizabeth wanted to laugh with derision but did not, realising it would make their situation more difficult.

"Then again, I suspect your opinion of me is already rather low," he added. "Do you know that it was Lady Catherine who informed Georgiana that Darcy was planning to propose?" She nodded, and he continued. "You have met my aunt, and I assume you can imagine she made it seem as though your marriage would be the worst thing that ever happened to our family, and she would not have stopped regardless of any signs of distress Georgiana displayed. When I saw her, she was..." He closed his eyes and shook his head. "I cannot describe it. I was furious with my aunt and with Wickham, though that was nothing new. Neither of them was nearby to bear the weight of my wrath, and so I directed it at Darcy for daring to want to marry the woman he loves. He and I argued, and I am ashamed to say that, for a time, I allowed myself to think very poorly of him. All I cared about was that it eased Georgiana's agitation to tell her that Darcy would forget the notion of proposing to you.

"When I learnt that you were in town, I was worried. I knew Darcy still loved you. What if he proposed or attempted to cajole Georgiana into saying she would not mind if he did? I had thought that she was beginning to improve, but with you here, her well-being was threatened anew. That meant that I treated you with unwarranted suspicion and hostility. Bramwell is quick to tell me how stupid I have been. You and he might like to discuss it." He gave an awkward chuckle, to which she did not respond. "I have not known what to do to help her. I ought to say that nothing I or any of us have done has helped her. Promising her she would not face the prospect of having—excuse me for calling you this—Wickham's sister as her own seemed to calm her. When I discovered this, I clung to it excessively."

"Did you encourage her to fear my presence?" Elizabeth interjected.

"No, no!" He shook his head vigorously. "If I did, it was *not* my intention. I simply agreed with her that it was reasonable to ask Darcy to forget you and assured her that she did not need to see you if she did not want to. I am sure I also agreed with her that she might encounter Wickham if you and Darcy married, even if it was inadvertently."

She regarded him for a long moment. There was a great deal she had intended to say to him, some of which she decided might be better kept to herself. He seemed to be sincere, which was satisfying and gave her hope that they could learn to be friends again. "I acknowledge that you believe you were acting in Miss Darcy's best interests, and I accept your apology, Colonel. But I want you to understand how difficult you made my situation. I was already desperately unhappy and trying to find a way to set aside my feelings for Mr Darcy. I never did succeed, as you are aware. It was bad enough that we were separated. To that, I had to add knowing Miss Darcy hated seeing me, and you, whom I had liked, began to treat me as though—" She stopped, knowing there was no need to remind him of his past behaviour. "I was miserable and confused."

"I am very, very sorry. I wish I could go back and do many things differently, for you, Darcy, and Georgiana."

She nodded. "Let us say nothing more about it. This should be a time for happiness. I hope you view it as such."

"I do."

"Good. Tell me, honestly, how is your cousin? Mr Darcy claims she is much improved, and the letter she wrote to me suggests as much, but I worry they both exaggerate. What is her true opinion of our engagement? Does it make her anxious? Understand, I shall do whatever I can to ease her concerns, but I can only do that if I know what they are."

Colonel Fitzwilliam shook his head and let out a heavy breath. "I feel like such a fool for ever doubting that you would be an excellent sister to Georgiana. I have spoken to her daily, and I assure you, with no pretence whatsoever, that she is thrilled—or as near to that state as she is currently capable of being. What you did for her in Buxton has convinced her that your presence in her life will do her a great deal of good, and she is aware of how much her brother loves you. It is possible she will experience some…setbacks along the way, but she is determined to confront and conquer them, knowing she can rely on her family—which includes you—to assist her."

It was just what Elizabeth had longed to hear. She and the colonel spoke a little more about Miss Darcy, and soon after, he took his leave.

Darcy came to see her later that afternoon, and as promised, she told him everything that had passed between Colonel Fitzwilliam and herself.

"You need have no concern," she assured him. "Recall that your cousin and I were friendly with each other when we met in Kent. We are both desirous of regaining that ease, and so we shall."

CHAPTER FORTY-EIGHT

It had been two days since Elizabeth, the Bingleys, and Darcy returned to town. At present, Darcy was doing his best not to pace near the front door of his London house. He was as nervous awaiting Elizabeth's arrival that morning as he had been the day he took Georgiana to Lambton to meet her for the first time. She was coming with the express purpose of seeing his sister.

Georgiana was waiting in the green drawing room, refreshments already laid out. A part of him thought he should have stayed with his sister, but he did not want his own anxiety to affect her. While she said she was well and only a little worried about seeing Elizabeth for the first time since Derbyshire, he suspected she felt it more deeply than that.

At last, he heard a carriage pull to a stop and, peeking out of the window, saw that it was Bingley's. The butler opened the door as Darcy approached it, and he was out of the house in time to hand Elizabeth down. She gave him a smile he was beginning to recognise as one conveying her love and pleasure at being with him. He adored it as much as he did the smiles she gave him when she was in a teasing mood or those when she was amused; then there were the ones she wore when she was simply happy... In truth, he simply rejoiced whenever she smiled.

They greeted each other and stepped into the house. When her lovely eyes took in the entryway as she removed her hat, he said, "I forgot. You have not been here before, have you?"

"I have not. I have been anticipating this visit for that reason, in addition to seeing you and Miss Darcy. After all, it will be my home."

"Not soon enough," he whispered as he led the way to the drawing room.

"Patience, my love. I am certain we shall be rewarded for waiting."

The reward in this case would be commencing their marriage knowing all their family rejoiced with them.

When they entered the drawing room, Georgiana was standing by the sofa, her hands clasped in front of her and her head lowered. Elizabeth offered Darcy a reassuring smile—another in her repertoire of expressions he loved—and stepped towards his sister.

"Miss Darcy, I am very glad to see you again."

Georgiana glanced at her, and Darcy saw that her eyes were bright with tears. Alarm shot through him. "Georg—" he began.

Elizabeth quickly closed the distance between herself and his sister, saying, "My dear, there is no need for that."

She took Georgiana's hand, and they sat side-by-side on the sofa. Georgiana buried her head on Elizabeth's shoulder, and she wrapped an arm around his sister's back. Darcy stood close enough to hear Georgiana's muffled words.

"I am so embarrassed. I have been dreadful to you, and I *am* sorry, and you have been so kind to me always. I hope that in time you can forgive me."

"I already have, though in truth, I do not feel I am owed any apology. You have done only what you needed to in order to be well."

Georgiana gave a single sob, and Elizabeth murmured soothing sounds. Although Darcy was mostly concerned with the present, he saw before him proof of what an excellent, caring mother she would be to their children. In some ways, Georgiana *was* his child; his responsibility to her had been that of a parent since she was ten years old.

"I cannot tell you how glad I was to receive your letter," Elizabeth said. "I had thought of you often, many times each day, praying that you were beginning to feel stronger. It was such a relief to read that you were, and now, I have the great pleasure of seeing it with my own eyes."

Georgiana sat up, sniffed, and wiped her nose with a hastily retrieved handkerchief. "Despite me making a fool of myself as soon as I saw you?" She accompanied her words with a bashful chuckle.

Elizabeth gave her a teasing smile. "Yes, despite that. Shall we speak of something else? I would like to hear what you have been doing since arriving in town. Your brother mentioned you have a new music master. What have you been learning?"

The conversation became more comfortable the longer it proceeded, and Darcy could have kissed Elizabeth—not only because he very, very much enjoyed doing so but because his love for her grew the more he watched her draw out his sister and help her set aside her worries for a time. He was not stupid;

he knew that as wonderful as his Elizabeth was, she was not the cure to what ailed Georgiana, but he was absolutely convinced she was part of what his sister needed. Elizabeth was already demonstrating that she would fight for Georgiana, let her cry when she needed to, and hold her hand when she was most lost to melancholia, but she would also help to pull her away from her darker thoughts and remind her that she could be happy.

They drank tea and ate sweet tarts, then Darcy and Georgiana took Elizabeth on a leisurely tour of the house. Soon after that, Elizabeth announced that she should depart.

"Jane will be expecting me. Bingley's sisters and Mr Hurst are coming to dinner."

"Do they know you and my brother are engaged?" Georgiana asked.

"Bingley intends to tell them, though whether he has yet, I do not know," Darcy said. "There is no immediate need, given the wedding is not until spring."

"Is that for my sake?"

"That is part of it," Elizabeth told her. "I do not want you to feel as though everything is changing too quickly, and I shall ask you to promise that if it is, you will tell me or your brother or the colonel. There is also Jane to consider, with the removal to Larch Lane and her happy expectations. She will require my assistance, and naturally, I wish to give it."

Georgiana nodded. "Will you see Mr and Mrs Gardiner soon?" She addressed her question as much to Darcy as Elizabeth.

"I hope to see them both before long," Darcy said. "Why do you ask?"

Georgiana's cheeks turned light pink, and her tone was diffident when she admitted, "I liked them both very much when we met last summer. When it is convenient, I would be happy to see them again."

Elizabeth met his gaze, and he saw the same satisfaction in hers that he felt. She understood what a remarkable step this was for his sister. It was also Georgiana's way of recognising their connexion to the Gardiners.

"They would be most pleased to see you. We shall arrange something." Elizabeth briefly clasped Georgiana's hand.

His sister nodded and, after a polite farewell, left them alone.

At once, Darcy had both of Elizabeth's hands in his and was kissing her. She made a noise of pleasure, and he anticipated hearing a great many of them in the future.

"That went better than I expected it would," she said.

"Are you generally dissatisfied with the manner in which I kiss you?" He was not certain his attempt at teasing her would succeed, but fortunately, she laughed.

"That is *exactly* what I meant, my darling Darcy." She tugged on his hands until he bent over enough for her to kiss him.

"To be serious, I agree," he said afterwards. "Georgiana has been acting resolute and brave, for lack of another way to describe it, but I have not known how much is an act rather than what she truly feels."

"I think she is as hopeful as we are." Elizabeth caressed his cheek with the tips of her fingers. "I am very happy. Incredibly so." He opened his mouth to respond, but before he could, she laughed and continued. "To be clear, I meant to be here with you, not just that your sister is doing so well. Upon occasion, we are allowed to think of ourselves, be selfish, and set aside consideration of everyone else."

"Such as my cousin or the Hursts and Miss Bingley? I shall

be thinking of you, your sister, and Bingley this evening and hoping his family behaves themselves."

Elizabeth rolled her eyes. "Is it wrong that I am preparing myself for them to be disagreeable? But I shall leave my brother to manage them. I also intend *not* to think of seeing the earl and countess tomorrow."

"Are you nervous?"

"A little, and we are doing it again—speaking of other people when I would rather use the last minute we have together today to think only of us."

"Oh?" he said as he lowered his head towards hers once again.

Elizabeth was warmly welcomed by the earl and countess when she, Jane, and Bingley dined with them.

"Georgiana told us what you did for her. I thank God for guiding her to you that day," the countess said, embracing her.

"We all thank you," the earl added. "You may not know it, but our niece, nephew, and sons have been singing your praises, as has my future daughter-in-law."

"The day we met in the park, I had the impression you were a kind, sensible young lady. I wish I had begun to reconsider the situation then, but everything has turned out as it should, and my husband and I are very pleased for Darcy and Georgiana, and for you, of course." Lady Romsley took her hand and led her to a sofa, where she insisted Elizabeth sit next to her.

Jane was not forgotten in their greeting, and for the hours they were together, the Romsleys and Colonel Fitzwilliam asked many questions about the Bennets, Longbourn, and Larch Lane. Lord Bramwell had fewer enquiries, but he was happy to speak to Elizabeth of Rebecca and once said, "I am glad all that fuss is *finally* behind us."

Talk naturally turned to plans for the coming months.

"Georgiana and I shall return to Pemberley in early November," Darcy said. The doctor whose advice had proved so helpful to Miss Darcy would be in town at the end of October; he and the colonel wanted Miss Darcy to see him in person once again. Elizabeth had insisted he remain in London until everything was properly completed.

"And you, Mrs Bingley, when do you expect to depart?" Lady Romsley asked.

"Sooner than Mr and Miss Darcy but only by a week or two."

Elizabeth knew this was because her sister and Bingley were anxious to commence the task of making Larch Lane their home.

"Have you and my cousin discussed when you would like to marry?" Colonel Fitzwilliam asked Elizabeth.

"We do not have an exact date yet because it depends on when my family can make the journey to Derbyshire without worrying about winter weather. It will be in the early spring."

"You will marry from Larch Lane?" Bramwell asked.

Elizabeth's cheeks warmed slightly. Explaining why required sharing news she was uncertain whether her sister was prepared to announce yet.

Bingley rescued her. "Jane and I hope there will be an addition to the family in the late winter, and Lizzy and Darcy cannot possibly be married unless *I* am there to witness it!" He laughed.

There were the usual congratulations, which made Jane blush.

Lord Bramwell pointed at Darcy and gave a bark of laughter. "I shall be a married man before you are." He and Rebecca would marry in December. They would go to Romsley Hall soon after.

"As though that makes you my superior," Darcy muttered.

The countess expressed a hope that they would see the Bingleys and Elizabeth over Christmas at either Romsley Hall or Larch Lane, depending on Jane's health and her willingness to travel.

During the separation of the sexes after dinner, Elizabeth sat with Miss Darcy. She said, "We have months before the wedding, and you do not have to make a decision immediately, but if you are agreeable, I would like you to be my bridesmaid."

"Would you?" Miss Darcy stared at her, her blue eyes opened wide.

"I would. We shall be sisters. Mary and Kitty were Jane's bridesmaids, and they will understand why I have asked you instead of them. But, if you decide you would not like to do it, I shall understand. There will be other ways you can assist with planning the wedding. I do not anticipate it being very large. Your family, my parents, Mary, Kitty, Jane and Bingley, naturally, and your brother might have a few friends or other relations he wishes to invite." Elizabeth's words were awkward, but she wanted to make it clear that Lydia and Wickham would *not* be present. It ought not to be necessary, but she knew Miss Darcy was prone to think less rationally of matters that made her uneasy at times.

"Thank you," Miss Darcy said, her voice little above a whisper.

Elizabeth decided to avoid further serious topics and spoke of music and novels until the gentlemen joined them quarter of an hour later.

The next few weeks were a whirlwind of activity for Elizabeth. She and Rebecca met, and the Bingleys, Darcys, and Elizabeth saw the Gardiners several times.

After much shopping and many amusements, Jane, Bingley, and Elizabeth began the trip north in the third week of October. Everything at Larch Lane was proceeding well, and Elizabeth spent the next weeks assisting Jane with ensuring the inside of the house was how she wanted it, while Bingley took to his duties as the new owner with great enthusiasm.

The Darcys followed them to Derbyshire a fortnight later, and over the coming weeks, the residents of Larch Lane and Pemberley were often together. Miss Darcy even spent a week at Larch Lane *without* Darcy. Nothing convinced Elizabeth that Miss Darcy had no reservations about her brother's forthcoming marriage more than her calm—at times even happy—demeanour throughout that visit.

CHAPTER FORTY-NINE

Darcy and Georgiana spent Christmas at Larch Lane. Afterwards, the family from Romsley Hall, including a new viscountess, joined them. They were a merry bunch, and on New Year's Eve, they celebrated the end of 1813 and beginning of 1814 with some of the Bingleys' new neighbours, whom they had invited to an evening party.

The neighbours left in time to reach their homes before midnight, and Mrs Bingley immediately went to her chamber, saying she felt fatigued after the day. Bingley had escorted his wife upstairs with a promise to return shortly. Soon after, Georgiana said that she would follow Mrs Bingley's example.

"Good night, Georgiana. You did very well tonight, and I am confident the new year will be a wonderful one for all of us." Darcy kissed his sister on the top of her head and continued to watch her as she said a few words to those who had decided to remain in the drawing room.

The earl and countess also elected to retire, Lord Romsley saying, "We shall leave you foolish young people to stay up far too late for no greater reason than that, beginning tomorrow, we must all remember to write 1814 on our correspondence. I would much rather be warm and snug in my bed."

There was general laughter, and Lady Romsley said, "I do not disagree with you, but you do make yourself sound like an old dullard."

"Dullard?" he said, feigning offence.

Georgiana quietly laughed. "She is teasing you, Uncle."

That was obvious to all, including the earl, but he made a point of tucking Georgiana under his arm, thanking her, and requesting she explain how she had spotted his wife's cruel trick as he led both her and the countess out of the room.

Darcy smiled, his gaze remaining on the door. It had been an agreeable evening, and having met some of the Bingleys' neighbours, he was even more pleased for them than he had been previously. Larch Lane was an excellent estate, and despite having lived there a short time, Mrs Bingley—Jane—had done an excellent job making the house comfortable and attractive. Elizabeth had assisted her, and he anticipated her creating the same cosy atmosphere at Pemberley once she was its mistress.

"What has you so distracted, Darcy?" Fitzwilliam called from the sofa across from him.

"I would have said he was pining for Elizabeth, but she is sitting next to him," Bramwell said.

"Do you think he forgot?" Fitzwilliam asked, his tone and expression mock-serious.

Bramwell guffawed. "Possibly. He has always been a stupid—"

"Oh stop, both of you!" Rebecca cried.

"Thank you," both he and Elizabeth said at the same time.

"Rebecca, you always have been my favourite cousin, and

this confirms it." Darcy stood and held out a hand to Elizabeth. "Shall we take a walk?"

"Yes, please." Her hand in his, she too rose.

"Where do you intend to go at this time of night?" the colonel said.

"Anywhere away from you will do." Elizabeth smiled sweetly at Fitzwilliam.

To Darcy's great pleasure—and relief—not only had his friendship with his cousin been restored, so had Elizabeth's. It had been easier for Fitzwilliam and him to set aside their disagreement, but Elizabeth had been as determined to forgive him as he was to earn her forgiveness. Elizabeth had once told Darcy that she had two very good incentives to establish an easy affinity with Fitzwilliam. The first was Georgiana; she did not want her to worry that her beloved cousin and future sister-in-law were at odds. The second was Darcy himself. Elizabeth knew they had long been close friends, and she wanted him to have that connexion again.

Every day, it seemed that he found another reason to appreciate and adore her, another something he could point to and say, "*That* is why she is the only woman I could ever love."

His three cousins laughed at Elizabeth's tease, and Rebecca said, "Please do not let my brother-in-law and husband frighten you away with their horrendous manners." She turned to Bramwell. "At least let her marry him before you call him stupid. What if she believed you and cried off?"

"You are just afraid you would lose your friend, my love." Bramwell kissed her hand.

"Please take me away from them," Darcy said to Elizabeth.

"Very well." To Rebecca, she added, "We shall return soon." Elizabeth and he walked through the house, and she described the Bingleys' intention to begin a collection of art and books, to create a legacy for their children.

"I believe Bingley is taking his inspiration from Pemberley, although Jane rightly reminds him that hoarding books is a Bennet family trait as well. Jane may not be as much of a reader as I am, and I doubt Lydia will ever voluntarily pick up a book, but Mary takes great comfort in them, and my father tells me Kitty is growing to as well," Elizabeth said.

"Is she?" To Darcy, the second youngest Miss Bennet had always appeared rather empty-headed.

"She is. To his credit, my father has been insisting she learn to be more serious, and it appears to be working."

Another time, he would ask whether she would like to invite either of her unmarried sisters to stay, whether in Derbyshire or London. They would have to ensure Georgiana was comfortable with the prospect, but she might like to befriend them.

After wandering for a while, they stood by a window in a smaller sitting room, looking out to the park. It was too cold to go out of doors, as evidenced by the frost on the glass. The night looked peaceful, and the sky was covered by a plethora of stars. The only light in the room was from the silver candlestick he had brought with them.

"It must be almost midnight." Elizabeth spoke softly.

She pulled her wool shawl more tightly against her. Darcy wound an arm across her shoulders to share his warmth and kissed her temple.

"It is almost 1814. The year I finally make you my wife," Darcy said.

Elizabeth made a happy chirping sound. "The year I finally make you my husband."

They both turned so that they were facing each other. Darcy

placed a tender kiss on her lips, restraining his impulse to pull her close and demonstrate how much he was anticipating their wedding, but he admitted it would be easy to go too far, given the stillness and darkness of the room and how long and deeply he had loved her.

"And it is the year I become an aunt and you an uncle," she said.

"One I can, at last, begin without feeling a dark, stormy cloud hanging over our heads."

Elizabeth covered his cheek with her warm hand and gifted him a soothing kiss, her lips soft and tasting of the wine she had been drinking earlier. "Remember my love, whatever transpires with Georgiana, or anything else in your life, you will not have to confront it alone. I shall always be by your side to share the burden."

Darcy embraced her. The desire to hold her, to feel her body pressed to his, was too great to overcome. She rested her head on his chest, and her arms wrapped around his waist. They stood like this for some time as he contemplated the import of her words. He was not alone any longer. They had been through rough weather these last years, and it had strained some of their relationships, none more than his and Fitzwilliam's.

His connexion with Lady Catherine had fared worse, but she and her daughter did not matter. She had not apologised for going to Longbourn and confronting Elizabeth or for telling Georgiana of his intentions to marry her. Georgiana had told him more of that dreadful day, and it—along with the disgusting letter Lady Catherine had written to him upon learning of his engagement—had meant the end of his connexion to the de Bourghs.

"Where do you think we shall be next New Year's Eve?" Elizabeth asked.

He kissed the top of her head and took a moment to contemplate. "At Pemberley, perhaps standing by a window as we are now and taking in a similar view. We shall speak of the year that has passed—the joys and, if we are fortunate, lack of sorrow—and our wishes for 1815. We might already be anticipating a child."

"I hope we are," she whispered.

"In the end, all that truly matters to me is that we shall be together."

"Just as we were always meant to be."

Elizabeth lifted her chin to gaze up at him, and he looked down into her beloved face and kissed her.

The beginning of the new year was both quiet and busy. Darcy and Georgiana continued to come to Larch Lane when the winter weather permitted, and Jane insisted Elizabeth go to Pemberley to stay with Georgiana while Darcy was in Manchester visiting an old friend of his father's, whose health was failing. Thus, Elizabeth went to her soon-to-be home and spent an agreeable week with Georgiana, who was steadily growing stronger.

"I do not know what it is or how it has come about, but I *do* feel so much lighter," Georgiana said to her one afternoon. They were enjoying tea and shortbread after discussing how one of the principal rooms should be renovated. "I can hardly believe that a year ago even the thought of seeing you made me afraid. Now, I wish you and my brother were already married so that you would not have to return to Larch Lane. I am trying very hard not to apologise for my past behaviour because I know you will tell me I need not."

"You are exactly right. I cannot express how glad I am to see you so well—or how delighted I am that the wedding will be soon." Elizabeth smiled warmly at her, and both ladies laughed. "To be serious, as much as your brother and I long to be married, I am glad we waited as we have. All of us—not just you—are happier now." She did not want to say outright that she was more confident in Georgiana's acceptance, but that was a significant part of it. The young woman had made remarkable progress and was determined to maintain the daily habits that seemed to contribute to her well-being. Between that and being embraced by Darcy's relations, Elizabeth would enter her new life as his wife free of the anxieties she would have had previously.

Mrs Annesley would remain with her after the wedding; it was Georgiana's request, not because she did not trust or want Elizabeth to keep her company and support her but because Mrs Annesley provided a different sort of assistance as she fought to maintain her well-being. Since Mrs Annesley was a pleasant, intelligent woman, Elizabeth had no objections, and it went without saying that Darcy would agree to anything his sister said she required to be healthy.

On the seventeenth of March, Jane presented her husband with a daughter, who, despite her young age, showed every promise that she shared her mother's beauty and both her mother and father's affable characters. Mr and Mrs Bennet, Mary, and Kitty arrived at Larch Lane a fortnight later to meet Miss Frances Elizabeth Bingley. As Elizabeth had expected would be the case, her mother was beside herself with joy at seeing Larch Lane and meeting her granddaughter, and when she saw Pemberley, she was almost too shocked to speak, quietly whispering to Elizabeth that she could not believe *her* daughter would live in such a place.

Then, a week after Easter—and two years from Darcy's first proposal—Elizabeth married her Mr Darcy on what was undoubtedly the happiest day of her life.

When they were alone in the carriage after the ceremony, driving back to Larch Lane for the wedding breakfast, she said, "I have you now, and I have no intention of ever letting you go."

Darcy chuckled and let out a relieved sigh. As he gathered her into his arms and lowered his mouth to hers for a kiss, he said, "I assure you, my darling, most beautiful Mrs Darcy—how I like calling you that!—I will never, *never* be parted from you again."

EPILOGUE

October 1838

I*t is good to be home,* Darcy thought as he strolled through Pemberley. He had no purpose in mind other than exercise. It was drizzling, which precluded outdoor activity. Besides, he should remain readily disposable to Elizabeth. She might require his opinion or simply his company, and despite all the years of their marriage, he hated the thought of disappointing her, even if it was a matter of her having to wait an hour or two to speak to him. He appreciated her efforts to include him in her current occupation—making final arrangements for the wedding of their daughter—but truth be told, he was happy to leave it to her and the other ladies.

It had been a busy year thus far, and they had returned to Derbyshire less than a week ago after having travelled south in the spring. Their first stop had been Meryton. Two of Elizabeth's sisters currently lived there—Mary, now the wife of the town's attorney, and Lydia. The latter had returned to her childhood home to live with Mary after Wickham had been killed in a brawl just before their tenth wedding anniversary. To everyone's surprise, the sisters had done well together, and presently their bond was almost as strong as that of Elizabeth and Jane. Fortunately, Lydia and Wickham had not been blessed with children, and she had told Elizabeth—who then told Darcy—that it was a relief to be free of a marriage that had become, in her words, 'disagreeable'. Three years after becoming a widow, she had married one of Charlotte Collins's younger brothers and appeared satisfied with her choice. Elizabeth had corresponded with Lydia for years, but it was only after Wickham's demise that they met again.

After spending a week in Meryton, Elizabeth, Darcy, and their four children had gone to town. During their months there, they had visited the newly opened National Gallery and celebrated the coronation of Queen Victoria. Darcy had experienced riding one of the country's great new railways; it had been equally exhilarating and terrifying. In many ways, it was a marvellous time to be alive. All around him, he saw progress—new discoveries that promised to change the lives of everyone in England. It was a shame to see some of the old ways fading into history—and he much preferred the ladies' fashions of earlier times, although Elizabeth looked beautiful no matter what she wore.

Tomorrow, the first of their children would be married. Jane Anne, aged twenty, was the Darcys' only daughter. 'Jenny' to her family, she was marrying Bingley and Jane's son, Bennet, who had been born a year after his sister Frances. Since his new son was also his nephew, Darcy's role was slightly confusing. His middle son, Thomas, would say it was old age nipping at his heels, but he had only recently turned four-and-fifty and felt 'old age' was a few years away still. *Though I might feel differently the day I become a grandfather.*

"There you are, my love."

The unexpected sound of another's voice made Darcy jump in shock. He turned to see Elizabeth walking towards him, one hand already outstretched. He took it in his when she was near enough and pulled it to his mouth for a kiss. This morning, she wore a deep-blue gown that seemed to accentuate the richness of her hair—despite the odd grey strand—and the brightness of her eyes, in which he could still easily become lost.

"Were you looking for me?" he asked.

"Always." She smiled, her look one of love and teasing. "I have been walking the corridors since I knew you would disapprove of me taking my exercise out of doors."

"If only we might. I do hope the rain ends today. I would like our girl to have a perfect wedding day."

Darcy wrapped her arm around his and led her towards the portrait gallery. She had been as excellent a mother to their four children as he had supposed she would be. In addition to their daughter and Thomas, they had two other boys, Hugh—named in honour of Darcy's own father—and Edward.

"If it is raining, we could always put it off," he grumbled. It had become something of a family joke that he was reluctant to give away his daughter, even to his nephew, whom he had known and loved his whole life.

Elizabeth laughed. "If I believed you were serious, I would give you a long lecture as to why *that* is never going to happen. Goodness, Jenny would not speak to you for a decade if you even suggested such a measure to her."

Darcy chuckled. He had accepted the young couple's wish to marry even though he believed Jenny might do better to wait until she was a year or two older. She and Bennet Bingley had seemed destined for the altar since they were adolescents, and Darcy's initial reluctance to grant his permission and blessing had ended abruptly when Elizabeth had challenged him to name the age at which he would be pleased to see his only daughter leave his care in favour of another man's. The answer had been never, and he knew that would be unfair and absurd.

"Is everything prepared to your satisfaction?" he asked.

"It is. Rooms for our guests are ready, Cook and I have reviewed the menu for dinner, and he promises everything at the wedding breakfast will be exactly as it should be. I have just come from Jenny. She *had* to try on her gown again because she was certain it would not fit—why, I do not know—but she seems reassured that she will be the most beautiful bride in history. Bennet will believe so, and that is all that truly matters to her."

"I am in a quandary," Darcy said. When Elizabeth gave him a quizzical look, he continued. "I have always believed *you* were the most beautiful bride ever. I could never say that to my daughter and have her think I consider her less lovely than her mother, which I do not, but how do I explain that to her? I am not sure I can sort it out myself. You are both beautiful to me but in different ways."

As they slowly strolled through the gallery, she rested her head against his shoulder. "You are a silly man."

When she said nothing further, he asked whether she intended to offer him counsel.

"I do not." She spoke each word carefully and stopped walking so that she could stand in front of him, holding both his hands. "I have spent all morning soothing our daughter's anxious nerves and offering her advice, and I am afraid, my darling husband, I have no more to give. Ask me again after dinner, and I might be sufficiently restocked by then to make a pithy comment or two." She kissed him.

"Where is Jenny now?"

"With Georgiana. I do not know what she has planned, but she assured me she would distract Jenny for the next hour or two. She has always had a wonderfully calming effect on the children, and I am glad it has lasted as they became adults."

Darcy agreed. His sister had remained single, always afraid of what the trials of marriage and motherhood would do to her well-being. She had attracted many admirers over the years, and once, Elizabeth and he had believed she might change her mind and marry a gentleman she had grown attached to, but she had been firm in her resolve that the risk was too great. Instead, she had remained a contented, healthy, dearly loved aunt; she was almost a second mother to Darcy and Elizabeth's four children.

Georgiana had experienced the occasional 'difficult period' as they called them over the years, none more challenging than when their aunt Lady Romsley had died and the old earl had followed her less than a year later. But his sister had drawn on her family for support—Elizabeth especially—and the helpful practices she had learnt in the past. Darcy had developed an interest in medical advances, determined to be aware of new treatments that might aid his sister. It was an interest his youngest son had adopted, and Elizabeth suspected he would, as she said, 'do something with it' when he finished university. What exactly that would mean, time would tell. Edward had a scholarly mind and might choose to undertake research into the causes and cures of mental illness, which would please Darcy and make him exceedingly proud. Not that he would tell his son that, lest he adopt a career he did not truly want just to earn his father's approbation.

"When will our guests arrive?" Darcy asked. Apart from the Larch Lane contingent—Jane, Bingley, their five daughters and one son—their family from Romsley Hall would join them to celebrate the first wedding amongst the younger generation. Unfortunately, Darcy's cousin Fitzwilliam was currently abroad with his Italian wife and their two young children.

"They should be here in about two hours."

"Where are the boys?"

"Thomas and Edward chose to accompany Hugh on the calls you asked him to make." There were a couple of neighbours he had business with or messages for, and one of them had to see the vicar to ensure he was prepared to perform the wedding ceremony. Darcy had asked Hugh to undertake the tasks since, eventually, such responsibilities would rest on his shoulders.

Darcy slowly smiled. "Do you mean to suggest I have you all to myself for the next two hours?"

Pleasure and love filled his beloved wife's countenance. "It does. What do you intend to do about it, my darling Mr Darcy?"

He answered her with a kiss.

ALSO BY LUCY MARIN

A Matter of Prudence

A Pinch of Salt

Being Mrs Darcy

Christmas at Blackthorn Manor

Her Sisterly Love

The Marriage Bargain

Mr Darcy: A Man with a Plan

Mrs Bennet Makes a Match

The Recovery of Fitzwilliam Darcy

The Truth About Family

Collaborations and Anthologies

Happily Ever After with Mr Darcy

'Tis the Season

ABOUT THE AUTHOR

Lucy Marin developed a love for reading at a young age and whiled away many hours imagining how stories might continue or what would happen if there was a change in the circumstances faced by the protagonists. After reading her first Austen novel, a lifelong ardent admiration was born. Lucy was introduced to the world of Austen variations after stumbling across one at a used bookstore while on holiday in London. This led to the discovery of the online world of Jane Austen Fan Fiction and, soon after, she picked up her pen and began to transfer the stories in her head to paper.

Lucy lives in Toronto, Canada, surrounded by hundreds of books and a loving family. She teaches environmental studies, loves animals and trees and exploring the world around her.

ACKNOWLEDGMENTS

My ongoing thanks to Amy, Jan, and everyone at Q&Q.

Made in United States
North Haven, CT
28 April 2024

51886927R00224